10/96

Foreign Devil

A Novel by Wang Ping

COFFEE HOUSE PRESS :: MINNEAPOLIS :: 1996

This project has been made possible through a major grant provided from the Star Tribune/Cowles Media Company. Additional support has been provided by the Minnesota State Arts Board, through an appropriation by the Minnesota State Legislature; the National Endowment for the Arts; the Lila Wallace-Reader's Digest Fund; The McKnight Foundation; Lannan Foundation; Jerome Foundation; Target Stores, Dayton's, and Mervyn's by the Dayton Hudson Foundation; General Mills Foundation; St. Paul Companies; Honeywell Foundation; James R. Thorpe Foundation; Dain Bosworth Foundation; Beverly J. and John A. Rollwagen Fund of The Minneapolis Foundation; Schwegman, Lundberg, Woessner & Kluth, P.A.; and The Andrew W. Mellon Foundation.

Coffee House Press books are available to the trade through our primary distributor, Consortium Book Sales & Distribution, 1045 Westgate Drive, St. Paul, MN 55114. For personal orders, catalogs or other information, write to: Coffee House Press, 27 North Fourth Street, Suite 400, Minneapolis, MN 55401.

Library of Congress CIP Data
Wang, Ping, 1957-
        Foreign devil : a novel / by Wang Ping.
                P.   CM.
        ISBN 1-56689-048-9
        I. Title.
PS3573.A4769F67   1996
813'.54—DC20   96-18427
                                                            CIP

10   9   8   7   6   5   4   3   2   1

c-/

For my father, Wang Zhaoqing

*For Lewis Warsh, who taught me
how to sing*

Chapter One

AT THE AGE OF TWENTY-TWO, I became a woman. Yan took my virginity. He was my first lover, a married man.

"Meimei, I want to hold you."

But you are, I thought, gasping for air under Yan's compact body. He had been lying on top of me for at least two hours like a mountain. His hip bones pressed and ground my abdomen with a slow, determined motion that made me feel that he wouldn't let me go until I was crushed and ground into dust. My stomach felt numb, as if I had been pressed under a nether millstone for days and nights. Where did he get this weight?

He was small, only two inches taller than I, with thin hairy legs, narrow hips, the ribs lined up on his chest like my grandma's washing board. When I asked him about this, he would point to his huge head with an ear-to-ear smile. I only needed to take a look at his black hair whirling around on the top in all directions and his chin always pointing to the sky, and I would burst out laughing. His most distinguished facial features, however, were his bony, hooked nose, which took up a third of his face, and underneath, his red, watery lips that hung like a new moon between his ears. Sometimes I teased him that his nose must weigh a pound. Yan argued that it was all his brain, which was at least twice as large and wrinkled as a normal person's brain. True. His round head looked so huge on top of his little neck that sometimes I imagined if I just flicked my fingers at his scalp, the blue veins that stood up along the neck would explode and his head would break off and roll on the ground. When Yan took my hand and put it inside his pants, I grasped something hot and sticky, trembling like a bloody newborn rabbit. What alarmed me the most was that this thing was expanding rapidly, and soon my fingers could no longer wrap around it. Was he going to penetrate me with this gigantic monster, thicker than my wrist, harder than my grandma's washing stick, and hotter than a red iron rod? The thought threw me into a panic and I withdrew my hand quickly.

"Meimei, my delicious Meimei, Gege wants to hold you and eat you up, little by little," Yan moaned as he pressed down harder, wrapping me with his long arms and legs like an octopus. I felt his heart thumping against my chest as he sucked my already-swollen lips deep into his mouth and cupped my breasts firmly with his hands.

Finally. I'm going to lose my virginity tonight, I said to myself. Why not tonight? It would have to happen, just a matter of time. If I tried to put it off again, he would be really mad at me. My roommate Wang Ying had left earlier in the afternoon to visit her aunt. It was now past eleven. She had missed the last bus back to school for the night. The door was locked. I had checked it twice before Yan pushed me down on the bed. No one must see what we were doing. To fool around with a man before marriage was bad enough. To fall in love with a married man could ruin both of us. Yan was leading my hand into his open fly again. At the touch of my cold fingers, the thing twitched like a live fish in a sizzling pan.

"I want you, Meimei, I want you," Yan murmured repeatedly as he chewed my ears and cheeks, his saliva dribbling all over my face. "I can't take it anymore. I'm going insane if I don't hold you tonight. You'll let me, Meimei, won't you, my sweet meimei?" His whisper smelled of garlic and fish. The thing in my hand was moving up and down, the way my father pounded garlic in a mortar with a stone pestle. My father ate garlic every day, either mashed or whole, always raw.

What did it look like? I had never seen a penis in my life. Not true. I did see one at a bus stop in the suburb of Shanghai when I was nine. It was a drizzling afternoon. The waiting shed had only three people—my mom, a bald old man, and me. My mother went to the bathroom. I took out *The Western Journey* to read. The Monkey King had transformed himself into a fly and entered the Iron-Fan Princess's stomach. The old man said, "Hey!"

I looked up. He had something red and rubbery sticking out through his open fly. *Why did he insert a rubber pipe between his legs?* I thought. *To suck out all the extra fat and water from his round tummy?* He circled his hand around it and began to pull and push it so hard that he made strange, painful noises, and his face was all contorted. Was he trying to peel the skin off the pipe? If it hurt so much, why did he do it? Suddenly, he bent over. White liquid gushed out from the tip of the red pipe and made an arc in the air before it fell on the ground. At this moment, something clicked in my mind. I blushed heavily but did not turn my back to him. By the time my mother returned, he had already buttoned up. I pointed at his back to my mother. "What?" she said. But the old man turned his face. His look scared me. I shook my head and ran to the other side of the waiting shed. My mother's voice chased me like a whip. "Why are you so red? Damn, who spit on the floor again? People are such pigs!"

"Why are you so stiff? Relax, Meimei. Gege wants to know you, and you want the same thing, don't you? The only way to do it is to go inside you. This will be our true union. No one can separate us again. Meimei, please breathe with me. Now, inhale, exhale. Again . . ."

I breathed deeply, in, out, in, out, but I just wanted to laugh. This was too much like having a baby. I saw my mother giving birth to my little sister at home. The nurse told her to breathe exactly like this. Instead of relaxing, I began to feel the cramps in my stomach. Funny that it always happened this way. I spent many sleepless nights in my dormitory bed, calling Yan's name in silence. I wanted him to come inside and make me die. But when he humped me with his swollen loins, I got all tight and crampy. Although I called his name in my bed, the images that answered my call were all different men. None of them had Yan's face. Maybe he was too ugly? Maybe I regarded him too much as my brother, father, and teacher?

About a month and a half ago, Yan called me meimei, sister, for the first time, while we were waiting for the beginning of 1980. He sat on Wang Ying's bed, me on my own, our fingers intertwined over the desk between us. We had just reached an agreement. I was going to take the 1980 college entrance exams in June and Yan would tutor me. He made a schedule for my daily study: 4:00–7:30 A.M.—Chinese and history; 5:30–11:00 P.M.—geometry and political science. I had to teach from 8:30–4:00 P.M. In the next five months, I had to catch up with all the junior high and high school courses I had missed during the Cultural Revolution.

"What you learned during those years is useless for the exams," Yan commented with a sneer when I told him I was a top student in high school. He was right. Because the Cultural Revolution began when I was in the third grade, I had spent most of my school years working in the countryside and factories, reading Mao's red book, and writing papers to criticize myself or others. "Don't you worry a bit about it," Yan said. "I'll help you from the very beginning. We'll make it, I'm sure." He waved his fist in the air, his Adam's apple rolling up and down along his neck. Yan was really excited.

He's helping me to realize my lifelong dream, I thought. *What can I do for him? If I really pass the exams, not only will I give him everything I have for the rest of my life, but also in my next life I'll become an ox or a horse to serve him.*

"What are you thinking about?" He squeezed my hand. Before

I could answer, the radio solemnly announced the arrival of the New Year. When the clock stroked the twelfth time, Yan stood up dramatically and embraced me across the desk. "Meimei, my little meimei, what am I going to do?" he moaned, his cheek burning like a hot wok against mine. Suddenly, he dropped my arms, stepped back, stared at me without seeing. "What am I doing? Oh, god, what am I doing?" In a second, he ran out of the room, leaving me totally bewildered.

The next day, he came back but refused to enter my room. "I come here to apologize for my behavior last night," he announced in a high-pitched voice, his manner still so dramatic but touched with melancholy.

"I don't get it, Yan Hua. Why did you run away like that?"

"I can't. I'm a married man, you know. You're still a virgin. I don't want to ruin your future."

"I don't have a future without you," I said, astonished at what I was saying and the way I said it. Yan's dramatic manner was influential. But what I was telling him came from the deep well of my body. The feeling had never surfaced before, even though we had been seeing each other every day for the past three months. But now words just poured out like spring water. "I don't care whether I'm a virgin or not. But I do care that you're married. I don't want to ruin your family. So let's be brother and sister, since you don't have a meimei, and I don't have a gege."

His eyes lit up. "You forgave me, Meimei? Oh, I'm so happy I'm going to die. All my life I've been longing for a little sister like you." He took me into his arms.

I rested my face against his green military jacket and realized how much my future depended on him.

YAN HAD PULLED DOWN MY PANTS. "Meimei," he whispered into my ear, "I'm going to come inside you now. It hurts a little, but if you relax, it won't be too bad. You'll open your door for your brother, won't you?"

Yes, I wanted more than anything else to let him in, to make him happy. But my door was tightly closed. Yan was drilling between my legs. *Gege, have mercy. You're cutting me into pieces. It's no use. The lock on my door has been rusted too long. Maybe I'm a shinu, a stone girl, whose hymen can never be broken. Don't poke me so hard, Gege. I'm going to scream.*

"I can't, I just can't." I pushed him away, shouting. "Why do we have to do this? I'm happy the way it was, gege and meimei."

Yan buttoned his fly and walked to the door without looking at me. I watched his slightly hunched back, my stomach twitching into a knot. The green silk lamp he gave me last year was shedding a soft light on the desk. This was the first birthday gift I'd ever received. Not that no one remembered my birthday. My paternal grandma Nainai always made her three best dishes that day. But instead of letting me eat them, she placed them under the elm tree in the yard, burned incense, and folded paper into the shape of money. She did all this, of course, at midnight, when everyone in the navy compound was asleep. On that day, June 14th, all the adults in my family—Nainai, Father, and Mother—treated me with silence and politeness. Even my two sisters stopped bugging me like flies. No one looked at me or talked to me, as if I were a ghost or a devil. In the beginning, I was delighted for getting away from the endless chores in the house, but soon I just wished that Nainai and Mother would curse and order me around as usual. Their politeness toward me did not come out of care but out of fear. It terrified me and sent me into endless daydreams and trances.

"Gege," I called.

"I'm afraid I won't be able to be your gege for long," he said, his hand on the lock.

I put my chin on my drawn-up knees. My head was buzzing with that familiar noise, as if an overwound clock was about to shatter at any moment, and time, instead of ticking forward, would slide backward in a bottomless tunnel at a dizzying speed. I'd been in that tunnel too many times. It was not fun at all.

Gege, give me your hand. Do not let me fall.

"Have you ever seen brothers and sisters live together forever?"

"What should we do?" my eyes asked in despair.

"We have to become lovers. We have to become husband and wife. I don't want to hurt you, Meimei, but this is the only way to keep us together. I'm not doing this for fun but for the plan I've been thinking about. I've made up my mind. I'm going to leave her and be with you for the rest of my life."

How are you going to do this? I said to myself. This society won't allow you to divorce her. You're a college student and she's only a factory worker on a small island. If you abandon her, you'll be cursed forever as a Chen Shimei, the legendary figure who abandoned his wife after he passed the official exams and had a government appointment, and you'll fall back to the place where you started. You'll never do that, Gege, because you're ambitious. You want a high place in this world.

"Once I break your virginity, I'll be your man forever. I'll have no retreat. Do you understand, Meimei?"

No, I don't understand, I thought. You mean if I were not a virgin, I would be less valuable to you? What about your responsibility to your wife? Didn't you take her virginity? But I do understand your point, Gege. The chance for an unmarried nonvirgin to find a husband is small. So you're burning the bridge for me. Take me if it makes you feel more secure. I'll endure the pain, no matter how bad it is. Have I told you I'll give you anything I have, no condition attached, because I love you?

"Say something, Meimei, please." Yan returned to the bed and held my head cautiously, as if holding a flower. "I never know what's going on inside your head. Your silence sometimes scares me, sometimes pisses me off. But maybe that's why I'm so crazy about you. I don't know."

I held his hand and still couldn't say a word. Everyone seemed to hate or fear silence. I couldn't even remember how many times my grandmas, mother, and teachers had cursed or punished me for not speaking and refusing to answer questions. *Either she is retarded or very bad-tempered for behaving like that,* they often commented. I grew up with different nicknames: *iron lips, wooden melon, mute mud, dead ghost.* I didn't give a shit about what they called me. Silence was the only way to keep one's dignity in this world, and I treasured the sacredness of sound and words more than anything else. Sounds should always be used to make things beautiful, like music, songs, poetry, expressions of emotions, making up and telling stories. The noises children made when they were playing could be beautiful even though they had no meaning. The sounds of sobbing or cursing, if they were done with true emotion and purpose, could also be beautiful. It was a crime to waste sounds, and worse, to pollute the earth with babbling nonsense and poisonous words. When adults got together, they immediately started chatting or arguing, as if they would be possessed by ghosts if they remained silent for a minute. I guarded my sounds and words like a miser except when I told stories, made up or real. To me, there was a very thin line between the two. How did we know what was real, what was made up? Most of the time it depended on our perception. The only person who didn't mind my quietness was my father. We could sit in one room, hike in the mountains, ride bicycles for hours without saying one word, and still feel comfortable. But those moments were too rare. Most of the time, he was away at sea. When he came home, he was besieged by Nainai, Mother, and my two sisters.

"MEIMEI, WHAT are you thinking about?" Yan's voice sounded distant and annoyed.

I gave him an apologetic look. This would be a crucial moment in my life. I would no longer be a girl after tonight. I must not let my mind wander too much. I removed my shoes, then my pants, which Yan had already pulled down below my knees. The idea of making love with clothing on made me feel cheap. People could say whatever they wanted about us—immoral morons, adulterers—but my feeling toward Yan was not cheap or light.

Wang Ying wouldn't come back tonight. It was not necessary to take precautions.

"Hold me, Gege," I said.

I had gone through all kinds of pain: my mother's whipping of bamboo sticks and belts, Nainai's pinching on the inner thighs, the hitting of washing sticks and rolling pins, and the burning of swollen knees and ankles from arthritis, but I had never experienced the pain of being sawed and drilled. Once he broke through my rusty door, would he pierce my womb, my stomach, and come out through my scalp? Like the Chinese baby on the bayonet of a Japanese soldier in one of those war movies? When I masturbated as a kid, all I felt was the dizzying pleasure mingled with shame and terror. Never had I imagined this kind of agony. Yan made weird noises through his clenched teeth, the kind of noise he made when he was having a hard time in the bathroom. It was funny, but I couldn't laugh. My stomach was turned upside down. Sweat poured down my face and arms, soaking the sheet underneath.

That weird ticking and buzzing in my ears again. Oh Mama, when will this end? Do not push me into the tunnel. Let me out. I can't breathe. It's dark and stuffy here. This time, I won't be able to come out alive. Who is the woman hung on a post at the entrance of the market? Her naked body is written all over with the character jian, adultery. It is in fact branded on her with a hot iron seal. Below her stands a donkey. A huge wooden block in the shape of a penis tied to the back of the donkey points up at the woman from between her legs. Two people come up and pull her legs apart. Then the person lets go of the rope that has been hoisting the woman in the air. She falls with a thud on the back of the donkey, the penis disappearing between her thighs. Blood spurts from the top of her scalp onto the heads of the staring crowd.

"I GOT IT, Meimei, I'm inside you," Yan shouted. The tearing pain pulled me out of the bloody pool, the tunnel, and sent me back to reality. Yan was thrashing on top of me, hurting me inside. *I'd rather die than go through this torment,* I cried to myself. *I don't want to be awakened.* Suddenly Yan shouted again: "Oh, I can't bear it anymore." He collapsed, his gripping hands and head now drooping like overcooked noodles.

I sat up slowly, my legs beneath me, my hand trying to cover my nakedness. How could I cool the burning between my legs? I inhaled and exhaled, my teeth still grinding against one another.

Yan wiped himself with my towel and knelt on the floor next to me, his arms clasped around my knees. He remained silent for a long time. I realized he was staring at something in the bed. I looked. On the white sheet, there was a dark spot. In the moonlight, it looked like an ink stain. Then I realized it was blood, my virgin blood.

"Meimei, Meimei," Yan cried passionately, burying his face in the sheet. "You're mine forever."

Chapter Two

I WAS A STRANGE GIRL. Everyone who knew me or just met me said so. It didn't bother me that much because I grew up hearing this comment, first from Waipo, my maternal grandma, from my aunts and uncle, then from my parents, my sisters, my neighbors and classmates, and now from my colleagues.

"How strange you are!" Waipo had said. She had been watching me sitting on a stool for hours, my eyes looking but not seeing. I was four years old and still hadn't seen my parents. I knew they lived on one of the fishing islands called Zhoushan. My father was a navy officer, my mother a dance teacher. Actually I had seen my mother once, her back. I was taking a nap and dreaming of a flood from too much rain. I heard Waipo say, "Leave. She's waking up." I opened my eyes and heard the crisp footsteps her leather shoes made on the wooden floor and stairways. I sat up and caught a glimpse of dark, dark hair cut straight above a long, snow-white neck.

"Mother Swan," I shouted, stretching out my hands as if to pull her back. I didn't know why I said it. My mother's neck was in fact neither extraordinarily long nor white like a swan's. But that was how I saw it. Waipo put her arms around me.

"Wake up, gua nuan, you're sleep-talking again," she said in a hushed voice. She called me gua nuan, obedient girl, only when she was extremely angry or pleased with me. What had I done in my dream? I rubbed my face with my hand. It was wet and it tasted bitter. So it wasn't just a dream. My mother did come to see me and wet my face with her tears. "Mother," I said. Waipo squeezed my arms.

"It was your aunt, gua nuan."

No, my mother, I insisted. She slapped the back of my head.

"Stubborn, stubborn, stubborn. Where did you get that from? Not from me, not from your mother. No wonder you were born with your feet out first."

I looked up at her. In my head, I was asking, "But what's wrong with that? Don't we all walk on our feet? Of course, we should all be born with our feet out first." When I finally opened my mouth, I said, "Really? But why?"

She seemed surprised by my second question. Her eyebrows knit together as she answered, "Perhaps you were anxious, or perhaps too proud to fall into this world head over heels. Whatever it was, you did have a pretty scary look on your face, as if you came into the world with a destination, a plan. And your cry was even more frightening. It sounded almost like a laugh, very sardonic, like this," she imitated, *"ha, ha, ha."* We both laughed, my head buried between Grandma's knees, her warm breath on my bare back. We laughed a long time until we fell into a longer silence.

"You were such a weird baby," she said again, "not only because of that funny cry, but also the full head of hair, dark and rough like a porcupine. Lots of things happened before and after your birth. It rained nonstop for weeks. All the rivers flooded and the ocean swallowed the beaches. People seemed to go insane, particular that Old One. She would have strangled you if I hadn't grabbed you from her. You should have seen her eyes, lit up like a flashlight with fear and hatred. And her mouth, open as wide as a basin, blood all over her face and hands, and curses spitting out like a snake spraying poison. She looked like a witch. I grabbed you and held you against my breasts. You were still bloody and naked, but I had already fallen in love with you, little helpless stubborn thing. 'This baby is mine now,' I said, glaring into that Old Thing's eyes. 'If you dare touch her, you'd have to step over my dead body first.'"

She stopped, then suddenly tightened her arms around me, as if protecting me from the grabbing of an evil spirit in the air. She was trembling. "Oh, baby, what are you going to do when it's time for you to leave your grandma and live with that Old One?"

I had endless questions. Why did "that Old One," my paternal grandma, hate me? What about my father and mother? If they didn't want to see me, why did my mother shed her tears on my face and run away when I woke up? Why was Waipo worried so much about my living with my other grandma? The thought of leaving Waipo's warm bosom tore my heart. When she was mad at me, she often threatened to send me back to Shandong, to the Old One's house, tomorrow. I hated the word *tomorrow*. It filled my heart with something I could name only much later: despair. But I said nothing, just buried my head in her lap. Waipo was combing my hair and braiding it into nine braids, which made me look like a bird with its wings open, getting ready to fly. Whenever she did that, she would tell me about the birds that lived their first two years on a Pacific island, then flew away to the ocean for twenty years, never landing, never returning to the island again until it was time to have babies and die. Those birds didn't build nests. They laid their eggs on barren rocks. The chicks had to learn how to live with nature on the day they were born. Many died, but those who survived grew up strong and tough. When the flying time came, they followed their parents to the top of the island. From there, they hopped down as fast as they could. Their hopping was awkward, but once they were in the air and their powerful wings wide open between the blue sky and the blue sea, they turned into the most magnificent creatures on earth. Thus they would keep flying over the ocean until they came back to have babies and die.

Except for the bird story and the braids, my memory of four years living with Waipo in Shanghai was misty, more like a waft of scent in the breeze. It came to me when I was not paying attention, but if I tried to grab it, it drifted away. When I was four years and three months, I finally got to live with my parents on the island. I cannot recall how I got there. I only remember my father picking me up from Waipo's arms and carrying me on his back to a ship named *Qingdao. We are going to Weihai, a beautiful place on the coast of the North China Sea,* Father murmured. How about Zhoushan? I wanted to ask, but dared not. Waipo told me you were taking me there to live with Mother and my sister. Suddenly I lifted my head. Someone was calling: "Gua nuan, gua nuan!" I turned my head and saw Waipo running along the dock. Her bun had come loose and the wind was blowing it up like a black flag.

"Where are you taking her, you liar, you country bumpkin?" she shouted as she ran up the bridge between the dock and ship. But the steward stopped her. "He's kidnapped my child. That guy up there kidnapped my child!" my grandma roared like a lioness.

"Waipo!" I shouted. She scared me. I'd never seen her like this. "Let me get off. I want to go with Waipo," I said to him, still not used to calling him father.

"No," he said firmly, "you're with me now." Then he turned to the security guard. "I apologize for this mess. My mother-in-law is very emotional. Sometimes she's a bit crazy. But she's harmless. Just make sure she doesn't come up here." I was kicking and punching my father's back. "Don't move," he shouted, and swung me to his chest. I opened my mouth. Before I called out to Waipo, he had already buried my face in his wool navy uniform.

What happened next was a mystery. It was like waking up in the morning: you knew so much had taken place in your dreams, but no matter how you wracked your brains, you couldn't retrieve any of it. My next memory was of me looking up at my mother, tall and dazzling, even when she was sitting. It was dinnertime. We each sat on a stool, our simple dinner set on a taller stool. It was rice gruel, fermented bean curd, and a chunk of fat pork floating on the congealed surface. In the middle of the stool was a half piece of steamed bread. Mother was wearing a white dress with black polka dots. Her soft hair covered her upper cheeks as she bent her head over the bowl, drinking the gruel. In an apartment with only two beds and a few chairs, we sat face to face, so close that our knees brushed against one another from time to time, and I didn't know how to respond. The dust was dancing up and down in the last rays of the sun. Suddenly I had some strange questions. *Who am I? What's this place? What am I doing here?*

"What are you staring at? Ghosts?" Mother asked. "Don't fidget with your food! You'll spill it."

I tried to swallow the rice and tears. What was Waipo doing? Was she still crying on the dock? What happened after she was pushed off the bridge? Did she have anything to eat? The rice and pork smelled good, and I was hungry. But I couldn't eat.

"What's your problem? You have a bone in your throat or what!"

"I can't swallow the fat pork and I don't like fermented bean curd."

"You ungrateful little ghost, you're lucky to have anything to put in your mouth at all. People are eating leaves and grass nowadays. Eat the pork now." She hit my head with her chopsticks.

The door flew open. A man in uniform came in with an old woman on his shoulders. Her eyes were puffy and red like rotten meat, with yellow puss congealed around the lids. They both looked like they'd been crawling in mud for days without any food. The woman's eyes brightened as she saw the food. She stumbled toward us.

"Oh, my heavens, the fucking steamed bread!" she roared, and fell to the ground.

"Niang, Niang, take it easy," the man shouted in a strange accent as he rushed to her. I recognized him from his voice. Father. What had happened to him? When he had entered Waipo's apartment that day, he looked awe inspiring. There was not a wrinkle in his gray uniform except for the straight "railway tracks" on his pants. Now his gray uniform, his face, even his dark curly hair were the color of dirt. He smelled different, too. I sniffed hard, searching for the smell of the sun and ocean his body had given off on our first encounter. But I found only the odor of vomit, mixed with something new, yet not unfamiliar. Later I realized it was the smell of the northern soil.

"Do we have more bread?" he asked Mother.

My mother looked at the old woman, now leaning again on Father's shoulder. Her eyes were filled with fear and contempt. Then she walked to the kitchen without a word. She had not greeted them.

"Ni Bing, come and say hello to your nainai."

I ignored Father's order. I couldn't take my eyes off this puffy, wheezing woman. I had never met her, yet I had seen her before. I immediately disliked her. She scared me, although she looked as if she would crumble onto the ground again at any moment. Something in her eyes when she looked at me through the swollen eyelids (she had only looked at me once since she came in) was not fun at all. It was more awful than the look Mother gave her. I smelled hatred in it. She was my nainai, my paternal grandma, whom Waipo called "that Old One."

He took my hand and pulled me close to her. "Ni Bing, from now on, you must learn to show respect to your elders. Call Nainai." His voice was low and stern; his hands pressed down on my shoulders until I collapsed on the floor. Nainai stood before me in her rags, like a tower burnt by the sun and fire, silent, ruined, yet still powerful. I lifted my head slowly, sitting on my legs like a mermaid. Our eyes met. This time her look told me clearly that we were enemies. Yes, she hated me, and yet we were connected by some invisible cord.

Later on, Nainai told me about the terrible droughts that had fallen on her homeland. "Three years, not a single drop of rain. Thousands of people died from hunger. Those who lived went crazy. We would eat anything—tree barks, grass, even soil.

In many places, people cut the meat from the dead bodies." She sighed heavily. The swelling in her face and the sores around her eyelids had gone, but her eyes still struck with horror and awe. "The old heaven was punishing us for something we did. It had to be, because the whole country has been suffering from droughts and floods for such a long period." She stared at me, sharp light shooting out from her contracted pupils, like a cat about to leap upon her prey. I shuddered. She made me feel I was the cause of all disasters.

I HAD BEEN STRANGE and lonely since I was a child. I didn't know how to make friends. When I was five, I brought a girl home for the first time. Her name was Jia Jia. I sat on the floor watching her fly my airplane all over the room. Jia Jia, what a nice name! And she was as beautiful as her name. Mama would be so proud of me: I could make friends at last. I was not as abnormal, stupid, unsociable as she thought me. Jia Jia fell. The wing cracked. Jia Jia's face turned white. "Don't worry," I consoled her, though I was trembling with fear myself. "See, I can fix it with some glue. Going home now? Come back tomorrow. The glue will be dry then, and we can fly again. Will you come back? Will you, Jia Jia?" I kept shouting long after she ran out the door.

At night, someone pulled me out of the quilt. I opened my eyes and saw Mother holding the broken plane in one hand, a bamboo stick in the other. She thrashed my thigh several times. "If you bring any wild kid home again," she said, "you can sleep on the streets."

Since then my entertainment was sitting by myself reading. I devoured any books I could lay my hands on. I also enjoyed leaning on the window when I finished my chores in the house, watching my sisters playing rubber band jump rope or hide-and-seek with their friends. Father sometimes urged me to go out and join in the game. I just smiled and shook my head.

When I was a freshman in high school, a girl moved into the apartment across the hallway. The next day she appeared in my class and was assigned to share the desk with me. Her name was Li Jia. I couldn't tear my eyes away from her. Everything about her showed that she was from the capital—her standard mandarin with Beijing accent, her clothing, her manner. What fascinated me most were her velvet shoes with the immaculately white plastic soles. I'd been wearing homemade shoes all my life.

We became inseparable. We lived across from each other, shared a desk in school, and did our homework together. I helped her with her homework and housework and she told me endless stories about Beijing. One day Mother saw me light a coal stove for Li Jia in the yard. She called me in and said, "That girl from Beijing is taking advantage of you. Who do you think you are, her maid? The older you get, the more stupid you become. You neglect your duty at home for someone who's not worth your friendship. How much do you know about her family? Did you know that her father was demoted from Beijing because of an affair with a young girl in his office? Her sister isn't much better. I heard she's had two abortions already. Li Jia herself is also a snob. Can't you see? She talks to you only because you can do her homework and light her stove."

I continued seeing Li Jia secretly. But one day, she wouldn't open her door. I knocked stubbornly, knowing she was home with Dongzhuo, the girl from upstairs whose father was the vice-commander at the navy base. I had heard them going in five minutes before. I stopped knocking and waited. Suddenly I heard the laughing from inside. I walked away. Something inside me was shattered. The next morning, I asked the teacher to transfer me to another desk. When I graduated, I received straight As, but I hadn't made a single friend.

I WAS TRAINED TO BE independent, useful, and hard working after I came to live with my parents. I learned how to clean the apartment, wash my own clothes, make rice and noodles, steam bread, haul rice and coal on a cart from stores, raise chickens, grow vegetables, and many other things.

I still remember the morning when Mother called me to her bedside and handed me a one-yuan bill and some ration coupons for meat and bean curd. "Go to the market now and get fifty fen of pork, twenty fen of bean curd, and the rest for any vegetables you like," she yawned, her body ready to slip back into the warm quilt.

I stared at the money. My hands were still covered with soot from lighting the stove. But that was not the reason why I didn't reach for Mother's hand.

"What's wrong, Ni Bing?"

"I promise I won't forget to sweep the corners next time. I'll wash all the stains off the clothes and dishes. I'll try my best not to burn the rice again. But don't send me to the market, please! I don't know how to bargain with peddlers. And I don't like it."

Mother sat up straight and exposed her naked behind. "Do you think I send you there because I'm lazy? Not at all. I'm training you to take care of this family. Who knows when those Red Guards will take me away for the training class? Once I'm in there, even God can't help us. Do you understand? Your father is always on the ocean. If anything happens to me, you, the eldest daughter, must take care of your two sisters. From now on, you must learn fast. How old are you this year—eight, nine? Not a little girl any more!"

I took the money and stepped into the dark morning. The silent rice fields surrounded me with unknown danger and the stream made weird noises like a monster weeping underground. I had fished there with my sisters after the rain. It never uttered this kind of sound during the day. But I couldn't run away from it. The stream flowed through the center of Dinghai County, where the market was located. I passed several sentry posts along the road. The guards were sound asleep. This was the quietest moment. From morning till late evening, bullets whizzed past our apartment building. Occasionally Red Guards hid at our doorway, aiming their guns, which they lifted to their sweaty faces, at the outside world. There were five bullet holes in our door. This was nothing compared to the upstairs, where almost all the windows were shattered or pierced by bullets. Frightened adults were talking about moving to the first floor apartments. At first the children were scared, then they got really excited. They bugged their parents to let their best friends move into their apartments. I was also scared. My fear had more to do with the food supply. It was more and more difficult to get rice or sweet potatoes, for most of the rice stores were closed or destroyed. Everything was rationed: rice, oil, meat, sugar, even matches. I could not feel at ease unless the rice jar was full and the sweet potatoes piled high in the kitchen corner. There was a little hand in my stomach. When the jar was half empty, or when I passed my regular mealtime, the little hand would start scratching, grabbing, punching, and pounding. The only thing I could do was to eat until the food had pushed the little dirty hand to the bottom of my tummy. I didn't know why I was like that. Mother and Nainai, even Waipo, called me an incarnation of a hungry ghost.

A Red Guard stepped out of his sandbag-and-wire shelter and pointed his bayonet at my chest. Dewdrops were sparkling on his thick beard. I raised my basket upside down, then showed him the one-yuan bill while pointing in the direction of the market with my thumb. He inspected my face for a while, then let me go with a friendly smile.

Soon I passed the Liberation Bridge and entered the free market area, where freshwater fish, shrimp, crabs, potatoes, grains, and vegetables were sold. I went directly to the huge, green plastic shed of the state market. Food like pork, tofu, and seafood were only available here with ration coupons. Mother told me to get pork first, before it was sold. When I saw the line that rounded the counter three times, my heart sank. Standing among the ferocious adults, who constantly pushed and elbowed one another, I prayed that there would be some pork left for me. Mother had to eat meat and seafood every day to keep up her spirit. After the needles had crawled around the clock on the wall, it was finally my turn. But I couldn't see the fat butcher's shiny scalp. The counter was too tall for me.

"What you want? What you want?" I heard him shouting impatiently. Someone lifted me and sat me down on the greasy counter. "Ha, you little sprout," the butcher shouted, amused by what he saw. "How old are you? What are you doing here? Where's Mom?"

"Meat for fifty fen," I said with all my courage, blushing as I imagined that everyone was looking at me. "Ha, fifty fen of pork for my sprout," he sang out loud, as he picked a piece of lean meat and threw it to the cashier. "Thank you, Uncle," I said with gratitude. He'd given me the best meat that was left on the counter.

I didn't bother to stand in the line for bean curd. There were only two boards of them left. Each had ten pieces. Even if everyone bought just one piece, only twenty customers could be served. I quickly counted the people ahead of me. There were at least forty-five in the line. I passed the fish stands. The rotting smell made me sick. This was the only thing that didn't require coupons. When the season came, the market was drowned with sea bass, belt fish, and squid. I hated seafood, hated its smell and its mushy meat, especially the white eyes of the fish when I washed and fried them in the wok for Mother. I bought some shrimp for her. Caught in the morning and boiled alive with salt water, the peddler claimed, his face as red as the boiled shrimp. I didn't bargain with the peddler. It was degrading, both for the buyer and the seller, but everyone who came to the free market was supposed to do it. Mother, Nainai, even my younger sister haggled. The only person who refused to bargain was my father. He just walked around in the crowd and stopped when he saw something good. If the price was not too bad, he immediately took out his wallet. Not a word was wasted. Unfortunately, I had only gone out with him twice. He was too busy.

The shrimp peddler seemed to be shocked by my manner. When I was leaving, he threw a handful of shrimp into my basket. "Enjoy, little sister," he said, his white teeth glistening in the first morning light. It made the rest of my shopping easier. I bought a jin of sprouts and a half jin of mustard pickles. Sprouts could make a big dish for lunch and dinner. Pickles sautéed with sliced potatoes were my favorite and cost only thirty fen. On the island, vegetables were double, even triple the price of seafood. Mother should be happy with this full basket. I would tell her that I had bargained hard this morning and cut the shrimp price down to only eighteen fen a jin. It would make her happy. She often complained that I didn't know how to bargain and had to pay more for the food. I started home. I had to let out the chickens from the bathroom and clean it before everybody got up. I had to pick and wash the vegetables before I went to school at seven-thirty. I had to hurry.

So I MADE MY first lie at the age of eight, a sweet lie to please my mother, to get praise from her. I was willing to do anything to get it out of her beautiful mouth. She was my idol, someone I had tried, was still trying, to get close to. As for my relation with my father, it was beyond words, beyond comprehension. I hadn't called him father for almost seven years, and we'd never written to each other since I left home six years ago, yet he was with me day and night. It was strange, but so was I.

Chapter Three

IT WAS MONDAY AFTERNOON, the day after I slept with Yan. I sat
with my colleagues in the conference room of Hangzhou
Teachers' School, waiting for Party Secretary Hong to begin a
meeting. It must be an important one because the entire faculty
and staff were summoned here. Even the cooks from the school
canteen, who were usually spared the Monday afternoon political study meeting, sat with sour faces in the back corner. When
the meeting was over, no matter how late, they still had to rush
back to prepare the dinner for the teachers and students. The
meeting was supposed to have started at two, but it was already
2:10, and the row of tables in front of the conference room,
which was reserved for Party Secretary Hong and his adminis-
trators, remained empty. By the front window, Li Ai, the former
party secretary of this school, sat alone on a stool. With her
drooping shoulders and short entangled hair, she looked like a
bird who had flown hundreds of miles only to find that her nest
had been destroyed and her babies killed. Apparently she would
be the main target of today's meeting. My roommate and colleague Wang Ying kept looking at her watch, murmuring that she
should have brought her students' homework to read. Ying and I
were new teachers in this school, where we had both graduated

the same year, but Ying was the serious one, much more stable and reliable. At least she appeared to be.

At 2:21, Party Secretary Hong came into the room, followed by the two newly appointed vice-party secretaries with files of documents under their arms. They didn't look in Li Ai's direction, but their expressions showed that they were aware of her presence. One of the vice secretaries took the microphone and told the audience to pay special attention to today's meeting. There was an extremely important document from the Central Party Committee to be relayed. Everyone became quiet. Behind their expressionless faces, I could see that their only interest was in having this meeting over as soon as possible. Hong put on his glasses and began to read from a crisp new document. It was about starting a new movement to eradicate the influence of the "Gang of Four." Everyone must work hard to dig up the hidden dregs and clear them out. People in the audience turned their eyes to Li Ai. No doubt she was part of the dregs. No one seemed surprised. Li Ai had enjoyed her days of glory for the past ten years. It was her turn to fall. The only problem was that the document in Hong's hands looked dreadfully thick. And his voice, still enthusiastic and firm after an hour's reading, became more and more droning. If I could only have some cotton balls to block my ears!

So I lost my virginity finally, at the age of twenty-two, I said to myself. The thought hit me once more like a foaming wave in a high tide. Did anyone here notice the change? It was said that once the hymen was broken, a woman's eyebrows would begin to disappear. I looked around. Most of my colleagues were marking papers; some were reading or napping. The cooks were nodding off, their greasy heads resting on the backs of the chairs in front of them. They all had their own agendas, which had little to do with the droning voice from the rostrum. The only person who seemed to be listening to Hong was Li Ai, whose fate was now in his hand. Or, to look at it from a different point of view, their futures depended on each other. Li Ai's downfall equaled Hong's security in his new position and a possible promotion.

After the meeting, I'll borrow Wang Ying's mirror to check my eyebrows, I thought. She sat next to me, her head slightly bent forward, as if she was absorbing Hong's speech. But only I knew that she was sleeping. I studied her sparse eyebrows. Surely she was still a virgin. But who could tell? How much did I really know about my roommate, who was widely admired for her good manners, maturity, and sedateness? We got along fine, but there was a glass wall between us. You thought you knew everything about her, but you didn't. For one thing, I'd never seen her legs, though we'd slept in the same room for a year and a half. Sometimes I couldn't help doing mischievous things, such as wiping the desk with her snow-white towel, leaving my dirty socks on her bed, just to see how she would react. She never said or did anything. But a few weeks ago, my friend Wu Jian came to see me and told me how lucky I was to share a room with the sainted Wang Ying. Once I lost my temper and shouted, "You're also becoming as tactful as she. What happened to your straightforwardness? I'd rather you tell me how awful I was to have done those things to Wang Ying. But let me ask you something, if she really was a saint, how did you know what I did inside this room?" She was struck dumb and never mentioned Wang Ying again. I knew she wouldn't. It had to mean something that she was my only girlfriend in this city.

What would Wang Ying and other colleagues think of me if they knew I had lost my virginity to an ugly married man?

Yan was so ugly. When we first met at Ma Ao People's Commune five years ago, I couldn't help laughing in his face. He came up to me with an enormous smile, the corners of his pink mouth almost touching his ears, which stood out like fans on each side of his head. His long, bony nose tilted to the left about half an inch. *A clown,* I thought. Even now I still avoided looking straight at him so as not to laugh.

What really mattered, however, was Yan's family: his wife, who worked in a soy sauce factory in Dinghai, and his two kids, who lived with his parents in Shanghai.

If they knew what happened last night, I'd be also sitting on a stool in the front, like Li Ai, a moral criminal for breaking up a good family, except that no one would be dozing or reading. My affair with Yan would attract far more attention than this new political movement. How strange! People regarded me as a young, bright teacher, although they were occasionally frightened by my sudden bursts of temper and energy. Even my bosses avoided me when they saw the sparks in my eyes, which meant that my head was filled with suggestions and ideas for change. Not that they were afraid of me. No. They avoided me because they knew things needed to be changed but they couldn't and didn't want to do anything. Once they discovered that I had fallen in love with a married man, I'd be a devil, one of the most disgraced human beings on earth. But nothing had changed yet. Nothing would. Virgin or woman, I was still Ni Bing, quiet and humble on the surface, fiery and defiant in my bones. I may have appeared obedient, but secretly I didn't give a damn how people looked at me. My grandparents and parents knew it. Even my bosses.

"Ni Bing," someone called out my name, loud and ferocious. I jumped in my seat. Now the Party Secretary Hong was shouting other names from his list.

"What's going on?" I asked Ying.

"Li Ai will start her training class tonight to make a clean breast of her relation with the 'Gang of Four.' We are both assigned to be her keeper for the first week."

Ying was frowning with annoyance. For a whole week, excepting teaching, we'd be spending all our time, day and night, with Li Ai, making sure she got what she needed, but most importantly, making sure she did not run away or kill herself. Things like that happened all the time. After a long period of isolation and interrogation, people often had nervous breakdowns. It was not fun to be a guard, losing our own freedom as well as watching another human being suffer. Somehow, though, I felt relieved. A week away from Yan. This was what I needed. The thought of making love again caused cramps in my stomach.

"It's not fair," Ying whimpered in my ear. "Why should we stay there for a week just because we're single?"

"Do you have anything to say about this arrangement?" Hong asked, his eyes narrowing as he stared in our direction.

Ying stood up. "No problem. We can move in right now. We're single and should contribute more to this great movement." Word by word, she made the pledge for both of us. Her smooth face radiated sincerity and determination. I looked away in shame. How could a person change so quickly? A minute ago, she had complained about the injustice; now, she was pledging her loyalty.

The meeting was over. Two teachers escorted Li Ai home to fetch her clothing and other necessities for her training class. No one knew how long she would be shut up there. It depended on how quickly she would confess. Ying and I would move in with her at six o'clock this evening. I lifted my wicker chair above my head and headed for the office.

The wood floor of the empty office was clean from Saturday afternoon's brushing and mopping. It smelled like a pine forest after a spring rain. Ten teachers for the seventh grade shared this big room on the second floor. It was 4:30. Supper in the canteen was at five. I put my feet on my desk and tilted my chair backward, my favorite position to relax.

So Yan had made me a woman. How had that happened? I had fantasized about all kinds of men I would go out with—all except Yan.

WE MET in Ma Ao People's Commune in 1975. I had just been appointed a model "educated youth" of the year and had been touring from school to school in the commune to give speeches about my work in the countryside. One day, a man came up to me with a sarcastic smile. He held his head so high that I could only see the whites of his eyes and his huge nostrils.

"A nice report, Comrade Ni, only I wish the story about the son of the landowner was fake."

I stared at him, my face flushed with fear. "What do you mean?" my eyes asked.

"You see, if it were fake, he wouldn't have to go through this hell. But I guess some people have to trample on others to climb up." He stalked out of the auditorium. He was small and skinny, but his steps shook the ground of the auditorium. I stood on the stage, trembling. He had touched my sore spot. I, too, wished the son of the landowner in my story was fake. But Ma Gang was real. He had gone through many critical meetings for trying to "corrupt" me, while I was given rewards for having resisted the temptation of the class enemy. People were leaving, but I couldn't move my feet. My guilt had nailed me on the stage, as if I were the target of public criticism.

MA GANG was my neighbor in Ma Ao Village. The first thing I had noticed about him was that he didn't look like a peasant. He was too tall, his skin too white, and he barely spoke unless someone asked him a question. Peasants respected him greatly because he knew everything about farming, and the worst-tempered buffalo became a sheep in his hands. But they kept a distance with him. I had tried to talk to him several times, yet lost my nerve whenever I approached him.

He came to me one day at dusk. I was sitting on the steps reading *Dream of the Red Chamber* in the last rays of the sun. He came and read the book over my shoulder. I turned and smiled at him. I had done the same thing as a kid and had gotten many dirty looks from the book owners. They didn't like a stranger bending over their heads. He blushed and murmured an apology. I was even more amused. A true peasant would never apologize. I stood up and handed him the book. "Too bad it's not complete. Have you read the other two volumes?" he asked.

He turned the pages with extreme care. It dawned on me that all the peasants in the village could barely write a simple letter. How was it possible that he could have read one of the most complicated books in Chinese literature?

"Yes, I have. I used to have three versions; my dad's, actually."
He turned to the front page to see the publisher and year of publication, only to find that I had torn off the cover and wrapped it with *Mao's Collected Works*. We smiled at each other like comrades.

"Ah, can you tell me the end of the story?" I asked.

He looked around the quiet yard and squatted on the steps. He was such a great storyteller that I didn't even hear Su Feng's footsteps. When I looked up, I saw her staring at us through the steam rising from the bowl of pickles and potatoes in her hands. She seemed to be on the verge of crying. I jumped up and tried to explain what we were doing. She just walked past us and entered my room. She had brought the dish for my supper, but I was sitting shoulder to shoulder with her beloved. I knew she was crazy about him, though she never said a word about it. Twice a week she would sneak into his room and collect his dirty clothing to wash in the stream before she came over to sleep with me. She admitted that he got mad sometimes, but she didn't care. She couldn't bear seeing a man do his own laundry. It was degrading. Ma Gang blushed like a girl and went back to his own place in a hurry.

I ran back home. Su Feng sprawled in my bed with her face down. I spent hours trying to make her talk, until I lost my patience and said, "Well, it doesn't solve any problem by lying here. If you like him, why don't you just go and tell him? This was the first time I ever talked to him. There's no need for you to feel jealousy."

She jumped up, shouting, "I can't! I can't! I can't bring misfortune to my family anymore."

I looked at her in bewilderment. What was she talking about?

"Oh, I wish I had the courage to love the son of a landlord," she wept.

No wonder all the melancholy and silence. What a curse to be born into such a class! He couldn't be older than twenty-five. When his father was classified as a landlord during the land reform, Ma Gang was still a child. He couldn't have exploited the peasants at that age. But for the rest of his life, he would be punished for his father's deeds.

"Where's his dad?"

"Dead. Starved to death in the sixties. My mom said he was a kind landlord. Never yelled at his tenants, loved to read and go to operas. When the land reform started, he gave up all his land and houses voluntarily. So we didn't torture him much."

"So Ma Gang learned how to read and write from his father?"

She nodded. "He knows everything. Whenever we have a problem, we go to him. He never talks about school. But I know he wants to go to college. And I know, and he knows, that it will never happen. My heart aches for him. Sometimes I wish he weren't so good looking, so intelligent. Perhaps he'd suffer less and so would I."

"Why don't you talk to your dad? He's wise and smart, and you're his favorite child. Perhaps he'll help you out."

"No, no," she screamed. "He'll kill me if he knows how I feel about Gang! If I married him, I'd drag my whole family to the bottom. I can't do that."

No more kerosene. The light flickered several times before it went out. I stroked Su Feng's hair and let her weep with her head on my lap. Finally she fell asleep. I sat in the dark, confused by the babble of words going round and round in my head. The whole thing seemed so unfair and incomprehensible. The only crime Ma Gang had committed was being born into his family. It would be easier for me to accept it if he looked like the class enemy I had read about in books or seen in films: mean-spirited, pig-eyed, wrinkled face, matted hair, walking with his head bent and hands behind his back. What if I were picked by some invisible power to be born into a family like this? I shuddered. Suddenly I remembered the scene of us sitting close to each other, reading a banned book. Would he tell anybody? Not likely. He would only make more trouble for himself. What should I do when I saw him again? Pretend that nothing had happened? No matter how much sympathy I felt for him, he was still the son of a landlord. Theoretically, he was my enemy.

I didn't see him, or I should say, I didn't encounter him face to face until the rice cake season in late autumn. By then, all the rice had been harvested, dried, and distributed to the peasants according to their annual workpoints. When the rain and northwest wind made field work impossible, each family took barrels of the new rice and gathered in the village mill to make rice cake. They would make hundreds of jin and soak them in huge water jars in melted snow water to preserve them until next summer's harvest season. For two weeks, the mill was jammed with people twenty-four hours a day. Children played hide-and-seek behind the barrels of soaked sweet rice lining the yard. Inside, four bathtub-size vats sprayed white steam and filled the room with sweet and sour odors. Two peasants lifted one of the vats and poured the hissing "snowflakes"—the white, puffed rice powder—into a huge stone mortar. Immediately, two half-naked young men began to pound the dough with wooden hammers, while a third turned it swiftly between each stroke. When the powder was pounded into firm dough, they threw it onto a long table where it was grabbed by a troop of women, rolled into small balls, and pressed into wooden molds. Then children peeled the two-inch-wide and six-inch-long cakes off the molds and sealed them with a red plum blossom or the character fu—happiness.

I had been eating and working in the mill for three days and nights without sleep, helping my friends' families with their rice cakes. We all helped one another. There was no class distinction during the season. Making rice cakes was collective work. My head was spinning with rainbow clouds, but I refused to go home and miss all the excitement until I had helped Su Feng's family. I was pulling a barrel of ground sweet rice to the steamer and saw Ma Gang's name on the bamboo basket. *Oh, it is his turn tonight,* I thought. Suddenly the barrel became much lighter. It was actually moving forward by itself. I looked up and saw him pushing the barrel from the other side. Our eyes met through the steam. I blushed. He moved his lips as if he had something to say, but nothing came out. I wiped my face with my sleeve and said, "Too hot here. I'm going out for some fresh air."

I stood in the yard looking at the moon. It had just untangled itself from dark clouds and was shedding cold light like a fluorescent lamp. I took a deep breath. The crisp air cleared my head. For three days, my heart had been pumping with excitement. Now it was filled with sadness and confusion. I really liked Ma Gang, but there was a wall between us, and I didn't have the strength to pull it down.

"Ni Bing," Ma Gang called from behind me. I jumped and turned to him. He was holding a bowl of snowflakes in his hands. The steam rising from the bowl blossomed into the shape of a white chrysanthemum. His hands shook, and the flower broke. "Ni Bing, would you taste my snowflake?" he asked, his face as pale as the moon.

I took the bowl without thinking. I'd had many bowls in the past three days. Whenever the steamer was uncovered, the owner would invite everyone present to have a bowl of snowflakes. To refuse was the biggest insult one could inflict on the owner. I pinched some from the puffy dough and brought it to my mouth, but then my ears started ticking like a time bomb, and a voice said: "Don't touch it, Ni Bing. Don't touch the poison from a class enemy. Give it back, back, back."

I bent my head. The bowl in my hands weighed more than the rice barrels. What should I say to him? What was I doing to him?

He sighed and my body froze. It was saddest sigh I'd ever heard, worse than sobbing or crying. I knew right away that I'd be haunted by his sigh for the rest of my life if I didn't do something. But I couldn't move or speak. He took the bowl gently from my hands and went back into the mill.

If he had cursed or hit me, I'd have felt less ashamed and less confused. I remembered having the same feelings I had when I saw the peasant women slap the Japanese devils with their shoes in the movie *The Tunnel War*. I knew I should hate those invaders and killers. But I couldn't stop shedding tears for them. My classmates reported this to our teacher, and I had to make a self-criticism in class. The teacher said, "There's proletarian humanity and there's bourgeois humanity. We must know for whom we cry. When Ni Bing shed tears for a Japanese invader, she not only stood on the side of the foreign devils, but she became one herself." That's when I got the nickname "foreign devil." What was the matter with me, I asked myself, recalling the expression of indignation and disgust on my teacher's face.

"Ni Bing, why are you standing here alone? Homesick?" It was Yue Niang, secretary of the Youth League in Ma Ao People's Commune. She was young and pretty, her skin white and smooth, unlike the dark and blotchy-faced country girls. She talked in a silky, authoritative voice. I had liked her the first time we met. Recently, she had been visiting me quite often. Each time she brought pamphlets and magazines to raise my political consciousness. I told her what had happened. Perhaps she could help me straighten things out.

"Excellent, Comrade Ni Bing!" she beamed. "Do you realize that you've just resisted the bomb coated with sweets from a class enemy? I have to report this to Comrade Lee and set you up as a model in our commune. We've been looking for one for the annual meeting in the county. I knew you'd not disappoint me. I've been keeping an eye on you for months."

"But perhaps he's been reformed," I argued. "He works harder than anyone else, and he hardly speaks. He gave me the snowflakes out of hospitality. It's just a local custom, you know." I began to worry that my stupidity might bring endless trouble to Ma Gang.

"A class enemy is always a class enemy, no matter what he's like and where he lives," Yue Niang said coldly. "Day and night they dream and plan to destroy our proletarian dictatorship. It's our great leader Chairman Mao's teaching, and we should never forget it."

I closed my eyes and mouth. How could I not remember this, having recited it hundreds of times in the past eight years? But I still couldn't see Ma Gang as an enemy. Not when his sigh kept echoing in my ears.

"Now, I want you to write a report about the whole event, from the beginning to the end. Dig into your soul and describe how you struggled against his evil purpose. Quote as many of Mao's words as possible. If you need materials, I can give you more magazines. Two days should be enough, eh? Remember, this task concerns your second life—your political career. Understand? I have to go now. I'll wait for you in my office in two days."

"Wait a minute, Yue Niang. I can't . . ." I cut my words short when I saw the coldness in her eyes and said instead, "I don't know how to write this kind of stuff. Besides, we're busy making rice cakes here. I've promised my friends to help."

"Comrade Ni Bing," she said, grabbing my shoulders and shaking me, "do you know that you're standing on a cliff? If you step forward, you have a broad road bathed in the golden sunlight for your future. But if you take just one step back, you'll be in the abyss for the rest of your life. You're a smart girl. You don't need me to tell you more. You must have guessed why I've brought you all the pamphlets about the Communist Party. We're thinking of you as a candidate to become a member. Here's your great chance to prove your loyalty. I hope you won't disappoint me."

She was gone, but her words continued to press down like stormy clouds. What she said was only half true: there was an abyss behind me and in front of me. How could I ever forgive myself if I wrote this report? But how could I let myself be stuck in the same pit with Ma Gang for the rest of my life?

Two days passed by, quickly and slowly. I tried to write something, but my brain was as blank as the paper. I went to Yue Niang's office empty-handed, ready to be punished. When she saw my face, she made a gesture to stop my talking and took a folder out of her drawer. "I wrote the report according to what you told me the other night. Tomorrow, you're going to Ma Ao Central Middle School to give a speech. All you have to do is to read it. Is it too much to ask? Day after tomorrow, you'll be in

Li Village Elementary School. Here's your schedule. Now I want you to read the report carefully and put some emotion into your reading. It's a mission the party has given you. You no longer represent just yourself but all the educated youths in Dinghai County. You can go now. Tomorrow at eight, I'll come to your place to take you to the school."

I walked out like a zombie. I *was* a zombie. What was left to the body when the soul was snatched away? The whole thing had gone beyond my choice. Ma Gang was in deep mud, whether I cooperated with the commune leaders or not. I was just a puppet in their hands.

I DON'T KNOW how long I stood on the stage. When I finally looked up, the whole auditorium was empty. I said aloud, as if Yan was still there, "What would you have done if you were in my situation?" Either criticize Liang and become a model educated youth or live in the countryside forever as a peasant—this was what the commune leader Li told me. I looked around the empty hall. If only the stranger was still there and could answer this question!

I quickly found out who he was. It was easy. As soon as I started describing his appearance, the peasants laughed and shouted, "Oh, Head-lifting Yan." He was an educated youth from Shanghai. They all knew him because he had taught their children at Ma Ao Elementary and Middle School. He taught everything: physics, Chinese, math, art, even English. What made him famous, however, was his house, which was haunted by his sister-in-law's ghost. Years ago, she had eloped with her lover to the island, hoping her sister, Yan's wife, would help them. No one knew what Yan's wife had told the desperate lovers, but they were found dead on White Spring Mountain near Ma Ao several weeks later, their bodies rotten but still intertwined. They had stolen Yan's wife's pesticide and drunk it with bottles of orange juice. They were buried where they died. Their parents didn't want to have anything to do with the bodies. Now, when the moon was full, Yan's wife would hear her sister calling and weeping, and the door would open and close on its own. Now she had problems seeing things.

I didn't see or hear about him again until that summer. Yan took his class to my village to help harvest rice. I avoided him. It was too embarrassing to encounter him, although I still wished I could explain what had happened between Ma Gang and me. One night, he suddenly appeared at my door, holding a pile of books in his arms.

"Xiao Ni, I'm here to say good-bye. I'm leaving tomorrow," he said with a smile, no sarcasm this time. He entered the room, put the books on my bed, then sat down on my stool. He acted as if we had known each other for years. I stood in the middle of the room, my eyes switching back and forth between Yan and the books.

"For you," he said. "When you finish, just come to my school for more. I'm the librarian. I have some good ones not available to the public." He winked.

I was not at all prepared for this sudden friendliness and intimacy. He sat on my only stool as if he were the owner of the room, one leg shaking comfortably on the other. His smile, which looked more like a leer, made me rather uneasy. Somehow, I preferred his stern, scolding look. At least I knew what he was up to. But the books. How did he know I was dying for new books? I had read all my old books more than ten times, including the little booklet on Jesus I had picked up from the garbage pile of Old Sao. He had died of TB two months before. The peasants threw all his belongings together, which were not much, and burned them. I grabbed the book before they set the fire. No one seemed to have noticed. If they had realized that Old Sao had been a Christian, what would they have done? Probably nothing. He was a gulao, someone who had no descendants, who had no son to cry at his funeral, the worst thing that could happen to a person. Anyway, I read even that booklet twice. Now I knew how Jesus

was born and how he practiced his miracles. The stories somehow touched me a great deal. When I was fifteen, I also believed
that I had become pregnant by staring at the boy I secretly loved.
Right now, I was just reading *The Complete Collection of Herbs*, eight
hundred pages. Occasionally, the weird prescriptions would
make my eyes open wide. Anything could be used as medicine—
feces, urine, hair, scabs, and the soot from the bottom of a wok.
But reading prescriptions was like nibbling at bland cookies. It
was not a real meal. I wanted fiction. I glanced at the pile on my
desk. The book on top was *Sunny Sky*. My heart jumped with
delight, as if a great gift had dropped into my lap from heaven. I
looked at Yan. *Oh, I would do anything for you,* I said to myself.

"I know what you're thinking about." He shook his finger at
me, his left leg crossed over his right, his foot drawing circles in
the air. "Let's not get into details now, OK? I just want to tell you
that my accusation about you the other day was wrong. You're
actually a sincere, hardworking girl, a bit too innocent sometimes. But that's also your advantage. I'm impressed by your
news bulletins. Great content, interesting style, direct and raw,
no bullshit. I like it. I've corrected some grammar mistakes.
Hope you don't mind. Oh, I'd better let you go to bed. You get
up at two in the morning, right? Don't worry, I won't tell anyone. Good spirit, but health is very important. In fact, it's the
most important. Don't do it too long, promise me?" He looked
at his watch. "It's eleven. You'll have three hours of sleep. Good
night, Xiao Ni. Should I close the door for you?"

"No, thanks," I said, feeling dizzy from the bombardment of
Yan's words.

He looked at the door closely. "You don't have a lock for the
door?" he asked in disbelief.

"What for? I have nothing worth stealing. Besides, I have to
leave my door open so my hen and duck can come in for food
while I'm in the fields."

He nodded his head. Suddenly, he held out his hand to me. "So
we're friends now, yes?"

I nodded.

He took my hand and covered my palm with his other hand. "Take care of yourself, Ni Bing, you have a long way to go." Then he turned to leave.

I stared at his back until it disappeared in the dark. He had just surprised me once more. But this time, it was a pleasant surprise. I felt a tremendous surge of gratitude for his forgiveness and understanding about Ma Gang. But how did he find out? Why was he so interested in me?

When I took the books to his school three weeks later, he was gone. "Back to Shanghai with his wife," the new librarian said, her eyes fixed on the sweater she was knitting.

"When will he be back?" I asked meekly, feeling an empty space in my heart.

"No idea. Depends on his wife. Depends whether they can get a good doctor. She's getting blind, you know. It's the ghost." She looked up. "Who are you? What's your relationship with Yan?"

I jumped and ran.

I DIDN'T SEE HIM again till 1977. I was studying at Hangzhou Teacher's School. That morning, I was pacing the campus road, memorizing an excerpt from *Sister Carrie* in a textbook of English.

"Good morning, Xiao Ni." A man called me from the other side of the road. The voice sounded familiar and intimate, but I didn't recognize it. I looked up reluctantly. Five minutes left for breakfast, and I hadn't learned the text by heart as I had planned. I didn't want to be disturbed. Through the branches of the Chinese parasols that neatly lined the road, I saw Yan and his raised chin. He ran towards me with his arms open. The faded blue navy jacket pressed against his bony chest.

"How nice to see you again!" He grabbed my hand and shook it vigorously. "I was really mad at you. How could you leave Ma Ao without saying good-bye?"

You left first without saying anything, I thought. But my face was smiling. I was genuinely happy to see him. "Well, you know the old story," I explained. "You're glad to leave the countryside, but at the same time you feel you've betrayed something or were betrayed. What? Can't put your finger on it. Your ideals, your beliefs? It's strange. When I was there, the only thing I could think about was how to get out. When I was leaving, I felt bad, terribly bad and sad. So I just took a bus quietly."

I was exploding with words. I talked like this only in extreme frustration or excitement. On Yan's chest was a badge of Hangzhou University. The red characters on the white background stabbed at my eyes. I, too, could have been a student there. The people's commune had actually recommended me. I had to compete with hundreds of candidates. In the end, only two passed numerous exams, me and a girl from the White Spring People's Commune. The final interview was conducted in English. I could tell one of the examiners was pleased with me. He beamed and nodded at every word I uttered. The younger one became more and more agitated. Finally he said, "Open your mouth."

I knew I was in trouble. He must have noticed my missing front upper tooth. It had had a bad cavity and needed a root canal. The young dentist from the navy hospital had somehow persuaded me to have it pulled. It was probably easier for him. He had also made me a new fake tooth, which tortured me for four months till one day it just broke into three pieces and fell out. I opened my mouth, trying to cover the empty space with my lip.

"Wider," he ordered and bent his head to look up into my mouth. "You see, I knew something was wrong with her," he shouted triumphantly to his colleague. "Her front tooth is missing. I was wondering where the hissing sounds came from."

"But it doesn't really affect her speaking, Comrade Mo," the older examiner said carefully. "In fact, her English sounds beautiful, hardly any accent."

"The hissing sound, Comrade Luo," he snapped, staring hard into the gray-haired man's eyes until the latter looked away. Apparently, Comrade Mo, though much younger, was in charge.

I stood up and left quietly. No use staying there any longer. I was not going to be accepted by the college. Before I went to the final exam, people had been telling me that the other girl, my last rival, had connections—her uncle was the party secretary in the English Department of Hangzhou University. I didn't want to believe it. I had to try my best. Now it was all over.

A month later, I received an admission letter from Hangzhou Teacher's School. The campus was right next to Hangzhou University. At least, I rationalized, it was better than spending another year in the countryside.

"OH, THIS," Yan patted his badge, noticing I'd been staring at it. "I'm in the Chinese Department there." He pointed to the tall gray brick buildings on the other side of the wall, his face lit with pride. "It wasn't easy. I had to compete with everyone who hadn't had a chance to go to college for the past ten years during the Cultural Revolution."

Fate, I told myself. If I had waited eight more months in the countryside, I could also have qualified for the exams. But how would I have known? When I decided to come to this school, no one had expected that the government would suddenly restore the college entrance exams policy. Now colleges were open to everyone under thirty, unmarried, except for me, stuck in this place to be trained as an elementary school teacher. The best thing I could do was to graduate and work for two more years before I would be qualified to take the exams for college.

"Congratulations! You must have done well," I said, forcing myself to smile.

"Well, my total score was the highest in Zhoushan, and my Chinese was number one in the whole province."

"You could have gone to Beijing University, at least to Fudan in Shanghai," I exclaimed. I was feeling sincere pride for him, and pity. What was he doing in this third-rate college with such a high score?

"If only I could!" he shouted on the verge of tears. "They

forced me to choose three colleges before I took the exams. I knew I could do well. But you never know. We can't always be in control. It's a real gamble. What if my grades couldn't reach the requirement of Fudan? Then I'd never be able to get out of the fucking haunted house in Ma Ao. I couldn't allow that to happen!" He waved his fist in the air. Suddenly he dropped his hand and stared at me weirdly. "You're smiling, Ni Bing. You're laughing at me. But I don't mind. I like your smile. Really sweet."

I blushed. I didn't realize I was smiling. His cursing amused me. It suddenly brought me back to the pungent days in Ma Ao. I hadn't heard this kind of bad words since coming to the city. I missed it. For the first time, I felt close to Yan. I noticed his voice. It was resonant and deep, confident, authoritative, yet also soothing.

The bell rang. "Time for breakfast," I said. "I've got to go. I hate standing in line. Nice seeing you again."

"Wait!" He caught me by the arm. "Do me a favor? My jacket is getting filthy. Would you wash it for me?"

I was too shocked to say a word. It was very bold of him to ask me to do his laundry. This was only our second, no, third meeting. Besides, I hated washing clothes. But I still nodded my head. I didn't understand. How much power did that weird guy have over me?

I SHIFTED UNEASILY in my chair. Blood flowed into my sleeping legs and my feet like thousands of ants nibbling at my flesh. Was the magic in his voice? Often I was content just to listen to him talking, my eyes closed, letting the waves of his sound wrap me and seep through my skin until all my internal organs were massaged.

Three gentle knocks on the door. The door was kicked open. Yan rushed in with a steaming pot in his hands. He dropped it down on the desk, then grabbed his ears to cool his fingers, hissing in pain as he jumped up and down. "Meimei," he said, his face still twisted from the burns on his hands, "Ying told me you didn't go to the canteen. I bought two bowls of noodles at the People's Restaurant on the corner. Pickle and pork, your favorite. Eat while it's hot. I've also brought you some Chinese and geography textbooks with a list of questions you should be able to answer after the reading. Not easy to get them in this season. Everyone was preparing for the exams. I guess I won't see you for the next week. I'll miss you. But you must work as hard, even harder, when I'm not around. Only two months left. Not much time. Meimei . . ."

I listened. No one had cared about me or loved me like this. "I can do anything for him, anything," I said to myself.

Chapter Four

I JUMPED AND hit my head on something hard when the school bell rang. The jolt sent my body back down on the bed. The pain awakened me. I realized I was lying in the bottom bunk bed in the interrogation room with Ying and Li Ai. Li was making sounds like a boiling kettle in her sleep. It must have entered my dream as the ringing of the school bell. I sat up slowly. Time to get up, anyway. I took out my watch from under the pillow and stared at it until the two green needles appeared in the dark. Four-thirty A.M., exactly as I had estimated. There was a clock ticking inside me, day and night. Wherever I went, no matter what I was doing, I always knew what time it was. People say time is invisible, abstract, something invented by human thoughts. To me, it was as real and concrete as my beating heart and the ground I stood on. I could feel it pushing, pulling, slipping by. Sometimes it raged like a creek in a flash flood and carried me to some really strange places, sometimes it cooed around me like pigeons in love. Most of the time, the ticking made me restless. I rushed around like a headless fly, hurrying to reach a destination that I knew nothing about. I knew time, but I still wore my Seagull watch. Its huge face pressed awkwardly against my thin wrist, its tight metal band bit into my skin. I wore it because it gave me a sense of being in control. When I held the watch, I was also holding time in my hand. It gave me the illusion that I could do anything with it. The needles always circled from right to left. After the short one had made two rounds inside the glass shell, people told themselves a day and night had passed. But I could see through the surface. On the other side of the watch, the needles could go any direction, any speed. Time was not bound by the twelve numbers or by the space. What a liberation! What a curse! When time ran back and forth like that, everything was a mess. I was forced to see and hear scenes of terror and misery. But I couldn't help it, just as I couldn't help tying time around my wrist and checking it every so often, as if I needed to prove my innate power.

In the dark, I gathered my jogging pants, sweatshirt, books I planned to read that morning, and two bowls to get breakfast for Li Ai and myself from the canteen, then walked out on tiptoes. In the dim light of the hallway, I put on my clothing and sneakers and ran downstairs. When I got outside, I turned left and headed toward the school sports ground for my half-hour jog before my morning studies. The first dawn light emerged above the classroom building. Its gray roof tiles and square windows made me think of the West Gate Village, the navy compound where I had spent ten years. For a decade, I got up before dawn, first with my father, then with Nainai, finally by myself, to light the small coal stove, fanning the hole at the bottom of the stove with an old palm leaf, watching golden sparks dance in the smoke. I had different names for them: fairies, angels, elves, stars, diamonds. When the black coal balls glowed red, I brought the stove in, put on a pot of rice and water to make porridge for breakfast, then went to the market with a basket on my arm.

I looked up at the tree top. It was about 5:15. I could tell the time by the color of the leaves, which, when I had arrived, were still dark, but which were now dyed silver-gray by the dawn light. I had run an extra five rounds this morning in addition to my usual ten, thus losing twelve minutes for reading. When I jogged, I paced myself at a regular rhythm: three minutes for each three hundred meter lap, not faster in the beginning, not slower in the end. Sometimes when running, I even fantasized that I had become one with time. My legs moved like a pendulum, but I had a much bigger space to run around in. Or did I, really? After all, didn't everything in this world, including my jogging, move in circles? If I kept jogging around the earth at this speed, I could actually measure its diameter by counting how much time I used. If I did this, did it mean that time and space were the same thing from different points of view? *Stop thinking,* I told myself, *and start reading the geography textbook right now.* I sat down under the scholar tree where I had hung my school bag and opened my book.

When I returned to the interrogation room with two bowls of rice gruel at 7:30, Ying was waiting at the door with her bag and an empty bowl. She looked at me, pointed at her watch, and rushed out without a word. "Sorry," I said to her back. I felt guilty for being late. Ying had to teach a class at eight o'clock.

"Li Ai, breakfast." I put the bowls on a stool and took two steamed buns from my bag. Then I pulled out two chairs. All the furniture in this room was small. The building used to be a kindergarten.

She didn't respond to my call but continued her morning exercise by the window. She was shaking her hands back and forth at such a speed that her arms seemed about to fall off her shoulders at any moment. I had seen my father do the same exercise. Before he discovered lingzhi, the magic mushroom in mythology, he had tried all kinds of weird folk prescriptions to cure his xinkou teng—heartache. This hand-shaking exercise was supposed to help circulate the blood and ease the tension if done properly. I coughed gently, hoping to get her attention so that I could tell her to take it easy. She did turn her head quickly. Her face startled me. I'd never seen anyone put so much faith into an exercise as Li Ai did. Her eyebrows, usually shaped like bee wings, were now twisted into triangles. Her soaked shirt stuck to her chest, revealing her drooping breast on the right and the empty space on the left. She had just had an operation for cancer. I heard that Hong had sent for her directly from the hospital. Would she be able to go through the interrogation process? I sat down on the baby chair. Let her finish. No need to rush her. I didn't have to teach till ten.

Finally she came over and sat down face-to-face with me. Our knees almost touched under the stool. I blew at the porridge. The congealed surface was pushed to one side and made wrinkles like the ones on Li Ai's forehead.

"There's a piece of fermented bean curd at the bottom of your bowl," I said.

She looked up and smiled. There was a thin scar across her chapped lips. Her eyelids were lined with brown spots. Gray strands of hair stood out sharply on top of her head and looked much coarser than the black hair. I heard she was only forty-five, but she appeared to be in her fifties. I suddenly had an urge to say something to her. I didn't know what, just anything, to comfort her. I had to bite my tongue to check myself. How could I feel sympathy for this woman who had tormented many teachers and exiled them during the Cultural Revolution? Perhaps it was this physical closeness that made me sentimental. Whenever I moved my legs, our knees touched.

Li Ai was making loud noises as she tried to suck the gruel from the bottom, her face buried in the white enamel container. Finally she took the bowl and poured what was left into her mouth. When she put it down on the stool, the inside of the bowl shined as if she had licked it clean. Not a single drop of rice left there. She took everything seriously, even her food. I heard footsteps and laughter. Hong and his committee were coming upstairs for their first session with Li Ai. Would she also take it seriously? Why did I have so much sympathy for her? Was there also an invisible cord between us?

The interrogators were at the door. I gathered the dirty bowls and hurried to the washroom to clean them. I had to get everything ready for the interrogation. Hong brought his own secretary today. I didn't need to stay to keep a record. I was going to my office to prepare my lessons. "What do you want for lunch?" I asked without looking at her.

"Two liang of rice and some green vegetables, please."

She wanted to tell me something. I could feel it in her voice. I turned. Our eyes met for the first time since we had moved into this kids' room. Her mouth opened, then shut suddenly, like a clam closing its shell when invaded by a hand. She made no sound, but I heard everything. The door was pushed open. They didn't knock. Interrogators never did. *Take care,* I said to her in my heart. She had turned her back to me to face Hong and his people. I slammed the door and ran downstairs.

At THE ENTRANCE to the canteen, Yan stopped me and slipped a book into my hand. "Here's the book you wanted to borrow, Ni Bing," he said, his chin nodding at me and the book several times. As soon as I returned to the interrogation room and handed lunch to Li Ai, I went to my bunk bed and took out the note between the pages. Yan had carefully folded it into a swallow.

"Meimei, wait for me at our place at eight. I must see you tonight. Something urgent."

At five to eight, I told Ying that I needed some clothing and books from my dormitory and slipped through the back door of the building. Our usual meeting place was at the northern corner of the wall that divided the two schools, right behind the interrogation building. We'd had lots of rain in Hangzhou this year. Grass had grown wild in this desolate corner. People had been avoiding it since a teacher jumped out of the window and died there in 1970. Yan had discovered a hole in the wall covered by waist-high grass and had decided to use it as our emergency meeting place. What had happened? I waited anxiously in the dark. I could see the yellow light from the third-floor window, the only light in the whole building. Ying was grading homework when I left the room, and Li Ai was reading Marx's *Manifesto of the Communist Party.* If Ying looked out the window, she could have seen me easily, but I knew she never would. She insisted on keeping the window shut even in the summer. We had constant, silent battles about opening and closing our window in the dormitory. Even if she did open the window, she couldn't stick her head out of the iron bars. They were installed there soon after the jumping incident. A black shadow crawled through the hole and held me in his tight arms.

"Meimei, Meimei, I miss you. What am I going to do without you?" Yan whispered, his face wet from sweat. He'd been running.

"What's wrong, Gege?"

"I'm going to Shanghai early in the morning. She must have another operation immediately, the doctor said, otherwise she'll go blind completely. They need my signature."

I sat down and clasped my knees. Yan crouched next to me, his arms around my shoulders. He rarely mentioned his wife, but she haunted us, just as she herself was haunted by her sister. She was the shadow of our love. The grass rustled in the wind. Someone was weeping in the distance. The sound came from above, faint and irregular, but consistent. It couldn't be Li Ai. It was hard to imagine her crying. "The ghost," I said.

"Yes, the ghost." Yan took my cold hand and warmed it between his palms. I was often amazed by the size of his hands. When he walked, he swung his arms back and forth with his huge hands open, as if he had tied two palm leaf fans around his wrists. In his loose jacket and baggy pants, he looked like a scarecrow. "Do you believe in ghosts?"

Did I believe in ghosts? Perhaps you should have asked me if I believed in souls. Ghosts were souls who had lost their bodies. Those good ones had been protecting me for twenty-two years. But the malicious ones had been trying to drag me into those dark tunnels of nightmare where they would have cut me into pieces hundreds of times. I knew thousands of ghost stories, Gege. In the summer evenings, we gathered in the square of the Western Gate

Village, kids and adults, competing among one another for the most frightening ghost stories. I always won. That was the most glorious moment in my childhood, when I was surrounded by kids and adults with drooping chins and scared eyes. I also liked to tell stories of love, jealousy, competition, and fights among ghosts. They were just like us. Not much difference. I grew up with them. Nainai called me "little ghost," and my mother preferred "dead ghost." Sometimes I myself believed I was one of them.

"Gege." I stroked his burning forehead with my free hand. "Tell me about your sister-in-law."

"She fell in love with her colleague in the No. 2 Textile Factory of Shanghai. It was unfortunate, because the guy was the son of a former capitalist. In fact, his father used to own the factory where they were working. Her mother threatened to kill herself if her daughter didn't stop seeing him. Her father threatened to disown her, but it only made her determined to marry him. The day before they went to register at the police station, her brothers locked her in the apartment. They tied her up with ropes and flogged her with belts until she promised never to see him again. As soon as they set her free, she escaped with her lover. We didn't know anything about it at that time. There was no telephone in our village. One night, around eleven, they suddenly knocked on our door. They both looked such a mess, exhausted and scared, her face and arms all bruised. Their eyes, however, burned with disturbing brightness. I let them in and tried to find out what had made them visit our village, but they wouldn't say anything. Then I went to cook dinner for them. They looked starved. When I returned with the noodles, they were gone. My wife was pacing the hall, agitated and indignant. *They eloped!* she shouted at me. *How shameless! They even had the nerve to ask me to lend them money and put them up for a few nights.*

"'What are you glaring at me like that for!' she shouted. 'What was I supposed to do? Let them soil our bed? No way! They don't care about losing face, but I do! I still want to go home and see my parents.' She was still babbling on when I slapped her. I'd never hit a woman in my life, Meimei, never! But I didn't regret slapping that monster. I ran after that poor couple. I shouted their names all over the place. I didn't know whether they went to the highway and got a ride or they didn't want to answer me. For the next few days, my eyelids kept trembling. Something bad was going to happen, I told my wife. We should report to the police. She still tried to tell me some bullshit like 'Domestic shame should not be made public.'

"'If something really happened to them, I'd never forgive you,' I said. Then I went to the police station in town by myself. As soon as I finished my story, they took me to the mortuary of the town hospital.

"'Glad you came. We found them two days ago. No ID or any other papers. The only thing we could tell was that they came from Shanghai. No one around here wears this kind of clothing and shoes. It was suicide.' I saw the two bodies underneath the white sheets and sank to the ground."

He grasped my hand, then brought it to his lips to suppress his sobbing. I stroked his hair with my other hand. Silence was my only way to console him. Yan wiped his tears and continued.

"Her mother didn't want to have anything to do with the body. The boy's parents had died in the sixties. My wife became completely hysterical when she heard the news. So I decided to bury them on the mountain where they died. You know the White Spring Mountain? Not far from Ma Ao. Full of pine trees. I figured they must like the place, since they chose it to end their lives. Soon they started visiting our house in the village. Our door would open by itself at night. My wife kept falling to the ground for no reason, as if someone invisible were tripping her. And she heard weeping voices wherever she went. A few months later, she started seeing blue light in everything, and her eyes hurt like crazy. I used to laugh at those who believed in supernatural things. But my sister-in-law's ghost really exists. If a ghost could swim, I'm sure she'd have crossed the East China Sea to haunt her mother and brothers. They killed her, the only good person in the family."

We sat in the dark silence, holding each other's hands. Finally he said again, his voice trembling with remorse, "My wife is a mean-spirited person."

I squeezed his hand to show my sympathy. *But you still had two kids with her in spite of that,* I said to myself. *Have you ever thought of a divorce? Are you going to live with her for the rest of your life? No matter how much you dislike her, you're still her husband. When she needs you, you still have to rush to her side. Will you rush to me when I'm sick? Can you?*

"I kept the marriage so as not to break my mom's heart," I heard Yan say as if he had read my mind. "Now things get really complicated. But Meimei, I'll be back as soon as the operation is done and she gets better."

He pulled me to his chest and unbuttoned my shirt while kissing my eyes and nose.

"Gege," I wiped his saliva off my cheeks, "are we going to be like this forever?" My face burned with shame.

His body stiffened. "Listen, Meimei," he said after a while, "you're a smart girl. You know the moment I ask for a divorce, I'll be expelled and sent back to Ma Ao or to live with my wife. No, I can't do that. College is my life, my future, my last chance to set up my career. I'm thirty-three, not young anymore. Besides, I can't live without you. If I go back to the island, I'll die."

"Is it that serious?"

"You're so innocent and pure! Oh, I want to protect you all my life."

"How can you protect me if we can see each other only in the dark?" *Why am I so sharp-tongued tonight?* I asked myself.

He seemed stunned by my question. Then he hugged and kissed me all over again as he said swiftly, "Meimei, sweet Meimei, trust me. I'll solve the problem some day. I'll think of a plan. Right now, I can only hold you. Will you let me?"

He pressed me down on the ground. Pointed stones cut into my back. I twisted my neck uncomfortably. Yan was unzipping my pants.

"Not here, Gege."

"Yes, yes, it's so romantic. Let the earth be our bed, and the sky our blanket. Come, lie on my jacket. I'll be gentle and slow."

He pushed himself in little by little. The wind blew on my naked hips and dried me from inside. He was pushing me into a bottomless pit that had no air. I was fading away with the pain. Suddenly he jerked, turned his head aside, and vomited.

I sat up and gazed at him in concern.

"Don't worry. I was just overexcited. I'm fine now." He sat up, wiping his mouth with a handkerchief.

"I must go. I told Ying I'd be away for only fifteen minutes."

"Meimei, look at me, please look at me carefully." He gripped my arms. "Gege has never failed in what he wants to do. I want you, you know that. I'm going to do something about it. Sooner or later, we'll be together openly. Just a matter of time. Trust me."

I nodded my head. He embraced me, then crawled through the hole and disappeared into the other side of the wall.

Chapter Five

PARTY SECRETARY HONG threw a pile of paper on the desk and said, "Let me tell you something, Li Ai. If you think you can fool around with me, you're making a big mistake. Who told you to copy Marx's *Manifesto of the Communist Party*, eh? I want your confession."

"I have nothing to confess," Li Ai said in a low, firm voice.

"Liar!" Hong banged the desk. His tea bottle fell and shattered at Li's feet. The hot brown liquid spread with white foam like a puddle of piss. I jumped in my seat at the noise and almost dropped my pen. But Li didn't move her feet or look up from her low chair, her face as blank as white paper. Was she nervous? I'd been asking myself this question as I lay in my bed listening to her breathing in the dark. She never showed any emotion, but her body couldn't pretend. She was losing weight fast. She was skinny when the interrogation began, and now she looked like a bag of old bones. Why didn't she write something and get out of this stupid room, so that I could go back to my own place? This was already my third turn. Smart-ass Ying had gotten away this time, saying that she had to take care of her aunt in the hospital. What a lie! I was sick of being here, recording these meaningless conversations. Always the same questions and answers, the same shouts and silence. Hong said he couldn't be fooled, but he seemed to be the biggest fool here, thinking of himself as a great hunter. Who was hunting whom? Sometimes I felt we were all being held prisoners like mice in a glass ball. We ran and the ball rolled with us. We thought we'd covered a great distance, but we were still trapped inside.

"Tell me how you followed the 'Gang of Four' during the Cultural Revolution," Hong said. He waited. When he got no response, he snorted, "Li Ai, even if you're made of granite, we still have a way to break you. Ni Bing, give me the file."

I handed him a heavy brown bag sealed with red wax. Hong broke the seal and picked out a blue file.

"You have two kids, eh, Li Jun and Li Shang, one in junior high, one in the fifth grade. Nice, nice," he said in a casual voice, as if chatting with a friend. "When was the last time you saw them? Don't you miss them?"

Her eyelids quivered. She folded her arms over her chest as if she was cold.

"Tomorrow we'll have a criticism meeting for you. We can arrange to bring your kids over. One stone kills two birds. You can see them, and they can get some education. Not a bad idea, eh?"

No! We both cried out at the same time. Li Ai leaped from her chair. I held out my hands to her. Hong was glaring at me in disbelief and anger. I couldn't care less. I held out my hand in Li Ai's direction, my eyes closed. Waves of the past rose inside me like layers of moving walls. *Please don't involve children, please,* I said, my strength fading. The walls were crashing down upon me, the sand under my feet was dissolving. I was going to be sucked into the waves at any moment. *Say something, Li Ai, for the children's sake. Don't let them be humiliated in public.* Angry waves in a sea of people.

The Red Guards stood at the door and ordered, "Chen Chun must go to the meetings right now and receive criticism from the revolutionary masses."

"Who's going to accompany your mother to the criticism meeting?" Nainai asked. "She should not go alone today. She's having fever." Nainai's eyes scanned the room like two searchlights and fixed on me. I'd been crouching in the corner since the Red Guards kicked open the door, hoping no one would notice me.

I stood up under the beam. "I'll go with you, Mama. Hold onto my shoulder."

Daughter of Chen Chun
Sautée her cunt with pickles

THREE BOYS across the street chanted at us with their arms on each other's shoulders. I recognized one of them, my classmate Snail. He got this nickname for his running nose. The yellow mucus hung under his nose all day long like the track left by a snail. "Woniu," I muttered. He understood that I was calling his nickname from the way my lips moved and threw a stone at me. It hit my forehead. They ran into a lane, laughing and chanting.

"Sorry, Ni Bing," Mother said.

I bit my lips to swallow the pain. Every time I walked on the street, this kind of attack occurred now that Mother had been criticized as a royalist and counterrevolutionist. It was a small town. People knew each other. In silence, we headed slowly toward Mother's school, where she was to be criticized by her students and colleagues. Big-character posters covered all the walls, trees, and fences. Names were written upside down in the shape of animals, then crossed out in red ink. The posters were glued on top of one another with flour paste. When the layers became too thick, the corners peeled off, beating against the walls in the wind. The noise made me think of the moaning of a dying old man I'd once seen when I peeked through a window with my sister. I shivered in my loose jacket. The cotton was old and hard like the posters. It couldn't keep me warm in this unusually cold winter. Mother's hand trembled on my shoulder. Was she also cold or just shivering from the fever? It felt weird to be so close to her, almost like being caressed.

We turned onto Liberty Street. A funeral parade was marching by. Women and children in white mourning costumes howled and bumped their heads against the coffins on the trucks. There had been a battle between the Iron Broom Faction and the Rebel Forever Against the Reactionaries Faction. The former lost three soldiers. They swore through the loudspeakers that blood would be avenged with blood. After much shouting and swearing, the loud-speakers blasted out a song set to Mao's poem, "Die Lian Hua."

> *I lost my wife Yang*
> *You lost your Liu*
> *The souls of Yang and Liu*
> *Soared up in heaven*
> *Dancing and singing*
> *Their tears poured*
> *onto the earth . . .*

I used to spend hours trying to learn how to sing the poem. When people played it at funerals and turned it into a dirge, it somehow lost the tone of its sadness to me. The singer's trembling voice cut through the frozen air and made passersby weep.

At the end of the street was the County Elementary School. Mother had been teaching dance and singing here since she moved to the island from Shanghai in 1958. From a distance, we could see the gray tiled roof of the school, one of the few two-storied buildings in town at that time. As we approached, I heard people shouting: "Down with Chen Chun!" "Chen Chun must be cut thousands of times!" Their stamping and screaming shook the whole building. I'd heard and read stories about what went on at criticism meetings, but I'd never seen one with my own eyes. My legs began to tremble under Mother's weight. She felt it and squeezed my shoulder as if to assure my safety.

A wall-size portrait of Mao hung above the gate. Two Red Guards stood on each side. I bowed to the portrait after Mother. When I looked up, she had already been taken away by two Red Guards, her feet dragging behind her. The shouting became louder and more fierce. I followed them into the auditorium. There were already three people kneeling on the stage, their heads bent so low that the signs around their necks touched the floor. I read each sign: "Liu Shaoqi's running dog Gao Gong," "Traitor Xi Min," and "the American spy Hao Yijin." What title would they give to Mother, I wondered.

She was shoved onto the stage. They pulled her hair to lift her head and turned it around to let the audience know that this was the right person. Then they pushed her head down to her knees. Without looking around, I recognized many familiar faces. They used to come to our house to visit Mother on weekends. They spent hours listening to her, their eyes full of admiration and respect. Some of them, including the two Red Guards holding my mother's arms, stayed for dinners I had made. I pushed my way toward the stage. I wanted to stare into their eyes to see if they knew the words *shame* and *conscience*.

Someone grabbed my shoulders. I looked back and saw Do, Mother's colleague and best friend. "Aunt Do," I called, suddenly on the verge of tears.

Do covered my mouth and pulled me out of the auditorium. "Go home, Ni Bing. This is not the place to hang around. Run back home, now." She changed her voice when she saw someone passing by. "Your mother has committed serious crimes. We're helping her to wake up and reform. You should draw a line between her and yourself." Before rushing back to the auditorium, she whispered, "Be a good girl, go home. Your mother will be all right."

I left the school and squatted in the doorway of a closed store across the street. I couldn't go home by myself. When I had walked out the door of our house with my mother leaning on my shoulder, Nainai had told me, "Ni Bing, you're already ten. You should know how to handle things. Whatever happens, you just make sure your mother comes home with you." The wind bit my hands and feet like a pack of hungry dogs. My ears hurt, the pain worse than when Nainai and Mother pulled them. I rubbed my hands over the felt gloves Nainai had lent me for this trip. I couldn't wear my own. My fingers were swollen from frostbite. Next year, I would take Nainai's advice and knit a pair of mittens for myself. It must be warm in the auditorium, packed with people shouting and waving their fists. Why did they hate Mother so much? As long as I could remember, she'd been elected a model teacher every year. The students worshipped her. How did she suddenly become a class enemy overnight? Strange that I should feel sleepy in this cold. I must not doze off here. Mother might need me at any moment.

A tearing pain in my ears. I looked up and saw Nainai. "I didn't do anything wrong, Nainai. Why are you punishing me?" I screamed. She said nothing and pulled me by the ear into a windowless room. The only light came from the fire in the middle of the kang, the bed made of mud and bricks with a stove built inside for cooking and warmth. I took another look at the fire and noticed that it had turned into the sun. Men and women knelt on the kang that took up half of the room, the skin on their backs peeling from the heat. Yet they were also shivering from the cold. Their bodies shook like containers with dice in them. They all knelt in the direction of the darkest corner of the room, chanting in muffled voices. Nainai put me on the kang and pushed my head three times toward the corner. A man picked me up by my feet, his head wrapped in a white towel. I was as light as a baby. The flames licked the top of the stove. Now the chanting became louder, joined by the drums in the middle of the courtyard. The square yard also swarmed with the kneeling peasants, half-naked. Nainai put a knife on my right ear. The side of the knife pressed into my neck and began melting. It was made of ice. A cluster of red firecrackers appeared at the door. A hand holding a stick of burning incense reached for the little string at the end of the crackers.

I jumped up. The firecrackers thrashed before my face like a snake on fire. They seemed to be exploding inside my ears. I screamed in agony, not only because I was jolted from my dream but also because my ears were extremely sensitive to drums and firecrackers. I had trouble hearing or understanding human conversations, but I could hear the piercing explosion of firecrackers miles away. The boy who was holding the cluster of firecrackers laughed like crazy when he saw the painful expression on my face. I snarled at him and tried to pick up a rock half buried in the ground. A drum started to thunder above my head. I looked up. The boy was gone.

Across the street was a parade, moving in slow motion from the school gate. It was led by four flatbeds. On each stood two Red Guards; one beat a drum and the other hit a gong. The drum, as big as the one in my dream, took up the whole surface of the wheelbarrow. The ends of the two sticks the drummer used were decorated with red silk, as in my dream. My heart stopped beating when I saw Gao Gang pulling the first flatbed like a cow. He was one of the people who had been kneeling on the stage. Around his neck was one of the wooden harnesses peasants used on cows and donkeys for ploughing and pulling carts. He wore a hat in the shape of cow dung and the new cardboard around his neck had a picture of a cow. A Red Guard walked before him, holding in his hand a rope that was tied around Gao Gang's neck.

I found Mother pulling the third cart. She was wearing a hat in the shape of a python with a human head. It had short hair and glasses. Apparently its image imitated Mother. It coiled up on the hat, a red tongue sticking from its mouth.

I looked at the other two people. The second had a ghost hat, and the last wore a hat painted like a kitchen god. It dawned on me that these four people represented niu gui she shen—cow, ghost, snake, and god, symbols for all the enemies of the proletarians in China.

I turned my eyes back to Mother. The shaft cut deeply into her shoulders. I couldn't see her face. Her upper body bent toward the ground as if to hide her shame. The drums were thundering like giants stalking down a mountain, their huge feet stamping on my scalp. I was in the dream again, being shaken upside down by the ankles, my limbs all out of joint. Would there ever be an end to all of this? *Dong qiang, dong dong qiang.* Every two beatings of the drums were followed by a gong, then a short silence. I was hearing words: *Tong tong qiangbi, tong tong qiangbi*—Shoot them all, shoot them all.

Suddenly the drums stopped. The Red Guards began beating the sides of the drums with their sticks in a fast tempo, accompanied by the stealthy, muffled sound of the gongs. The audience on the sidewalks who had been shouting and laughing now quieted down. *Some new trick is up,* I thought. The Red Guard by the first flatbed pulled the rope three times. The man with the cow hat raised the little gong in his hand and hit it with a little stick. "I'm a cow, a rightist cow. I'm here to be punished for my crimes," he chanted to the rhythm of the drums and gongs. The Red Guard beside him kept poking at his behind to make him speak louder. When the cow finished, the ghost went on. The beating of the sticks on the wood sounded like bullets. Perhaps it was better to be shot than humiliated like this. Now it was Mother's turn. She raised her gong and stick. I didn't want to hear, but words shot through me without mercy. "I'm a snake, a beauty snake." The audience, who had been quiet during the first two confessions, now burst into laughter. Kids ran around wild, clapping and chanting, "I'm a snake, a beauty snake." *Oh, Mother, Mother,* I stood in the doorway, numb all over my body, *how could you let them do such things to you? How are you going to live on after this? Why don't you just drop dead on the street, now?*

The parade went on. Thousands of feet rumbled like a gigantic stone roller going around the thrashing ground. Grains of wheat screeched underneath. Either they let themselves be husked or be crushed into powder. I did not cry. I cried only in my dreams. Tears were not for the public. Faces passed before me. Faces I had greeted every day: Aunt Do, Aunt Lao, Uncle Wang, Grandpa Shen, Little Wu, Brother Xu. . . . Faces laughing, shouting, and fists waving in the air. *We are nothing but grains,* I thought, *yet we are all in such a hurry to crush one another and to be smashed into powder under this roller. What was the matter with us?*

"No, you can't touch my children." Li Ai's shrieking voice cut the air into pieces. "Do whatever you want with me. I'm old and my life is over. But please leave my kids alone. I beg you, Secretary Hong." She stepped forward all of a sudden, throwing the chair and herself on the floor. "Don't touch my children," she cried.

Hong signaled me to start taking notes, then strolled toward Li Ai, still sprawled on the floor. Had he been staring at me all the time since I cried out with Li Ai? It seemed so. The look he had just given me was full of suspicion and shock. I needed to be careful. This was not the place or time for indulging myself in the past. I lifted my pen. Hong picked up the chair and helped Li Ai up from the floor. "Sit," he patted her on the shoulder. "Your life is not over yet. Once you tell us everything, you can start all over again." He waited till she stopped sobbing. "Now, tell me how Comrade Geng Hai died."

Li shivered on her chair, her face aghast. "He committed suicide. He alienated himself from Chairman Mao and the revolutionary people." Her voice sounded like a tape recorder.

"You and your assistants locked him up in this room for three months and interrogated him day and night. When he started spitting blood, you wouldn't let him see a doctor, saying he was faking it. And you brought his wife and two daughters to his criticism meeting to watch the Red Guards shave his head on the stage. Is that true?"

I had to force myself not to burst out laughing. This whole thing was a play: Li trembling on the dwarf chair, Hong pacing around her with his hands behind his back. The problem was that it had been played so much, with exactly same words, same roles and same plot, that it was just funny. Twelve years had passed since I had watched my mother being paraded in that snake hat, half of her head shaved. But nothing had changed. Hong was doing exactly the same thing Li had done to Geng Hai. Who would be Hong's executioner in the near future?

Hong strolled to the window and shook the iron bars with his fat white hands. "He jumped from this window when he came back from the meeting, didn't he?"

Li Ai dropped her head in her palms. "I don't know. I don't remember."

"And you didn't let his wife see the body. You said he made himself a class enemy by alienating himself from the revolutionary masses. You organized a criticism meeting on the spot, his blood still all over the place. After that, you threw his family out of their apartment. His wife went crazy right away and is still locked up in an asylum. And we still don't know where his daughters are. What do you think of that? You're a mother yourself, and a wife."

"I'm sorry, I'm sorry," Li Ai wept. "I was young and hot-blooded. I only thought of defending Chairman Mao's revolutionary line."

Hong spat with indignation. "Li Ai, you never represented Mao's lines. You were just a faithful running dog for the 'Gang of Four.'"

She dropped her arms to her sides, speechless.

Hong returned to his seat. "Li Ai, why did you persecute Geng Hai?"

"He was a capitalist degenerate. His two books of love poetry were full of poison. They corrupted hundreds of young students. His apartment was decorated with paintings of disgusting nudes and his bookshelves stuffed with books from the West. His wife even used lipstick and blush. He was known to have intimate relations with beautiful women." As she talked, her confidence and anger returned. She glared into space, her back straight again, her eyebrows knitted together, as if Geng Hai were standing in front of her.

"Where were you the night Geng jumped the window?" Hong noticed the change in Li Ai and shot the question at her with a malicious smile.

Li Ai sank again as if someone had pulled out her backbone. She looked around wildly like a trapped animal searching for an escape.

"You weren't home. Your assistants went to Master Chen's apartment and found you in bed with him. What were you two doing in bed? Carrying out Chairman Mao's revolutionary lines, eh?" Hong's stomach and shoulders shook as he laughed.

I ran out of the room. I was going to throw up. The little hand in my stomach was scratching inside me again. I had to vomit everything I had eaten this morning, the steamed bread, the rice porridge, the fermented bean curd, and everything else, to clean out my stomach, my liver, my heart. When would we stop grinding and crushing each other? Waipo said that people seemed to go crazy on the day I was born. But it seemed people were crazy every day. What went wrong? Time or just us? They say time goes only in one direction: straight forward. But it's not true. Time goes forward and backward, sometimes sideways. But none of us is prepared for this.

Chapter Six

"MOTHER, I'VE REGISTERED to go to Ma Ao to receive re-education from peasants," I said, clenching my fists in my pockets. I'd been rehearsing this line for half a month, and I couldn't put it off any more. In another week, I had to report to the commune.

"You what?" Mother's face changed from shock to anger. "Have you eaten the tiger's balls? Who gave you the authority?" She saw the look on my face and quickly changed her tone. "What's wrong with staying home, reading, learning, and doing whatever you like? I wish we could exchange places, you go teaching every day and I stay home."

No, Mother, you don't, I said in silence. *You'd die if you spent your days shopping, cooking, cleaning, and washing, and the only reward you get is some knuckles knocking on the head. Do whatever I like? By the time I sit down at my desk, I'm so damn tired that I just doze off over my books. Look at me, the coarse hands, the stained apron. I'm your maid, Mother, a free maid you can yell at and hit anytime you feel like it.*

"Look," Mother said, her hands open, "it's not my fault you can't find a job in town. Every factory and government office has stopped hiring new people. If you hadn't turned down the job at the arsenal, you'd be making at least thirty yuan a month. I should have known better than to listen to your silly teachers and let you have your whim."

She stopped when she saw the despair in my eyes. In my senior semester, a rumor had spread over the island that the college entrance exams would be restored and high school graduates could go to college without having to work in factories, the countryside, or serving in the army for two years. I got up at four o'clock every morning to study math, Chinese, and the history of the Chinese Communist Party before I began my household chores. When Mother handed me the job application form, I just looked at her. She knew I was determined to take the exams. I went directly to my English and math teachers. They had given me books to study. I told them what had happened, and they immediately went to my home and persuaded Mother to let me finish my degree and try my luck. I don't know what they promised her; Mother was quite supportive for a while. She even made my sister go to the market in the morning so that I would have more time to read.

But there was no exam. It had just been a rumor. Deng Xiaoping, who raised the issue of reopening the colleges to high school graduates, was kicked out of the Central Committee before the semester was over. Mother started calling me "fallen phoenix" in a sarcastic tone. My teachers must have told her that I might become a phoenix rising from a chicken coop.

"Be patient, Ni Bing. Maybe the factories will need more people next year. I'll try my best to get you a job."

"I'm going to Ma Ao, Mother," I said.

"No, you are not. You're not even sixteen yet. You're still a little girl. What can you do in the countryside? Sit on the grass and sing for the peasants? You can't even sing well."

"Whatever I do there can't be worse than what I'm doing now. Mother, do you realize I've been pulling a cart with five hundred jin of coal on it and carrying fifty jin of sweet potatoes on my back for miles since I was twelve? I started working in this house when I came to live with you at the age of five. How come you never used the words 'little girl' then?"

She slapped my face. "Go, I don't care. Just don't come back crying and begging for money."

"Never!" I said, holding my burning cheek. "Someone in our family has to go, right? Shuang is graduating next year, and Hao in three years. No one will get a job unless one of us goes to the countryside. You don't want to see the three of us idling at home, dependent on you and Father, do you? Among the three of us, who should go? Me, of course. Since I have to go sooner or later, I'd rather go now. If I work hard and if I'm lucky, maybe I can be recommended to college."

"Forget about college, OK?" Mother had been listening until she heard the word. "How can you still be fixed on that crazy idea? I know you did well in your high school. So what! The world has changed. It's no longer the place and time for your dream. Intellectuals are chou lao jiu—stinky No. 9, the lowest of all the class enemies in this country, worse than thieves and murderers. Look at me. My education has brought me nothing but bad luck. But why am I wasting my time? You know everything."

I stared out of the window. The gray backyard was jammed with chicken sheds, pieces of wood, broken furniture, and other junk. Outside the wall was the mud street that led to the sea port, lined with gray navy ships and fishing boats. Dark clouds pressed down upon the peak of the Western Hill. When the sun didn't come out, this island was bleached of color. The hubbub of bargaining peddlers, bicycle bells, and the whistle of a departing ship was faintly audible. Nothing had changed since I came here except for the wrinkles at the corners of Mother's eyes after she was released from the training class.

"Are you happy, Mother?"

"What?" She looked at me as if I were crazy. We barely talked, or, I should say, I had never communicated so many words to her. When she gave me orders or instructions, I listened with my eyes cast down, then turned away in silence to carry out the tasks. Except for occasional explosions on my part, I hardly called her Mother. "What's wrong with my life?" Her voice was menacing.

"Do you regret having children? You're a talented dancer and singer, and you're so beautiful. You could have been a famous star. Waipo told me that."

But what I really want to know, Mother, is whether you regret having me at such a young age. You're thirty-three. So you were pregnant when you were only sixteen. How could that be? Waipo and Waigong had lots of hope for you. They still keep the prizes you won for your high school. Among them is an admission letter to the Central Dance and Opera Institute of Beijing in the spring of 1958. What happened? Did you not go because you were pregnant with me? Did I ruin your life? Is that why you're always so mad at me and I can't feel close to you? Oh, this awful wall between us—but it's more than a wall. It's something else. Am I really your daughter? I shuddered. *You must stop thinking nonsense, Ni Bing,* I told myself.

Mother put her hand on my wrist, gingerly, as if she were feeling my pulse. Her fingers were cool and wet. She was sweating. Had she read my mind? Gradually the trembling stopped. Mother squeezed my hand before she let it go.

"Your waipo has a big mouth." She sighed. "Do I have regrets? Sure, I do. Who doesn't? But I couldn't have made another choice. I would have followed your father to the end of the earth at that time. You're too young to understand this." She looked into my eyes.

We looked at each other until I cast my eyes down first. She was not telling me the whole truth. She was hiding something from me, just the way Waipo hid part of the story about my birth. But I recognized the fire that flashed across Mother's face. She had loved once, and that had made her life meaningful.

"But you and Father fight almost every day, over money, over Nainai. You could have been a great artist, living in Beijing or Shanghai. Now you have to calculate every fen in your pocket, and your students call you chou lao jiu, stinky No. 9. I can't follow your steps, Mother, not that I have talents like yours. I have to leave this island. The only way out is through college. And the only way to go to college is to become a farmer first. I may never

be recommended for school, but I don't care. I have to get out
of here. I have to. Nothing will stop me!"

I breathed heavily. Talking at such length was exhausting.
Mother gazed at me like a stranger. "So you've made up your
mind, you stubborn donkey."

I nodded. "This is my only chance."

THE SMELL of curry beef and potatoes, fried fish, sautéed onions,
and other food mixed with the coal smoke drifted into my nostrils. Then I heard spatulas clanking against woks in the hallway.
My neighbors were making dinner. I looked up. The needle was
pointing to five to six on my clock. So I'd been sitting on the
floor of my dormitory for the past three hours, doing nothing but
thinking about the past since returning from the office to register for the entrance exams. Seven years. How many nights and
days were there in seven years? And how many dreams and daydreams had I had for this final moment—to take the exams and
become a college student? Till three o'clock this afternoon, I was
sure I would make it this time. But it was over now, all over.

So simple. They just summoned me by the phone to the registration office on Wulin Gate Road and told me that I was no
longer eligible for the entrance exams. In a croaking voice, I
managed to ask them why. The woman shrugged her shoulders.
"You've passed the age limit for English major," she said without
looking up from her paper.

"How can that be?" I asked, sweat pouring down my forehead.
"You set the age at July 30, 1958. And I was born on August 24."

She looked up with a sneer. "It's not true. We were informed
your birthday is July 15."

I covered my mouth with my fist to stifle my scream. "But
that's the lunar calendar. My birthday, according to the
Gregorian calendar, is August 24. Please, Comrade, don't cross
me out. This is my last opportunity. I've been preparing for this
moment since I was a child," I pleaded. At that moment, I felt I

would do anything to make her change her mind, even if I had to kneel or kowtow. She waved.

"Comrade Ni Bing, we do things according to rules. Now the rule says that anyone born earlier than July 30, 1958 is not eligible for the entrance exams, and your birthday on the residence registration is July 15, 1958. What do you want me to do? You're lucky that we're too busy to do anything about your lying. Just go home and think about your behavior." She bent over her papers and never looked up again.

I don't remember how I walked all the way home; I was in a daze. Even three hours later, her words still cut me like scissors. I clenched my teeth and waved my fists, as if the woman were still in front of me. "How could you do this to me!" I shouted.

The alarm went off. Out of my habit, I leaped up and grabbed the world geography textbook. It was six. According to the new schedule Yan had made for me, I should have memorized a Tang poem, read a chapter of Chinese history, and learned the names of all the mountains and cities in North America. "This is your final sprint," Yan had said before he'd left for Shanghai for the third of his wife's operations. "One more month left. From now till the exams, every minute counts. No matter what happens, even if the sky collapses, you must keep this schedule." I looked at the book on my lap, wishing I could cry. Perhaps tears could soothe my burning eyes. Time had suddenly stopped meaning anything. This was worse than the falling sky. Seven years. Nothing had changed. I was still as desperate and helpless. The only difference was that I had no more hope. It was over. While I was dashing toward the tape, I was disqualified from the race.

The alarm went on. Nothing could stop it until it had rung for five minutes. It was set that way. *Just to make sure you won't go back to sleep,* Yan had said when he gave me the clock. He had used it for himself when he was preparing for the exams. My head was on the verge of exploding. That damn clock. It wouldn't even let me mourn in peace. I picked it up and flung it against the wall. It hit the books I had piled up neatly in the corner. The pile tumbled down and scattered on the floor. For the past three months, I'd been getting up before dawn to read and memorize those books. Thirty-six of them. Piled on top of one another, they reached my stomach. Three months and seven years collapsed just like this at one fling. The alarm was still rattling, its face on the floor like an abandoned woman weeping in the dark. Oh, what was time, anyway? It was a piece of paper that was folded back and forth in a magician's hands. You were promised a bird, but it turned out to be a toad or a monkey.

July 15, gui jie on the moon calendar. There were 365 days in a year. Why did I choose that day to be born? It was a day when the gate of the underground opened and the dead came out to take care of their business and to declare their existence. The living must surrender and pay respect to the world of ghosts. Was I a ghost? Sometimes I felt like one, especially on my birthday, when no one talked to me or saw me, when Nainai lit the incense and kowtowed all day long to the west. Mother said the whole idea was just an old fart. No one believed in this kind of superstition anymore in the new society. But I could smell the fear in her. On July 15, fear filled the air like bats circling the silent sky at dusk. I was born on the wrong date, doomed to bad fate. Nothing could change that, even if I switched my birthday from the moon calendar to the Gregorian one.

And who had informed the registration office about my birthday? Hong? I remembered the funny smile on his face when he told me about the telephone message from the registration office. It must have been him. Only he had access to my file to check out my birth date. I knew that he would punish me one way or another. The day I walked out on Li Ai's interrogation, he discharged me at once as a guard and made me perform a series of self-criticism speeches at the weekly party meetings. He wouldn't have let me off the hook if Principal Shu hadn't reminded him that the school had no money to hire a substitute to replace me. But I was glad to have distracted his attention away from Li Ai. Her children never did show up at her criticism meetings. Soon Hong announced that the Party had helped Li Ai confess all her crimes and had sent her to a farm on the southwestern border. I heard she had recently been released to receive medical treatment. The cancer in her breast had spread and she had only a few months to live.

I wasn't surprised. Li had lost her will to go on. She really believed that what she had done in the past was for the revolutionary cause. Besides, she was dying to save her children. If she had continued living on the farm, Hong would have forced her children to join her, and that would have been the end of their future. Now that she was dying at home, Hong couldn't send them to the farm without their mother. Once she died, her children would be able to maintain their city residency.

The perfume from the cape jasmine blossoms outside the window was suffocating me. I stood up and looked out at the campus. White jasmine and red pomegranate flowers swayed in the May breeze. Narrow cement roads appeared here and there among tall Chinese parasols. In heaven there was a paradise, and on earth there was Hangzhou, people always said. Hangzhou Teacher's School had a beautiful campus in the city of paradise on earth. When I asked Shu to write me the permission letter to register for the entrance exams, he had laughed incredulously, thinking it was a joke, until he realized how serious I was.

"But why? Are you trying to get away from someone? Trust me, no one will touch you as long as I'm the principal here. I need teachers like you."

I just smiled and shook my head. Suddenly he laughed again. "I see, Little Ni. You're upset that Wang Ying was chosen to be trained in Hangzhou University. Don't worry." He patted me on the shoulders with his plump hand. "Next time, you'll go, I promise. How old are you? Twenty-two? Time for your own family. I'll introduce you to some fine young man. In a few years, our new apartment building will be completed. I'll make sure you have an apartment. How's that?"

"Thank you, Principal Shu," I said, trying not to stutter.

Sometimes I find it easier to deal with hostility than hospitality. "I really appreciate your help. But I've made up my mind. This is my last chance. I don't know if I'll pass. But if I don't try, I won't be able to live the rest of my life in peace."

Shu shook his head, wrote the letter, stamped it, and handed it to me. "You're crazy," he said, his eyes blinking in bewilderment behind thick glasses.

Su Fen, my girlfriend at Ma Ao, had the same bewildered look when she woke me up from my sleepwalk. "You're crazy, crazy," she murmured sleepily as she tried to mend the hole in the mosquito net I had torn under the dim kerosene lamp. "You'll kill yourself soon, working like this. I don't understand."

I could only smile to apologize for waking her up. In the summer harvest, every minute counted. We spent at least eighteen hours in the fields, cutting and planting rice before the season was over. For three weeks, we had had about four or five hours of sleep each night. And I slept even less. As the leader of the Youth Shock Team, I got up at three every morning, an hour earlier than the peasants, to pull the seedlings for the planting. I also published news on the bulletin board every three days. I was so exhausted that I began to hallucinate. I could no longer tell the difference between day and night, between reality and dream. Everything was blurred; every day blended with the next. In my sleep, I always carried two barrels of rice on the dark mountain road. The yoke cut deep into my shoulders, and stones scraped my bare feet, pus oozing out of the infected wounds in the soles. I groaned loudly in my dream, not because of the pain. Exhaust had numbed every sensation in my body. In the dark, I was groaning impatiently for light. I looked at my clock. Twenty to three. Since I was already up, I might as well get going. There was no difference between sleeping and working for me, anyway. I coiled my braid around my head and found my yoke, barrels, and sickle behind the door.

"Where are you going at this hour?" Su Fen screamed, and jumped from beneath the net to grab me. "Forget about becoming a model educated youth! Your life is more important than that, for god's sake." I loosened her fingers one by one and walked out the door like a sleepwalker. I was grateful to her for sleeping with me. She was worried that I might hurt myself when I walked around in my sleep. Yet I couldn't tell her about my secret obsession with college. Not that I didn't trust her. But if anyone knew my motivation for working hard, I'd never be able to get out of Ma Ao.

Outside, it was as dark as my dreams. The lamp I carried illuminated an area on the road only as big as a basin, but I had walked to the rice fields behind the mountain so many hundreds of times that I could have gotten there with my eyes closed. The light was just a symbol, a companion. It had rained in the night. My feet sank deep into the ooze of the mud and the droppings of cows, pigs, chickens. The fermented manure felt warm and comforting to my wounds. How I winced and danced around to avoid stepping on them the first day I walked on the country road! To this day, Su Feng still makes fun of me, even though I had become used to making manure balls with my hands and inserting them under vegetable roots in the fields. I was learning everything about farming—planting, weeding, ploughing, harvesting. The only thing I couldn't learn well was to walk barefooted. My soles were too sensitive. Stones and rice stubs cut them easily. Often I walked as if on a road full of knives and broken glass, and I couldn't help feeling like the little mermaid who had just turned into a human. As she walked on the beach, each of her steps was full of agony. She endured the pain for love. And me? I walked on the road of knives that might lead me to college. *It is the only path I have, and it is worth it,* I kept telling myself in the dark.

I passed the threshing ground. On the wall of the barn hung the news bulletin board. I don't know why I insisted on doing it. Most peasants were illiterate. They did appreciate my handwriting and drawings, which comforted me. Perhaps I also wanted to please the commune leaders? Yue Qing, the Youth League secretary, praised me enthusiastically. "You're wonderful," she beamed with excitement. "I'll report this to Comrade Li. We're looking for a model educated youth. Keep up the good work." *Did I want that honor?* I had asked myself several times. Not really. I was never ambitious politically. But if it would help me get into a college, I wouldn't mind. For my dream, I would do anything, anything.

Soon I arrived at the seedling fields at the foot of Xiao Lu Mountain. I waded in. The cool water massaged my legs gently. Someone had left a small stool in the middle of the fields. I took it and sat down before the dark green blanket of seedlings. The stool sank and stopped just an inch above water. I hung my lamp on a stick. Slowly I moved my fingers under the roots, rubbing them swiftly as I pulled them from the soil. When my hands were full, I drew a rice straw from the bundle at my waist and tied the bundle with a slipknot. A good bundle had to be tight, since it would be thrown several times from the seedling bed to rice paddies before being planted. The roots had to be loose and clean so that planters could quickly remove half a dozen seedlings from the bundle at a time.

Of all the farming work, I loved planting rice best. It was satisfying to turn and look at the six straight lines of seedlings I had just planted. Within two weeks, I had not only learned to plant, but I had also beat the best peasant in the village in the contest. Only I knew how much pain I endured in my back!

Soon I had dug a passage in the seedling bed. Inch by inch, I was getting closer to my destination. Leeches sucked blood from my calves and my right wrist. They hung together on one cut—sometimes two, sometimes six—drawing blood until their bodies bulged and became dark like bottles filled with soy sauce. I had also become used to them, no longer screaming or jumping or pulling them off my skin in vain as I had when I first encountered them. Once they had sucked enough blood, they'd fall off by themselves. In fact, I admired their persistence and cunning.

"LITTLE NI, LITTLE NI," Principal Shu called me softly, his fingers stroking my wrist, as gently as the sucking of leeches. "Go ahead and try, just don't kill yourself. I heard that you get up at four o'clock every morning. I admire your will, but still, health is the most important."

I withdrew my hand slowly. No need to hurt his feelings. His wife had been away in Africa for five years, helping the Africans to build a dam. He was the only person in this school I had told about my preparation for the entrance exams. But could he understand the obsession I'd had ever since I was a first grader? Every morning on my way to school, I would squeeze my head between the iron bars of Zhoushan Oceanology Institute, gazing at the shadows of the students reading quietly in the library. *That's where I want to be,* I told myself.

I looked at the books I had collected, read, and memorized for the past three months. They were scattered on the floor, dog-eared and torn, like baby turtles whose heads had been snatched off by seagulls before they could reach the ocean. I wasn't mad at Hong. He did what he was supposed to do, to avenge my unfaithfulness to the Party. The question was, Who informed him? The only person to whom I had told the truth was Shu, who wrote me the permission letter for registration. Wang Ying would have guessed what I'd been doing. We shared the room, after all. But why would she care? She was being trained at Hangzhou University and would come back with a certificate. She couldn't have so degraded herself.

The door opened gently. It must be Ying. I turned away. I didn't want her to see my anger. Her smiling moon face seemed to be lecturing me: "You see, troublemaker, it's no good to be too smart. You want to control your own life? You want to be a college student through your own effort? What for? Look, I'm the one who's going to college, and I don't need to get up at four and go to bed at midnight."

"Ni Bing," Ying said, "Isn't Yan coming back from Shanghai this evening? The telegram said the train would be here at seven. Maybe he can help you out. He's older and more experienced. Perhaps he could do something about your birth date."

I jumped up and ran out the door, forgetting to thank Ying or to question how she knew the details of my trouble. Certainly Yan could do something. He had a mouth that could bring the dead back to life and make hens crow.

"MEIMEI, HOW DETERMINED are you about going to college?"

"If I can't make it, my eyes won't be closed when I die," I replied without hesitation.

"Are you ready to take a serious risk? Not your life, of course, but pretty close?"

I walked to the kerosene stove and picked it up. "My mother gave me this stove when I went to the countryside six years ago. It's the most valuable and sentimental thing I have. Now I'm going to destroy it."

"What are you doing?" Yan leaped at me and grabbed my hand.

"Puofu chengzhou."

He nodded. Puofu chengzhou—break the cauldrons and sink the boats, a story from *Spring and Autumn*. An army was about to fight an enemy that was much better equipped. The general ordered all the cauldrons broken and the boats sunk after the troops had crossed the river. There was to be no retreat—either win or die. The soldiers fought savagely for their lives and won the battle.

"Good. Look what I've got for you."

The permission certificate. I cried out, breathless, "How did you get it back?"

"I've cut off your retreat, Meimei. Either you pass the exams and go to college or you go back to the countryside."

I thought, *even if the baby turtle made it to the ocean, that didn't mean it was out of danger.*

"I showed the office woman the affidavit of your corrected birthday, but she wouldn't change her mind. She's such a dry piece of bread. I talked to her the whole afternoon, used up all the sweet words I knew. Useless. She's a stone in the latrine pit, hard and smelly. Finally, I began shouting: *You're throwing away one of the best candidates in Zhejiang Province.* That worked. She was a serious worker. It's her responsibility and honor to have as many people as possible enter good colleges. I noticed the change in her mind and grabbed the opportunity. 'Let's make a deal,' I said, throwing your diploma on her desk. 'You give the permission certificate back to Ni Bing, and I'll leave this to you as security. If she fails the exams, she'll give up her diploma and her job, and go back to where she's from—Ma Ao.' She laughed and took the certificate out of her drawer. That dry bread." Yan rubbed his hands with a smile. "She became a good old sport toward the end."

I slipped my hand into his palms. Their moist warmth filled me with safety and confidence. I looked at the dark bags under his eyes. He hadn't gotten much sleep since I met him at the train station. When I had told him the situation, he gave me his baggage and went directly to his friend who worked in the police station. After he got the affidavit in the morning, he went to the office and stayed there till six o'clock.

I pressed my cheek on his hand. No one had ever run around for me like this. "I love you, Gege," I murmured. "How can I ever return what you've done for me?" Yan stroked my head, his fingers combing my hair with tenderness. Gradually, he moved his hands onto my breasts.

My body became stiff with the anticipation of pain. "Please, Gege, please, not here, not now. Ying may come back." *What's the matter with me?* I thought as I writhed in his arms, keeping his chest away with my hands. *This is the only thing I can give him, yet I'm pushing him away. How shameful!*

Someone inserted a key in the lock and turned it. We both heard the click and froze in terror. It was Wang Ying. I turned off the light, dashed back to the bed and threw down the mosquito net. The door opened. Ying walked in and groped for the switch in the dark.

"I'm sleeping, Ying. Please don't turn on the light." I ducked my head out the net, pleading.

"Oh, I'm sorry. I didn't know you were here. I'm going down-stairs to wash up," she said quickly, and rushed out with a basin.

We looked at each other in terror. It was the full moon. The room was bathed in the moonlight. Ying must have seen every-thing: Yan's shoes in the middle of the floor, his pants near the bed. Otherwise she wouldn't have run out in a hurry. Was she really washing her face? Would she report this to Hong?

"Leave now. I'll meet you at our place in five minutes," I whis-pered, as if Ying were listening outside the door. I waited for a while to make sure no one would see us together, then I tiptoed downstairs to the washing room. Ying was brushing her teeth slowly, as if she had a toothache. I walked away quietly. If she didn't report to Hong now, I'd be OK. As long as they didn't catch us naked in bed, I could always deny our relationship.

By the time I got to our place, Yan was waiting on the grass, his head bent in deep thought, a white handkerchief spread on the ground next to him. He looked sad and tired. For the first time, I was aware of the twelve-year difference in our age. I rubbed his head gently. He grabbed my hand and pressed it on his mouth for a long time, shaking like a malaria patient.

"Gege, don't worry about it," I said.

"Let's get out of here, Meimei."

What do you mean? I thought. *Out of this meeting place, this city, or this awkward situation?*

"Let's go to America."

I laughed in the dark. My hands kept kneading his scalp.

"I'm not joking or having a fever. I want to be with you, but there's no way I can get a divorce in this country. In America, people can do whatever they want. There are opportunities everywhere."

It can't be that simple, I said to myself. *Besides, how are you going to get yourself there?* But I just said, "You don't speak English, Gege."

"I'm learning. You must start giving me lessons after the exams. Once I get there, I can teach Chinese language and literature, anywhere—high school, college, I don't care. I heard there is a great need. I also know how to fix cars. At worst, I can be a mechanic. Anything will be better than our present situation."

"I agree, if you can get there."

"I don't blame you for doubting," he said. "Listen to my plan. Remember the cousin I told you about? The one whose parents fled to Hong Kong in 1950 and left their son to my mother?"

"Vaguely. Did he swim across the border between Canton and Hong Kong in the sixties to look for his parents there?"

"That's him. Last week my mom got a letter from him. We all thought he had drowned in the river. Hundreds of people drown there each year. He's made it in New York, two antique stores in Manhattan. He said he owes all his success to her. He'll give her anything she wants."

That's great, I said to myself. *You think your mother will want to go to New York at her age?*

"You still don't get it, Meimei, do you?" He laughed with excitement. "If he will do anything for my mom, it means he'll do anything for me. Understand? Because my mom will do anything to make me happy. She's going to ask him to be my sponsor."

"For what?"

"Are you playing dumb or you really don't know? You need a sponsor to go to America and study."

"You mean you're going to study Chinese in New York?"

"That's not the point." He became impatient. "The point is I must leave this damn country so that I can get my damn divorce and live with you. I don't care what I do there, clean streets, wash dishes, anything. You think it will be easy to throw away what I've done here? No! Believe me! If I continue working like this, I'll become a top intellectual in a few years, I am sure. But the more successful I become, the more difficult it is to get a divorce. You know all about that, Meimei. Why do you make me repeat everything?"

I said nothing. His head weighed like a rock in my hands.

"I'm sorry, Meimei." He took my hands and pulled me onto his lap. "I didn't mean to yell, I just got carried away. Hey, you know what I'm going to buy when I make my first American dollars? A white dress and a red car for my little bride. I can see how you'll look there. Yes, a car and a house, with our own bedroom, kitchen, and bathroom, no more sharing with strangers, no more stinky public latrine pit. And our house will be air-conditioned."

"And our bathroom will have hot water, and I can take a bath every day?" I was infected by his intoxication.

"You can take as many baths as you want, my little baboon, ten times a day if you want." He pinched my nose.

We sat in silence, our hands intertwined. In the moonlight, Yan's face glowed with hope.

"They say the American moon is bigger and rounder. That's bullshit. But I do believe that over there people have equal opportunities. I'm going to fight with all my strength, for us, for our future."

I tightened my arms around his neck. If things could move as easy as the rolling of words! But why not? Why not indulge for a moment in our fantasies? Perhaps that was the only thing left for us.

"You want to know my immediate wish, Meimei?" he whispered in my ear, his breath tickling my earlobe. "When you're done with your exams, I'll find a room where we can spend a night like husband and wife."

Chapter Seven

I STOOD AT THE WINDOW looking at the Monument to the People's Heroes on the top of the Western Hill. In my childhood memory, the tower was the most magnificent architecture on earth. But now it looked shabby and out of place. Even the mountain, which I had climbed hundreds of times, looked like a dwarf. I hadn't been back home for three and a half years, ever since I left Ma Ao and went to Hangzhou Teachers' School. I always thought I had nothing to come back for. Also, I had sworn to myself that I would return to this island only as a college student. But when I sat on the bed I had shared with my sisters and grandma for ten years, the past overwhelmed me like the mud sliding down the side of a mountain. The two hand imprints in the wooden windowsill were still there. I had often climbed in and out of the apartment through the window to avoid passing my parents' room. I remembered how I needed a chair when I started using the window, then I only needed to pop my hands on the sill and lift myself onto it. That was how I got my hand-prints on the frame.

From a distance, a ship was blasting its way into the port. Between the horns, I could hear Nainai's thread being pulled through the sole made of old cloth and flour paste. She was making shoes that no one would wear anymore. She spent her days and nights in bed now, except when she went to the bathroom on her crutches. How did she become so old within four years? Yet her eyes were still frighteningly bright when they fixed on me. Father was rewinding the tape again. He had been playing the same song repeatedly this morning. There were only three of us in the apartment. Mother and my two sisters had gone to work. For a second, I thought I was a teenager again, washing the dishes and vegetables in a hurry so as not to be late for school while Nainai and Father whispered in each other's ears. Everything remained in the same place, but time had left its traces. Nainai had lost all her teeth, Father's hair had become completely gray, and I was a student of Beijing University instead of a mute, sullen girl in the local middle school.

Beijing University. I still couldn't believe I had made it. During the three days of the entrance exams, the temperature in Hangzhou rose to forty-three centigrade, breaking the record of the past hundred years. I had to tie a towel around my forehead to prevent the sweat from pouring into my eyes, and I used another under my wrist so as not to soak the exam papers. Everyday, people fainted and had to be carried out of the room. After it was over, I spent a whole day in the air-conditioned movie theater with Yan, until the three days of fire and sweat froze in my memory. Yan was stunned when the scores came out. I made it to the top list and could choose any college in the country. Yan hinted I should consider Hangzhou University but immediately told me to make my own choice. He knew he had no reason to keep me in Hangzhou. First of all, it would be dangerous for both of us to be in the same school. Besides, he himself had applied to a graduate school in Dalian, a city far away in the north, for the next year. He also knew he would have picked Beijing University if he were in my position. *Go to Beijing,* he said. *No one there knows about my marriage and we can see each other openly.*

Hong had played his last trick on me. He intercepted the admission letter from Beijing University and kept it in his drawer for a week. Yan accompanied me to the office of the entrance exams and told the "dry bread" about the situation. She picked up the phone and ordered Hong to hand out the notice. There were only five candidates in Zhejiang Province who had been accepted into Beijing University. It was a great honor for everybody. How could Hong, a party member and secretary, be so selfish and nearsighted? The woman lectured him on the phone in a serious voice. I went directly back to Hong's office. He threw the letter on his desk.

"Two choices," he said sternly. "You can take the letter and get out of our school tomorrow. Remember, your birthday is still a problem. If you're thrown out of the campus, don't come back here. Ma Ao is where you'll belong. Or you can forget about this admission letter, stay with us, and I'll make sure you get trained in Hangzhou University."

"I want my admission letter, Secretary Hong," I said.

He flung it across the desk. I picked up the opened envelope from the floor and almost sobbed over the red seal of Beijing University. At last! The baby turtle had made the ocean after the journey of seven years!

The thousand-year-old iron tree suddenly burst into blossoms,
the deaf-mute finally opens her mouth to speak.
Thanks to Chairman Mao, thanks to acupuncture.

The singer's voice was so high-pitched that it sounded like a loud squeak. Perhaps she was the deaf-mute in the song who suddenly began to open her mouth. When the song came out, everybody learned how to sing it. They stretched their necks to reach the highest pitch. If a needle could make a deaf-mute speak, then anything was possible. We all loved miracles, but only the person on whom the miracle had fallen could really feel the wonder and joy.

I had only a week left to pack for my journey to Beijing. But still I had come home to say good-bye to my family. When I had shown them my admission letter, Father said nothing; he just stared at the red seal as if to check that it was real. Mother said "good," then added, "Now we have to tighten our belts for four years." I blushed, my heart filled with the familiar helplessness and guilt.

For the first time, I became aware of their money problem. For the next four years, my family would have to support me. The tuition and dormitory were free at college. But I had to eat and buy books. It was shameful to still be depending on parents at my age. My sisters said, "Don't worry, Mother. We're both working now. Together, we'll help our sister to get through school. She's the first college student in our family. We'd be happy to tighten our belts." Their support made me feel worse. I was not doing what the eldest should do for the family.

That night, Mother took me to visit her friend, the best English expert on this island, she claimed. As soon as we sat down, the expert started the conversation in English. He had a funny accent and used words that appeared only in the novels of the eighteenth century. He was eager to discuss international affairs in his absurd vocabulary. I tried my best to keep up with him out of politeness, wondering what this was about, when I saw Mother exchanging looks with the expert. I saw the sneer on her face. *She is testing me,* I thought furiously. *She is jealous of my going to college.* I shut my mouth and refused to answer any more questions. When I followed Mother out the door, I felt only sadness. I could never make her happy. She was not a mother. She was not my mother.

But the next morning, before she left for school, she slipped a roll into my hand and said, "Make good use of it." I opened my palm and saw five ten-yuan notes.

"It's too much," I stammered, not daring to look at her. I was ashamed of what I had been thinking about her. "Thirty will be plenty."

"Take it," she said firmly. "You need it to buy tickets for the ship and train to get to Beijing. Besides, you should buy yourself some new clothing. You don't want to look like a country bumpkin in the capital. From now on, I'll send you twenty yuan a month. That should be enough, yes? I know you'll also have some stipend from the university because you've worked for two years as a teacher. It's a new policy, my friend told me. If it's true, you'll have plenty even to buy books."

I nodded my head. What could I say? Mother had been in charge of the family finances since I could remember. She was capable, experienced. If only she could soften her voice. But there was tenderness beneath the matter-of-fact tone when I listened carefully. "I have a meeting this evening. So I won't be able to see you off tonight. Your father and sisters will be there. Take care of yourself. Eat well and don't work too hard. You don't need my advice. You know what to do." She stopped, her head tilted to the right as if trying to remember something.

Suddenly she stepped forward and put her hand on my shoulder. "How old are you, Ni Bing, twenty-two? You're still young. You should concentrate on your studies for the next few years. It's not easy to get where you are, and more difficult to keep what you have. I assume you're not seeing any boy right now. Good. I'll give you only one piece of advice: Don't talk love before you're twenty-five." Her trembling fingers dug deep into my shoulder. I was about to cry out in pain, when she released me abruptly. "Good-bye, Ni Bing," she said, and rode off on her bike.

Does she love me or not? The question had haunted me ever since I first met my mother at the age of five. Perhaps it was just a question of perception: it all depended on how I looked at and interpreted things. My youngest sister Ni Hao told me that Mother had always favored me. Seeing the shock in my eyes, she listed a number of things Mother had done for me, including the way she had used me as a model to make my sisters work harder. "I've decided to try the entrance exams next year, too," Hao declared, "just to shut her up. I'm tired of hearing her praise you day and night. If you can do it, so can I. Will you lend me the books you've studied to prepare? You don't need them anymore."

I nodded my head. Hao was not only the most beautiful but also the most intelligent of us three girls. I had wondered why she didn't take the exams earlier. She was even more talkative than Mother. When my two sisters and Mother got together, they took over the whole space, turning Nainai, Father, and me into mere shadows. The three of us were nontalkers. Not true. When Mother wasn't around, Nainai had endless things to say to Father. But she would whisper only in his ear, as if she were afraid Mother could hear, even when she was miles away. The only true nontalkers were Father and I. Hao was the only person in the family who dared talk back to Mother. I once heard Hao say "dog fart" to her. I thought Mother would slap her, but she just laughed and said, "You filthy little mouth." Was this not a miracle?

"Ni Bing, I want you to come with me," Father said. I jumped up from the window and stared at him, as if seeing a ghost. In his new navy uniform, he looked as if he was on his way to his office, but he was wearing a pair of old, muddy sneakers and a hat. A green military canteen and bag hung across his shoulders, making a big x on his chest. He held a new hat in his hand. "Put it on," he said, and threw it to me. I caught the hat and followed him without a word.

Chapter Eight

I FOLLOWED MY FATHER out of the apartment, out of the navy compound, and out onto the street that led to the Western Mountain. He was taking me there to pick linzhi, a magic herb he had been searching for and gathering for years. The creek along the road was still running, but the water had become green and smelled foul. I used to fish here with my sisters during the summer floods. My father once joined us and we came home with a full basin of loach. We sautéed them with red sauce, the most delicious food I'd ever eaten, and fed the rest to the chickens. The hens laid many double-yolk eggs after the feast.

The morning sun shone right into my eyes. It would be another hot day. I walked behind my father, keeping a distance of ten meters. He marched forward without looking back, knowing I was there. We had walked like this for eight years. I hadn't called him "father," hadn't spoken a word to him since he beat me to make me talk about Mother's affair with Uncle Gao. I had been fourteen years old.

THAT, TOO, HAD BEEN a sunny morning. My mother and two sisters had rushed off to school earlier than usual, having sensed something awful was about to happen. Father had been drinking since I got up and was still drinking after I came back from the market. By the time I had finished my chores and was ready for school, he was gulping from his second bottle of cheap red sorghum spirit. I tiptoed to the door, hoping he was too drunk to see me. When I reached for the door handle, I heard him say, "No, you're not going to school. Not yet, Ni Bing. I need to talk to you."

I turned to Father, cursing myself. *I knew it! I knew it! You should have left through the window, you damn fool!* Father sat cross-legged with his shoes on, glaring at me with his glassy eyes. His nose quivered like a flayed mouse. Hiccups wrenched his foamy lips, saliva spurted all over my face. His breath smelled of overnight garlic and an upset stomach. I stood still against the door, unable to lift my fingers to wipe off his slime, too petrified to turn my eyes away. In the space of two weeks, my father had become a gray old man. And he looked dangerous, insane.

I knew what he wanted from me. He'd been grilling Mother for two weeks to find out who had jumped out of the window in the children's room the night when he returned unexpectedly from a Beijing opera movie. He knew it was Gao, his colleague in the Department of Navy Navigation, whom he had first brought home to dinner six years ago. He wanted Mother to say Gao's name. But she had flatly denied that anyone ever visited her. He must have been hallucinating. Every night, after ten o'clock, Father closed the door to their bedroom and I lay in bed till dawn listening to their intense murmuring which, from time to time, would burst into a ferocious howl or mad laugh.

In the morning, Mother went to school on her bike, looking exhausted. Father took sick leave from the office. Most of the time, he just sat in bed with his mother, drinking and smoking cigarettes through a cored apple, a folk prescription for stomach ulcers, while she mended socks and whispered advice into his ear. Even though she stopped talking whenever I passed by, I knew what she was telling him: get a divorce and marry someone from Shandong, someone who would take care of him and the household with diligence and who would never betray him, someone who would not talk back to her mother-in-law. He was only forty-five, could have his pick of beautiful virgins, those juicy "yellow flower girls."

There was a constant war between Nainai and Mother. Waipo told me that Nainai had burst into tears the first time she and Mother met. She believed the bride from Shanghai was made of nothing but perfumed water. How long could anyone hold onto liquid fragrance? I grew up watching Father being tugged in two directions as he struggled to be a loving husband and a filial son. When I was old enough to do the housework, I, too, was pulled into the whirlpool of the power struggle. Soon I figured out that Mother was the one who held the real reins in this household, no matter how hard Nainai yelled and hit me all day. Mother had taken charge of the finances, and that was the key to power. It made her the pivot of the family.

Now the pivot was wobbling, and Nainai was applying leverage to undermine Mother's position. She had been encouraging her son to make his wife talk. Once Mother confessed, he would have her tail in his hand for the rest of his life. He could divorce her or at least puncture her arrogance. Since Mother wouldn't talk, it was I who now had to tell the truth. I was the only witness to that night. But I would not be used as the lever that would topple my family. I would not allow that to happen.

"Did you hear me, Bing? Father is talking to you. Come over here, right now."

I lifted my left foot, then the other. I was walking on clouds. My head, however, seemed to be filled with lead. I moved with great care, lest I topple over and fall through the mist. Bing. No one called me by my given name except Waipo and occasionally Uncle Gao. I liked my first name, Bing—ice, but I hated it when combined with my family name. "Ni" had the same sound as mud. My classmates and sisters often called me muddy ice. I always hoped that people would call me Bing, but it sounded full of menace now, coming from Father's contorted mouth.

I stopped at the desk next to the bed, fixing my eyes on the stain on the chest of my father's gray wool navy uniform.

Ni Bing, you heard nothing, you saw nothing, you know nothing, so you say nothing, I told myself over and over again.

"What did you say, Ni Bing?"

"What did you say?" I repeated after him, lifting my eyes from his chest to his nose. I was looking at my father, but I did not see him. Milky fog rose and gathered in front of my face, a black hole in the middle. I must watch it carefully. I did not want to fall into this abyss. I repeated the question again. I heard him clearly, but understood nothing. When the fog appeared between my eyes, I shut all the doors of my senses.

"Bi yangde," he cursed.

"What did you say, Father?"

Something flashed past my face. A whiff of wind and the smell of cheap cigarettes. It was father's raised arm. He was about to strike, but he checked himself. *Pay attention, Ni Bing,* I warned myself, *do not withdraw into the blank space yet. You need to handle this with a clear mind.*

I refocussed my eyes, and slowly Father's face came into sight. The black hair quivered on top of the mole on the right side of his nose as his nostrils flared. He took a deep drag from his cigarette. His face disappeared momentarily as he sucked in his cheeks to inhale. The end of the cigarette brightened, then dimmed, leaving a quarter inch of ash hanging. The room was quiet. I could hear Nainai's needle and thread piercing through the shoe sole. I waited. How was he going to start the interrogation?

"Open the drawer," he said.

I jumped and put my hand between my breasts, where the keys hung on a black string. How did he know I had access to this drawer? Only about a month ago, Mother had called me into her room after a long visit from Uncle Gao and handed me a key and a five-yuan note. "You're fourteen," she said. "Time for your own drawer and more responsibility for the family. I'm really tired of giving you money every day to buy food. From now on, you'll have five yuan each week to plan the daily meals. Should be enough, no?" I stood straight before her like a fool, not knowing what to say.

Mother's pine desk had four drawers. Two contained things like scissors, screwdrivers, buttons, pins, and other junk. The other two were locked and only Mother had the keys. What had I done to deserve such trust? Even Shuang and Hao, Mother's favorites, had not gained that privilege. Mother looked radiant. Her cheeks, usually pale and yellowish, flushed with rosy color. And how dark and watery her eyes! Uncle Gao had magic power over her.

Why did Father want to see the drawer? What did it have to do with Gao? I wished he could just ask his damn question about that night and get it over with. I wanted to get away.

A storm had gathered behind Father's sodden face. I quickly pulled the key out from between my jacket buttons and knelt to unlock the second drawer on the right side of the desk. Then I stepped aside, the "Forever" lock dangling on my chest. Father jerked the drawer open. Coins rolled around, jingling against portrait pins of Chairman Mao. He grabbed a roll of money from the inside corner and threw it on the desk.

"You'd better explain this, Daughter."

I closed my eyes in despair. Without looking, I knew exactly how much was in that bundle. One five-yuan bill, one five-jiao bill, three two-jiao bills, five one-jiao bills, and five-fen, two-fen, and one-fen coins—a total of six yuan, eighty jiao, and two fen. Twice a day I counted the money, wondering what to do with my 1.82 yuan surplus. Mother never said I could keep it. And I dared not spend it without permission, though I was dying to know what a banana tasted like. What should I tell him about this huge sum of money?

"Who gave you this? Speak! Are you a deaf-mute? Was it your mom or Uncle Gao?"

Blood rushed to my face. My father suspected that I had been bribed to keep their secret. Even if I had a thousand mouths, I wouldn't be able to clear myself. Father would never believe my story. He ground his teeth as he mentioned the name, as if he were chewing Gao's flesh and breaking his bones. They used to be best friends. I still remembered the afternoon when Father came home shouting in the hallway that they had a special guest from his department. We all ran out. Gao stood next to Father, smiling and nodding to everyone. I had always thought of my father as the best-looking guy until this moment. Gao overshadowed Father, not because he was taller and more neatly dressed, his gray uniform without a single spot or wrinkle, but because his manner was more refined. *He must have had a college education,* I thought.

And I was right. Uncle Gao had graduated from Beijing Foreign Languages Institute. I noticed his big, liquid eyes fix momentarily on Mother. She blushed faintly, then offered her hand to him. Father told us to call him Uncle Gao. He patted our heads and shook our hands, then hoisted Hao on his shoulders. "Isn't he great?" Father shouted as we entered the apartment. "He's also from Weihai. I'm not boasting, but only my native home can produce such a good-looking guy." Thereafter Gao dropped by every weekend for dinner, poker, and music. Mother always sang or played accordion when he requested. When Father was away at sea, he asked Gao to keep an eye on his family. At such times, Gao visited at least twice, sometimes three or four times a week. His wife and son lived in Weihai. He saw them only once a year. He showed us a picture of them. Secretly, we all agreed that his wife was not even half as good-looking as he. Soon, he had become part of our family. Father often patted him on his back after a few drinks, sighing, "Old Gao, I really don't know what I would do without you. You're dearer than a brother."

Now he was ready to eat his dearer-than-a-brother friend alive. I must be careful. I didn't want to be torn into pieces in this fight. *Speak, Ni Bing, speak. Open your mouth and tell him that Mother gave you the five-yuan bill last night to buy food for the coming week and the rest is just leftover change.*

"Bi yangde, you think you can still fool me, eh? You think if you don't talk, I won't know they gave you the money to cover up their foulness, eh? No way! Father is determined. Today the whole thing must come to light." He began to rake the drawer with his trembling fingers. "Let me see, what else did that couple of bi yangde give you to seal your mouth?"

I almost tittered and quickly bowed my head to hide my smile. Recently I had discovered in a book that babies were born through vaginas, reversing my belief that we came into this world by tearing open our mothers' bellies. This new discovery made Father's curse sound extremely funny. Bi yangde—you that were born of a cunt! Did he realize that he himself also came from that place? Every time he cursed others, he was in fact cursing himself.

"What is this?" he roared. "A golden Hero fountain pen! Where did you get this? Ah, here's Gao's name. So he gave you his pen. Why? Why such an expensive gift? What have you done for him? You won't speak to me? Fine. Now watch this."

He flung the pen against the wall. It sprang back in an arc, then fell to the floor by his feet. I leaped forward to retrieve it, but his black military leather boot got there before my hand. A loud crack. Slowly he lifted his foot. I knelt on the cement floor in front of my Hero. The golden nib was bent and split, the black shaft, which had been rubbed so bright and smooth by my hands and mouth, was shattered into pieces, exposing the limp ink bladder inside. I used to squeeze it with my fingers, sometimes with my teeth, watching the ink ooze or spurt out through the golden nib until one day the rubber tore and red ink splashed all over my mouth. Before Mother had given me the key to the drawer, I had carried the pen with me for six years wherever I went, day and night, close to my skin.

"So you still have the face to cry, you whore," Father's voice thundered above me. "Then go ahead and cry." The slap.

Clouds poured in from eight directions, like cotton balls stuffing my nose, mouth, ears, and eyes. I held my breath and blew my nose as hard as I could. Blood spurted out, blood as red as the sunset.

It was like that bloody dusk when Uncle Gao had come to me. I was sitting on the windowsill, gazing at the sun inching down behind the Memorial Tower to the Revolutionary Martyrs on the Western Mountain. The sky looked like someone had spilled jars of paint over red velvet. Bats and crows darted in and out of the sharp golden rays, their bodies so dark they seemed to have been singed by the fierce sun. The whole navy compound was quiet. Every one had gone to watch the movie *The Tunnel War* in the courtyard of the navy headquarters. Each family had eaten dinner early so they could get a good spot near the screen. I had to stay behind because I was being punished for breaking a bowl. Gao was supposed to come to dinner and go to the movie with us. But he didn't show up or send a message of explanation, which was rare. Mother got more and more agitated. When I dropped the bowl, she threw herself upon me, pinching my arms and thighs and cursing viciously until Nainai pulled her away. "Don't let me see your ugly face tonight," Mother said, and banged the door shut. I climbed onto the windowsill and watched my family walk into the scarlet dusk. Father was at sea. If he had been home, he would have put in a word for me. If Uncle Gao had come to dinner, Mother would not have hit me so hard. If I were as pretty and smart as my sisters, would I stop suffering? The crows cawed in the distance. My eyes were too dry to weep. The sun set everything on fire. I looked at it through my palms. The rays pierced the spaces between my fingers. My hands were also burning. Oh, when I grew up and had children, I would never let them weep like this!

"What's the matter, Xiao Bing?"

I removed my hands from my eyes. Uncle Gao stood in front of me against the setting sun, his slim body edged with an orange halo. I looked up at his face from my windowsill. He called me Xiao Bing—little ice, Xiao Bingquai—little ice cube, or simply Bingbing, when Mother was not around. It made me feel that maybe I wasn't as ugly as the others thought. He and Waipo were the only two people who could make me laugh. How deep, yet how soft his voice was! Like ocean waves. I wanted to close my eyes and bathe in it.

"Your nose is bleeding, Xiao Bing. And where did you get that bruise on your cheek?" He took out his white handkerchief.

My eyes suddenly felt hot. I quickly looked away. "Nothing, Uncle Gao. I broke a bowl this evening."

He sighed and turned my face gently toward his. "Bingbing, try not to be mad at your mother. Your father is often away. She misses him. Sometimes she gets impatient."

I stared at him. *She got mad because you didn't come to dinner,* I wanted to say, but kept quiet.

"I had to take care of an emergency this afternoon and I couldn't find anyone to send a message. I came as soon as I finished up, hoping someone might be still here. See, I was right. My Xiao Bingquai is still waiting for me."

He lifted me off the sill and spun me around, holding me above his head. I opened my arms and legs. A flying bird. The sun passed and returned swiftly. It had fallen at the foot of the tower, half-hidden behind the peak. Suddenly I fell and landed on his chest, my arms around his neck, my chin on his shoulder. Uncle Gao's hair and jacket smelled of the sun—the smell that seeped into cotton fabric after a day of exposure to the clear sky. Father also smelled of the sun when he returned from the sea. I buried my face in his collar.

"Bingbing, Bingbing," he murmured as he stroked my back. "It's not too late to go to the movie. Don't worry about your mom. She won't see us there in the crowd. When the movie is over, we'll run back before everyone else. You can sit on my shoulders. You're as light as a little swallow. How old are you, Xiao Bing?"

"Eight," I said into his ear.

He put me down on the windowsill again and held both my wrists in one hand. "I must talk to your father," he said in a low voice as if whispering to himself. "You shouldn't carry heavy things at your age. Your bones are still frail. And you must eat more so you can grow fast. Now, my little Xiao Bingquai, are you ready for the movie?"

How I loved the way he called me "xiao bingquai." I felt myself melting in his embrace. He was about to lift me when I jumped up. "Wait a second," I said, and leaped back into the apartment. I reappeared on the windowsill in a red velvet skirt. It was Mother's hand-me-down from her mother. She had just trimmed its frayed hem and altered the waist for Shuang's birthday. Shuang was a year and two months younger, but three inches taller than me. The skirt reached my ankles and I could slip my hand easily into the waistband. I lifted it with my right hand and smiled up at Uncle Gao.

"Xiao Bing, you have such a cute smile, do you know that?" he said. I smiled more broadly, then remembered my missing front tooth. I quickly covered my mouth with my hand. Laughing, he hoisted me onto his shoulders.

The sun had gone down. The sky was now orange, smudged here and there with dark gray strokes. Sitting high up, I could see a few moviegoers carrying bamboo chairs on their shoulders and turning left into the street that led to the headquarters. The stream along the road and the gravel under Uncle Gao's boots sounded like singing. I began to tell him how many fish my sisters and I had caught in the stream, how many worms we had picked from tree leaves to feed the chickens, how many more eggs they had laid after eating the worms, and how one of the hens wouldn't desist from hatching her eggs no matter how my grandma tortured her. My hands were busy at the same time. I coiled locks of his hair around each of my fingers, kneaded his ears, wrapped my skirt around his head and neck, until he told me that I was quite a naughty girl. I laughed, kicking at his chest with my heels as I shouted, "Run, run, horse, run all the way to the headquarters." He neighed and galloped like a horse, then stopped and panted, pretending he was out of breath. We both shrieked with laughter. Suddenly I realized that if I hadn't broken the bowl and had to stay home, all this would not have happened.

Uncle Gao had never paid so much attention to me. He only talked to Mother and let Shuang and Hao sit on his shoulders.

"I want to walk," I said.

"Why? I'm not tired," he protested, but nevertheless lowered me down gently onto the road. I gazed up into his face, its dark pupils half hidden behind his thick eyelashes as he looked down at me. The gravel gave my feet a firm grip on the ground. I put my hand into his. It wasn't as big as Father's, but it was much warmer and softer. From time to time, he squeezed my hand, and I looked up at him with a smile. When our eyes met, I cried to myself: *If we could just continue walking like this forever! I would do anything for him, anything!*

We walked into the square, into the ren shan ren hai—the seas and mountains of people. On the huge screen, Mao was waving to the Red Guards from the rostrum of Tiananmen. They all screamed on and on, jumping up and down, their twisted faces smeared with tears. The audience clapped whenever Mao appeared, then immediately continued chatting and cracking their sunflower, pumpkin, or watermelon seeds. The ground was covered with a thick layer of nutshells, candy wrappers, pop-corn, and popped rice. This biweekly open-air movie had become a festival for the navy families. They turned up to enjoy the few movies that were allowed to be shown, even though they had seen them at least ten times. But what they loved even more was the occasion for a gathering during which they were not obliged to shout slogans or wave fists. The whole square was packed. Those nearest the screen sat on the ground, and then, somewhat further back, the rest occupied rows of bamboo chairs, and behind them the benches. The latecomers had to stand on benches in order to see from the outer fringes of the crowd. I was too short to see anything even if I had a bench to stand on. Uncle Gao picked me up. I protested. He could see nothing from here. Besides, I couldn't let him hold me up through the movie. I looked around and pointed to the steps to the auditorium.

"Let's sit over there, Uncle Gao."

We were the only people sitting there. From the top step, we had a good view of the screen, though the faces were a bit blurred by the distance. I stretched out between Uncle Gao's legs, my skirt spread around my feet. The wind blew, rubbing the soft, silky velvet against my bare thighs. The movie started. The crowd quieted down as the shouts of "The ghosts are entering the village, the ghosts are entering the village," echoed above the dark heads. The Japanese soldiers crashed in, raiding the village and killing the peasants they found hiding in water jars, barns, and cellars. It was a story about peasants in northern China fighting off the Japanese invaders during the Second World War. In the beginning, the peasants lacked the weapons and other resources to wage war. Then they got in touch with Mao's guerrillas, and after reading Mao's books, they found a way to fight the Jap ghosts: the tunnel war.

The wind blew harder as evening fell. I embraced Uncle Gao's arm for warmth. I had forgotten to bring a sweater for the mid-September night. Uncle Gao lifted me onto his lap, enclosing me with his long arms. But I was still shivering in my thin white shirt. He unbuttoned his jacket and enfolded me. I rode on his lap, the key chain and wallet in his pants pocket caused a strange sensation on the inside of my thighs, something itchy and yet not exactly itchy. My body was bathed in his sweaty warmth and the aroma of Fan soap. His hands moved up and down on my belly. It was ticklish in the beginning but soon felt nice. I cast a languid look at the screen. The peasants had started digging the first tunnel to connect two houses. Stoves were used as tunnel entrances and exits. He rocked slightly. I closed my eyes. It was like sleeping in a cradle.

Soon the cradle turned into a ship tossing about in a storm. The waves opened their foamy jaws. The wind tried to blow me into endless dark holes. I clung to a mast with each of my hands. They somehow turned into boa constrictors and entrapped my chest. I woke up gasping for air. Uncle Gao was rocking me in a frightening manner. His arms clapped around my waist like an iron hoop, lifting me up and down, up and down. My legs were firmly clamped between his thighs, my skirt lifted and my underwear pushed down to my knees. There was something funny between my thighs. It felt like a huge bone, yet it was also fleshy; it was hard and silky smooth at the same time. He hoisted me up and down, rubbing this hot stick between my legs. I looked down and had a glimpse of something shaped like a rubber tube protruding between my closed thighs. In the moonlight, it looked frighteningly red, trembling like a flayed rat. His breathing became faster and faster, like Nainai gasping for air during one of her asthma attacks. I smelled something similar to Father's garlic breath. The shaking made me dizzy. I grasped at his arms on my chest for some support, trying to focus my eyes on the screen. The whole village had started digging like mad. All the houses had been connected by tunnels. Every hole inside and outside the houses—be it under a stove, a well, or a chicken shed—had become a loophole for weapons as well as an entrance to the underground world. The Jap ghosts were totally baffled. The bullets were coming from everywhere, but there was nobody in sight.

Suddenly, Uncle Gao pitched forward in a convulsion, his arms tightening around my stomach. "Bingbing, oh Bingbing, I'm dying," he moaned, filling my ear with his hot wet breath. He was no longer rocking, and the rod between my thighs shrunk rapidly. He trembled, as if he were suffering from malaria. Slowly he sat up, moved me aside to button his fly, his shirt, and his jacket. As I pulled up my underwear, I found something sticky and white on my thighs, like a bowl of spilled sweet rice porridge. It smelled of the piss odor that always lingered in my parents' room when I made their bed in the morning. Uncle Gao wiped me with a white handkerchief. I suddenly remembered the white towel stained with this creamy stuff that I often found in my parents' quilt. Blood rushed to my cheeks. I didn't know what he had just done with me, but it was something I would never tell anyone about. It was a secret between us. He wiped me clean, straightened my skirt, and put me on the stone step. Two Jap ghosts had been captured by the villagers. A group of angry women were slapping their cheeks with the soles of cotton shoes. The cheers of the peasants on the screen mingled with the applause from the audience. I flinched at each slap, my face burning with shame and pity.

"Would you like to go home, Xiao Bing?" He knelt before me, his hands holding my shoulders. When I looked up, he quickly moved his eyes away. How pale he looked! And how he trembled!

"Yes," I whispered. He turned, motioning me to climb on his back. On the road, we could still hear the woman singing sweetly through the loudspeaker: "The sun comes out shining everywhere. Chairman Mao's thoughts are kept within our hearts . . ." He carried me on his back in silence all the way home.

He put me down on the windowsill, then opened the unlatched window. His hand rested on my head for a long time, while his eyes looked vacantly into the empty apartment. I sat still, waiting for him to speak. Finally, he pulled the black Golden Hero pen from his breast pocket and laid it in my hand. I trembled with excitement. Uncle Gao had won this pen in a chess tournament. When he had showed it to Mother, she had pouted and wriggled as she begged him to give it to her. He had laughed and told her she would have to prove herself a good girl to get it. But now he wanted me to have this pen. Was I a good girl?

"Keep this to yourself, Xiao Bing," he whispered.

I nodded. The black Hero pen was thick. I could feel its solid shaft in my fist. Before I turned to leap back into the apartment, Uncle Gao reached out his hands to hold my cheeks and planted a long kiss on my forehead.

"GET UP, Ni Bing, don't just lie there like you're dead. You can't fool me. Wipe your nose and talk. Don't think you can just walk out of this door today without saying anything."

I opened my eyes. Father was squatting over me, wiping the

dry blood off my face with a yellowish handkerchief that stank of snot and sweat. I sat up to dodge his hand. Father's face and shoes spun like wheels. Warm blood trickled down my nose to my lips. I didn't bleed easily, but once the blood started, it wouldn't stop. It dropped silently onto the front of my blue-and-white polka dot padded jacket.

"Hold it, hold it up to your nose," Father screamed, waving his pathetic rag. His tone was still harsh, yet I could see concern, fear, and shame in his eyes. He rarely hit his children unless we did something really wrong. The only two times he had beaten me were for stealing rubber bands from a store and for reading dirty books. And he often scolded Mother for punishing us too much. I had always regarded him as my protector, even though he was away from home most of the time.

I took the handkerchief from him and pressed it under my nose, holding my breath to avoid the smell. He wouldn't have slapped me like this if Mother hadn't pushed him into the corner. I touched my forehead with the handkerchief. Uncle Gao's lips were permanently imprinted there. Ever since he had kissed me that night, I had gotten into the habit of pressing my forehead from time to time, as if there was a window there that might suddenly pop open, exposing all my unspeakable secrets to the world if I didn't take constant care to keep it closed.

"Ni Bing, I'm sorry I hit you. I was totally out of my mind." Father helped me to a chair, then paced back and forth as he wheeled me. "You must help me. Your mother won't tell me the truth. I know I wasn't hallucinating as she claimed. I saw him. I saw him jumping out of the window, all unbuttoned and barefooted. If I hadn't shouted, he probably wouldn't have taken the risk of leaping across the ditch to make his escape. Oh, I wish I had never brought that grandson of a turtle home. I wish I hadn't gone to that idiotic opera movie. I wish that stupid projector hadn't broken down and we had all sat through the whole movie instead of coming back earlier. I wish I hadn't spoiled your mother. I wish, oh, how could she betray me like this? How could he have done this to me after I've tried my best to get him promoted in the department? I wish I could believe her story. I didn't want this war, I didn't. But everyone saw the shadow that night. If I don't do anything, I'll never be able to show my face in the office or in this compound again."

He circled the chair I was sitting on. I listened, my hands crossed behind the back of the chair, my sympathy swinging back and forth like a pendulum. Was I a clock? If I was, who was the hand that wound the time that was locked inside? Not Father, not Mother. Morally, I should tell him what had happened, not only because I had always felt closer to him than to Mother, but also because she had gone too far. No one in the world could treat her as preciously as Father. He never returned home without a bundle of presents for her—clothing, food, seashells, and odds and ends from the different ports his ship had visited. He gave her all of his salary, taking only ten yuan for his own pocket money and two for his mother. And even that money went mostly to Mother's collection of clothing. When he married her, he had quit smoking and drinking so that she could send more money to her mother. Only recently had he started smoking and drinking herbal spirits again to cure his ulcer, and then he had plunged all the way in. Within a few months, he was drinking from morning till night and spending five more yuan from his salary on liquor and tobacco. Mother screamed and cursed, but his need to drink was insatiable.

I knew I should tell him the truth because he had been a kind and fair father and he was the one I loved the best in the entire family. But if I told, I would lose Mother, probably forever. Yesterday, she had tried to kill herself with a kitchen knife. I was frying belt fish on the stove when Shuang ran to me screaming: "Jiejie, Jiejie, Mom sharpened a knife and hid it in her bag." I was initially too shocked for her words to sink in. Shuang had never called me older sister before. It sounded strange yet immediately made me aware of my responsibilities as the eldest. I grasped her wrists to keep her from jumping up and down.

"Where is the bag?" I asked. "Un, un, un, under the bed," she stuttered nervously. I ran into the bedroom. Mother lay in bed with a blanket covering her from head to toe. I stole the bag and returned to the kitchen. After hiding the knife under the coal basket, I told Shuang to keep an eye on Mother and make sure she stayed at home while I ran two miles to get Aunt Do, one of Mother's colleagues and best friends.

Aunt Do rushed over on her bike. When I finally got home, I found my parents in tears and Aunt Do sitting between them holding forth on harmony between husband and wife, based on unconditional trust and responsibility. She talked on until they both promised her to behave like sensible adults and stop torturing each other with foolish words or acts. That night, a sinister peace settled over the house.

No, I would never be able to live with myself if the family broke up and something happened to Mother because of me. What about Father, then? He seemed on the verge of weeping, tortured by his gnawing desire to know the truth and by his fear of actually discovering it. His eyes were so bloodshot that if he really cried, he would probably shed blood instead of tears. Could I carry the terrible burden of this secret for the rest of my life?

"Ni Bing, my life depends on you now," he pleaded. "Tell me it was Gao who jumped out of your window that night. You must have seen him. Even if you were asleep, all the noise outside the door would have awakened you. You don't even have to say his name. Just nod yes, please."

I looked up at him. A wave of pity and sadness surged over me. My father looked pathetic in his wrinkled jacket and matted hair, an apple in one hand and a bottle in the other, his eyes shining with cunning and despair. He was no longer the handsome, radiant young man in the wedding picture hanging on the wall above his head. Where was his pride, now that he was begging his daughter to talk about his wife's affair with another man? I needed to say something, anything, to get us out of this awful situation. I couldn't bear watching my father lose his dignity. *Say something, Ni Bing.*

"Who do you think you're protecting?" Nainai's voice shot through the room from her bed next to the kitchen, loud and clear. "Let me tell you something, that turtle egg, whose name I don't even want to mention, and that mother of yours are shameless. They care nothing about their honor, but we still do and so should you. You're fourteen, still have a long way to go. You don't want to live your life faceless, do you? Your father didn't work so hard just to raise an unfilial child. Speak up, it's time you defended your father's honor."

I covered my forehead with my hand. Shameless! I had kept my forehead unwashed for three weeks after Uncle Gao had kissed me on the windowsill. I wanted to show him how I treasured him. But he never came to visit again. Mother was furious at everybody in the family. When Father returned from the sea, she complained bitterly about his friend's inexplicable estrangement until he went to the office and dragged Uncle Gao home. During the meal, Uncle Gao talked only to Father, Mother, and Nainai. His eyes never turned to me, no matter how many times I walked past him. His pen, for which I had knit a special holder and belt so I could hang it around my waist under my shorts, rubbed against my belly. This was our secret. No one could take it away, even though he refused to talk or look at me. Father patted me on my head as I put a fish casserole on the table with a smile and praised me for my diligence.

That night, my parents went to bed soon after Uncle Gao left. I listened to the sounds from their bedroom. The rustling, moaning, and creaking of the bed were not unfamiliar to me. I had heard them many times in the evenings, in the mornings, and in my dreams. But this time, they had a new meaning. I drew my knees up to my chest and put my arms around them. On my left, Shuang and Hong ground their teeth in their sleep; on the right lay Nainai's bound feet, which always smelled like a mixture of salted fish, rotten egg, and stinky tofu. But they no longer bothered me as I lay on my back, imagining myself wrapped in Uncle Gao's shirt and the aroma of Fan soap. I stroked his secret fountain pen on my belly. It was round and smooth and firm. I was back on the ocean. My ship rocked me into a bottomless dream in which I slept in a coffin with Uncle Gao. It was big enough just to hold our two naked bodies.

Oh, shameless! His lips were burning through the back of my hand on my forehead. I wanted to be with him so much that I prayed every night. Old heavens, make me as beautiful as my mother and as lively as my sisters so that Uncle Gao might smile at me as he smiles at Mother and lift me in the air as he lifts my sisters Shuang and Hao.

I prayed religiously. When I was eleven, my prayers were finally answered. I was staying in Shanghai with Waipo that summer. After the first three weeks of excitement, I began to feel restless. The alley kids were big snobs. They wouldn't let me hang around with them unless I was willing to cater to their whims by running to the store for candy, delivering messages to kids from other streets, or holding their rubber band jump rope. No way. I would rather die of boredom than degrade myself by putting myself at their service. Thus I was slumped in the sagging chair in Grandma's one-room apartment, my real uncle Zhong's copy of *Tess of the D'Urbervilles* on my lap, thinking madly about the mountains I'd roamed around in that island countryside, sometimes alone, sometimes with my father and sisters, the trees I'd climbed to pick cocoons for my chickens, and the mud beach my fingers had combed to dig for those delicious miniature clams called ocean seeds.

Then I heard his footsteps, firm and solid, not too slow, not too fast, the footsteps of someone who knew where he was going. I looked up from my chair, which faced the door and staircase. First his cap, then his eyes, nose, and lips appeared in the door frame. His smile froze at the corners of his mouth when he saw me. So did his voice. He stood on the landing, his hand gripping the staircase banister, hesitating. He hadn't expected to see me here because he had sailed with his ship a few weeks before Mother had suddenly decided to send me to Shanghai for the summer. Waipo came to his rescue as she descended from the bathroom on the roof porch. She called out his name with genuine affection and joy. Uncle Gao always arrived with a present for her, and he could provide such charming, pleasant conversations, she often said, so unlike your country bumpkin father. She ushered him in and made him sit in her own wooden antique chair.

"Get a clean towel for Uncle Gao, Ni Bing," she shouted. "Bring him lunch. Take out all the dishes I've just made, including the fried fish. Don't worry about your aunt's dinner. I can go to the market later. By the way, did you say hello to Uncle Gao? When are you ever going to learn manners?" Grandma chirped on, laughing and spooning food into his rice bowl.

I served him with my eyes cast downward, then went back to my chair and buried my face in *Tess*. My lips moved in silence to pronounce each character fully and correctly, but the words did not convey any meaning, for my ears were trying to catch every sound that issued from his mouth. Sweat seeped through his khaki uniform, but instead of the sour odor of perspiration, he still had that familiar sun smell to him, accented by the salt of seawater—the same smell emitted by my father's clothing when he came home from his long voyages. I felt dizzy again.

Uncle Gao said very little during the meal. Waipo sat on the edge of her bed chatting on and on, sometimes leaning over to whisper in his ear. Finally he put down his chopsticks and said he wanted to go out for a stroll and to do some shopping for his friends. Waipo insisted he take a nap first. It would be bad for his health to walk around in the blazing sun with a full stomach. Besides, all the stores were closed from noon to two. "Ni Bing," she said, "take Uncle Gao to your uncle's room in the next building and tidy up the bed a little bit. Your uncle is such a pig."

I remained seated in my chair. My body felt as if it had been struck by a thunderbolt. My heart was shouting: *Go, Ni Bing, go get the key and take him over there,* but my legs wouldn't move. Waipo called again. I heard Uncle Gao tell her that he could find his way by himself since he'd been there twice already, and I watched him rush out of the apartment.

The room was quiet again. Waipo snored lightly on her bed. The heat poured in through the bamboo shades, melting everything into a blur—the table, the chairs, the posters of Mao, and my little brain. I gnawed away at my arms. *What a fool!* God had given me this opportunity, and I was in the process of throwing it away. My teeth sank deep into my flesh until I flinched with pain. *Serves you right, you fool.* I examined the reddish tooth marks that marched neatly up my arms from my wrists to my shoulders. *Tess* fell between my knees and landed with a loud thud on the floor. Waipo groaned and turned her back to me. I picked up the book and looked at the page my fingers had happened to open. D'Urberville had just rescued Tess from the drunkards. On his white horse, they roamed through the woods, Tess half asleep in the arms of D'Urberville, until they at last were lost in the pitch dark.

I stood up and moved toward the bed. Underneath her huge pillow, Waipo kept hundreds of coins and her gigantic key chain. I had once counted the keys on it. Thirty-six in all. She kept the keys to every apartment she had ever lived in. One of them opened the room where Uncle Gao was now sleeping. I slid my hand between the coins and cotton fabric. I pinched the tip of a key between my fingers and gingerly pulled the whole chain toward me. Waipo's head lay on the other side of the pillow. My heart was beating like mad. I hoped she wouldn't hear. But her body didn't stir in the least when I finally got hold of the chain. It weighed heavily in my palm. I drifted out of the room like a sleepwalker.

Outside the door of my uncle's room, I took a deep breath. My brain was a pot of rice gruel bubbling on a stove. My body was an empty cave in which a voice echoed back and forth: *Open the door. This is your last chance.* I looked down at the keys in my palm and picked out a white one with two teeth protruding from its shaft— a New Peace brand. The lock clicked and turned. Uncle Gao, wearing a sleeveless undershirt, sat in bed with his back against the wall, facing the door, a cigarette burning between his fingers.

"Hi, Ni Bing, so here you are," he said, as if he knew I was coming.

I couldn't look him in the eye. My face was burning and my head splitting into two at the place his lips had once touched. I walked to the desk, murmuring that Grandma had sent me to clean up the room. My uncle had a pile of old magazines on the corner of his desk. I put all the *China Youths* on the left, and the *Red Flags* on the right. My back was turned to Uncle Gao, but I knew he was watching me. My nostrils itched from the dust and smoke. I dared not sneeze, lest I disturb the terrible silence between us. Suddenly he spoke. His voice made me jump.

"Come over and nap with me, Xiao Bing," he said.

I hung my head on my chest, my hand buried among the *China Youths* and *Red Flags*. How could I turn? How could I not? This time, not even God could help me. But Uncle Gao's hands had already lifted me in the air. He carried me to the bed and laid me down gently. I closed my eyes. The room was spinning around like a merry-go-round. I closed my eyes to fix in my memory forever the face I'd just seen, his chin blue from shaving, the curve of his lips. He put me down and watched me for a while. Then the sound of a belt being unbuckled. He lay down next to me, his hand on my stomach. Through my thin white cotton dress, I felt the hot, wet current flowing from his palm. If he moved his hand up two more inches, he would touch my breasts, which bulged like baby's cheeks with cherry nipples. For months, they'd been hurting and itching persistently. I didn't want to mention anything to mother because she might scold me for making a fuss over nothing. Several days ago, however, when I was carrying a pot of hot rice porridge from the kitchen downstairs to Grandma's apartment, I happened to look down into my T-shirt and saw the swelling of my breasts. I ran all the way to the fourth floor, leaving the pot on the second-floor landing, and shouted to my grandma that I had breast cancer. Everyone in the room, my aunts, uncle, grandpa and grandma, laughed hysterically. "But it's true," I screamed, "feel the lumps there. They really hurt." Amid all the laughing and hiccuping, my grandma finally told me not to worry. "You're just growing like a normal ten-year-old girl."

So I had grown. In the past two years, since Uncle Gao had kissed me, I had grown four inches taller and ten pounds heavier, and my shoe size was five and a half. I could carry thirty-five pounds of rice two miles from the store and pull the cart with three hundred pounds of coal in it.

The hair on his leg tickled my skin. It was soft and thick, quite unlike my father's rough, dark hair. I too had black hair shooting from my underarms. Why didn't he rub my belly as he did last time? I wanted to show him the pen holder I'd knitted for his Hero. I turned to him. His chest hair was rubbing against my nose and lips. The warmth of his heaving chest and the hot humid air of his breathing surrounded me, lifting me up to the sky in a hot air balloon. He drew his arm more tightly around my waist. *Take me, Uncle Gao. I've grown.*

"Ni Bing, are you up there? Ni Bing, come down right this moment," Waipo's call came from the alley, her voice shrill and anxious. I ran to the window. She was standing in the hot sun, a paper fan covering her forehead as she looked up.

"What are you doing in there?" she asked sternly as soon as she saw me.

"Nothing, I'm just cleaning the room as you told me." Before she said anything else, I withdrew from the window and headed to the door. Uncle Gao had already turned to the wall. I closed the door behind me without a word.

"TAKE YOUR HAND off your stupid forehead and look at me," Father roared into my face, his fingers poking into my collarbones as he shook me awake from my stupor. "Tell me, now, did Gao come that night? Did they sleep together? How many times? Tell me, if you're still my daughter. How much did they give you to keep their dirty secret? Say something. What can I do to make you talk? Do you want money also? I have money. I make four times what your mother makes. Is that what you want, you shameless bitch?" He was shaking me like a snare drum. His nails dug deep into my shoulders, as if he wanted to squeeze my lungs out of my chest. But I still managed to spit into his face when I heard that curse. He loosened his grip in his shock.

"I know nothing about them, I'm no shameless bitch, and I'm nobody's daughter," I shouted as hard as I could, but my voice came out broken and hoarse. My father stood in front of me dumbfounded, his face as white as a ghost's. He seemed to have been petrified into a white rock. What had I said to make him look like this?

"Fanle, fanle!" Nainai jumped up and down on her bound feet in the doorway. "What a little upstart! And you, my son, what are you waiting for? Beat this bi yangde."

He lifted his foot like a puppet. His soul had left him. The empty shell of his body was now controlled by an invisible thread in Nainai's hands. He kicked me in my shin. The steel-tipped shoe drove into the bone like a nail and sent me to the ground in a heap. My breathing stopped for a moment. The pain emptied my brain of thought and speech, leaving only a dark fury in the shape of clouds shooting forth from an abyss. I tried to look up at my father. *Sorry I hurt you with my words, but you hurt me worse. Now we're even. Sorry I have to keep the secret. I just have no right to tell you what I have seen, Father.*

"Look at this little upstart. She's still looking at you with the whites of her eyes. Do something, if you're still the head of this family. How can you handle your wife if you can't deal with your daughter? Do something. Teach her a lesson."

He grabbed my braid and started dragging me through the apartment, knocking over a chair and a lamp along the way. I heard tearing sounds as my hair was ripped from my scalp. I clawed at his hands to reduce this blinding pain. My foot hooked onto something. It was Nainai's ankle and her stump of a foot. She was holding the door to the kitchen. Quickly I bent my knee and kicked out with all the strength left in me. She fell like a withered tree.

He leaped back and forth between the two bodies sprawling on the floor, strange noises hooting from his mouth. "Mom, Mom, what's the matter with you? What a unfilial son I am!" He knelt next to his mother and tried to pull her up. She groaned and moaned, her trembling finger pointing in my direction. He jumped up, lifted me by my hair and collar, and threw me on the sink. "Die, die, die, everyone die! You don't let me live, so I won't let you live," he shouted, hitting both my head and his against the cement sink. I was seeing golden stars. Suddenly he threw me to the floor again and ran to the stove and coal basket. I heard a clanking of metal. I wheeled around and had time only to get a glimpse of a black poker poised high above my head before it came swinging down.

Yeah Daddy you want to know what whose hard dark thing this is and what he is doing here You know it already Why this torment You want the detail that's right I know everything even though he never talked to me or looked at me again after we came back from Shanghai But I heard the squeaking bed and the crying through the latched door She pretended she had strained her back Not true Only a trick And you're so easy to fool because you loved her too much you're blinded by your passion and obsession Her words are holy and you only hear her no one else nothing else But I heard the screeching two insane dogs biting tearing each other apart and I lay on my back listening I knew he'd come that's why I stayed home. And I knew when you knocked on the door my window was the only way out for him So I sat up in bed waiting He couldn't unlatch the chain so he broke the door open with his shoulders and dashed in That dark thing in the middle standing bolt upright between his thighs his mouth in the shape of O her mouth in the shape of O I closed my eyes this is too much too much too much Do you really want to hear all the details Can I ever put them into words turn them into sounds Forgive me Daddy I had to betray you I wanted him more than my own life and I had promised to follow him to the end of the world if he just gave me a look even if not Do not pull us apart Daddy see how happy we are in this coffin his breasts pressing against mine his lips sucking the hole in my forehead he and his shadows all over me top bottom left right nothing between us in this coffin rocking in this cradle do not pull us apart

"Oh, baby, baby, wake up, don't die on me, don't die!" Father's crying came to me, the sound of waves splashing on rocks. Cold water on my face. I opened my eyes. Grandma stood above me with a bowl in her hand, father knelt next to me holding my head in his hands. I struggled to get to my feet. My brain sloshed in my skull. I looked into the small splintered mirror above the sink. Blood and water all over my face, my hair, fresh blood still oozing from the split on my forehead. I pinched it shut with my fingertips and put my head under the tap. I let the water run until the fog in my head cleared. After I dried my face and hair with my towel, I rebuttoned my jacket and straightened the school satchel that hung across my shoulder. They watched me in complete silence. But when I headed to the door, Nainai spoke: "If you say a word to your mother about this, we'll kill you."

I turned in the direction of the voice, knowing he was by her side. I looked but could not see. His figure had blurred into gray mist, his facial features a gob of phlegm. I opened the window near my bed and climbed onto the sill. A chicken coop stood against the wall under the window; beyond lay a ditch bound by a wire mesh fence which divided the Zhoushan Middle School from the navy compound.

Once I crossed the ditch, I was a different person in a different world. On the wall of the white tower of the main building was a slogan in red paint: "Chairman Mao's sayings, each word equivalent to ten thousand." Underneath was a huge blackboard used as the school news bulletin board. I was the senior editor. This afternoon I had to take my volleyball team to another school for a match. Since I'd been appointed captain a year and a half ago, the youngest captain of any team, we had won almost every game. I had never gotten a grade lower than A- in any subject over the past three years. All my teachers praised me and entrusted me with tasks they couldn't assign to other students. But I had no friends. How could I? I rarely hung out with them and never brought them home. And how could I ever bring anyone back to this world?

The chickens crowded under the window, cooing for me to

come down to the coop and pet them as usual. Normally, I would slide down the window sill and play with my eleven red hens and one white rooster for a while before I crawled over to school through the hole in the wire. Today I was not going to crawl. I wanted to leap clear over the chicken coop, clear over the ditch, clear over the wire mesh fence. I wanted to soar. Perhaps a phoenix would rise from the chicken coop.

I turned to take a last look at my father. He was staring up at me, his mouth wide open as if he were about to scream, his hands held out as if to grasp something. I looked up at the sky to fight back the sudden surge of tears. The thick, bony hand that reached over my body to play with Mother's breasts. Me lying between them, hearing their soft talk and muffled laughter in my half sleep. His arm arched over my chest like a bridge across a brook, its hair tickling my skin, leaving an unspeakable sensation. Occasionally he also pinched my cheek. How I loved this hand! And his back that smelled of the sun, that protected me from the wind and rain as I sat in the backseat of his bike on our way to the Western Mountain to climb the Memorial Tower to the Revolutionary Martyrs. This was my first memory of my father and would be the last. *Sorry, Daddy, I don't want to leave you, but I can't help it. You've been fair and kind, but you're too far away, and he's so near. Daddy, oh Daddy, hear my call. This is the last time I'll speak to you.*

I looked at the sky. The sun had disappeared behind the clouds. The memorial tower could not be seen, only its steeple shining crooked through the mist. Facing the rusted needle in the distance, I uttered the first curse in my life: "Bi yàngde."

And I leaped from the window.

EIGHT YEARS. I thought the pain had been well buried, or healed like my sprained ankle from that jump. But walking with my father had opened the past unexpectedly. It sprang out like the ghosts let loose on July 15th of the moon calendar, rushing around, taking care of business in a limited time. It came out full of edges and thorns, cutting through my body without mercy. I was bleeding inside. But somehow I welcomed the pain. Could the past really be buried like the dead? If not, it was necessary to bring it out again. Sometimes a broken bone may appear to have healed, but it has actually knitted together wrong. In order to correct it, one must rebreak it to put it right. This was the day when we should settle the past.

We approached the gate of the navy headquarters. The guards saluted Father. He saluted back and passed by. So we were not going to the office. I quickened my steps to keep up with him. Soon we were again walking in the same rhythm, our sneakers crunching on the gravel in unison. Yan had told me he liked my way of walking: big steps, arms swinging back and forth without boundaries like a boy. Walking shoulder to shoulder with my father, the road between us, I discovered I walked just like he did. Perhaps I was a soldier by nature. We continued west and soon arrived at the foot of the Western Mountain. Father stopped to tighten his belt and drink from his canteen. Then he handed the canteen to me.

It was chrysanthemum tea with sugar. He had made the tea especially for me; he disliked sweets. Only women liked sweet things, he would say whenever Mother offered him cookies or candies. He had the same attitude to all fruits except for the Guoguang apple, a specialty of his homeland. In winter, he would ask his brother at Weihai to mail him a basket. He would wrap each fruit in straw and tissue paper and hide the basket under the bed. When we were really good, he would cut an apple into three and tell us to eat it slowly so the fragrance would sink in. As a child, I had often crawled under the bed and put my nose against the basket. My mouth watered so, but I never dared steal one. Father knew exactly how many apples were left in there. At the end of the winter, they began to rot. The room would fill with a funny smell. Only then was Father willing to finish them. In Hangzhou, I bought the same brand of apples, but they never tasted as sweet as Father's. After I stopped talking to him, he had given me a whole one on New Year's Day. I just looked at it and turned my back to him. I could see, with my back toward him, how hurt he was. No one had ever refused his sacred fruit.

The sweet tea was soothing. "Keep it," he said, when I handed back the canteen. "You'll need it more." From his bag, he took out something that resembled a dried mushroom, the top of its umbrellalike canopy covered with chocolate powder, the belly tinged with a tender yellow like the down of a baby duckling. Linzhi, I murmured. His eyes sparkled with delight. From hearing my voice or the name of this magic herb being called? Shuang told me Father became insanely obsessed with linzhi. He had taken a long leave of absence from his office to roam around the mountains searching for mushrooms. He had collected a full trunk under his bed. When I heard that, I immediately recalled the apples that slowly rotted toward the end of the winter in the basket under the bed. He put it under my nose. A pungent smell of earth and plants hit me. I sneezed. He smiled. "Strong, eh? It has absorbed the essence of all good elements in nature. Takes years for it to grow. This one is still young. See the yellow color? Probably ten years old. They say a thousand-year-old linzhi can change its shape into anything and can bring the dead back to life, but they're impossible to find. Even a young one like this is often guarded by snakes."

I looked carefully at the linzhi my father had placed in my hands. This mythological herb did have some magic power. It had suddenly transformed my father from a silent, exhausted, about-to-retire officer into an eloquent, passionate man. I looked into his eyes for the first time since our fatal conflict. Golden sparks jumped back and forth between his pupils. Yes, his hair was still the gray of eight years ago, and his face was more wrinkled, but youth had returned to his eyes. His feet were planted firmly in the yellow soil of the path, his back was as straight and solid as the pine trees that surrounded us, and his shoulders against the brown rock were thick and square. *My father has come back to me,* I said to myself.

"Linzhi may look different from this one," he said. "It can be dark, white, and brown. And the shape may vary. But you can't make a mistake about the smell. Nothing on earth has the same smell as linzhi: pungent, sweet, and bitter at the same time. It opens one's mind. You'll understand it after you've smelled it long enough. When you look for it, use your nose, your heart, and your guts more than your eyes. Otherwise, you'll never find one. And watch out for snakes. They're guardian angels for the magic herb. There's always some truth about mythology," he said with a mysterious smile like a naughty boy. "Don't panic when you see them. It's good news. It means you're close to the nest. Also, drink the tea slowly so that you'll have something when you really need it. Don't worry about me, though. I can go without water for a whole day. Now, you're ready? Take this path and turn to your right. It's a promising spot. Now get going."

I didn't move. My father sending me out on my own just like this? What if I got lost, or lost contact with him, or encountered a snake? He smiled again and patted me on the head. "Don't worry, Ni Bing. I won't lose you. Trust me?" I nodded, suddenly feeling in touch with the ground, the mountain, as if his patting had hammered me several inches down into the soil and filled me with confidence.

I followed the path for a while, then turned into an aspen wood. I was drawn to these trees by some mysterious force. Compared to the pines and firs around them, they looked like dwarves, with their round, tender green leaves. But they had the passion the bigger trees didn't have. Their tiny leaves trembled like young women calling their estranged lovers. There was no wind in the air. What force made them shake so violently? I caught a branch. My breath seemed to make the leaves move more rapidly. If they had a voice, the sound would be either sobbing or laughing. The leaves were not as round as I had thought. Each had a tip like the curve of a baby's upper lip. Funny that the trees had such youthful leaves while their trunks were twisted and bent like a hundred-year-old man. The sun shot through the treetops, spreading golden coins on the ground. They, too, quivered as if burning and melting in an invisible fire. I looked up and down, then around. Not a person, not a sound. Even the birds had stopped chirping. Where was linzhi? Where was Father?

As if my questions were being answered, I heard a call from underground, muffled and urgent, a call for help. It was my father. Did he fall off a cliff? I ran in the direction of the call and halted suddenly at the edge of a pit that looked like a grave. My father was rolling inside, his face buried in old leaves and pieces of rotten coffin wood, his fingers digging deep into the brown, moist dirt. My first thought was that my father was digging for some treasure in the ground. But no, he was pushing his stomach against something hard, his back slightly arched in the center. He was suffering from his old xinkou teng—heartache again. No doctor or pills could help him stop the pain. The only thing he could do was to press his stomach against a rock, the edge of a bed, a chair, anything with a corner to dig into the inflamed organ, and wait for the agony to go away.

So linzhi hadn't cured him, as my sister had told me. My father groaned and dug into the dirt. I wanted to jump in. At least I could wipe away his sweat, as I had often done as a kid. But the pit was big enough for just one person. I didn't want to land on top of his tortured body. Spasms rolled over his back like waves, no, more like the spasmodic trembling of aspen leaves. *No, still not that,* I thought. It was more like my father was having an intense sexual relationship with the earth. He was trying to dig his way into the ground, to become part of the soil. I smelled something pungent and bittersweet, the same odor that came from linzhi. Was that how the magic herb came into being? A fruit of passion between earth and plants, between life and death? I lay down on the ground, my arm reaching into the pit. "Father, Father," I called. "Father, come back," I shouted. It wasn't as hard as I had imagined. For eight years, the word *father* had become a block of lead hanging on my heart, pulling everything inside me down.

The spasms ebbed gradually. He heard me, I thought, as I held my breath to wait for his recovery. Little by little, he lifted his back up, his hands still inserted in the wood and dirt. He pushed himself up like a gigantic mushroom, or like a linzhi? He straightened up but had to press his face against the grave wall to get his breath back. I grabbed his hand, which reached above his head, and called again, "Father."

He looked up. I almost fell into the pit. His face had become unrecognizable from the swell and patches of blue and purple. His puffy lips had opened wide for breathing when his nostrils had closed up. He was baring his teeth at me. From the glint that shot through the slits of his eyes, I realized that he was smiling. I felt the grip in his hand and pulled. As soon as he climbed out, he pulled something out of his shirt. "Look what I've got, Daughter," he said in a squeaky voice. His throat must have also become swollen.

"A mushroom," I said.

"No," he squeaked, "it's white linzhi, the most precious kind. It grows only in ancient graves. You brought us good luck, Daughter." I looked into the pit. A yellowish skull lay in the center. My father had pressed against that to stop the pain. Still, how did his face get swollen and discolored like this? "It grew right out of its mouth," he said, pointing at the skull. "I could hardly believe my good luck when I found it. I got so carried away that I forgot about its guardian angel. Phew, it was huge. The biggest cobra I've ever seen. It rose as tall as me on its tail and spat into my face before I drove it away with my stick. I must look a mess, eh? It's worth it. Oh, all those linzhi addicts will be so jealous of me."

I took a close look at the herb for which my father had risked his life. At first glance, it didn't look much different from a dried mushroom. Then I saw the dense rings on its back like the annual rings of an old tree. Its smell was more pungent than the big brown linzhi my father had shown me. It had the same quality of being young and old at once.

"At least two hundred years old," he said.

I looked at his deformed, glowing face. So ugly his face, yet so beautiful! I turned my eyes to the frail-looking magic mushroom.

It came out of death, yet it was meant to save life. Perhaps these two were not supposed to be different? And my past hatred for my father, was it also love?

"For you." He put it in my hand. I closed my fingers around its long stem. It was unexpectedly heavy for its size, like a dwarf star or a flower that suddenly bloomed out of my fist. "I insist," he added quickly, knowing I was going to refuse to take this precious herb. "Without you, I couldn't have found this white treasure. It's meant to belong to you. It will bring you good luck. I don't know when I'll see you next time. I'm sure you'll be fine, but still, Beijing is so far away.

"Ni Bing," he hesitated.

Oh, please don't say 'forgive me' or things like this, I said to myself, my eyes closed. *I can't take it.*

"Ni Bing," he repeated, "I want you to know that Father has always been proud of you. You're my phoenix from the chicken coop."

We stood so close to each other that I could hear his heart beating with a powerful force. I tilted my head against his chest, listening to the stubborn drumming of his heart. The poison hadn't touched that spot. It dawned on me that this was what I'd been waiting for the past eight years: to lean against my father's thick chest, to listen to his heart beat, and to inhale the mixed smell of ocean and soil from his navy uniform.

Chapter Nine

I SLEPT AN EXTRA HOUR on Sunday and didn't get up till seven. I washed my face with cold water in the public bathroom across the dorm and rushed to Canteen 3 to grab a steamed bread on my way to the library. The northern bread was twice as big as the bread in the south and more solid. Everything here looked much bigger and more rugged, full of edges, unlike the delicate, refined south. The square bread weighed like a white brick in my hand. It would be my fuel for four straight hours of study in the library.

I had been in Beijing for five weeks and many things had already taken place. As soon I arrived at the campus and settled down in the dorm room, which I shared with nine other students, I was summoned to the English Department and told that I had been nominated as monitor of the 1980 English class, as student secretary of the Youth League of the English Department, and two other titles. When I recovered from the first shock, I tried to decline the offers. Yan had given me three rules: during my four years of studies at Beijing, I must not participate in any political or social activities, must not see movies or plays, and must not go to parties of any kind. "This is the only way to concentrate on your studies," he had said. "You must never forget how you got where you are."

So I stammered to the secretary Li Tong about how inexperienced I was as a leader, trying not to leave a bad impression on my first day. But Li waved his hand and said, "You're the only Party member we admitted this year. Of course you have to do more. Tomorrow all the new students will arrive. I want you to hold a welcome meeting for them. Some sophomore students and I will attend. We'll introduce and explain things to them."

I left the office feeling proud and bewildered. I was glad to be trusted, but I was also a new, confused student. Li Gang seemed to have forgotten that.

The next shocking thing was that the department promoted me to the sophomore level soon after classes began. I had to go through several tests whose purpose was kept secret from me. Of the five students chosen for the tests, only two passed. I felt really honored and didn't realize the challenge until I started taking the real classes. All the sophomore courses were taught by laowai—old foreigners, an endearing term the students gave to the Western professors. They came from America, Canada, and Europe and spoke English with accents. I could only figure out about thirty percent of what they said. Most of the courses—the history of English literature, Shakespeare, and American literature—required an endless amount of reading. And I could read only two pages an hour. After two weeks, my only wish was to have forty-eight hours a day to finish my homework, go to meetings, and get more sleep. I went to bed at one in the morning and woke up with the loudspeaker blasting the song "Red Is the Sun" at six. When my roommates took naps at noon, I read or memorized new vocabulary in the hallway. My daily route was between dormitory, classroom buildings, canteen, library, and meeting rooms. I followed it like a clock, except for my trips to the campus post office and bookstore. For a month, I did not step outside the campus. I didn't have time or money to go around Beijing. Besides, Yan wanted me to save sightseeing for his visit in the winter.

I missed him terribly but also enjoyed our separation.

Somehow, his absence romanticized my emotions. I could think of him much more as a lover, less as a brother.

We wrote to each other every day. In letters, I could talk more freely. Yan always wrote about his remembrance of our days in Hangzhou, about the night we passed together in his friend's apartment.

He had introduced me as his wife. We were both a bit drunk. Yan had taken me to an expensive restaurant that evening and made me drink a full glass of wine. "Meimei," he had said in tears, "tonight is our first time together like husband and wife. I want you to enjoy me. If it still hurts you like before, I'll never touch you again."

Perhaps the wine helped. I didn't feel much pain. Yan's appetite was frightening. He had to "hold" me eight times that night. Yan recalled that night with details in each of his letters. I hid them inside my pillow case, the only private place in the dorm. We had only two desks and six drawers for ten people. Things always got mixed up. Fortunately, I slept in an upper bunk bed, so it was not easy for anyone to climb there to search my pillow case. Yan said he'd collect the letters when he came to Beijing. He had much more privacy in his dorm. Or maybe he'd leave them in his mother's place.

I nibbled at my bread as I headed toward the library. There were few students in the dormitory building on Sunday morning. Half of them had gone home for the weekend. All college students were required to live on campus, even if their families lived just a few blocks away. Ten dorm buildings clustered around the public bath and hot water center. Girls stood outside the bathroom waiting for the open time, their braids loosened over their shoulders, each holding a basin that contained towels and soap and clean underwear. I usually went there after eight on Sunday, when there weren't so many bathers. I passed the dorm area and approached the post office. A crowd had gathered in front of the main bulletin board across the street. Since the first election declaration came out on the third of October, the place had become the center for propaganda. It was surrounded by the bookstore, post office, the Big Canteen, which was also used as the movie theater, and Buildings 24 and 27, where students of law, political science, and economics lived. These were the most politically conscious and active students at the University. The bulletin board used to be covered with posters, lost or found notices, and ads for used book sales. Now, every few hours, new big-character posters replaced old ones. During lunch and dinner hours, the place was packed with students eating and reading. Everybody was excited about this first election in China since 1949. They believed the door to democracy had finally opened.

I avoided this place because it reminded me too much of the Cultural Revolution. But something on today's new poster drew my attention. Under the title "On Freedom of Speech" was the author's name written in red ink—Huang Ming. I pushed into the crowd, ignoring the dirty looks from the other girls. The twelve-page-long poster took the whole space of the bulletin board and extended to the walls of the Big Canteen. I read eagerly:

Freedom of speech is the most urgent issue for human rights in China. Authorities punish speakers and thinkers in order to wipe out potential threats. In such an atmosphere, only those who keep silent can be safe, and those who are engaged in double-dealing and conspiracy are trusted.

A regime that has the right to forbid any opposing opinions is supported forever by its "people" because it excludes those who are against it. When a regime pledges that it will be loyal to its people, and at the same time decides who the people are, this regime is enforcing the dictum: Absolute power makes truth. Such power eliminates every possibility of self-regulation and leads a country to disaster.

Authorities always start literary inquisitions by suppressing opinions that most people truly believe are reactionary so that people will not realize that they are helping to deprive themselves of their right of free speech. Once they force this on others, they put themselves in a position where no laws can protect them. The more they feel their freedom is restricted, the more they will deprive others of their right. The Anti-Rightist Struggle of '57, the Four-Clean-up Movement in the 60s, the

Cultural Revolution, and the nationwide rallies in '76 to protest the con-
demnation of the Tiananmen Square counter-revolutionary event, are just
products of the literary inquisition . . .

I let myself be pushed out of the circle before finishing the
whole thing. My strength suddenly went away. The crowd had
grown three times bigger and a lot more tense. People in the
back were standing on chairs they had taken from classrooms and
dorms.

I could see from their wide-open eyes the worry, admiration,
and excitement. I was trembling myself. Never in my life had I
read anything so daring and to the point. It was a bomb that
blasted a hole in the wall of a windowless room. Suddenly I could
breathe. How I loathed the endless political study meetings to
unify our thinking and speech! And how I hated myself for saying
things against my will and conscience to avoid troubles!

"Huang Ming." I called his name silently. I still couldn't believe
this person was interested in me. He could pick any girl he wanted. Besides all the titles he had—the vice president of the students' union of the university, the student party secretary of the
Political Science Department, the board member of the election
campaign, to name just a few—he was a great-looking guy. The
first time I had met him in the union meeting, I was shocked by
the thick, swordlike eyebrows above his deep-set eyes. They
sparkled with intelligence and wisdom and courage. *Only a god can
have eyes like that,* I told myself, blushing deeply when he saw my
stare. He nodded to me as if we had known each other for a long
time and continued his speech on the preparation of the campaign.

It had been only the previous afternoon when we first talked to
each other. The meeting was about cleaning the dormitories. The
university spent a fortune hiring professionals to clean the hallways
and public bathrooms in the ten dorm buildings. But the smell got
worse and garbage was still scattered everywhere. The administra-
tors were finally fed up and told the student union that it was their
job to solve the problem. Huang came up with the idea of "self-
autonomy": hiring students to take care of the buildings. They

could earn some money; more important, they would think twice before they littered the place they had just cleaned themselves. The union leaders were all for it, but no one wanted the job. Not a single student worked to support him- or herself. It was considered degrading, especially a job like cleaning bathrooms. I raised my hand after a long, awkward silence. I couldn't stand the disappointed look on his face. *What the hell!* I said to myself. In the countryside, I had to deal with shit every day, and I never thought it demeaning or shameful. Why couldn't I handle it here? Beside, it wouldn't take too much of my time, and I could get ten extra yuan a month for books and better meals. Again, Huang had nodded at me like an old friend. After the meeting, he gave me some forms to fill out for the job and said, "Thank you, Ni Bing."

I smiled across the table and bent my head over the paper. His eyes were too bright for me. When I handed him the forms and was about to leave, he said, "Have you been to Yuanming Yuan Palace?"

I shook my head. I wanted to tell him that I hadn't been anyplace since I came to the city, that I hadn't stepped out of the campus for the past month, but I couldn't. What if he laughed at me? The palace was actually not far from here. It was a royal garden, looted and burned down about two hundred years ago.

"It's only a ten-minute ride by bike. I'm going there tomorrow afternoon. If you're interested, meet me in front of the southern gate at four," he said, then immediately bent his head to continue his work, as if he didn't care about my answer or feared that I'd say no. I left without a word, feeling grateful that I didn't have to respond.

After reading the article, I decided to go. His poster excited and worried me at the same time. The old guys from Beijing University and Central Committee would never tolerate this kind of freedom of speech. They had many secret ways to eliminate the people they disliked. Would he think of me as a coward if I told him to be careful?

IT WAS FIVE TO EIGHT in the morning. The reading rooms in the library hadn't opened yet. I sat down on the lawn. No need to stand on line at the gate. On Sunday, there should be enough seats for everyone. I took a deep breath of the crisp autumn air. The library was the only example of modern architecture on the campus. Around its gray walls, chrysanthemums were blooming under well-trimmed Chinese ilex. A statue of Mao stood forty-five feet high in front of the eastern gate, waving its arm as if Mao were still saluting his Red Guards. Strange that Beijing University, the center of new thoughts and the cradle of all the radical movements, still kept this idol in such a prominent place; Mao's statues had been destroyed everywhere else. The pine trees behind it almost reached to his shoulders. Beyond the lawns were classroom buildings, their red walls shadowed by the branches of the orange maple trees. The upturned eaves of the buildings expanded aggressively, keeping the sun from shining into the small, square windows. The rooms had to be lit even during the day. The huge roofs made these three-story buildings look higher and bigger than their real size. They surrounded the library and the statue like guards in uniform. The library was the center, highlighted by Mao's figure.

I stretched my legs on the grass. It was rare that I could relax like this. Something hard in my pants pocket pushed against my thigh. I jumped with guilt. I had forgotten to mail the letter to Yan and to read his letter. This had never happened before. Last night, when I returned to the dormitory from the library, I picked up the mail on the table outside the window of the janitor's room. I hadn't turned on the light for fear of disturbing my roommates. This was not uncommon. But what made me forget both to open his letter and to mail mine this morning? Was it Huang Ming's invitation and his campaign declaration?

I tore open the letter.

Dear Meimei:

I can't believe you've broken your promises within such a short time. Remember how we cried in each other's arms with the admission letter against our hearts? You said you would value it and devote all your time

*to studies. But now you've taken four positions. How are you going to find
time to sit in the library? Yes, your dream has come true. But this is only
the beginning. You want to do well at college? You must work ten times,
twenty times harder. Why? Because you didn't have a good foundation for
your high school education, and you're older than most of the students.
That means you have less energy, and more distractions. Don't be deceived
by your promotion. It's based solely on your English. If you want to be a
good scholar, you need more than that. So I still hope, though I know it's
probably useless, that you'll quit all your social commitments and concentrate on your real work.*

*More importantly, your involvement in the election is most dangerous.
Don't be deceived by the false tolerance of the Central Committee. There
has never been such a thing as free speech in China, and there won't be
any within this century. Take my word for it, Meimei. For your own sake,
for our sake, please withdraw from everything before it's too late. I need
you. I can't live without you. Our only hope to live together is to go to
America. To do that, your political record must be clean, otherwise the
police will never give you a passport. Remember it!*

I kiss you a thousand times,

Gege

*P.S. Who's the person whose name you crossed out? There should be no
secret between us, right?*

I clasped my hands around my legs and rested my chin
between my knees. Yan was right about everything, but that still
didn't stop me from feeling angry. Why did I mention Huang
Ming's name, then cross it out in the letter? We had not even
spoken to each other yet. Was I interested in him without admit-
ting it to myself? I took out the letter I had written to Yan last
night and tore it into pieces. I had mentioned Huang's invitation
to the park in it and asked him if it was appropriate for me to go.
Of course he would say no and give me another long lecture. I'd
heard enough of that. As long as I studied hard, I should have the
freedom to decide what to do in my spare time. No one should
accuse me of being lazy if I read eight hours on Sunday, then visited a historical park for an hour or two with a friend. No

secrets? I would have told him anything if he'd just stop lecturing me. Even my father didn't do that. Of course, I would try to resign my positions in a year. Yan had a point. If I wanted to go abroad with him, I would have to keep my political record clean.

As SOON AS I SAW Huang Ming, I regretted having changed into my best clothes: I wore blue jeans, a beige turtleneck sweater, and blue sneakers. I had even brushed my hair again and tied it in two ponytails behind my ears. Huang just wore his usual faded yellow uniform, which fit his broad shoulders and thick chest. When our eyes met, I smiled, getting ready for the greeting and hand shaking. Huang nodded at me and mounted his Pigeon bike.

"Get onto the backseat," he said, pedaling slowly to keep the balance.

When he felt my weight in back, he shot off with a sudden jerk. I grabbed his jacket. As soon as I got my balance back, I let go. "You can hold onto my waist. It's safer," he said. I blushed and bent my head to avoid the curious eyes from students returning from home or shopping. Soon we turned into a bumpy country road. Huang had to pedal hard, for the road went uphill. His breathing made me think of my ride with Father. He also had a Pigeon bike. Often my two sisters sat in the front, chatting and singing in his arms, and I in the back, sullen with jealousy. But none of us had ever thought about getting off and helping him push the bike up the hill.

"Shall I get off and walk?" I offered Huang Ming.

"Don't move. I can do two more hills like this."

We passed a few country houses. The flat roofs were covered with golden wheat, and on the mud walls hung braids of purple corns, white garlic, and scarlet peppers. To add more color, brown chickens and white geese pecked for food and honked in each yard. I thought about the chickens and ducks I had raised in Ma Ao Village. When I left, I had asked Uncle Ma to take care of them for me. He promised not to eat them and to let them live full lives. Would he keep his words? Even if he did, they had probably all died. Almost four years. These tamed animals couldn't live that long.

Gradually the land became barer, nothing growing except for the wild reeds in dried ponds. Their yellow leaves rustled in the wind. Huang made a sharp turn and slowed down. I jumped off and looked around. In front of me lay the vast ruins of Yuanming Yuan Palace. The carved stone columns were half buried in the ground. Only the stone frame of a gate remained standing under the speckless autumn sky.

I moved forward as if hypnotized by some mysterious power from the dragons carved on the gate's two columns. Huang Ming opened his arms and embraced one. I pressed myself on the other side and stretched my arms. Our hands couldn't touch. The stone was burning hot from the afternoon sun.

"It's still burning." His voice seemed to come from far away.

I knew what he meant. Yuanming Yuan had been burning since the Eight-Power Allied Forces invaded China and suppressed the anti-imperialist Yihetuan Movement in 1900. After they captured Beijing, they looted this palace and set fire to it. It had been used to store thousands of years of royal collections of art, books, jewelry, and other treasures. The fire lasted a whole week until it collapsed in its own ashes.

"Listen," he said. His muffled voice traveled around the column.

I pressed my ears against the stone but heard only the howling of the wind. Winter came earlier in Beijing than in the south.

"Listen this way." He came over and pressed my chest against the stone. "Listen with your heart."

I heard hooting, sometimes low and deep, sometimes shrill.

"The dragon is roaring." He stroked the tail on the column. "It's thirsty for blood."

The hatred in his voice shocked me. Dragons were the sacred symbol of China. They appeared everywhere, from quilt cover designs to palace columns.

"It's a symbol of authority," he continued. "In the feudal society, the dragon was the son of heaven, and the son of heaven was the emperor." He stepped back. "Come and look at the column from here."

I went over and saw the clouds carved in concave lines, barely recognizable compared to the raised, detailed carving of the dragon.

"Look how triumphantly he speeds across the sky. He lives in clouds, plays in clouds, exercises his power in clouds. People are their clouds and sky. Nothing ever changes, whether we're ruled by dynasties or by a communist regime."

I opened my eyes wide. Was he really comparing the party leaders to emperors? I had always believed that communism was the best system and ideology for China. I heard him say, "Since 1949, the Party has become the bearer of the people's will and their personality. We truly believe it's our honor and duty to sacrifice our own thinking for the benefit of others. We've learned to take the interests of the whole country into account. Look at Zhou Enlai . . ."

"He was the most beloved premier," I interrupted.

"Because he sacrificed the most?"

I nodded.

"But as a prime minister, he should have spoken up for people, not the abstract people, but concrete individuals. It was his job to correct Mao's mistakes and fight against the political swindlers and careerists. But he didn't. Nor did he support those who dared to speak and were tortured to death: Liu Shaoqi, Peng Dehuai, Luo Luiqing . . ."

"He had no choice," I cut in again. "If he'd spoken out, he'd have been suppressed, too, and wouldn't have been able to help out others secretly as he did during the Cultural Revolution."

"If he had spoken out, if the whole country had done that, the party could not have obtained absolute power, and many disasters would never have happened." He waved his fist. I stepped back. He hit his own forehead when he saw me moving away, and lowered his voice. "The tragedy is that Zhou really believed he was doing good for the party and China. We have been taught to forget our individuality and submit ourselves to the highest monarchy. Loyalty to monarch, to father . . . the feudalist mentality is deep in our blood."

My cheeks flushed with anger. Huang's remark put Premier Zhou on the same level with Li Ai, who had also believed she'd faithfully carried out Mao's idealism. But how could these two people be compared? And the feudalist mentality? I immediately thought about Yan's advice that I should not get involved in the election and let others speak. Now I blushed with shame.

"Sorry, Ni Bing, I didn't bring you here to argue. We've done enough on the campus. Let's sit here for a while before the sun goes down."

He touched my shoulder gently and led me to a broken column half buried in the ground. I sat on the hot stone like a schoolgirl, my hands on my knees. Awkwardness had suddenly returned to me when we stopped arguing. If Yan had known I was sitting in this wild place alone with another man, he'd have eaten me up alive.

"What happened to your hands, Ni Bing?"

I hid them between my knees. Huang grabbed my right hand and stroked each of the scarred fingers tenderly, as if flattening a piece of wrinkled silk.

"It's from frostbite," I said, trying to keep my voice steady. "We don't have heat or hot water in the south. Things get really cold and damp in winter, especially when we wash vegetables and clothing in icy water. My hands were always swollen and covered with pus. I couldn't even wear gloves. At night, I had to keep my arms out of the quilt so that the pus wouldn't stain the sheet. Sometimes it got to the bone and affected its growth."

I untangled myself from his grasp and put my hands up to his face. All the fingers, except the thumbs, were out of shape. The joints protruded sharply and the backs of my hands were covered with purple scars. My left little finger was half an inch shorter than the other.

"It's really gross, isn't it?" I asked with a bitter smile. *Why am I doing this?* I asked myself. I really liked Huang and wanted to keep him attracted and interested, but I was displaying the most disgusting part of myself to him. Why was I talking so fast? "Almost everyone has frostbite. My sisters and I used to call ourselves rotten winter melons. My mother has frostbite on her cheeks and ears. That's awful."

He closed my fingers in his palms like a sandwich. Unlike Yan's damp hands, Huang's were dry and rough with calluses. If he rubbed them, sparks and electricity would probably flow out. I should withdraw my hands, I said to myself, but I didn't move. It was warm and comfortable there like the inside a new cotton mitten.

"I like scars," he whispered, our faces so close that our breathing intertwined like our hands did between our chests. "A scarless person is always a little suspicious to me." He kneaded my fingers, his eyes fixed on my face. I noticed the deep wrinkles on his forehead and the shallow ones in the corners of his eyes. He had to be younger than Yan, though he looked older. I had never realized that wrinkles could add so much attraction to a man. I wished I had the guts to feel them one by one, the way he stroked my fingers. Should I tell him that a man without wrinkles seemed suspicious? His facial features reminded me of northern bread: heavy, thick, solid. Nothing decorative, but you knew you could rely on it.

"Are you from the north?" I finally managed to ask.

"Shenyang, the real north. I'm the youngest of seven children."

"You don't look like one. Usually the youngest child is badly spoiled. Did you fight a lot with your siblings?"

He laughed. "We didn't have time for that. My family was really poor. As soon as I started walking, I followed them to pick coal cinders and vegetable leaves from garbage cans at markets. My father had lost his vegetable stall after the liberation and had been assigned to a job pulling a coal cart. He wasn't made for that type of labor and had to quit after a few months. Everyone in the family worked to get food and clothes. At school we were called little beggars. Any kid could beat us up. My brothers and sisters all dropped out of school after two or three years, but insisted that I continue to go until I got into college. They took turns escorting me from home to school. But I still got beaten up during breaks. I never told anyone. What was the use? It would only make them feel anxious and worried. They wanted me to finish school, so did I. That was my only way to return their care and love for me. I grew up poor, but never lacked warmth and support.

"And you? I'm sure your parents love you very much. How could they not? You're so beautiful. No, beauty is not the word for you. You make me think of a bamboo tree, clean and delicate, yet unbreakable. The first time I met you, my heart suddenly became clear. *This is the girl I want to know,* I told myself. I was so happy to see you at the gate. I barely slept last night, wondering if you'd come. Ni Bing, Ni Bing," he whispered my name, "forgive my boldness. I didn't know what to do. I've never asked any girl out before." He pressed my fingertips to his mouth and stroked my palms with his burning lips. When he held my cheeks with his hands, I closed my eyes and sighed with satisfaction. I wanted to lie in his callused hands like this forever. He breathed heavily above my half-open lips. I inhaled his pine-scented breath, waiting. *Burn me and melt me into the golden sunset,* I called silently, my hands clasping around his chest.

Then Yan's face, contorted with anger, came to me. His chapped lips trembled. "How could you betray our love, Meimei?" he said with sadness. I dropped my hands. "I must go back to school," I said.

He blinked his eyes, his thick eyelashes wet and heavy like the wings of a butterfly in the early morning. I turned my back to him. Better to hurt him now than later. "I'm sorry, Huang Ming, I have someone in the south," I said. I could see with the back of my head how he turned pale. My heart ached. *You shameless woman, I told myself, you should have told him earlier. You should never have accepted his invitation or let him hold your hands. Now you're finished in his eyes. You're not a bamboo, but some cheap grass on the wall letting the wind blow you in any direction.*

We did not speak on our way back. Outside the campus gate, I jumped off the back of his bike and ran to my dormitory.

"But we can still be friends, yes?" he shouted after me. I looked back, nodded, and continued my running.

Chapter Ten

"How is everything, Ni Bing?" You Shan asked when I entered the office of the English Department. She pointed to a chair for me to sit down. Her assistant, vice secretary Jiang, looked up from his desk with a grunt and went back to his document.

"Fine, thank you, Secretary You." I sat at the edge to the chair, wondering why she wanted to talk to me. You Shan was the only female departmental party secretary in Beijing University, well respected for her administrative efficiency and her support for students. She was only forty-five, the youngest party secretary, but her face was a web of wrinkles and her hair all gray. She had been tortured during the Cultural Revolution and rehabilitated in a May Seventh Cadre School for seven years. The hard labor had aged her face, yet her eyes still sparkled with sharp intelligence.

"I heard that you're doing well in your sophomore class and that you're active in student affairs. That's marvelous."

"It's nothing," I murmured. It was weird to be praised by the authorities. I was supposed to tell her that I owed my success to the party's education, but I couldn't bring myself to make such a phony speech. "I just love studying and serving students," I said in a low voice, blushing with embarrassment. Even that sounded pretty fake.

"Well said. Now tell me about the election. I've missed several debates and lots of the big-character posters. What a pity! Too many unnecessary meetings. A waste of time. I wish I were a student again to participate in this campaign. It will be recorded in history."

You Shan's sincere, enthusiastic look took me off guard. I began to tell all I knew about the election, adding my own interpretation here and there. She listened with full attention, nodding occasionally in approval. I talked more fluently, waving my hands to reinforce my statement. Someone coughed. I stopped abruptly and saw the frown on Jiang's face.

"Very good, Ni Bing. Your understanding and memory are excellent. I want you to tell me what Huang Ming has to say about the election. I did have a chance to read his article. Very interesting."

Aha, now she was aiming at the target. I must do everything to protect him. "I'm not sure I can help much, Secretary You. I barely speak to him." *This is not exactly lying,* I told myself. *It's true the only time we talked was at Yuanming Yuan. And I haven't seem him once after that.*

"Liar!" Jiang shouted from his desk. "You went to Yuanming Yuan on the back of his bike last Sunday, didn't you? I saw it with my own eyes."

He was lying. I had scanned every passerby from the bike that afternoon and didn't see any familiar face. It had to be someone who knew Huang Ming and reported it. Was he in trouble? Anger and worry hit my head. "So what? It was strictly personal and had nothing to do with the election."

He had jumped out of his chair—now he sat back down with a grunt as You Shan waved her forefinger at him.

"Be patient, Old Jiang. Ni Bing is just being shy about her date. We were young once, too. Remember?" she laughed. Her voice gave me the creeps.

"Really, Secretary You, I told the truth. I haven't even seen him again since the trip."

"Well, tell me about the trip, then."

I closed my mouth tightly. How could I tell her what had happened toward the end of the visit? I'd gone over the scene and his words in my mind hundreds of times, and each time my cheeks burned with excitement and shame.

"Well, I'm waiting."

I heard a touch of annoyance in her voice. I must be pulling a blank face again. "When you put on that blank face," my mother used to tell me, "I feel I no longer exist in your world and I can't stop hitting and screaming at you." *You must be careful,* I told myself. *You Shan could turn this place into a hell for me. If I don't get her angry, I can protect Huang Ming better.*

"Nothing important, Secretary You. We just talked about the history of the palace. Oh yes, we talked about our childhood."

"Is that all?" Jiang squeezed each word through his teeth, a sarcastic smile hanging at the corners of his mouth. His expression was saying: *Don't be a smartass. You can't fool an old revolutionary like me.*

I looked at the loose purple bags under his eyes, his sallow cheeks, his red, alcoholic's nose with dirty black hair sticking out of the inflamed nostrils, and his gray zhongshan suit, tightly buttoned to his neck. For a second, he turned into Party Secretary Hong, and I into Li Ai. I was being interrogated. The thought made me tremble.

"Comrade Ni Bing." You Shan's voice had lost its gentle touch. "You're a party member. Your first principle is to be loyal to the party and to keep no secrets. Huang Ming is the most active campaigner in this election. It's hard to believe that he didn't say a word about it during the three hours in Yuanming Yuan."

They even knew how long we had stayed there. But certainly they couldn't have known the content of our conversation, otherwise I wouldn't be sitting here. I had to say something to get myself out of there.

"We didn't have time to talk about the election. The place was deserted, so we . . ."

I stole a glance at Jiang and You Shan. Jiang's eyes brightened up. He was hooked.

"What did you do?" he asked eagerly.

"We held hands."

"And?" Jiang asked, his upper body leaning across the desk. You Shan watched me coldly. I licked my dried lips.

"We kissed."

"Go on, go on." Jiang was getting more excited.

"We kissed again."

"Then you did it, didn't you?"

I looked at him with wide eyes, pretending not to understand his question and his obscene gestures. This dirty old goat, I cursed silently.

"Enough, Old Jiang," You Shan spoke in a stern voice. "Comrade Ni Bing, you're disappointing today. Do you know how much we've invested in you? We appointed you to the important positions, arranged the promotion tests for you, and we're even considering sending you to Columbia University in New York for the exchange program next year. We gave you honor, but you reciprocated with lies. Let me tell you something: it's too easy to slip down a hill."

"I thought I was doing my best to be a good student, Secretary You," I finally managed to say. Sending me to Columbia University? It must be a hoax.

"You should be a good party member first. You should know where you stand, on the side of the party or with someone who has serious problems."

"You're talking about Huang Ming, I assume?" I looked into her eyes. "But he's from a poor family. He studies hard and works day and night for the benefit of students. Besides, he's also a party member."

"He's drifted away from the party," Jiang said with indignation. "He criticized Chairman Mao and other leaders, criticized the socialist system. We'll never allow such a dangerous person to be elected as the people's representative in our district. Here's the

instruction from the City Party Committee to investigate him."
He waved a white sheet with triumph.

"Old Jiang, we'll call a meeting to transmit the document
later. Ni Bing," she turned to me, "do you realize the consequences your stubbornness will bring you?"

We stared at each other. I bit my tongue to prevent the boiling
blood inside me from spitting out. The hell with consequences! I
was sick of hearing this warning. Life was more than that. How
smart she was. In such a short time, she had already sensed my
"bull personality," the stubbornness that had brought tons of
trouble and beatings in my childhood.

You Shan averted her eyes. "Think the matter over and come
back after you've sorted this out. But no later than the day of the
election."

As I walked toward the door, she said, "By the way, I want to
remind you that a party member should always lead a rigorous
and moral life. There're some rumors about your association
with a certain foreign professor on the campus. Look at the way
you dress." She scanned my jeans and turtleneck sweater with
utter contempt. "You're a Chinese, a party member, not a foreign
devil. You must be aware of the policies on the behavior toward
foreign people. Don't get too close to them, even if they're your
professors. I heard," she paused, knocking her pen on the arm of
her chair, "that you had dinner with Professor Steinberg?"

Are they also investigating me? I asked myself, aware that she was
watching me and that I must stop sweating like this. Steinberg
was the first Western professor I had encountered. When I entered the sophomore composition class, I was quite startled to
see a blond giant with green eyes hidden under bushy red eyebrows, pacing down the aisle between desks. When he saw me
standing like a log at the door, he came over immediately, smiling. I saw the golden sparks shooting from the thick bushes.
When I introduced myself, and he extended his dustpan-size
hand, I saw soft, golden hair crawling in curls from his fingers to
his arms. *A golden bear*, I said to myself, holding back my impulse
to touch the dense, furry arm.

My first sophomore class ended disastrously. The students were assigned to write about eclipses. It was the first time I had ever head the word "eclipse" in English, and I was too scared or ashamed to ask anyone for help. So I spent the two hours just staring at the blackboard and wiping away my sweat, avoiding the golden bear whenever he looked in my direction. After everyone had left the classroom, I walked up to him and told him I couldn't give him anything because I knew nothing about the subject. He smiled. "Good. I admire your honesty. I'd rather you write nothing than make up some nonsense. Why don't you write about something you know, anything, as long as it's what you care about? Take your time and leave it in my mailbox in the department."

So I wrote a long story about the wedding of my girlfriend Su Feng in Ma Ao Village, about her tragic love for the son of a landlord, her decision to marry a stranger so that her brother could use her bridal gift money for his engagement. It took me three days and nights. During this time, I heard the story about Steinberg. He came from Columbia University in New York. Apart from teaching composition, he also taught the modern American literature course. In his first semester, he used Kurt Vonnegut's *Breakfast of Champions* as an introduction. For weeks, the sophomore students talked about nothing but the sizes of penises and vaginas and passed the book along to their favorite lower-grade students. The department threatened to discontinue the contract if he didn't withdraw the books immediately. Soon the copies were collected and never seen again. This semester, he had introduced the course with Hemingway's *The Sun Also Rises*. They said he had mellowed down a lot. But I felt the fire was still burning quietly behind his green eyes.

He loved my story. He typed my handwritten manuscript and made copies for the class to read and discuss. We had quite a heated argument about human rights and the situation of women in China. Lulu, a girl who took eight classes each semester and asked the strangest questions, cried as she talked about her frustration as a woman with too much energy and intelligence. No one wanted to leave the room when the bell rang. Steinberg had to promise to continue the discussion the following week. After the class, he invited me to have dinner in the canteen for foreign professors and students. He told me about his enthusiasm for the Cultural Revolution. He had read all of Mao's works that had been translated into English and French. There had to be some solution for the misery and torture in this world, since capitalism had failed to bring equality and happiness to people. He had been a Red Guard when he studied in Paris, breaking windows and fighting with police, but nothing had come of it. He had planned for years to come to China. He had told his wife and kids that if this worked out, he might move the family here permanently. I listened and watched the green sparks flash and fade under his eyebrows. I didn't need to tell him anything. What he had seen and experienced here was enough to shatter his illusions. It was obvious that he was heartbroken, though he didn't say a word about it. I wanted to tell him there was always hope somewhere. And it was that hope that had been keeping us Chinese going, no matter how much we suffered. But I didn't say anything. It was up to him to figure it out. When we walked out of the canteen, he asked me if I wanted some coffee. I hesitated a moment and shook my head. There was no other place to have coffee on the campus except his apartment. Not that I didn't trust him or myself. But I didn't want to register my name at the entrance of the building for foreigners. Better to be cautious.

But I was not cautious enough. I was still caught. For what, though? They couldn't put me in jail for having supper with a foreign professor. I looked straight into You Shan's eyes. A menacing light flashed behind her glasses. She saw the challenge in my look. She nodded. "I hope, Comrade Ni Bing, you'll start behaving like a party member. You may go now."

I wandered around the Weiming Hu, the unnamed lake. The campus had suddenly shrunk, leaving no air for breathing. How much did they know? There was no way they could have heard my conversations with Huang Ming and Steinberg. They couldn't have bugged the palace or the canteen. Was Huang in danger? My first instinct was to look for him and warn him about the situation. But he must be aware of it. They must have interrogated other people around him. I needed to be careful not to drag him into deeper trouble.

Things happened exactly as Huang had pointed out in his article: people were treated like suspects, enemies, including Huang Ming and myself, both party members. Were You Shan and Jiang trusted by their authorities? The party—who controlled the party? It seemed that the fates of a billion people were being tossed around at the will of a few.

I felt cheated for the first time in my life. I'd believed, like Steinberg, that Mao was one of the greatest leaders of the century and that the Communist Party was the only hope for China. When I was accepted as a member, I had told myself that I had gained a new life that was much more glorious and meaningful than the life my parents had given me. I had been disgusted by the greed and corruption around me, but I'd never doubted the correctness of the party. I'd always cherished that belief somewhere in my heart. Now I felt as if my backbone had been pulled out.

What should I do? If I didn't go back to You Shan with information about Huang Ming, there would be serious consequences. What if they expelled me from the school? I closed my eyes and shivered. No, I would never let that happen. But to betray Huang Ming, as I had betrayed Ma Gang six years ago? *Never,* I screamed, and was startled by my own voice. I opened my eyes. Fortunately there was no one around the lake in midday. Students were in either the library or the classrooms. Feeling a sudden weakness in my knees, I sat down on a blanket of red leaves. "Ma Gang," I whispered the name, "will I ever be able to forgive myself?"

How hard i had worked that winter! Except for touring around schools to give lectures, I had gone to the fields every day, enduring the silence and dirty looks the peasants gave me after I was appointed the "model educated youth" by the commune leaders. Su Feng no longer came to me in the evenings. Usually there wasn't much work to do outside in winter. But that year, the whole country was frantic about Dazhai, a model village in Shanxi Province set up by Mao's wife Jiang Qing and the Party Central Committee. Everywhere mounds were shovelled and ditches filled to make terrace fields, and rivers straightened to beautify the landscapes. Ma Ao Village had also started to flatten a hill and fill up a ditch as its own Dazhai site. It was strenuous and obviously wasted labor. The peasants cursed whenever the head of the village was not around, but I welcomed the work. The mechanical digging and carrying somehow numbed my pain. Besides, I had nowhere else to go. I didn't have the courage to visit any peasant in the village. I couldn't even go to my parents' place for the Spring Festival. I couldn't face my family with my bad conscience.

On the eve of the Spring Festival, I went to work on the Dazhai site. I carried two baskets of yellow soil on my yoke, trying to resist the desire to sit or lie on the ground. The swelling in my ankles and wrists was getting really bad. I often dreamed of being burned and cut into pieces alive, and woke up feeling my limbs on fire. I had tied them with layers of elastic bands to numb the pain. It had helped only for a day, and then the agony returned with a doubled force. I bit my lips to suppress moans as my feet touched the ground.

"Are you all right?" Grandpa Ding, a former landlord, stepped toward me, his hands reaching out to give me some support, but he stopped about two feet away. Apparently he didn't want to get too close. *He has learned the lesson from Ma Gang,* I told myself. I didn't blame him. But what about the peasants who were not class enemies? And my best friend Su Feng? I glanced around. Ma Gang was digging furiously with a mattock on the other side of the ditch.

"I'm fine," I mumbled.

"You should be with your parents on the eve of the Spring Festival. We class enemies have no choice. We have to work on holidays to reform our souls. But why are you here?"

For the first time, I noticed that the nine peasants on the Dazhai site were all from the cursed classes of the landlord, rich peasants, and loafers. If not for the ten-meter-long red banner, and the loudspeaker through which the Commune Party Secretary was urging people to learn from Dazhai and have a revolutionary New Year, the scene would have looked exactly like one of the monthly reform-through-labor meetings for the class enemy. But everybody was supposed to show up here after the afternoon snack and work voluntarily from five to nine in the evening. When the village party secretary announced the decision in the morning, the peasants laughed openly, as if they had heard a good joke. Apparently no one took it seriously except for me and people like Ma Gang and Ding. They had no choice, as Ding had just said. Did I? I was here to redeem myself, to get a sign of forgiveness from Ma Gang. The thought that he would hate me all his life had made my nights and days miserable.

"Well, I don't want to go home like this," I said loudly, hoping to attract Ma Gang's attention, as I pointed to my lice-infected hair. "Isn't it disgusting? My mother will force me to cut my braids."

"That'll be a pity," Ding said. Ma Gang continued flinging his mattock into the ground. I suddenly felt a sharp pain in my chest.

"I wonder if it's time for dinner," I said to Ding. If he had dared to invite me to dinner, I would not have hesitated for a second. But Ding resumed his work as if he hadn't heard anything.

It was twenty past nine when I returned to my cold room. Uncle Ma, the village party secretary, had invited me to his family dinner, but I had declined. On my way home, I passed Su Feng's house. Through the open door, I saw the family sitting around the table full of steaming dishes and rice bowls. The smoke of incense rose slowly toward the portrait of Mao and a picture of the kitchen god that I had never seen there before. A boiled pig's head was placed on a plate at the foot of the altar, its eyes staring blankly at me over the heads of the family. I hurried away before anyone noticed me.

I warmed up the leftover vegetable rice and fed my hen and duck. Under the dim oil lamp, I kept telling myself it was better to eat alone than spend the holiday at home. There was endless preparation, shopping, washing, cooking for weeks. The banquets often started at nine in the morning and didn't end till eleven at night. By the time people staggered out of the apartment, I was still washing the greasy dishes at the public tap, cursing the pain from the frostbite festering on my hands, cursing the Spring Festival. The guests would mutter some praise at my back, while my mother ordered me to greet the uncles and aunts and thank them for the compliments that I probably didn't deserve. She would babble on until I lost my control, turned around, and gave her a blank glare. It always drove her nuts.

Someone was knocking on the window. I leapt from my desk, thinking it might be Ma Gang. The door was pushed open. "Are you home, Ni Bing?" the party secretary shouted. I sat back with a sharp disappointment, then stood up immediately to meet him. Secretary Ma had already walked through the kitchen and entered the bedroom. His face was flushed from the homemade rice wine.

"Sit, sit," he said. "I just want to make sure you're enjoying your holiday. Do you need anything?" He sat down on my bed, leaning comfortably on my folded quilt. He was wearing his best outfit for the festival, a navy blue Mao jacket, green army pants. His starched collar made a dark red circle around his brown neck. He had just gotten a haircut from the travelling barber Old Lan, and he was clean-shaven from the base of his neck to his ears, with a perfect round bush of black hair on top. It looked like the cover for a brand-new chamber pot. Old Lan came to the village every three months, rattling his little drum to announce his arrival. He lit his little coal stove in the village ancestral hall, and by the time the water began to boil, a long line had formed in the yard. Then for a week or two, all the male peasants walked around carrying a chamber pot cover on their heads. It had always amused me, but not this time, not when Boar Ma, famous for having seduced almost every woman in the village, lounged on my bed at ten-thirty in the evening in his drunkeness. I stood in the middle of the room, searching my brain to find something to say that would send him away without offence.

"Why are you standing? Sit next to me and relax," he said, leaning over suddenly. Before I could jump away, he had already entangled his long arm around my waist and pushed me on the bed.

We wrestled silently. I didn't want to disturb my neighbors. Not only did I not want to become a laughing stock in the village and the commune, but I also couldn't afford a scandal that could cost me the opportunity to be recommended to colleges. The benches under the bed shook and squeaked. I wished I could cry. Perhaps tears would soften his heart.

"Let me go, Uncle Ma. I'm only sixteen, too young, too skinny, too ugly. My mother will give you anything you want— watch, wool fabric, cigarettes, sugar. Let me go."

He laughed. His mouth opened so wide I could see his dark red tonsils. "Uncle Ma doesn't want watch, wool, or cigarettes. He wants to taste the sweet model educated youth. If you're good enough for the commune party secretary, then you're good enough for me."

I screamed and banged my forehead into his nose. He released his grip to cover his face with his hands. I jumped off the bed, grabbed the certificate of the model educated youth from the desk, and tore it into pieces. "Fuck this!" I shouted. "Fuck all of this! I never wanted it. But you, and those from the commune, forced this on me. Now I'm a bad girl, eh? Yes, I am bad, bad, bad! That's why you're here to fuck me? Come over here—fuck me, then." I tore open my shirt and banged my head against the

wall. It felt good to scream and bang like this, to feel blood trickling down along the sides of my ears onto my shoulder blades. I
screamed as loud as I could. Suddenly nothing mattered. I had
probably screwed up everything. Might as well. Let me sink to
the bottom. Let me die in front of his face. Ma jumped up and
held my arms. I struggled until I exhausted myself. When I finally
stopped howling, my ears ached from my own high-pitched
sounds.

"I'm sorry, Ni Bing." His voice was no longer drunken. "I
should have known better. I shouldn't have been so hard on you.
You are just a sixteen-year-old girl, too young and innocent to
play the political game. Don't feel too bad about Ma Gang. He
never blamed you. And ignore what the peasants said about your
relation with the commune leaders. I never really believed those
shitty rumors. I've always thought you're a good girl and still
think so."

I looked at him in disbelief. I couldn't be hallucinating. But if
it were true, on whose side was the party secretary? Was he
speaking for Ma Gang, the party, or me? My head started wheel-
ing.

"Don't think too much, girl. Someday, you'll understand.
What are you eating for the New Year? Not this kind of shit. I'll
have my mother send you some goose meat and fish. Eat it all and
then rest. You worked hard today. I'll also send Su Feng to you
tonight. Happy New Year, Ni Bing," he winked at me and closed
the door behind him.

I STROKED THE SCAR on the top of my head, hidden under my
thick hair. Till this day, I still didn't understand how I had got
away from Boar Ma's violation, how my crazy reaction had
changed his attitude toward me. He never touched me again
after the scene. Instead, he treated me like a strict, kind father,
making sure that I ate well and slept enough hours every day. He
also got me out of the school touring. Uncle Ma's forgiveness had

lifted the ban for me in the village. Peasants and my best friend Su Feng began to be friendly to me again, but no one could lift the ban from my conscience. For two years, I had almost worked myself to death in Ma Ao. I had volunteered to do the hardest and dirtiest jobs that were assigned to the former landlords and rich peasants who needed to be reformed through labor. I, too, had to redeem my conscience through labor. In Ma Gang's case, I could still excuse myself for being only sixteen.

But not with Huang Ming. I had passed my twenty-third birthday. And he was not a class enemy but a party member, a student leader, and my beloved. Beloved. That thought made me dumbfounded. My lover was Yan. My feelings toward Huang were just ones of respect and admiration. As a friend and comrade, I should warn him of the coming danger. I didn't know if my silence would help him get through this difficult situation. Even if You Shan and Jiang couldn't find a single person to betray Huang, they could still make up something. But at least I could choose not to let my soul get lost again.

I walked into the student conference room where Huang Ming usually worked from four to six in the afternoon. Only a stranger sat there reading a newspaper. She looked me up and down before she told me that Huang hadn't shown up for days. I went to his dormitory. At the building entrance, I realized I didn't know his room number. A group of boys returned with bowls in their hands. It was nap time. They stared at me weirdly as they passed by. I left. Tomorrow I'd go to the conference room again. If he still wasn't there, I'd come back to find out his room number. It shouldn't be difficult, since Huang was a well-known figure on the campus.

I went back to my room and lay down on my bunk bed. Too late for lunch, and I had no appetite anyway. Where could he be? The election campaign was in its final stage. New posters came out every two or three hours, and every night there were several debates going on at the same time. Those who were running for the election had stopped attending classes to write posters and prepare their speeches. Only six days left. How could he have disappeared from the campus? Had they already arrested him?

"Ni Bing, Ni Bing," a man called outside the window in a muffled voice. I jumped up and hit my head on the ceiling. It couldn't be true! It was impossible! He was hundreds of miles away. The call stopped for a few seconds, then started again, low, persistent, and demanding. I lifted the upper corner of the curtain from my bed. Yan was standing outside the window.

Chapter Eleven

I RAN OUT BAREFOOTED. He tried to smile, but there was a frown on his face. *Why is he here?* I asked myself.

"Meimei, don't stare at me like that. I got a research grant for my graduate thesis. Didn't you receive the letter I mailed a week ago? I waited an hour at the train station. Never mind. Here I am, Meimei." He opened his arms.

I took his hand, my heart filled with guilt. His letter was still in my pocket, unopened. I had picked it up when I got back from the lake, but my mind was too preoccupied with Huang Ming to open it. "I wish you had sent me a telegram, Gege."

"Don't worry about it. I'm glad I've saved you several hours on the buses and in the waiting room." He pulled me to his chest and kissed me. "Tell me, my little sister, did you miss me?"

I felt his heart beating fast. I looked around the empty road before I spoke, "Of course, Gege. What a surprise you gave me! Did you eat?"

"Starved. The train was so crowded I couldn't push my way to the dining car. You look pale. Did you also miss your lunch? There's a restaurant across the street. Let's get something."

He pointed in the direction of Haidian Restaurant outside the campus wall, which the students called Canteen Eleven. Those who could afford it came here once or twice a week to get away from the campus food.

Yan lifted the heavy cotton curtain. A strong smell of garlic and burnt oil poured out. A few clients were finishing up. A waitress was sweeping the cement floor, driving flies from table to table.

"Closed. Come back at three," she yelled without looking up.

Yan walked over and whispered something in her ear. She slapped him on his shoulder, laughing like a hen who had just laid a twin-yolk egg and pointed to a table with her broom.

Two guys were sitting there on opposite sides of the table, one eating dumplings and the other diced chicken with pepper. Yan dusted the bench with his handkerchief before he let me sit down.

What did he say to her? I wondered. Within a second, he had turned a tigress into a pussycat. He made life so easy. Wherever he went, he could smooth out anything and anybody, whereas I seemed to get in trouble everywhere. If I had come by myself, the waitress would have thrown me out right away. Not that I would have come to a restaurant by myself. In fact, before I met Yan, I'd never entered a restaurant.

He ordered liver and sliced pork in brown sauce, two bowls of rice, and a beer. The waitress took the five yuan from Yan and walked to the kitchen. Yan fetched the chopsticks from the counter and bought a small dish of boiled peanuts to go with the beer. He wiped the chopsticks with his handkerchief.

"Eat."

I tried to pick up a peanut, but it kept slipping away from the tips of the chopsticks.

Yan took my hand under the table and gave it a gentle squeeze. "What's the matter, Meimei? Something is bothering you. Tell me. Gege will try his best to help."

His voice ran over my burnt body like a soothing stream. If I couldn't tell Yan, who else could I go to for help? Surely he'd support me. Hadn't he shown his contempt for my betrayal of Ma Gang the first time we met? Surely he'd understand that my relation with Huang Ming was just friendship. I took a deep breath and told him about my trip to Yuanming Yuan with Huang Ming and my talk with You Shan.

The waitress brought the food. The receipt and change were clamped on the edge of the dish. Yan snapped it off and pocketed the greasy money in his gray sport jacket. He took a big sip of beer from the bowl. I couldn't see his face but could feel his smoking rage.

"Why did you keep it secret in your letters?" he said in a stern voice. Before I responded, he waved his hand and went on. "Going out to a deserted place with a man. No wonder You Shan suspected you. Anybody would. Not that I'm jealous, OK? But you're here to study, not to be gossiped about as if you were a loose woman. How many times did I tell you not to get involved in politics or personal scandals? You don't listen. You never listen. You're stubborn like a mule. Now you're in mud up to your eyebrows. I had a feeling that you were in trouble. That's why I hurried here. Now how are you going to join me at Hangzhou when you graduate? How are you going to live your four years here while You Shan holds your braid in her hand? Ni Bing, when will you grow up? When are you going to learn to think before you jump?"

I looked across his shoulders into the kitchen, where chefs in white hats scurried around. The two men at our table were nibbling at their food and listening to us. "I didn't get involved in politics," I murmured. "I didn't write a poster or give a speech . . . politics came to me."

"I know you didn't mean to," he said, his expression softened. "But you're too innocent to choose a friend, particularly a male friend. They can easily take advantage of you."

I frowned. Huang Ming take advantage of me? How? I glanced at Yan's face, twisted with suspicion and jealousy. Huang Ming would never talk to me as if I were a three-year-old.

"Eat, Meimei. Let's not talk about these unpleasant matters on our reunion." He poured some beer into an empty bowl and handed it to me. "Cheers. May we live together soon and never part again."

The beer tasted bitter. I tried to smile, but my mind was racing to figure out a way to contact Huang Ming in the afternoon.

"Don't worry anymore, Meimei. Gege is here. He'll smooth things over for you. Tomorrow I'll have a talk with You Shan and explain the situation. You should know my ability by now. What class do you have in the afternoon?"

"History of the Chinese Communist Party."

"Skip it. I'm taking you to Wangfujing, the biggest shopping center in Beijing. You need a jacket for the fall. Then we'll eat in Donglaishun. Their instant boiled mutton is the best in the country. Maybe we'll go to a movie in the evening, if we can get tickets."

"But where did you get the money?"

"My department gave me some for the trip. My mom also gave me twenty yuan when she came to the station to meet me. You know the train always stops in Shanghai for half an hour."

I stood up obediently with him. He had arranged things so perfectly. With him, life became just smooth and pleasant. What else could I do but follow him?

As SOON AS the world literature class was over, I hurried back to the dormitory. Yan wanted me to meet him at Beijing Library at five-thirty, then we'd go to a well-known dumpling restaurant in the center of Beijing. I stopped at the student conference room on my way, but Huang Ming was still not there. I'd been looking for him for five days since my talk with You Shan. No one knew where he was. He seemed to have disappeared into thin air.

"Ni Bing," someone called as I was entering my building.

"Huang Ming!" I turned around sharply and grabbed his arms. I held onto him as if holding onto a gift dropped unexpectedly from the sky. "I've been looking for you all over the place."

"Shh, don't say a word. Jump on the backseat."

His bloodshot eyes, tangled hair, and the strong tobacco smell from his wrinkled clothing told me something terrible had happened. Without a second thought, I got onto his bike. As we rode out of the campus gate, I suddenly remembered my appointment with Yan. *But this is more important than having dumplings,* I told myself. *I must find out what is going on with Huang Ming.*

Within ten minutes, we arrived at People's University. He stopped in front of a dormitory building and led me to the second floor. The dim corridor was lined with stoves, coal baskets, wood, and kitchen cabinets. Pungent smells of curry and fried onions filled the air as people cooked their suppers in the hallway. The building, designed and built for students, was now used as apartments for professors and their families. Huang Ming opened the door at the end of the corridor. Books were scattered on the table and floor. Something was cooking on the kerosene stove; steam puffed out rattlingly from the metal cover. A queen-size bed near the window took up a third of the room. On the wall there was a wedding picture of a young couple.

"My friend," Huang Ming explained. "He's in Guangzhou right now and let me have his apartment for the campaign. His wife is a middle school teacher in Shanghai."

So this was where he'd been hiding. I sat down on the edge of the bed. "I really worried about you. You Shan called me to her office and asked many questions about our trip to Yuanming Yuan. You must be careful."

He lit a cigarette and took a deep puff, his eyes fixed on me silently. I began to feel uneasy under his gaze when he said, "Ni Bing, I'm leaving for Tibet tomorrow."

I leaped to my feet. "You're kidding. Tell me you're just kidding!" I shouted.

He shook his head. Our faces were so close that I could feel his hot breath on my forehead.

"How about the election? Most Beijing University students are going to vote for you. You can't run away like this. Are you scared of the authorities?" I stopped. What was I talking about?

"I'm leaving so that the election can continue," he said slowly, as if he wanted to make sure I would understand. "The authorities are determined not to let me be elected. They will use all their means to stop me, even at the cost of canceling the election on our campus. If that happens, all our efforts will be wasted. So I must leave. At least one of my comrades can become the people's representative."

"Is it your personal decision?"

"No, it's the decision of our campaign committee."

"But why Tibet?" I felt the stinging in my eyes at the thought that I might not see him again after tomorrow. "Why can't you simply announce your withdrawal from the election?"

He smiled bitterly. "Have you heard of the saying: *Lead the life of a whore and build a monument to her chastity?* They hate me and want me to disappear from the campaign, but they don't want to make it look ugly. So it's better that I go to Tibet as a volunteer. I'm sure they'll give me a lot of publicity after I leave. They can afford celebrating me as a hero in my absence."

"But you're not a Tibetan. You're not used to the high altitude and harsh life there. Many people have died."

"Don't worry, Ni Bing. I'm as strong as a mule. I'm used to hardship, remember? It's only a four-year service. By the time I come back, you'll be a college graduate. I hope you'll still remember me."

"Four years, four years is a long time," I said in a trembling voice.

He put his hands on my shoulders. I felt I was going to collapse on the floor under their weight. "You'll miss me, won't you?" he whispered in my ear.

I buried my face in his chest, inhaling greedily the smell of his flesh. *This is my home,* I told myself as I wrapped my arms around his waist and pressed my breasts against his warm body. *This is where I should be.*

He groaned, held my face in his hands and looked into my eyes. "This time, I won't let you run away."

He bent his head and brushed his lips along the nape of my

neck. The tickling spread like little streams to the top of my head, to the tips of my fingers and toes. I trembled with pleasure. I thought of Yan but did not feel the slightest guilt or shame. Even if we made love tonight, it would still be all right. One did not feel ashamed to get pleasure from bathing in the sun. My feeling for Huang Ming was based on zhengqi—a positive force. No evil thought could get near us. It wasn't a coincidence that he was murmuring "my sunlight" at me. We were each other's sunshine. His lips burned like a little torch, making permanent impressions on my skin. Oh, it was possible to feel close, to enter each other's skin without sexual intercourse.

He stopped behind my right ear. There was a scar that extended from there along my jaw. It was barely visible. When I got excited or frightened, it rose like a little worm crawling out of the earth. I had been intimate with Yan for so long, naked, half-naked, but he had never noticed it.

"How did that happen?" He touched it with his fingertips.

"I don't know. I never paid attention to it. Is it ugly?"

"No, it's not. But that's not the point. It doesn't look like you cut yourself in an accident or a medical operation. You should find out what happened to you as a child. Everything we do or say now goes back to our earliest years. Sometimes it can be unpleasant, even scary, but it's necessary. Because the deeper you try to bury it, the harder it will get back at you. It's just a question of time."

I pressed the scar into the skin. He was right. I was frightened of asking, though I knew no one in my family would tell me if I did. Somehow I knew that behind the scar there was a bloody story that had to do with my birth.

He smiled. "Sorry, I sound like a lecturer again. I'm sure you know more about this theory than me. You're majoring in Western literature. Ah, the tea eggs are done. Are you hungry?"

The fragrance of the tea and soy sauce suddenly entered my nose. I nodded my head. It was hard to imagine that Huang Ming could cook. He lifted the pot cover and picked out a bowl of eggs with chopsticks. I peeled an egg. The shells had been cracked during the cooking so that the tea and soy sauce flavor could seep into the eggs. The cracks had left dark brown geometric patterns on the light brown background. I touched the smooth egg with my lips. It was too good to be true. So I was in a dream. Tomorrow, I'd wake up and he would be gone. I choked with sadness.

"Don't go away, Ming, don't go away. I'm just getting to know you."

He wrapped me in his warm body. I looked up and stared into his eyes. There were two suns burning there. No, one was the sun and the other, the moon. Someday, the sun and moon would meet, and there would be Ming—bright, brilliant, and clear—on earth.

WHEN I RETURNED to my room, Yan was chatting and laughing with Huli, Leilei, and the other girls like an old friend. "Here she is," they called out, and stood up to leave. It was almost ten o'clock. Too late to go out for their evening studies. Apparently they were leaving to make space for us. I grabbed their hands and begged them to stay. How was I going to face Yan alone tonight? But they just slipped out of my hands laughing. "Bye, enjoy," they said, winking at Yan.

"Where have you been?" He pounded on me like an angry sea as soon as the door was shut.

I stood at the door in silence. If things got bad, I could just run.

"Where the hell have you been?" he roared. "You won't talk, eh? So you think I won't know? How stupid! In China, nothing can be hidden. You were with Huang Ming, weren't you?"

One of my roommates must have seen us and told Yan. They were the only people he knew on this campus.

"This Huang Ming is your hero, eh? You can't stop thinking about him day and night, ha!" He waved a red velvet notebook in front of my nose. So my roommates had let him climb onto my bunk bed and take my journal from under my pillow. He had the ability to make the dead stand up from their graves and dance.

"Tell me, did you also think about him when you were shopping and eating dinner with me?" He slapped the notebook as if slapping an enemy. I stared at him but couldn't focus my eyes on the blurred figure jumping up and down before me. "I don't care what you think of me. I just want to know the truth. Tell me, did you sleep with Huang Ming?"

I laughed. I knew I shouldn't, but I couldn't help myself. This was the only thing he cared about. I laughed so that I didn't have to talk. He'd never believe that we didn't sleep together.

His face turned from pale white to green. Suddenly he dropped to the floor and cried like a little boy. "My only hope, my only hope," he said between his sobs, "gone, gone forever. What's the point in living?"

I squatted next to him and handed him my handkerchief. He grabbed my hand. "Meimei, let's perish together."

He jumped to his feet and unscrewed the switch on the wall. Placing his fingers two inches away from the red and black wires in the socket, he stared at me with a crazy leer and asked in a dramatic, false voice, "Are you ready to perish with me?"

I dragged him away from the switch. He struggled in my arms, shouting, "I don't want to live! I don't want to live!"

"Sshh, someone is coming."

The footsteps passed our door and entered the bathroom. I looked at my watch. It was 10:15. "People are coming back from the library. Let's go out."

He stalked into the hallway. I screwed the cover back on the light switch and tidied the room before I left.

The late autumn wind blew sharply against my face and chest. I had forgotten to put on the jacket Yan had just bought for me at Wangfujing Department Store. It was bright green, with pointed collars and a zipper in front. It cost twenty-eight yuan, my monthly salary when I taught at Hangzhou. If it had been up to me, I'd never have bought it. But Yan said it was worth it: I looked like a green peony in the jacket. He walked ahead of me, then turned into the Zhongguanchun Restaurant. When I lifted the greasy curtain, Yan was already seated at a table, staring at a bottle of gaoliang spirit in front of him. I bought a dish of boiled peanuts at the counter and put it next to the bottle. He poured a full cup and drank to the bottom.

"Peanuts, Gege," I said, moving the dish closer to him. He swept his hand over the dish and overturned it. Round peanuts rolled to the other side of the table where four men were scalding thin slices of mutton in the boiling water. They stared curiously at us through the steam from the stove on the table. Yan poured another cup.

"Gege, you shouldn't drink any more." I covered the cup with my hand. "It's bad for your liver."

"Mind your own business, biaozii." He banged his bottle on the table. The whole restaurant looked in our direction. My face burned as if I had been slapped a hundred times. No one had ever called me whore in public or private. But tonight I could endure anything. Yan raised his voice when he saw that he had everyone's attention. "Father wants to be drunk. What are you doing here? Why don't go back to Huang Ming and fuck more?"

I stood up and left. The wind was blowing harder. I hugged my shoulders for warmth. A bus slowed down at the stop across the street. Yan came out with the bottle. When he saw me still waiting at the door, he tried to throw himself under the bus wheels. I caught the tail of his jacket and pulled him back to the sidewalk. The bus braked with a harsh squeak. The driver leaned out of the window, cursing and mocking at us at the top of his lungs. Beijing residents were known for their mocking skills. They could make every part of your organs bleed in shame. A crowd gathered around us. I started laughing again. When you were insulted and angered to the extreme, the only thing you could do was to laugh. The driver stopped his melodious cursing and looked at me as if I were crazy. Then he spat at us and rolled up his window. Yan had calmed down and let himself be pushed onto the next bus.

We got off at the zoo. On top of the gate was a gigantic map with green turtles painted as advertisements. "Turtle," he shouted, pointing to the sign with his shaking finger. "Turtle, I'm a fucking green hat turtle." He ran blindly away from the zoo. I tried my best to keep up with him. My strength was fading. All I had eaten today was a steamed bread and half of a tea egg.

I finally caught up with him at the end of a small lane. We stared at each other like strangers. I bent over and vomited against the wall.

"Let's go back, Gege," I said, wiping my mouth with my sleeve. He shook his head. "The train station."

He was insane. It was already after eleven o'clock. The last bus back to school was 11:45. If we missed that, we'd have to spend the night on the street or in the station. Why did he want to go there? To go back to Hangzhou? His luggage was still in his hotel near Beijing University. He started moving. I followed him without asking.

In the waiting room of Beijing Train Station, Yan fell asleep on my lap. I watched his arched eyebrows and crooked nose. In his sleep, he resumed his old, familiar, gentle look. Would he resume his dignity and reason when he woke up? Would he resume his love for me? Could I love him as I used to after what had happened tonight?

The clock on the tower above the station stroked six. Peddlers and beggars who the police had thrown out last night were now returning to the benches for more sleep. Lines began to form at each entrance, where two conductors were punching tickets. Was Huang Ming in one of the lines? I looked for the sign for Tibet, then realized that there was no direct train from Beijing to Tibet. He had to go first to Sichuan or Qinhai, then take buses from Chendu or Xining for another week. I wasn't sure if I'd ever see him or hear from him again. But I knew that we'd never forget each other.

Chapter Twelve

On new year's eve, Jia and his wife brought the color TV out to the yard so that the residents of the navy compound could watch the final game between the Chinese and Cuban women's volleyball teams. Since their son had bought the set from the Shanghai Television Factory where he worked, the Jias had suddenly become the most desirable and respected family in the compound.

I stood at the entrance of the yard, watching the audience screaming, stamping, and applauding for the Chinese team. Somehow, it was easier to let oneself go in front of the screen, be it TV or movie. To my surprise, I found Mother sitting behind the Jia couple. She barely talked to her neighbors, who were mostly peasant women. In her opinion, these housewives did nothing but gossip and poke their noses into other people's business. She particularly disliked Mrs. Jia because she had been Nainai's best friend.

What a change! Mother had never washed dishes in my memory, not before I left for Ma Ao at fifteen. Now she went to the market every morning, cooked meals, and shouted in the crowd in front of the TV. Had she also mellowed with age?

She had sent me money at the end of the fall semester so that I could have a reunion with the family. *Haven't seen you for a year and a half,* she wrote. *We all miss you.* I read the letter several times to get used to the tenderness. As soon as finals were over, I took the train to Shanghai and boarded the night ship to Dinghai. Waipo was quite unhappy when she couldn't persuade me to stay overnight, even though I promised to stay for a week with her before I went back to Beijing. When I got home the next morning, Father had gone into the mountains and Mother was about to go to school. She pulled me into her room and closed the door.

"Glad you came so quickly. I want you to take your nainai away," she whispered. "Take her to Shanghai where she can take the ship for Shading."

"Mother," I said, but words suddenly failed me. The only thought I had was the saying Ku xiao bu de—Don't know whether to laugh or cry. My mother never changed except for her thickening stomach and waist. Finally I managed to say, "I thought Nainai was going to live with us till . . ."

"I know, I know," she cut in. "I don't want to send her back to her native place in her condition. But old and weak as she is, she still tries to separate your father and me."

"How can that be possible, Mother?"

"I heard it with my own ears." She raised her voice. "You know your father is about to retire from the navy. He can either stay on the island or go back to Shading, his native land. Your nainai is persuading him to return to Shading. Oh, if I could ignore it. But you know your father can be stubborn and crazy like a donkey. For all these years, he never stops thinking of his Shading, though he hardly mentions it. What if he really chooses to go back to the north? I won't say this island is a paradise. But your old mother is not going to the cold and impoverished north. So the only choice will be separation or divorce. What a joke! At our ages. And you children will have endless suffering if this family falls apart. You're my first daughter. The old saying is *Maintain the army for a thousand years to use it for an hour.* It's time for you to do something for the family.

"I've thought about it for a long time. If no one whispers evil advice in your father's ear every day, your father will stay with me. We've been husband and wife for twenty-four years, after all. You know what rubbish she tells your father? He can still marry a virgin in his native land with his retirement pay. Yuk, I want to puke. He's going to be fifty-two. Take her away as soon as possible. You can do it. She's in such awe of you now, the first college student in the Ni family." She smiled, but I couldn't tell if she was being sarcastic. "Tell her I'll increase her allowance to twenty yuan a month. With that amount, she can live comfortably in her hometown. I've had the money ready, your fare to go back to Beijing, and two months allowance. Just tell me when you're ready. She leaves, you leave."

APPLAUSE EXPLODED among the audience. Long Ping, the Iron Hammer of the Chinese team, had just pounded the ball on the rival's ground. My mother jumped up and down like a little girl. Suddenly she turned her head in my direction. I winced and left the crowd at once. For a week, I'd been avoiding her. I dared not tell her that I hadn't talked to Nainai about her leaving. I felt I was under house arrest. Every day was like a year. I wanted to leave as soon as possible, but Mother had made it clear that I couldn't leave without Nainai. But how was I going to start the conversation with Nainai? Why must I be the bad guy? Why couldn't she or her other two daughters tell her? They lived with her, anyway, not me. Mother said she didn't want to be involved because she didn't want Father to hate her for the rest of his life. How about me?

Nainai could barely walk in her present condition. The shortest route to Shading would take five days. If she had an asthma attack on the trip, it would be hard for her to survive. Who was to blame if that happened? It seemed that my life was a series of choices, not between good and evil, which wouldn't be difficult, but between two bad ends.

I passed my parents' room and entered the children's room. No matter how old I grew, I would always be a child here. Nainai sat on her bed with her legs crossed, trying to thread a needle. She had her glasses on but was unaware that the thread missed the needle by more than an inch. Her mouth closed tight in concentration, threading the needle slowly and carefully, as if the whole room had become the needle hole. Her bed stood in what had originally been designed as a closet. Father had taken off the shelves and door and turned it into a semiprivate bedroom for his mother. A full-size bed fit perfectly, half hidden by the walls on both sides. Underneath it, Nainai kept her trunks and other belongings that she would bring to her laojia someday, her native town. She must have shrunk another three or four inches since I had seen her last. In my memory, her head could almost touch the ceiling when she crouched on the bed and her body seemed to overfill the closet space. Now it was like an extra-large jacket on a kid's body, yet somehow it seemed right. She looked like one of the two funny-looking harmony gods on the traditional New Year's pictures.

I took the needle from her hands and threaded it in one try. She laughed silently, exposing her toothless gums. When I was seven, her teeth had become so bad that she had to have them all pulled and replaced with false teeth. At night, she soaked them in a glass of water. I had often stared at the pink gums and white teeth at the bottom of the glass, longing to touch them but afraid they might clamp down and bite my finger off. Sometimes when Nainai beat me or gave me a hard time for no reason, I would spit into the water. Now her gums had shrunk and the old set no longer fit. She looked up at me, her face more wrinkled than a walnut shell. "Nainai is really old," she said.

"Nonsense. What does it have to do with age? It's too dark here to see anything," I said. "Do you want to move to our bed? It's bigger and brighter, since it's near the light."

"Don't bother, child. Your sisters may come back soon. I don't really need much light to do what I'm doing. I've made so many pairs of shoes I can work with my eyes closed." She waved the black velvet cotton shoe.

I took it from her hand to look at the red peony embroidered on green leaves. It was beautiful, but who would wear this kind of shoe nowadays?

"It's for you. I hope I can finish them before we leave."

"What do you mean? Leave? Where?" I asked in a hoarse voice, my cheeks burning with shame. I knew exactly what she was talking about. I'd been planning to discuss this with her for a whole week. Was I being hypocritical? But why did my heart cramp with so much pain? "You're not going anywhere, Nainai. This is your home."

She looked at me with her dim eyes. "Bing Ah," she said. I trembled. My grandma had never attached an endearing "Ah" to my name. It sounded strange and familiar at the same time, as if I was meeting an old, old friend unexpectedly in a foreign country. "Bing Ah," she repeated my name, "your father is a good son, and you three girls are great granddaughters. I've had a lot of happiness here. But I've been away from my native homeland too long. They're all calling me. I must go back before it's too late."

I suddenly felt like crying, as if I was about to lose my best friend. But why? I had grown up hating and cursing her, especially when she beat me. Most of the time I had been terrified of her. After I left home, I managed to put her out of my mind. It wasn't too hard because I was busy and didn't need to deal with her directly. I didn't understand why I felt this way now.

"You must be cold, Nainai," I said quickly. "Let me bring you some hot water to warm up your feet." I got a basin and filled it with hot water. Mother and my sisters would get mad when they found out there was no more hot water left in the flask, but I didn't care. I put the steaming basin on the floor near the bed, watching Nainai untie the bandages from her bound feet.

"When did you start binding your feet again?" Although I often called her "bound-feet old lady" behind her back in my anger, I had never actually seen her bind them. She had liberated her feet in the late forties.

"A few months ago. My feet had grown much bigger and out of shape since I stopped binding. Your grandpa wouldn't like it. I'm afraid I won't be able to restore them to the original size. But at least I can make them more shapely."

My grandpa had died when Nainai was twenty-eight. What was she talking about? I bit my lip. I must plead with Mother to let Nainai stay. She had untied the bandage and exposed her foot. It was much less puffy than I remembered. And the toes, except for the big one, which turned upward slightly, were firmly locked into the flesh of the sole. The heel was huge and round in contrast with the pointed front, its skin pink and tender due to the wrapping. I reached out my hand, but withdrew it quickly before I touched her foot. *What was life like when one had to walk on a pair of feet three or four inches long?* I wanted to know, but I was afraid to ask.

"When did you start binding?" I asked.

"At six, the best age for binding. The bones have grown, but are still soft enough to be reshaped. And I was old enough to know the importance of beauty to be able to endure the pain. I still cried day and night in the first three months. When my toe bones were broken and the flesh rotted, I begged my mom to loosen the bandages. But she stuffed her ears with cotton balls. She hit me with a stick and made me hop around in the backyard to speed up the rotting and breaking."

"Why was she so cruel?"

She smiled. "She wasn't. If she had loosened my bandages, I wouldn't have had a perfect pair of lotus feet and wouldn't have married well. In those days, even a poor peasant wanted his wife to have a pair of tiny feet. My mother was really good to me. I married at sixteen. Your grandpa loved my feet so much that he wouldn't let me work in the fields. Of course, he could afford it. I had quite a few years of good life before he passed away. I guess it's my fate. It's been over forty years, but sometimes it feels like just yesterday. I've been dreaming about him recently. I think he's calling me to join him."

I wanted to tell her that she could live for a hundred years, but I couldn't. She didn't need this kind of cheap solace. Death might sound frightening to me but not necessarily to her. Still, I shuddered as I suddenly saw that the closet looked like a tomb and that Nainai sat in it like a mummy. Would I also dry up and shrink when I grew old? Ten years ago, she had had so much fire and energy, trotting on her tiny feet in the house and on the streets like a horse. She could walk two miles to the navy headquarters for a movie, carrying a heavy bamboo chair, and I sometimes had to run to keep up with her.

"Why do you call bound feet 'golden lotus'?" I asked, hoping the change of subject would drive away my fearful thought.

She pondered for a second, then crawled to the trunk at the end of her bed against the wall. She groped at the bottom and took out a pair of red embroidered shoes. They were about three inches long. The toe pointed delicately like Nainai's. At first glance, I thought they were toys. No human feet could possibly fit into them. They certainly didn't match Nainai's feet.

"My last pair," she said in a proud voice. "It took me a whole month to embroider them. My feet grew after I stopped binding, and I had to throw out my old shoes. But I kept this pair. They're too pretty."

I played with the shoes. They were only half the size of my palm, grotesquely beautiful and sensual, like a pair of pointed peppers. So this was what Chinese men had been obsessed with for a thousand years. This was the wonder that Chinese women had created within this tiny space.

Nainai took the shoes and put them beside her feet. "I can't wear them anymore, but I'll bring them with me when I go." She lifted her foot and turned the toe around. "Thanks to Chairman Mao, you girls no longer go through this anymore. I wonder sometimes if anyone nowadays can take that kind of pain. But pain is not always bad, you know. It's good to chiku—eat bitterness, a lot of it, when you're young, so you can appreciate sweetness when you're older. It also makes you strong. If my mom hadn't put me through the torture, I probably couldn't have survived the loss of your grandpa. It wasn't easy to be a widow with two young boys. Thank god I had two sons so I could hold onto the land my husband left us. I learned to do all the work in the fields, learned to be a midwife. Hundreds of babies have come out through my hands. After the liberation, I learned how to read and write. I was elected the head of the Women's Liberation Group because I was the best singer and dancer in my village. Hey, your nainai was a famous woman when she was young."

We laughed together, clasping each other's hands. Nainai's toothless mouth opened wide like a black hole. I suddenly remembered the last time we had laughed together like this. I was twelve.

That summer, my mother had gone to see Waipo on Father's ship. As the soldiers started lifting the bridge away from the dock, my sister Hong started crying. Her tears moved my mother and allowed her to get on the ship. I stood on the dock watching the ship disappear beyond the horizon, ignoring Nainai's call. The strong sea wind blew straight into my eyes, but not a single tear came. Nainai went away. When she came back, she pulled my sleeve to show me what she had just bought. "Banana," I cried out. I had only tasted one in my dreams. It was overripe, its yellow skin covered with dark patches. My nostrils trembled at the fragrance. "Let's go home and make pork and vegetable buns for dinner. This banana will be our desert," she said.

Nainai let me take the first bite. I almost fainted with the taste, which was soft, fragrant, and sweet at the same time. The sensation was too much to bear. Nainai took out her fake teeth to feel the full taste of the banana. She smacked her lips and moaned like a baby. I burst out laughing; she joined in, her mouth wide and toothless. Tears streaked down our cheeks. When laughter was scarce, it had to be accompanied by tears, which were equally precious. So we took a bite of the banana, laughed, took another bite, and laughed more. It took us a whole hour to finish it.

Nainai stopped laughing, wiped her tears, and bowed. I jumped to my feet and straightened her up. "What are you doing, Nainai, what are you doing?" I cried out in shock.

"I did things that hurt you when you were young," she said with her head bent. "Sometimes I did it deliberately, sometimes I couldn't help myself. I don't want to blame what I did on others or society. Nainai has made many mistakes in her life because of her personal faults. You don't hold any grudge against me, which makes me feel more ashamed. Will you accept my apology?"

"I'm the one to blame, Nainai. I was clumsy and stubborn. I still am. I have caused you a lot of stress. I should apologize to you."

She stared at me for a long time before she spoke again. "Bing Ah, when you grow older, you'll know more things that happened to our family. Probably not everything. I hope by then you'll be able to understand them. Perhaps you'll understand why Nainai acted the way she did. Now, Bing Ah, you must tell your mother that I'm ready to go home. As soon as possible. I don't have many days left. I feel it. I must hurry. I'll tell your father about my leaving. He'll be sad, but will understand. Bing Ah, will you write to me? Just once a month? Just a few words? It will really make me happy to hear your letters read aloud in my last days."

"Ni bing, how could you forget the past so thoroughly?" Waipo threw a bowl of green peppers into the hot wok and stirred them angrily. "Don't you remember how she abused you physically and verbally when you were a child? I remember every story you told me. They made me cry endlessly, and now you're treating her as if she were your mother. I don't understand."

I put down the young soy bean pods I was shelling on the table and embraced her from her behind. "Waipo," I said, pressing my cheek on her pitch-black hair, "no one has loved me like you, and no one can replace you in my heart. Remember, it was you who I called mother first? I haven't forgotten the past, Waipo, not at all. But she's going home. And she's sick. This may be her last trip. I want to make it as pleasant as possible."

"I know, I know. Do you think your waipo is a heartless old woman? But it just makes me angry whenever I think of her pinching and clubbing you. And you don't have to squander all your money on her. It's your allowance. What are you going to buy food with when you get back to Beijing? Drink the west wind?"

I became quiet. We'd been in Shanghai for three days, waiting for the ship to Qingdao, from which Nainai would take a long-distance bus to Weihai City, then a local bus to Datiandong Village. Father wanted to travel with her, but Mother reminded him that he shouldn't take off while he was waiting for his retirement papers. He had to think about the future of his family. She suggested that he make the trip to Shading after everything was settled so that he would have some money and plenty of time to make a comfortable home for his mother.

When I saw my father holding Nainai's hand and crying like a boy, I told myself that I must do my best to make her happy in Shanghai. We stayed in Waipo's apartment. Going to a hotel was beyond our means. Waipo received Nainai with extreme politeness, though there had been much bad blood between the two women in the past. Yan had offered to buy the ticket. He stood on the line all night for a fifth-class ticket, the only kind we could afford. The ship was leaving the next day. For the past three days, I'd been taking Nainai out every morning, strolling along Huaihai Road and Nanjing Road, the two busiest streets in Shanghai. We stopped at famous bakeries and dairy stores, and I forced her to choose things she had never tasted. It was a pleasure mixed with pain. Everything was new to her. The delicious smells confused her eyes but not her instinct. She would praise every item, yet when I took out the purse, she would clutch my hand to stop me from buying anything. I practically yelled at her to make her eat. However, as soon as her tongue touched the ice cream or chocolate cookies, she seemed to melt with delight, and tears would come out of her eyes. Wherever we went, people stared at us with curiosity: me in a flashy red down jacket with the badge of Beijing University on my chest, accompanied by a small peasant woman in a black velvet hat and black lotus shoes embroidered with red flowers. We looked funny together, but I couldn't have cared less. With Nainai, the normal standards for behavior no longer applied. The snobbish attitude from the store girls could not make me mad anymore, nor did I feel embarrassed shuffling along with Nainai in the crowd. Finally we entered the Second Department Store of Shanghai. She stopped at the silk counter, her eyes fixed on a roll of black silk with rose patterns. I told the saleswoman to cut a piece of silk big enough to make a jacket and pants. She took a glance at Nainai before she measured the cloth and tore it off. The sound of tearing silk sent sparkles into Nainai's dim eyes. For the first time, she didn't protest or try to stop the purchase. When I put the silk in her hands, she clutched it to her chest, murmuring, "Nainai is lucky. Nainai is lucky."

I didn't know what to tell Waipo. I didn't understand why I was squandering money on Nainai as if I were paying a debt I had owed in my previous life. I couldn't explain why I wanted to please her so much instead of holding onto the old grudges.

"She's had a hard life," I said to Waipo. "Her husband died when she was twenty-eight and she had to bring up two boys all by herself. Since she couldn't get along with her two daughters-in-law, she kept getting shuffled back and forth between Dinghai and Shading. She's certainly not as lucky as you, Waipo. All your five children treat you like a queen, and Waigong is still strong and healthy. I feel bad that she has to go back to the north at her age. Maybe that's why I want to make things pleasant for her. I want to make her happy."

"Who does she have to blame but herself?" Waipo again flared up with jealousy. "She thought she could exercise her authority in her son's house as she did in her village. That was her mistake. She chose the wrong time, wrong place, and wrong person. Why should your mother, well educated and sophisticated, bow her head to that country bumpkin? She kept telling me that she was a big shot in her native place. So what? That witch! You don't remember how she kidnapped you to Shading and almost killed you when you were five, hmm? But I do. You'd have been dead years ago if I hadn't followed you to that evil village and grabbed you from the knife."

The scar behind my ear was rising again. The pulsing in my neck was like an awakened dragon, roaring and stretching, ready to tear through the skin and let all the blood spurt out. The drums were beating inside my ears, and the sun was blinding my eyes. *Waipo, tell me more about what happened then. I've lost that part of my memory. Memories can evaporate as easily as dreams. Help me crystallize it.*

"*Xiao nuan, xiao nuan,*" Waipo shouted in my ear. She hadn't called me "little girl" for years. She was holding my face in her hands, her mouth close as if she were trying to breathe life into me. *Waipo was mad. She lost her head. Forget about her nonsense.*

I looked into her eyes. "Waipo, Father said we were going to Dinghai to see my mother. But when we boarded the ship, you were running after us. I heard you scream 'kidnapper.' Then Father covered my face with his jacket, and the next thing I remember is eating dinner with Mother. So what happened in between? Where did he take me? You must tell me, Waipo. I've grown up."

She sighed, letting go of my face. "Ni Bing is not a xiao nuan any more," she murmured to herself. She turned off the gas stove and sat down on the stool.

"Your father took you away in a rush. He wouldn't let me see you off, not even downstairs. His ship was waiting for him. But I followed him surreptitiously to the street. He jumped onto Bus 42. That bus didn't go to the military port! What was going on? I got into a sanlun and told the driver to follow that bus. It wasn't hard for a bike to follow a bus in Shanghai. The traffic has always been bad.

"He got off at Huangpu Port and entered the waiting hall. If he was going to take you home on a civil ship, why did he have to lie about it? I went to the ticket office and asked the girl what port the ship for Dinghai was docked at. She said there was no ship going in that destination today or tomorrow. I panicked. What the hell was going on? Where was he taking you? I searched the waiting hall, shouting your name. Then I realized something. I went back to the window and asked for the ship going to Qingdao. It was leaving in ten minutes. I ran to the dock. It was really far. When I got there, I discovered I had forgotten to buy a platform ticket. It took me another five minutes to persuade the guards to let me in. But it was too late. The ship was leaving already.

"That bastard! Why was he bringing you to Shandong secretly? The more I thought about it, the more I believed that something was wrong. I immediately sent a telegram to your mother on the island and with a loan bought a ticket for the next ship to Qingdao. It wouldn't leave till four days later. I jumped up and down but could do nothing about it. I just prayed that nothing would happen to my baby before I got there. So you really don't remember anything? Perhaps it's better this way. Are you sure you want to hear the whole story? What good will it do?"

I nodded my head. I wanted to tell her that I remembered everything in my bloody dreams. Sometimes they even haunted me during the day when I was not careful. But I checked myself. I didn't want to sound melodramatic.

"It was the worst journey I'd ever made, three days and nights at the bottom of a ship, sleeping on a piece of straw mattress on the floor with hundreds of dirty, stinky strangers, using a plastic bag for vomit. When I finally got off the ship, I was half dead. Then I couldn't find the bus. No one could understand my Shanghai accent, and I couldn't understand their Shandong dialect.

"It was a miracle that I found that small village. Actually, it was the drums that led me there after I got off the bus. I had never heard such powerful drums. They went directly to the heart and brain. I was just sucked into the vibration, sucked into the ancestral hall where hundreds of peasants knelt in the sun and chanted in unison. The men were all half-naked, the skin on their backs peeled. They knelt in front of the statue of a god. Under his feet was a bowl of water. It dawned on me that these people must be offering a ceremony to the sky to request rain. There was obviously a bad drought in the north. On the bus I had seen miles of cracked fields and withered crops. Suddenly the drums and chanting became really fast. So did my heartbeat.

"A woman in a red-and-golden gown came out and danced with a sword. It was your nainai. She looked like a demon. I shouldn't use the word *dance*. It was more like someone having a fit. She rolled her eyes and head, twitched and shook her body, leaped up and down like a monkey. Then she rolled on the ground, her face covered with white foam. She raised her sword up to the sky. Two men came out, holding a child upside down by her ankles.

"'Ni Bing, my baby,' I called out, but couldn't make a sound. I couldn't tell if you were still alive, because you didn't struggle or make any noise. You just hung there upside down, like one of the piglets in the window of the Cantonese restaurant waiting to be roasted in the oven. They brought you to the statue and lifted you above the water bowl. That witch got up from the ground and wriggled her evil body near you. She put the sword on your neck. Blood trickled down your head into the bowl and dyed the water scarlet. She knelt down and raised the bowl to the sun. The chanting became louder. Somehow the sight of your blood freed me from my trance and my voice came back. I screamed and cursed at the top of my voice, and ran to you while tearing off my jacket. 'Take my blood, if you want, you devils! Take mine!' I pounded and scratched my naked chest.

"Perhaps it was my Shanghai accent, perhaps it was the white spots of vitiligo on my body that scared them. They probably thought I was a ghost or goddess becoming manifest. Anyway, no one moved when I snatched you from their hands and ran to the bus station. By the time they recovered from the shock and started chasing me, I had already reached the highway. They couldn't do anything to me there.

"What they were doing was superstition. It was illegal. They could have gotten themselves arrested. I should have reported them to the police right then, but I was anxious to get you out of there. I took the buses and the ship and brought you directly to Dinghai. Your mother could protect you better because she had the legal right. To my surprise, your father had already arrived. I snarled at him and cursed him with the most vicious words. After I told your mother the whole story, she dashed at him like a tigress, her claws wide open. She would have eaten him alive if I hadn't torn her away. He didn't fight back or dodge. He just murmured with wide eyes, 'I didn't know. I didn't know. I thought my mother just wanted her to live in our native land for a few months, to cleanse her sins before her name was written in our family record.'"

She stopped. I waited for her to continue. At the same time, I wanted to know why Nainai wanted to cleanse my sins. What sins had I committed as a baby? But Waipo looked pale. The story had exhausted all her energy. I myself was shaking. Almost all the details had appeared in my dreams and were now confirmed as real memories.

"I made your father promise that his mother would not come to live with them until you were fifteen, otherwise I'd report everything to the government. He swore, but a month later, he rushed back to Shandong and brought her to the island. He claimed that his mother was dying of hunger and he'd rather stay in prison than be an unfilial son. Besides, he argued, his mother had never intended to do you any harm. She just needed some blood of a four-year-old girl who was born in July of the lunar calendar. You fit right in, even your birthday. Bullshit! But what could I say, especially when your own mother had agreed? She's very soft-hearted, although she may appear harsh. But I had always kept my eyes on you, my baby. Every time you came to Shanghai and showed me the bruises and scars that old witch had inflicted on you, I felt just like strangling her. That's why it shocks me to see you treat her so kindly. I know I shouldn't feel that way. One shouldn't bear a grudge against a dying person. But I guess the past has poisoned my heart a little bit."

I took Waipo's hand and put it on my cheek. She had such soft skin. All those years of rubbing and washing hadn't hardened it at all. Everybody said that Waipo was plain looking. But in my eyes, she was the most beautiful woman on earth. Her skin was so smooth and silky that I just wanted to be in her embrace forever. Even the vitiligo patches, which made others into monsters, looked like flowers on her delicate body. There had always been so much intimacy and tenderness between us. I should have hated Nainai after hearing the story, yet I didn't.

"Waipo, why did Nainai want to cleanse my sins? What had I done? What had happened before and after my birth?" I wanted to ask, "Who is my mother?" But I didn't dare. If my mother was not my real mother, in what position would I put Waipo? Waipo had to be real, no matter what!

She covered my mouth as if she had guessed my next question, her pale face now turned green. She was shaking. "Don't think nonsense!" she said sternly. "There's nothing amiss about your birth. And remember, sometimes it's better not to poke your nose into everything. I've told you enough today, my child. Now I want you to bring these dishes upstairs. It's past lunchtime. She must be hungry." She took off her apron and headed for the door.

"Where are going? Aren't you having lunch with us?"

"I'll get some desserts from Qiaojiashan Bakery. She likes their rice cakes with red beans."

I watched her walk along the narrow lane, and said, "You're the best waipo in the world."

YAN AND I STOOD in the middle of the street trying to get a taxi. Nainai sat on her trunk on the sidewalk. Her ship, which had been scheduled at Port 16, was switched to a wharf fifteen blocks away. No bus went there. We had only thirty-five minutes before it embarked. How could we get Nainai, her two trunks, and her five parcels there that fast? It would be a miracle if we got a taxi. Occasionally, some Japanese and German cars zoomed through the streets. The passengers, however, were always foreigners or overseas Chinese businessmen. I wanted to tell Yan to give up the bizarre idea when a Toyota braked in front of us and the driver in sunglasses leaned out the window in obvious irritation.

"What are you standing in the middle of the street for? Tired of living or what?"

"Shifu," Yan said with a smile, handing him a cigarette. People in Shanghai often called strangers shifu—master—to start a conversation or ask for a favor. "My grandma has to catch a ship. She can't walk fast because of her tiny feet. Please take us there. It's only fifteen blocks. I'll pay you triple price."

"Take the bus," he said, the corners of his mouth dropping as he saw Nainai's bound feet.

"There is none. Shifu, just consider it as a good deed. If we miss the ship, she'll be stuck here for another week."

"I only take foreign exchange money," he said arrogantly. I saw the disgusted expression on his face when he heard "good deed" and I knew Yan had just blown his chance. "No? I knew it. Get out of my way, country bumpkin. Go home and take a look at yourself in your own piss before you give people any advice." The car glided away.

Yan cursed and waved his fist at the dust. I returned to the sidewalk and said, "Let's walk, Nainai."

She picked up two parcels. Yan turned a last look to the road and lifted the trunks. I tied two parcels together, flung them on my shoulders, one front, one back, and picked up the last parcel with my left hand while supporting Nainai on my right arm. We walked slowly against the wind.

Soon she started panting. The phlegm in her throat rumbled painfully. She opened her mouth wide to gasp for air. Her lips and cheeks turned purple.

I stopped. "Take a break, Nainai. We have time."

"No. We must go on. I must not miss the ship." She gasped for more air.

I put her arm around my neck and half carried her. We'd never been so close physically, though we'd shared the same bed and slept under the same quilt for years. Her soft breast pressed against my side and part of my back, and I liked it. *But shouldn't I hate her?* I asked myself. Her breathing sounded like a whistling kettle. I couldn't take the pain anymore. I tied all the parcels together and threw them onto Yan's shoulders. I squatted before Nainai.

"Get on my back," I ordered.

"No, no, I can't. I'm too heavy. Sinful, it's sinful."

I grabbed her hands and put them around my neck. Then I held her legs and stood up. She was surprisingly heavy for her shrunken body. *The dwarf star,* I thought, recalling the magic herb my father had given me. I was carrying a star on my back. Through my jacket, I could feel her breasts. I had never touched her breasts before, but I felt I had known them as well as my own. Her heart was beating against mine in the same rhythm. I should hate her, but our hearts were beating together. There was some strange connection between us. The wind blew hard. I moved forward with all my strength. I was taking Nainai home.

My aunt was waiting at the iron gate, holding a box of chocolate cake. "Three minutes left," she shouted at us. I suddenly lost my power. My knees shook. I put Nainai down and my aunt took her right arm. We carried her to the floating dock. Some seamen were untying the rope from the gangplank. Yan shouted, "One more passenger." A young crewman carried Nainai's luggage on board, then came down to get Nainai.

We embraced.

"Bing Ah, write to me."

I nodded. It was impossible for me to utter a word at the moment.

"Bing Ah," she paused for a second, "come to see your lao jia someday."

I gave her another nod. Lao jia—old home. My native home was Weihai, which I had inherited from my father the way I had inherited his blood. I could wander into the farthest corner on earth, but that place would always be my umbilical home.

She took out a red package from her bosom and pressed it into my hand. The crewman carried her on board and she disappeared into the bottom of the ship.

The ship blasted three times before it set sail. It made a left turn and was gone from my sight forever. I opened the embroidered silk wrapping. Inside were Nainai's lotus shoes, three inches long, pointed and narrow, one embroidered with a dragon, the other with a phoenix.

Chapter Thirteen

THE REGISTRATION for graduate entrance exams in 1983 started at the beginning of the spring semester. The professors in the English Department made a special appeal to the university administration for me to take the exams with the class of 1979. I was still registered with the class of 1980, although I'd been exempted from the freshman courses and had completed all the required credits for graduation. When I got the news, I wrote to Yan and my family. If I passed the exams, I'd be the first graduate student in the Ni and Chen families.

Yan wrote back immediately. "What about our plans to get together? You promised to go back to Hangzhou after you get your BA," he wrote indignantly. "And I'll try my best to find a position in Hangzhou when I finish my graduate program in Dalian. Do you know that our reunion is the only thing that keeps me going? How could you break my heart over and over again? It's not that I don't want you to get into the graduate program. I'm just worried that I'll never see you again if you stay in Beijing much longer."

I pleaded that this opportunity was a gift from heaven. If I didn't take the exam, I would have to wait till 1984 to get my bachelor's degree. But if I got into the graduate program, I could get a master's degree in 1985. "If you can endure one more year,

Gege," I wrote in my letter, "I'll be grateful to you for the rest of my life. It means a lot to me. I don't want to sound greedy, but I like school as much as you do, and I'm good at it. Why should-n't I take an opportunity when I have one? If I throw it away, how will I face my professors who fought hard with You Shan?"

The next week, I got an express mail letter. When I opened the envelope, I cried out. Xueshu—a blood letter. Yan had stabbed his fingertips and written the letter with blood.

"I have cancer, Meimei, liver cancer," I read anxiously. The congealed blood had wrinkled the paper and made the characters crooked and writhing. "I've been feeling a sharp pain in my liver for a long time. The doctor won't tell me what's wrong but just advised me to eat whatever I want and to take a vacation. What can be more clear? I'm not stupid. Meimei, I have probably only three months to live. After you read this letter, you're free. I love you too much to make myself a burden to you. Good-bye, Meimei. When I die, throw my ashes into the East China Sea near Shanghai, my birthplace."

I went directly to my advisor Professor Wang and asked for a leave of absence. My fiancé was dying of cancer, I said. He looked at me as if I were insane, and asked me if I realized the conse-quence of my absence. I would miss the entrance exams that the department had taken so much trouble to arrange for me. He and other professors had guaranteed You Shan that I wouldn't dis-appoint them this time. If I took off, my career would be finished at Beijing University. Besides, there was no such a thing as taking three months leave unless I, not my fiancé, was hospitalized.

I returned to my room and counted my money. I had the twen-ty yuan my mother had sent me yesterday, plus the five yuan nutrition fee from my gymnastic training. Enough for a hard-seat ticket to Dalian. I loaded in my bag a copy of *Moby Dick* and the steamed bread I had just bought for the next day's breakfast and rushed to the bus stop. It was five past six. If I was lucky, I could catch the eight o'clock train and by tomorrow afternoon I would be with Yan.

The tickets for Dalian were sold out. I bought a platform ticket to get into the station and the track where the train parked and sneaked into the carriage by helping an old lady with her luggage. Ten minutes after the train started, I went to the conductor's desk. I had to pay an extra two yuan as a penalty for getting on the train with the platform ticket. Now all I had was five fen in coins. I took a look at the packed car and settled down behind the public tea bucket next to the bathroom with some peasant peddlers.

The train was five hours late. When I got out of the station, it was already dark. The three peddlers with whom I had crouched together for twenty-four hours were pulled into a minivan by three giggling girls. Their powdered cheeks were heavily rouged. Yan once told me that prostitutes had popped up everywhere like mushrooms since Dalian reopened its port to the West. Dalian girls, considered to be the most beautiful in northern China, had tall slim bodies, brown eyes, curly hair, and light complexions. Many of them had White Russian blood. I watched the van drive away until the red characters of Golden Flower Hotel faded in the dark, then walked to the No. 3 bus stop, playing with the coins in my pocket. Should I spend the five fen on food or on the bus? The only thing I had eaten in the past 24 hours was the steamed bread. I stepped into the pork bun restaurant nearby, lured by the irresistible smell from the steamer. At the end of the line, I saw the sign above the counter: Tianjing pork bun—ten fen each. I sighed and returned to the bus stop.

When the bus came, I bought a five-fen ticket. The fare to Yan's school cost six. If I was lucky, the conductor might not notice me; otherwise, I would have to get off and walk the last two stops.

Luckily, the bus was crowded and the conductor didn't pay attention to me. I registered at the gate of Dalian Teachers' College and headed to the building where Yan shared a room with two philosophy graduates. I had made friends with them when I stayed here last summer as Yan's cousin.

I stopped outside the building and looked up at his room on the second floor. Was he moaning in bed? They said that cancer could cause tremendous pain in its last stages. Yan said that he'd rather die in his own bed surrounded by his books and papers than in a hospital. I stood in the shadow, trying to decide what to do. I couldn't walk into his room anymore, not since Yan's wife had written to the dean of his department accusing her husband of abandonment and neglect. She hadn't seen her husband for more than two years. What did he do at school during the summer? What stopped him from coming home during the three-month vacation? The dean summoned Yan to his office and asked him about his relationship with the "cousin" who had spent the summer in his room, then warned him not to let his personal life interfere with studies and degree. In his panic, Yan wrote warning me never to appear at his school again.

Students came in and out of the building, talking and laughing heartily. I took out my journal book and wrote: "Gege, I'm outside your building." I tore off the page, folded it into a swallow shape, and put it between the pages of *Moby Dick*. When I saw an honest-looking young man, I stopped him politely.

"Excuse me, comrade, could you pass this book to Yan Hua in Room 206?"

He was startled by my sudden appearance out of the dark. He looked at the book, then at me, his eyes asking, "Why don't you go in yourself?"

I forced a grin. "Well, it's kind of late for me to enter a boys' dormitory."

He took the book. "All right, I'll pass it to him."

In a minute, Yan will run out and cry in my arms, I told myself. *I'll comfort him and then I'll get something to eat.* I stepped back into the shadows to wait.

Ten minutes passed. Then twenty. My neck became stiff from straining to look at his window. If he was too sick to come out himself, at least he could send someone else to me. It had been almost an hour since the boy delivered my book. It suddenly occurred to me that he might have been sent to hospital. I knew I had to do something to find out where he was.

I threw a handful of sand at the window, waited a moment, then threw another handful. Someone turned off the music and light, opened the window, and shouted, "Get out of here, hoodlum!"

It wasn't Yan's voice. I retreated into the bush and sat down. My knees and ankles hurt as if thousands of needles were pricking them. My eyelids felt heavy, as if full of unsheddable tears. So I was a hoodlum sneaking around under a married man's window, breaking up his family. Yan had been telling me how awful his wife was and that I shouldn't feel too bad about her. What about his children? They didn't do anything wrong. Yan had begun to have his five-year-old son adopted by a distant relative in Canada so that he might be able to immigrate there some day. I had met Yan's daughter at the train station once. She leaned on her grandma's stomach, stealing angry glances at me. She knew something was going on between her father and me. I had touched her pigtail and had asked her if she made the beautiful braid by herself. She stepped back, her eyes filled with tears and hatred.

I shuddered. The temperature had dropped quickly since I had arrived. Ten past eleven. I needed to do something if I didn't want to spend the night out in the cold.

"Yan Hua, Yan Hua!" I called in a false, shrieking voice that cut the night into pieces.

The window opened. The man who had just shouted at me leaned out. "He's not here."

I almost asked him which hospital Yan was in when he spoke again, looking in my direction, but unable to see who I was. "Well, I don't think he'll come back tonight. He went to a concert with the dean's daughter at the city hall. He told me not to stay up to open the door for him. Come back tomorrow." He closed the window.

I stood in the bush until all the lights in the building went out and then I walked toward the iron gate of the campus. The night had frozen me inside out. How could I get back to Beijing? The thought of seeing Yan and asking for money was nauseating. I roamed the suburban streets of Dalian. If I could die tonight so that I wouldn't have to face him tomorrow! I fell into a ditch. It was much warmer down there than up on the surface. I curled up and waited for the dawn.

I fell asleep and had the dream that had been haunting me every night for the past year. I was groping in a deep valley, then a cave, then a mine. Dark water ran underneath my feet. I climbed among the sharp rocks, inch by inch, my nails cracked and worn out, my blood dyeing the rocks scarlet. Each time I reached the top, a pale man without eyes or nose or mouth stamped on my fingers, dancing wildly as I fell into the abyss.

I woke up hearing Yan sobbing over my stiff body. As soon as he saw me open my eyes, he began rubbing me from head to toe until I could move my joints and crawl out of the ditch. He took me to a restaurant nearby and ordered my favorite breakfast: boiling soy milk with dried shrimp and scallions with three drops of hot red pepper oil. I sipped the milk, listening to his babble of explanations. His dean was a powerful man who could get him assigned back to Hangzhou after he graduated. He went to the concert with the dean's daughter just to please him. If he'd known I was coming that night, he'd never have left his room. The fat girl was nothing to him.

Would I forgive him for faking the liver cancer? He wasn't himself when he wrote the letter. He didn't know I'd come all the way to see him. But he was so happy! He was reassured that I loved him and would do anything for him. He talked, sobbed, and laughed, and I watched him as if watching a stand-up comedian. Nothing mattered and everything mattered in the show. It all depended on the audience. The boiling milk brought some color to my face. But inside me, the iceberg was still there.

Yan found a place in the basement of an abandoned building and I stayed there for a week. During the day, he took me to different restaurants for the famous Dalian seafood. At night he made love to me with urgency, as if we were never going to see each other again. He talked on and on, day and night, and I listened in silence, my face a mask set in a perpetual faint smile. I'd passed the deadline to register for the graduate entrance exams, but nothing seemed to matter anymore. Somehow there was a kind of pleasure in abandoning myself completely for a while.

But it would be just a while.

Chapter Fourteen

A YEAR WENT BY quickly. It was again the week to register for the graduate entrance exams. Yan had arrived in Beijing without warning and checked into a small hotel near the campus. He claimed he had come to do his final research for his master's thesis. I said nothing. He knew, and I knew, why he was here. Last year, when I was in Dalian, I had agreed to go back to Hangzhou after my graduation, either as a graduate student or as an employee. But Yan didn't trust me. He had come to Beijing to make sure I would not register for the entrance exams for Beijing University. So far, he hadn't mentioned a word about it. He just visited me every day with all sorts of fruit and food.

One afternoon, he rushed in without knocking on the door. "Meimei, put on your green jacket and get ready to go. I want you to meet somebody. Hurry."

"Who?" I asked without looking up from my book.

"Mr. Zhou. Come on, we have to be there at five o'clock." He took the book away from my hand.

"Who is he?" I asked impatiently.

"Mr. Zhou, my cousin from America. He came here to buy antiques for his stores in New York. Where's your memory? Finally I can meet him. This was why I rushed to Beijing. I didn't tell you because I wanted to surprise you."

"Where's he staying?"

"The Great Wall. Isn't he something? Oh, I feel so excited. We have a lot of hope, Meimei. I'm sure he'll sponsor me to go to America."

I stopped combing my hair. The Great Wall Hotel, the largest and fanciest hotel in Beijing, had caused a lot of excitement and controversy when it was completed a few months ago.

"Can we get in? It's only for foreigners and Hong Kong businessmen."

"Yes, if we register. Don't braid your hair too tight. Loosen it a little bit. There now, it looks really sexy. OK, let's go." He pulled me out of the dormitory.

Though I had heard much about the elegance and luxury of the hotel, I was still shocked at the sight of the illuminated glass edifice towering above the low gray residential houses nearby. A piece of the replica of the Great Wall stood at the entrance, surrounded by fountains spraying water in firework patterns under the light.

"How much did it cost to build this?" I wondered, thinking of the dormitory room I shared with nine roommates, of Waipo's room with three generations packed together, and of the millions of lovers who had been waiting for years for the government to assign them a room for their marriages.

The guard at the door checked our IDs and told us to write down our address, school, telephone number, age, time and reason for visit, name of person we wanted to meet, his age, occupation, and room number. While Yan was filling out the form, I looked at the exquisite Mongolian carpets on the floor and walls. There was a strong smell of musk and rose in the air that tightened my throat.

"Are you nervous?" Yan elbowed me as we walked towards the elevator. "I am, but we'll get used to it soon. Our house in America will also look this." His voice sounded muffled and fake. I didn't respond.

"Call him cousin, as I do. You're my girlfriend and will be my wife. We're all relatives." I gave him a look. Since when did Zhou and Yan become relatives? They had called each other cousins while Zhou was living with Yan's family only for the reason that the police would not suspect Zhou was the son of an escaped capitalist couple.

Zhou was on the phone when we entered the room. He made a gesture for us to sit on the sofa and continued his phone conversation. He wore steel-framed glasses. His cheeks puffed like a squirrel. His skin was pale and smooth. He looked younger than Yan at first glance. Soon he put down the phone and shook my hand. "Good, good, I've heard a lot about you. You must be talented to get into Beijing University." He smiled warmly, his face wrinkled like worn-out silk.

Yan winced at his remark but immediately started talking about the mischievous things they had done together in their childhood. Zhou listened and laughed like a child.

"Cousin," he patted Yan's shoulder, "I'm not boasting, but when I fled China with forty jin of rice coupons, who would believe someday I'd come back a millionaire, a big capitalist with two antique stores in Manhattan? I was considered dull, remember? I was dull. To swim across the border with those rice coupons at the risk of my life, only to find out they were worthless in Hong Kong! Who would believe that you, Yan Hua, the smartest boy at school, would greet me in this hotel?" He laughed till he was out of breath. "It's fate, pure fate, my dear cousin. If I had stayed here, I might be laying bricks for this hotel."

"That's right, Ah Ge," Yan said, changing cousin to brother in a natural tone. "Luck and opportunity, plus talent and encouragement. What do you think of me, Ah Ge?" He thrust out his chest. "I'm not stupid. I work hard. And I'm willing to take risks. All I need is an opportunity, which only you, Ah Ge, can give me. You can change my life."

Zhou gave him a quick look through his thick glasses, then glanced at me. "Mm, your background isn't bad. I'll think about it. Well, I'm sure your pretty girlfriend is hungry. It's our first meeting, so I must give her a big treat. Ah Lan!" he hollered.

A woman in her mid-thirties stepped out of the bedroom, rubbing her hair with a white towel. She wore a fluffy white bathrobe that was loosely tied around the waist. Her face was pink and fresh from the steam. She stood at the door for a second when she saw the guests, then moved languidly towards Zhou.

"What's going on, Jimmy?" She smiled at Yan and rested her arm on the back of Zhou's chair. Yan's eye grew wide as he watched her massaging Zhou's neck affectionately.

"My secretary, Miss Lan. My cousins Yan Hua and Ni Bing," Zhou introduced us briefly. "Know any good restaurants around here?"

She tilted her head, her hair floating over her shoulder and arm. I noticed a little black mole at the nape of her neck. It made her skin look milky and tender. Yan couldn't tear his eyes away from the spot.

"Mmm, I think Maxim's at Congwenmeng would be a good place, the best French gourmet in Beijing. The ingredients are imported from Paris. I know the manager there. But the place . . ."

Zhou waved his hand. "Money, small peanuts. I want to have some fun tonight. Would you call your friend for a table? I'm starving."

She glanced at me. "That's not what I was thinking about, Jimmy. I'm afraid we have to be dressed up for that restaurant."

My cheeks burned with embarrassment. Both Yan and Zhou had their ties on. I was wearing my jeans, the only decent pants I had. What did she mean by *dressed up?* What was I supposed to wear?

"Gege," I turned to Yan. "Maybe you and your cousin should go. I'll go back to school."

"Nonsense," Zhou shouted. "The party is for you. Ah Lan, do something for her."

Lan beckoned to me and led me into her room. She opened a box filled with bottles and tubes, then her suitcase.

"Let's see your sweater," she said, her eyes searching for something suitable in the suitcase.

I took off my green jacket. Even my best clothing looked cheap in the mirror.

"Not too bad," she murmured, pulling at the beige turtleneck. "Your boots will go well with brown. All right, try this." She fished a brown corduroy skirt out of the suitcase and threw it on the bed. "Put it on quickly. I have to do your hair."

I stared at the skirt and didn't move. No one wore a skirt in March in Beijing. But the idea was really exciting.

"You can use the bathroom," she pointed at the door in the corner, thinking I was too shy to change in front of her. Without men around, her movements became crisp and aggressive.

The spotlessly clean toilet and bathtub shocked me. If only I could jump in the tub and have a bath! I couldn't remember the last time I had had the luxury of a bath. I changed quickly.

"Not bad at all." Lan turned me around to see the skirt, tugging it at the waist. "A bit too big here, eh? You're young and slim, like I used to be. Doesn't matter. Your sweater will cover it. Now sit down here."

In the mirror, I noticed that Ah Lan had blown her hair into a wavy shape over her shoulders, put on her lipstick, and rouged her cheeks while I was in the bathroom. *That was quick,* I thought, holding my breath as she pulled my hair back tightly to make a braid.

"There you go," she finally said, holding a mirror behind me to let me see what she had done. The braid began from the middle of my head and went down to the waist. It was so tight that my eyes were pulled upward like those of a woman on an antique vase.

"You look good in a French braid. Put on some rouge." She dabbed at my cheeks so suddenly that I backed away in surprise.

"Sit still. You have good skin. I used to have skin like that. Young girl, don't waste your youth. It doesn't last long." She looked at me and herself in the mirror, her hands still in the air.

I didn't know how to respond to her advice. In the awkward silence, I asked, "Am I done, Miss Lan?"

She jumped. "Wait a minute. You can't go to the restaurant bare-legged. Take this."

She opened a drawer and pulled out a pair of black panty hose. It was surprising to discover that such thin material could make me feel much warmer. Today I had had many firsts—the rouge and lipstick, the French braid, the skirt in early spring, the stockings.

"You look good," Zhou said as soon as we came out. I blushed, wondering if Zhou was praising Miss Lan or me. Yan came over and put his arm around my shoulders, as if claiming me as his belonging.

When we left the hotel, a taxi appeared out of the darkness and stopped alongside us. We got in without questions or bargains. It was understood that Zhou would pay the driver in foreign exchange money. When we got to the restaurant, he handed him a ten-yuan note and waved off the change. Lan's friend Tony, the manager, greeted us in the lobby and helped us take off our coats. We sat down at a small round table with a rose and a red candle. A band was playing upstairs. On the walls were imitations of Renaissance paintings.

"Something to drink?" Tony asked. He gestured to a waiter, who immediately brought out a bottle of red wine. "On the house," he said.

"How's business, Tony?" Lan asked. Both Zhou and this Chinese manager had Western names. Did all Chinese change their names when they lived abroad?

"Not so good," he sighed. "The food is overpriced. Most of the foreigners here are tourists. Of course they prefer Chinese food, which is inexpensive, tasty, and exotic. Why should they spend a fortune on French food in China? And the silly rule for ties and dresses. Who wants to be dressed up for a casual dinner? It's Beijing, not Paris. I suggested to the French manager that we should be more adaptable. We should accept yuan so the Chinese can come. They are the ones who are really interested in French gourmet. It's suicide to take only foreign exchange money. But he won't listen."

Lan took out a cigarette. Tony lit it for her with a silver lighter.

"How long have you been open?" She puffed the smoke elegantly.

"Eight months. Time passes slowly here, and the nights are long. Nowhere to go after eleven. Everything closed. I'm tired of complaining. Ready for dinner?"

We went upstairs. The dining room was even more luxuriously decorated. The band—piano, drums and bass—was playing on a stage in the back. I had never seen these instruments play together. The music they created sounded strange, sad, and exciting at the same time. As I stared at the long-haired musicians, a girl in a black velvet evening dress came over to greet us. She had smooth olive skin, her big almond-shaped eyes outlined with long and curly eyelashes, a mixture of oriental and Western features. Her hair was straight and short, the left side an inch shorter than the right. A pair of moon-and-star earrings hung over her bare shoulders.

"My hostess, Miss Chow," Tony introduced her as he kissed her hand. "Without her, my life here would be a desert."

"Miss Chow is the most beautiful Asian girl I've seen," Lan said.

"Only half. My father is French." Her voice was deep and proud. I couldn't keep my eyes off her.

Five waiters came up from behind us. I moved my chair to sit down when a waiter rushed forward. What did he want? I gave him a look as I sat down.

"Excuse me," he said, his hands gripping the back of my chair.

"Sorry," I said, then thought maybe I should thank him. Suddenly he grunted and left. I sighed and tried to put my elbows on the table to relax. Then I realized my problem. My chair was half a foot away from the table. The waiter had been trying to move my chair closer to the table, but I had sat down too quickly and had been too dumb to let him fix it. I stretched my back and bent forward. My elbows barely reached the edge of the table. I dared not move my chair. All the waiters stood in a line behind me, all in black tails, watching. I glanced at Yan. He had become quiet since we entered Maxim's, carefully watching how Zhou and Lan put the napkins on their knees. Zhou ordered beef steak. He wanted it rare.

"The same for me," Yan told the waiter.

I stared at the menu. None of the names meant anything to me.

"Miss Ni, what would you like?" Lan said from across the table. I looked up and met the mocking eyes of the waiter who had tried to adjust my chair. He was holding his order book.

"Sole filet, please." But what the hell was that?

"What soup would you like?" he asked patiently.

"Soup? No soup, please."

I immediately sensed I had made another mistake. Lan exchanged a look with Zhou and smiled.

"Miss Ni, French soup is very special. You'll like it."

I picked up the menu again. Everyone was watching. My stomach began to twitch with a sharp pain. Damn it. What I was doing here? I wished that I was sitting in the campus canteen eating steamed bread and corn porridge with my roommates.

"Vegetable soup, please." I finally found something I could identify.

"Good choice," Lan approved. The waiter brought me a colorful plate of green, red, orange, and yellow stuff mashed and arranged neatly in the shape of a flower. I couldn't believe this was my soup. At least this was not my idea of a soup. It looked more like thick porridge or the homemade glue my grandma used to make shoe soles. I waited until everyone else picked up their spoons. At first, my glue tasted like nothing. Gradually, I recognized spinach, carrots, and celery.

"How's the soup, Miss Ni?" Tony asked. I nodded my head. "Good," I said, but my stomach cramps were getting worse.

The main course came.

"Excellent, excellent," Zhou said while cutting his steak, blood oozing from the meat. I turned my eyes away. How could Yan eat this kind of meat? "Your chef is number one, better than my master in Paris."

"I didn't know you've been to Paris, Ah Ge," Yan asked in surprise.

"Name a place I haven't been to. None! Europe, Southeast

Asia, South America, even Africa. When I got off the plane at
J.F.K. in New York, I had only six bucks in my pocket. I started
as a busboy, a dishwasher, then a waiter, chef, chief chef."

"Ah Ge, but you look so young and well preserved. Who could
believe you've been through so much hardship?" Yan's voice was
full of admiration.

"Hardship?" He stared at Yan. "Are you kidding? The second
day I arrived in New York, my agency sent me to a Chinese
restaurant in New Jersey to wash dishes. I got off at the wrong
station. I didn't speak English. I had only two bucks left. The
snow was up to my knees. Was it hardship? No, it was a dog's life.
You want to succeed in America? Be a dog first. Remember,
you're a foreigner, a chink. You have no money, no visa, you
speak no English, you must start at the dirtiest, lowest, humblest
job. Then, someday, if you're lucky, you can sit here with your
relatives and friends to enjoy your money." Zhou waved his fork
and knife around as if he were fighting against an invisible enemy,
his eyes as bloody as the steak. Yan kept nodding his head.

I cut my filet with my fork. It must be fish, then, since it
looked like a fish. But it had no bones. The chef must have taken
them out, mashed the flesh, and restored its original shape. What
was the purpose of all that trouble? The cramps were giving me
such a terrible pain. I wished I could lie down on my small bunk
bed. I forced myself to eat because Tony was looking at my plate
with sadness. The creamy taste of the fish made me sick.

"Do you like it?" he asked.

"Yes. Can I have something hot to drink?"

"Sure. Tea?"

"Please. Thanks."

Tony signaled to a waiter and told him to get the madam a cup
of tea. I didn't care that everyone turned to me in surprise, or
that my steaming tea made them rush their meals. I just wanted
to get rid of my pain.

Two waiters wheeled in the desserts on a cart. Each chose
one, but I shook my head.

"Try some chocolates. They're very good," Tony said gently, and put two pieces on my plate. "You don't have to eat if you don't like them."

I smiled to him gratefully. He was the only one who hadn't given up on me. The tea had made me feel much better. I bit the chocolate and finished it all. Tony was really pleased. He called a waiter and whispered something to him.

"You did well," Ah Lan told me as we walked downstairs. "First Western dinner for you, right?"

In the lobby, a waiter handed me a package in the shape of a Beijing duck.

"It's made of the chocolate you like," Tony said.

Lan looked at me as if to say, "I told you."

Zhou gave me a red envelope. "Sorry I didn't bring you anything from New York. I didn't know I was going to meet you. Take this and get whatever you like. It's my first-time-meeting present."

I looked at Yan. He made a gesture for me to open the envelope. Inside was a hundred-dollar bill. It was more than my entire annual salary when I taught in Hangzhou.

Chapter Fifteen

YAN WAS GOING BACK to Dalian on Sunday. He had finished his research and had no reason to stay in Beijing any longer. He hadn't mentioned a word about my registering for the graduate exams, which were to end at five on Saturday. I had almost convinced myself that perhaps he had changed his mind about them when he asked if he could have a serious talk with me on Friday night. We went to the Weiming Lake.

Yan patted the white handkerchief he had spread on the ground and said, "Sit here, Meimei."

Finally, I thought, leaning against a tree to support myself. *Ni Bing,* I told myself, *don't be afraid. He's not your mother or father. Tell him what you want and everything will be fine.*

He sighed when he saw that I was determined not to sit next to him. "Did you have a good time with your friend at People's University?"

"Yes," I answered with hesitation, surprised by this unexpected question. I looked down and saw his nose quivering, a sign of fury. I shifted my feet from side to side, my nails digging into the tree bark.

"Really?" he said sarcastically. "I met your roommate Huli this afternoon. She saw you in the library the whole afternoon.

Besides, she didn't know you have any friend at People's University. Can you explain that?"

I pressed against the tree, wishing to become part of it. Trees had no need to talk.

"I don't understand why you told me lies. If you'd told me you just wanted to study, I wouldn't have had any problem with that. I have a lot to do here myself. Tell me why you did this to me. This isn't your first time. I didn't want to talk about it because I had been hoping you might change. Now, would you please explain?"

I stared into the lake. Nothing there except for its immense darkness. What could I say? I didn't know why I had to lie about everything to Yan. I just felt like it. It made me feel good.

"Are you ashamed? I'd feel terrible if I lied to you. I always believe there should be no secrets between us. It's a matter of honesty."

I burst out laughing into his face. Honesty. This from the guy who faked liver cancer to stop me from going to the graduate school. "Honesty, since when have you believed in it? You taught me to tell lies to my family and friends. I'm your cousin to your colleagues and classmates. To my family, you're a good friend. And here, where no one knows your background, we're lovers. I'm getting really good after all these years of practice. I can tell lies without blushing. You want to know why I tell you lies? Well, lying has become part of my nature."

"You're cynical, Meimei." He sounded as if he were mourning my death.

"Cynical? No, I'm lonely. I don't have friends anymore. I've lost contact with reality. I don't go out except when you take me. I live in a room with nine people, but we have nothing to say to each other. As soon as I enter the room, they stop talking and laughing. The only person still talking to me is Huli."

"Meimei," he held out his hands. "What about me, what about our love?"

"What about it? Our love is nothing but lies and shame. Can we tell anyone about it? You couldn't even tell Zhou that you're married, and he's supposed to have seen the world and have an open mind."

"Meimei," he said in despair, "you have to believe in our love, our future. That's the only thing left for us."

"How dare you mention the word future! If you had really cared, you'd have divorced your wife. Or you'd have controlled your stupid jealousy and anger when Zhou kissed me good-bye at the airport. What the hell was on your mind when you pushed him away and cursed him? You cut the only hope for our future, so stop telling me about love or honesty or future! It makes me sick."

In the dead silence, I heard him sobbing. I clenched my fists, but my voice softened against my will.

"I have the same nightmare every night, Gege. As soon as I close my eyes, I dream of being pushed off a cliff. I'm afraid of the night. Gege, if you really love me, give me two more years. Let me finish the graduate program in Beijing University. The best university, the best faculty, the best library. And my thesis advisor Yang Han wants me to be in his program. He's seventy-nine. I'll be his last student. It's a great honor. He's the best scholar on Western literature in China. If he wants me, the department will have nothing to say. He's the only person who has some faith in me, do you understand? Everyone else in the department thinks I'm a good-for-nothing after what happened last year. Gege, this is something I really want. It's the first and last favor I ask you. Please!"

"I can't live without you, Meimei," he said after a long silence.

I jumped up and screamed. "Yes, you can, you can! We've never lived together, and never will. You know it better than I. You'll never risk your reputation for our relationship. You've wiped away every single trace of us. If I were to tell your wife or boss that we've been lovers, I couldn't even prove it because you've taken back every fucking letter you wrote me. Why the hell do you want me to go to Hangzhou? First of all, you're still in Dalian. How can you be sure that you'll be assigned back to Hangzhou when you graduate? Even if you are, everyone in that city knows you're married. Can we walk in the streets together? Can you visit me and spend time with me as you do here? I can't stand sneaking around any more. I'm twenty-six. I need a normal life. Have you ever thought about it?" I paused for a moment, my throat burning from talking so much and so fast. Yan had stopped sobbing.

"Listen, Gege, listen carefully, because I'm telling you the truth. This morning I registered for the graduate program at Beijing University. I'm not going to change my mind no matter what you say or do. Nor am I going to see you during the next two years unless you get a divorce. For once in my life, I have to think about myself."

I planted my feet firmly on the ground, ready for a scene. Yan sat motionless, clasping his knees. I looked at the dark water, then at Yan. *I must leave now,* I told myself.

"Good-bye, Gege, I wish we truly were brother and sister."

I walked away quickly. Before I turned, I looked back. The street lamp extended my shadow all the way to the rock where Yan was sitting. He raised his foot and stamped down. I ducked my head and he missed the shadow.

I WAITED TWO DAYS for Yan's reaction. To my surprise, he didn't call or come. I began to ask myself if I had been too cruel to him, worried that he might do something stupid to himself, although I kept telling myself that his absence was just one of his tricks. On the third night, I was thinking of going to Yan's hotel to see if he had checked out, when Huli came and said she had some-thing important to tell me. We strolled along the campus road. Neither spoke for a while.

"I've been thinking about you and Yan these days," she said finally. "I think that I was naive and that my opinion about Yan was one-sided."

I gave her an anxious look. I had told Huli briefly about my breakup with Yan. When she heard that Yan was trying to stop me from entering the graduate program at Beijing University, she

got excited. Yan had no right to make me sacrifice my indepen-
dence and education. If he really loved me, he should encourage
me to take advantage of this opportunity. Love should be mutu-
al and balanced, based on consideration and respect. Who did he
think I was? Some meek, traditional girl born and bred to
sacrifice? She would give Yan a piece of her mind! She had talked
on and on, waving her fist in indignation. That was three days
ago. Now she was singing a different tune.

"I think," she said in a high-pitched voice, "you should go to
Hangzhou and join Yan."

I couldn't believe my ears. Was she the same person who had
suggested I should carry a pair of scissors or a knife in case Yan
lost his temper?

"Have you been seeing Yan?" I asked.

She nodded solemnly. "He wrote me a letter the other day.
After I read it, I went to his hotel and we talked for two
evenings. He told me everything."

Everything! I looked at Huli sadly. She was four years younger
than I, twenty-two, the age when Yan took my virginity. I was
probably even more naive and dramatic at that age.

"He talked a lot about his life, how you two helped and loved
each other during the difficult periods. Ni Bing, I think he's
right. You can't be complete without each other."

I felt like knocking my only friend down, then running to Yan's
hotel to shoot him. In two evenings, he had turned my only ally
into his loudspeaker. I sighed. Huli was an easy target. She was
madly in love with her father, claiming he was the greatest, the
best-looking, the most brilliant and talented man on earth who
admired her as the perfect beauty except for her dark skin. But
even dark skin was becoming fashionable these days. "My dad said
that all Western women would die to have tan skin like mine," she
said with such seriousness that all the girls in the dormitory
laughed. I admired her for her innocent seriousness and warmth.
We'd taken many after-dinner walks around the campus.

"Yan is great." The passion in her voice reminded me of the

times when she had talked about her father. "His letter made me cry. You should read it." She took a thick envelope out of her bag.

I didn't want to read it, but my hand took the letter against my will. I was dying to know how Yan had converted Huli into his disciple. It began with his childhood, his adolescence, his youth during the Cultural Revolution, and his years in the countryside, the same stories that had attracted me to him. In spite of my disgust, I had to admit that he was a great storyteller.

Huli said, "Ni Bing, I may be too young to tell you this, but as you have often said, a woman can be happy and complete only when she has found her true love, the other half. Ni Bing, you've found your other half, and you should do all you can to keep him."

Did I say that? The other half, true love—those were Yan's favorite remarks.

"I know how you love him without reservation. You've turned yourself into him. You are he and he is you. It's too late to deny him because it would mean denying yourself. How can you throw away your past and present?"

I bent my head. Yan had completely hypnotized Huli and was exercising his power through her. How could I deny my past? It was true that I had loved him as my other half. Breaking up with him was like killing myself. At twenty-six, I had passed the golden age for girls. Without Yan, I'd become a social problem—an old maid. There were thousands of single female intellectuals about my age in Beijing. The party and youth league organizations tried to match them up with men by giving dance parties. As long as I continued having a boyfriend, at least no one would try to persuade me to go to those awful parties.

"Tell him," I said, my face turned away from Huli, "if he can transfer my registration from Beijing University to Hangzhou, it must be my fate to follow him and I'll submit to it. Tell him I don't want to see him before the exams. I want to concentrate on my preparation."

Huli ran away to give Yan the good news. I looked up to the sky and shouted to myself: "Old heavens, help me! Don't let him succeed." The strict regulation for applying to graduate school was my last hope. It was forbidden to change schools once the applicant registered. But Yan was smart. Nothing stopped him. Once again, I let myself fall into his trap. I hit my head against a tree trunk. No, I was not going to let him control my life anymore. I must stay in Beijing at any cost, even if it meant I had to give up graduate school! Even if I had to fail the graduate entrance exams deliberately!

Chapter Sixteen

WE DINED IN THE WESTERN ROOM of the Great Wall Hotel. Zhou ordered a hamburger for me after he watched me stare at the menu helplessly for ten minutes. I took a bite and almost threw up from the bloody grease oozing out of the ground beef. The bread tasted fresh. I decided to eat that first.

"Why are you eating bread with a fork?" Zhou asked with amusement.

"Oh, I thought I should use a knife and fork for everything in a Western restaurant." I chuckled to cover my embarrassment, put down the fork, and leaned back in my chair. In a corner of the restaurant, a woman was playing a Chopin serenade.

It was quite a shock when Zhou called me from the hotel. After Yan had made such an awful scene at the airport, I assumed I would never see him again. Yan had pulled me away from Zhou's embrace, cursing like a lunatic. He'd have hit him in the face if Lan hadn't caught his hand. Zhou gave Yan a contemptuous look and said, "Brother, you'll never make it."

On the phone, Zhou told me casually that he had just arrived in Beijing to buy more antique porcelain and asked if I had time to have dinner with him. I hesitated for a moment. I was still ashamed of what Yan had done. Then I thought perhaps I could take the opportunity to explain things to him for Yan.

Sitting across each other at the table, we didn't mention Yan's name, but both of us were conscious of his absence.

"Well, Jimmy, how was your meeting this afternoon?" I asked. Zhou had insisted that I call him Gege. "Or simply Jimmy," he said, laughing heartily.

"I signed an extraordinary contract, two million dollars worth of vases. Guess how much I paid?" He held out his palm. "Fifty grand. Unbelievable!" He cut into his pork chop vigorously. "It's too easy—a few cartons of Marlboros, a few bottles of whiskey, some cash. Those cheap, corrupted wastrels. They sell priceless vases like they're throwing out garbage. Ignorant! Greedy!" He shook his head sadly, as if worried about the future of his native country. "How many more antiques can they trade for limousines, color TVs and whiskey?

"Anyway," he raised his beer glass, "let's not spoil the fun for tonight. Lucky that those vases fell into my hands. I like art. I treat it with respect. Thank you for coming to see me." He touched my glass with his and drank up. "Ask me a favor, anything, while I'm in a good mood. It makes me happy to do something for you. Make a wish, quick."

"Forgive Yan and help him to go to America," I said without thinking. I couldn't believe it was my own voice. Why was I doing this when I hated him so?

Zhou poured himself another glass of beer. "You must be kidding," he said after taking a big sip.

"I'm not. He wants to go abroad really bad. You're the only one who can help him. I know he acted stupid at the airport. You must forgive him. He couldn't control his jealousy because he loves me too much."

"Do you really believe he loves you? Why on earth didn't he get a divorce?"

I almost jumped. How did he know the truth? Yan had warned me not to say a word about his marriage so that Zhou wouldn't think badly of him.

"He must have also promised to help you go there after him," he went on, waving his hand impatiently. "Do you realize you'll never see him again once he's out? Even if he has the intention of bringing you over later, which I very much doubt, there's not much he can do unless he has a green card. It will take him at least five or six years to get one, if he's lucky. Most people I know have been living there illegally over ten years. Even when he has one, he still can't help you because you're not his wife. Do you understand? He's writing you a bad check."

I poked at my hamburger with the fork. His words stabbed my heart. Although I had known all this, part of me still clung to Yan and his promises. But Zhou had destroyed the last illusion.

"Tell me how you met. Tell me everything before I can make a decision."

The sincerity in his voice touched me. I looked up at him. For the first time, I didn't see sarcasm in his eyes. He seemed to really care about me. Perhaps he could pull me out of the dark water. I placed my hands between my knees like an elementary school student and began to talk. By the time I had finished, the restaurant was empty except for our table. A waitress approached with a polite smile and asked if we needed anything else.

"Just the check, please." Zhou's eyes followed her slim waist and the curve of her legs beneath her tight white qipao uniform. "Pretty," he muttered.

For a second, I regretted having told so much to person I'd met only twice. Why should he care?

"I think you should stop seeing him." Zhou turned to me, each word sounding like the pounding of a hammer. "You're too good for him. Understand? You're an intelligent woman. You shouldn't waste your talent on a jerk."

Each new statement was more shocking than the last. Yan a jerk? Was he reaching a conclusion too soon? And me, talented? For all these years, Yan had told me I could do nothing without him.

"Trust me," he said, amused by the shock on my face. "I'm good at judging people, having seen so many of them. He's definitely a jerk, and you're very gifted. It makes me mad to see people like you being dominated by people like Yan. I want to help you." He paused, then said, "Do you want to study in New York?"

My brain went blank for a second. I had never thought about it, although Yan had constantly talked about going to the United States and helping me get there. It was just too unrealistic. Finally I stammered, "Of cour-course I do. But what about Yan?"

He waved his hand in disgust. "You don't want to wake up, do you? Can't you see? He's too clever. Everything he does is for his own benefit. You may be blinded by love, but he can't deceive me. Someday he'll be ruined by his own cleverness. Ni Bing, you've got to think about yourself, at least sometimes, if you want to survive and succeed. I want to train someone I can trust and feel comfortable with, someone like you, smart, reliable. Don't think I'm helping you out of charity or sympathy. I'm making a good investment in my own interest."

I stared at him in disbelief. "But what can I do for you in America? I have no business experience; I'm just a bookworm. The only thing I know is literature."

"Lots of things. You're attractive and intelligent. I'm thinking of training you to be my manager. Eventually, you'll do the traveling for me. I'm getting old. I want to spend more time with my family. Want to see my children?"

He fished a photo from his wallet and handed it to me. A boy and girl sat on the lap of a woman wearing heavy makeup and permed hair. Zhou pointed to her.

"My wife. She's from Taiwan. She married me the year she got her Ph.D. I'm still puzzled why she fell in love with an uncouth fellow like me. My children are going to college, like you, like my wife. It's for them that I'm working like a slave."

"They're lovely," I said, watching him put the photo back with care.

"Well, what do you say about my proposal?"

"Are you sure I can do well in business?"

"Trust me. I can make jade out of you. Of course, no one can guarantee anything. We all have to take risks. But you know what?" He winked. "No risk, no big money, and I like to add, no fun." He raised his glass. "So I assume that you've accepted my proposal. Let's toast to our future."

He clinked my glass and drank up. "Now we're going to talk business. I heard that Dinghai, the island where your parents live, is buying and selling used ships. I want to look into that. Since I'm going to Shanghai for more antique dealings, I'd like to make a trip there. Do you think you can go with me? Can you take a week off?"

I quickly thought about the possibility. It was early June. I'd taken the graduate entrance exams about three weeks ago and had finished my graduate thesis. No one would notice my absence, since I no longer had any friends at Beijing University. Huli and I had become distant since she had become Yan's ally. No one would care.

"Yes," I said with great sadness and excitement. "When do we leave?"

THE NO. 13 EXPRESS from Shanghai to Beijing stopped at Nanjing Station. I shook hands with Zhou and watched him climb into the car sent by the Nanjing Antique Art Export Company. He was going to do more business here before flying to New York.

I stretched out across the soft bed. Without Zhou and his foreign exchange money, I'd never have been able to get into this first-class car, which was open only to foreigners, high-ranking officials, and their children. Compared to the hard-berth and hard-seat cars, it was like heaven. Clean, quiet, plenty of room to move around, no suffocating smoke from the beginning to the end of the trip. And you didn't have to crawl over passengers' heads to get to the bathroom or dining car. What was more, you didn't have to feel guilty for having a seat while some older people without seats stood in front of you, shifting their weight on their sore legs. When people couldn't get tickets, they often sneaked onto the train with platform tickets. I'd done that many times. It was a real ordeal to travel from one place to another. The government claimed more trains and railways were being made every year, but it made no difference. China was too big and too crowded.

The trip to Dinghai hadn't been successful. I introduced Zhou to some dealers who sold the parts of machines from old ships. But they asked for too much money for Zhou to make a profit. Zhou comforted me and said that no one could guarantee that each trip would be a success. He was glad to meet my parents and my sisters, glad that I had my first taste of the business world. Before he left, he gave me his card, home address and telephone number, and assured me that he would send me application forms for graduate schools as soon as he got back to New York.

But why? I kept asking myself. It would cost him a fortune to pay the first-year tuition and living expenditures, plus my plane ticket to New York. He said that he was tired of flying back and forth between New York and China, leaving his family behind. He seemed to be sincere about training me and always treated me with respect. He flirted with waitresses and service girls whenever he had a chance, but he never made a pass at me.

I doubted my potential as a businesswoman. I couldn't even count my own money well. I used to be quite proud of myself for not being tempted by wealth after having grown up in poverty, but now I began to doubt that also, for I truly enjoyed the privileges that Zhou's money could buy.

The door opened. I sat up in my bed and saw two white men at the door. The tall one in a brown leather jacket nodded at me and entered with a suitcase. After putting it carefully onto the luggage rack, he took the small case for the short man and laid it on the bed across from me. They were talking to each other in a language I didn't know. From their looks and gestures, I guessed they were wondering if the two upper beds had been taken. I pointed at them and said *Empty* in English.

Their faces lit up. "Oh, you speak English," they both cried out. The tall man quickly introduced himself. "I'm John and this is Bruno. Bruno is going to Beijing. Are you going there also?"

I nodded. He pulled me aside immediately. "Bruno is my boss, a very important man from Fiat. Do you know Fiat, an Italian car company? No? What a pity! Bruno has to go to Beijing for some important business, but all the airplane tickets are sold out. He's upset that he has to take the train. I'm so glad you're here. Will you take care of him? He doesn't speak Chinese at all."

I glanced at Bruno and his bald head, disappointed that John wasn't going. He seemed much easier to talk with than his boss, who had been standing against the wall as if nailed there. An army officer pushed the door open and stuck his head into the car with his hand on the knob. The sight of two white men startled him. He withdrew quickly and slammed the door behind him.

Two lao wai in that room, I heard him telling his companions.

Bruno began talking to John at a fast speed. He looked anxious and irritated.

"Are those beds taken?" John asked me.

I shook my head. "They've been empty since the train started from Shanghai. But someone may come in at any station, just as you did. You never know."

"We want to buy the two beds to make sure that no soldier shares a room with us," he said as he walked out.

It was my turn to be startled. A first-class ticket was worth a half-year of my salary. John came back with the head of the train crew. He didn't speak English, and John asked me to interpret for him. I explained the situation, telling him that the gentleman was not used to sharing a room with strangers, and asking if it were possible for him to buy the two beds. The crewman stared at them, his jaws moving as if he were chewing something. Finally he said it was against the rules, but if the gentleman wasn't feeling well, they could talk it over. He gave John a look before he walked out. John grabbed his bag and followed him. Five minutes later, he returned with a new conductor.

"We made it," he called to his boss in English. "It was easy. All I needed was cigarettes and whiskey."

I blushed, feeling ashamed and offended. Bruno noticed it. "It's the same everywhere," he said. I smiled at him with appreciation and started interpreting for John and the conductor. The two tickets cost seven hundred sixty yuan in foreign exchange money. John was forty yuan short. The conductor waited with a smile on his face. John took out a handful of colorful Italian money and handed it to him. "Would you take this?"

He shook his head. "Only foreign exchange money, cash, no check, nothing." He spoke perfect English. He must have heard what John had said about cigarettes and whiskey. It was his turn to laugh. Bruno turned to me.

"I have forty yuan," I said, touched by his desperate look, wondering at the same time if I was doing the right thing to lend my only cash to these strangers. "If you don't mind, you can borrow it and return it to me when you get to Beijing."

"Great. I can't thank you enough for your generosity." John jumped up as if he were going to hug me. The conductor grunted as he took the money from me, handed John two tickets, and left without saying another word.

The train started moving. Bruno and I sat on our own beds, trying to make conversation. The train crew came in three times without knocking. Each time, Bruno jumped and became moodier. Finally we gave up and took out books to read. The conductor came in for the fourth time to check our tickets.

"How come you got on the train at Shanghai Station?" His eyebrows lifted.

"What do you mean? I started my journey at Shanghai."

"Aren't you together?" he pointed to Bruno with his chin. I looked at him, puzzled. "I mean, don't you work for him? Aren't you his interpreter or something?"

"Oh, no!" I said, still unaware of the coming danger. "I don't work for him. We just met on this train."

He grunted with satisfaction and left. Before I had time to tell Bruno what had happened, he returned and beckoned me out.

"The chief conductor wants to speak to you. Come with me."

There was no chief conductor in the office. Instead, two men in police uniforms were waiting for me. One pointed at a bench for me. As soon as I sat down, he began his questions, and the other took notes in his book.

"Did you know Bruno before?"

"No."

"Why did you lend him forty yuan, then? It's a lot of money for a student."

I shrugged my shoulders. "I don't know. When I saw he was desperate, I felt sorry and offered my help. I'm sure he'll give it back to me. No big deal."

"Desperate for what?" He rolled his eyes. "To get rid of other passengers so he can be with you alone all night?"

"What?" I couldn't believe what he was hinting at. "He just didn't want to share a room with soldiers, because one of them had already entered our room without knocking. I'm sure he'd like to have the room to himself. But I was there before him, and he can't throw me out, right? Besides," I suddenly thought of something, "if you suspected that he intended to do something with me, why did you let him buy the two beds? It would have been so easy for you to refuse him—just say they were booked." My anger rose as I spoke.

"We thought you worked for him. It was Comrade Zhang," he pointed to the conductor, "who discovered that you had never met him before. He reported to us immediately. Comrade Zhang has high vigilance. We all should learn from him."

Right, learn from him how to push himself into other people's rooms without knocking, I said to myself. "But there would have been two of us anyway," I said, trying not to sound angry. "Apparently the two beds weren't booked, otherwise you wouldn't have let him buy them. This kind of thing happens all the time on trains, a woman and man sharing a room. You don't interfere with every case, do you?"

"Not unless someone, especially a foreigner, insists on having a room to himself with a young girl. You're too innocent about these things. You don't know how complicated society is. We're here to protect you, to prevent you from making a serious mistake. He pats his ass and leaves after enjoying you, but what about you? If anything goes wrong, where can you find him?"

"Thanks for your concern." I forced myself not to laugh. "I'm old enough to take care of myself. I've been on my own since I was fifteen and have seen people much worse than Bruno. So please don't worry too much about me. Can I go now?" I stood up.

"Wait. I don't think you should go back there and spend a night with a foreign stranger. We could have put some passengers in it, but since he has bought the two beds, we can't do anything except move you to another room."

"Please do," I said with a sneer, my arms folded on my chest.

Zhang stepped forward and whispered something in the cop's ear. He frowned, then turned to me. "Sorry there're no more empty beds in the soft-berth cars. Since it's out of the question for you to go back to your room, I'm afraid you'll have to go to the hard-berth carriage."

"No. I paid for the first class, I'll stay in the first class."

"You can get your money back."

"Right now, from here?"

"We can't do it here. You have to go to the general office at Beijing Station. You're getting off there, anyway."

"You think I'll believe your promise? You think I'll get my money back? Forget it. I'd rather stick to my old room."

"Absolutely impossible."

"Why?" I snarled.

"It's against the law. You're not entitled to stay in the first class."

"Ah, I see," I finally lost control and cried out sarcastically. "It's the law, the law of the People's Republic of China, that an ordinary Chinese citizen is not entitled to travel in first class. I thought everyone was supposed to be equal in this socialist country. My mistake. I should have remembered the sign on the gate of the Shanghai park in the forties: *Dogs and Chinese Are Forbidden.*"

"Watch your mouth, young lady," the policeman said coldly.

I stopped, realizing that they could easily put me in jail for what I had just said. *What had gotten into me today?* I asked myself. "All right," I backed off, "I'll move out. Just tell me where I should go."

"How are you going to explain to Bruno?"

"Why, the party has been teaching me to be frank and honest, so I'm going to do so. Shouldn't I?" I couldn't help being sarcastic again.

"Well, policy and tact should always go together. You can tell him you have to get off earlier for some urgent business, so he won't be upset. We should leave him a good impression about our country, so he'll come back and do more business with us.

"It's almost dinnertime," he looked at his watch. "Before you move out, why don't you have dinner with him in the dining car and smooth things over? Dinner is free for the first-class passengers."

"Why don't you go and give him a good impression yourself?" I told him. *How can this guy kick me out and then expect me to gild gold on his ass?* I thought, with anger and amusement. "Not me, sorry," I said aloud. "Do you think he's a baby? The moment I move out, he'll know what's going on. Lying will only make things worse. The best thing for me to do is to get out as soon as possible."

I went back to my car and started packing. Bruno watched me in puzzlement and remorse. Finally he stood up. "I'm going to talk to the head of the train crew."

"You won't find him," I said to his back.

He stopped at the door, throwing up his hands with a moan. "I don't understand this. Is there any justice? Are there any rules to follow?"

I didn't respond. No matter how ashamed and angry I felt, I still didn't want to share my feelings with a Western stranger. Besides, someone might be listening outside the door— Comrade Zhang, probably, although he wouldn't understand a word. Bruno grabbed my arm when I picked up my bag.

"Say you'll wait for me at the Beijing Station. Please. I have to return the money. Let me see you again in a different environment. Please."

I pulled my arm out slowly. "Not at the Beijing Station. They might follow me."

He took out his notebook and scribbled something down. "Call me," he whispered, handing me the sheet he tore off from the book along with his business card. I glanced at the paper. He was staying at the Beijing Hotel. I nodded to Bruno and opened the door.

There stood Comrade Zhang with his oily smile on his greasy face. Behind him were a Hong Kong tourist couple, round eyes, round noses, round cheeks, and round bodies.

"I waited outside because I didn't want to interrupt your packing," he explained in a hurry.

"Which car?" I asked without looking at him.

"Oh, I'll take you there. This Miss is very, very nice," he said to the couple. "When she heard your wife isn't feeling well, she offered to exchange her ticket with you."

I almost burst out laughing in his face. Did they know the word shame? I brushed Zhang's hand off my bag and marched away by myself.

Chapter Seventeen

THREE DAYS AFTER I returned to Beijing, I went to visit Bruno at
the Peace Hotel. He took me to the hotel restaurant. I had
spaghetti with white clams. The simple, earthy style of Italian
food and its garlic taste truly pleased me. Bruno was delighted to
see me enjoy my meal. My story about my first Western meal at
Maxim's made him laugh. He asked me if I would climb the
Great Wall with him the next day in his rented car. I accepted his
invitation. As we were drinking coffee, a young man came over
and introduced himself as Bruno's driver. He suggested in broken
English that we leave at five A.M. and come back early because it
would be a very hot day tomorrow and his car had no air-condi-
tioning. Bruno seemed to be confused and amused at the same
time. He turned to me. I shook my head. To get to the hotel at
five, I would have to leave school at three in the morning. The bus
didn't run until five o'clock. We tried to tell him that we would
like to leave around seven, but he wouldn't budge.

"Five or no go," he repeated. He knew that Bruno didn't have
time to rent another car for tomorrow.

We looked at each other, then he said, "Would you stay here if
I get a room for you?"

I thought for a moment. "Why not!" I said. "If you get the room under my name."

"Sure, I can arrange that." He didn't mention the bill, but it was understood that he would pay for it. I didn't have that kind of money. In the lobby, I handed the service man my ID and watched him put all the information in his record book. They gave me a twenty percent discount because I was Chinese.

"Miss Ni stays only one night," Bruno said. "Should I pay when she leaves or just charge it to my bill?"

The service man looked up and smiled. "Sure, I can put her bill under your name. Save you lots of trouble."

The look in his eyes troubled me a great deal, but I didn't say anything to Bruno. I wanted him to enjoy his trip.

It went well. We climbed the wall, went underground to see the coffin of Emperor Wanli from the Ming Dynasty, and had dinner in the Royal Court Restaurant, which was open only to foreigners and overseas Chinese. As I watched the sweating tourists standing on line for watermelons, juice, and bread, I felt a tinge of guilt. But it didn't stop me from taking a long bath in my hotel room before I returned to school. Everything seemed to have run smoothly.

Bruno was scheduled to leave for Nanjing on Thursday, so I called him to say good-bye the day before. He was delighted to hear my voice and immediately invited me to dinner to celebrate the deal he had just made with the China Bank that afternoon. Fiat was going to build an auto factory in Nanjing.

It was almost four o'clock when I arrived. Someone in the lobby called me. It was the service man who had registered me for my room.

"I've something to tell you," he whispered. "Wait for me at the newspaper stand in the northeastern corner outside the hotel. I'll be out in a minute."

"But I don't know you. Besides, my friend is expecting me," I said, seized by the same uneasiness I had felt when I first met him.

"Tell him to wait. This is more important. See you." He went into a room behind the counter.

I picked up a phone on the wall and dialed Bruno's number.

"Hi, Ni Bing, are you downstairs? Come up. I've some champagne."

"Sorry. A clerk downstairs wants to talk to me. He sounds weird, but I've got to find out what he wants. Give me five to ten minutes? Twenty at most."

"Sure. Want me to go with you?"

"Oh, no, I can handle it. Thanks."

I waited at the stand for almost ten minutes and was about to give up when the man from the hotel appeared from behind on a bike like a vulture.

"Get on the backseat," he said.

"You're out of your mind. Why should I go with you? Who are you, anyway? Why don't you spill out what you have to say? I don't have a whole day to fool around."

"This isn't a good place to hear what I'm going to tell you."

I looked at the crowd around me and sighed. "You could at least tell me where we're going."

"Tiananmen Square."

I walked. He followed me pushing his bike. The place was only a few minutes from the Peace Hotel. We sat down under the shade of a big pine tree in the back of Mao's Memorial Hall. I waited for him to start. He was about twenty-five, good looking and well dressed, but his closely knit eyebrows and eyes gave him a greedy, mean look. He took a torn plastic bag from his chest pocket.

"Recognize this?" he asked.

It looked like a medicine bag with foreign letters on it. I shook my head.

"Yes, you know. It's a condom bag. I found it under your friend's bed."

"So?" I shrugged my shoulders but became alert inside.

"I checked with my coworker who cleaned up on the floor

where you and your friend stayed. Since Saturday night, your room has had no sign of being slept in. We made a thorough cleaning in his room and found this. So we concluded that you must have stayed in his room for the last three nights and that he's been screwing you."

"What!" I started laughing. It sounded too ridiculous to make me feel mad. "Perhaps I went back to my school three days ago?"

"Impossible!" he cried. "You never checked out. The room is still under your name, and the bill is still going up. Of course he's paying for everything."

"Are you serious?" I jumped up. "When I took the room, I told you I needed it only for one night. I remember clearly having asked you if I should pay on the day I leave or put the bill under Bruno's name. You said he can pay the day he leaves."

"But you never checked out, my dear," he said with such a triumphant smile.

"You set this trap for me! But it won't work. I can prove that I slept in my dormitory those nights."

"Who would believe you? Your party secretary? First of all, you college students aren't supposed to sleep outside the campus unless your family is in Beijing. Second, the hotel you stayed in is open only to foreigners and overseas Chinese. If this were reported to your department, you would never be trusted again, even if you had a hundred mouths to defend yourself."

"Why did you give me the room, then?" I stared at his squinting eyes and cursed him silently. It occurred to me that I had asked the same kind of question on the train. "I must go," I said in disgust.

"Where are you going? I'm not through with you yet." He grabbed me and pulled me toward him.

"Let me go. I must go back to the hotel and check out. I also want to talk to the manager about this whole dirty trick. Why should my friend pay for those nights?"

"I'll check you out. As for the manager, I advise you to give up. We have a profit target every month. The more customers, the more bonuses. I know my boss too well. He never lets a piece of fat pork slip out of his mouth, so I'm afraid your friend has to pay. But I'm worried about you. You're too naive to see things clearly, though you're a college student. You should never let anyone know you've spent nights with a foreigner. It ruins your reputation."

"I never slept with him. We're just friends."

"Are you acting or are you really so innocent? But I do care about you. I want to be your friend. I can help you open your eyes to reality." He put his arm around my waist. "May I kiss you?" he asked, imitating the gallant lover in Western movies.

"You're pathetic," I said as I pushed him away.

"What's wrong with you?" he shouted. "I'm much younger than that old stinky foreign devil, stronger and cleaner. Why can't we have some fun? I can make you happier. Oh, I see, I don't have the foreign exchange money, is that it?"

"You asshole, you asshole." It was all I could say as I backed away from him. Then I turned to run till I was out of breath. Finally I came across a red public phone booth. I dialed the hotel.

"Bruno," my voice choked as soon as I heard his greeting.

"Where are you, Ni Bing? I was really worried. You've been gone for a long time. What happened?"

"Can you come out? I'll meet you at the corner of the hotel. No, I can't explain on the phone. See you."

WE SAT SPEECHLESS on a stone bench in the Purple Bamboo Park, staring out at the vast lotus pond. He remained silent after I had told him what had happened. Finally he said, "I'm sorry to get you into trouble again. I wish you would let me help. I don't understand why I can't make a complaint about that serviceman. He told me he'd check you out and that he would transfer the bill to my account. I have you as my witness. In any other place, he'd be fired on the spot. In fact, no one would dare to play such a stupid game."

"This is China. We have a saying that when a scholar meets a soldier, there's no way to talk reason. All the big hotels are secured by the police. Who do you think the police would believe? Him or me? I'm the worst witness you could have."

"But the manager seems reasonable and considerate."

"To foreigners, yes. If you make a complaint, he might apologize and cancel the bill. But when you leave, he will crush me with a phone call to the police station. No, the best thing you can do for me is to pay the money and keep quiet."

"Is there any law in your country?"

"The party is our law."

We again sat in silence. A frog jumped off a lotus leaf, breaking one water drop into three. They rolled back and forth on the trembling round leaf. I thought of Huang Ming. He was speaking through me when I told Bruno that the party was our law. How was he doing in Tibet now? At one of the student union meetings, I had overheard that he was coughing blood. He never wrote to me, but I didn't feel abandoned. Our connection was not through letters or phone calls.

"You like Dante?" he broke the silence.

"Yes, Dante and his *Divine Comedy*." I began to recite the beginning of *Inferno*:

> *Midway on our life's journey, I found myself*
> *In dark woods, the right road lost.*

I spoke it in Chinese, but somehow he understood. "God," he grabbed my hand, "you've got to hear it in Italian. Listen, Ni Bing. I'm returning to Nanjing tonight, then I'll fly back to Rome the next day. But I'll be back here in two weeks. Can I call you at school? I'll change hotels. Please, I want to read Dante to you in Italian."

Two weeks passed by quickly. I became more relaxed when I heard nothing from the department about the Peace Hotel incident. Obviously the clerk didn't report it to the hotel security or police. The library closed at nine P.M. on Friday. As I walked to the dormitory building, I heard the phone ringing on the table at the entrance and saw the old concierge dragging her fat body out of the door. *Answer it,* I told myself, *it must be Bruno.* I ran up the steps and grabbed the receiver before the concierge could get to it. She gave me a dirty look and withdrew into her room.

"Hello," I said.

"Ni Bing?" he recognized my voice but still couldn't believe his luck. "I've been trying to reach you the whole evening. I'm staying at the Xiyuan Hotel, the nearest one I could find to your campus. Can I see you tonight? Can I send you a taxi?"

I looked around as if Bruno's voice could be heard through the whole building.

"Bruno," I whispered in English, "please, I can't come at this hour."

"But it's not that late. I'm sending you a taxi. Why don't you wait at the gate? Please, I need to see you. I brought Dante."

"No taxi, then," I said quickly. If anyone saw me climb into a cab at ten at night, there'd be a serious investigation and interrogation. "I'll take my bike. I know where the hotel is. It's only a half-hour ride. See you soon."

I dropped the phone as if it were a hot iron. I was lucky that the concierge spoke only Chinese. If I saw Bruno for an hour and came back before she locked the building, no one would suspect anything.

The road from the campus to the city was the busiest one in Beijing, but at night it was sensationally quiet and beautiful. The air was thick with the fragrance of lilac blossoms and pine needles on the sides of the road. This area used to be all wheat fields. Now it was packed with universities, academic institutes, computer research centers, markets, and other science organizations and commercial stores. At night, when the darkness hid the buildings in the vast fields and a few dim lights sparkled along the road, I felt the solid calmness of the countryside again. How amazing life was! Nine years ago, when I had climbed over the mountains to teach peasants how to read and write at night school, scared by the green, flickering ghost fire over the graves, I had never imagined a night like this.

I entered the Xiyuan Hotel quite easily. The security there seemed more casual than at the Peace Hotel. No guards around the gate. The clerk didn't even look at the form I filled out. Bruno smiled happily as he opened the door. He took out a package from his suitcase. I opened the carefully wrapped paper and saw Dante's *Inferno.*

"It's beautiful." I stroked the brown leather cover.

He turned to the first page. "Can I?" he asked, and began to read in Italian. After a few sentences, he put down the book and recited the rest of the stanza, his blue eyes fixed on my face.

"What a song!" I sighed when he finished.

He didn't respond, but continued to gaze at me until I bent my head. "Your eyes are the dark forest in which I lost my way," he murmured, finally breaking the silence, his tone dreamy, as if he were still reciting Dante. "They're so deep, yet so clear. I'm lost in them. Ni Bing, you made me happy. Would you accept this book?" He held it out to me with both hands.

I reached out, hypnotized by the intense light in his eyes. He took my wrists firmly.

"Thank you," he said.

I withdrew my hands gently, trying to stay calm. I had often wondered about making love to a Western man. But now I was frightened by the threat of punishment from my school, the police, and rumors. Bruno had already caused enough trouble for me.

"Would you take me to the rotating top of the building?" I said. "I've always wanted to look at Beijing from there."

The sparks in his eyes disappeared. Silently he opened the door and made a gesture for me to leave before him. We headed for the elevator together. The rotating top was used as a dance hall. Rock music exploded into my face when the elevator door opened. The hall was dark, except for a few dim green and yellow blinking bulbs. Bruno held my hand and led me to a small table near the glass wall.

"Beer or Coke?" he asked.

I was looking out eagerly at the brightly illuminated city. I recognized the Peace Hotel, the big clock on top of the telephone building, all falling away as the hall turned slowly.

"Can I have some orange juice?"

A beautiful waitress came over to take our order. The drinks arrived quickly. I sipped the juice. It was fresh and real, not made of artificial dye and sugar like the bottles sold in stores and streets.

Bruno shouted something in my ear, but his words got lost in the thundering music. I nodded at him, pretending that I understood. When my eyes became accustomed to the darkness, I found that almost all the dancing women were Chinese and most of the men were white and black foreigners. I tapped my foot to the rhythm and watched them with envy. Bruno asked if I wanted to dance; I smiled and shook my head. I didn't feel free enough to dance like the girls here. They were spinning as if the waxed floor were an ice rink, their tight pants glittering, their hair flying in all directions. A girl in silver tights and a loose scarlet top caught everyone's attention. She whirled like a wild animal who had just been let out of a cage. Her movements were grotesquely exaggerated and dramatic, as if she were acting out a ritual, each gesture signifying an event in her life that had ended tragically. One by one, the other dancers, including her partner, stopped to watch. Bruno shrugged his shoulders and poured more Qingdao beer into his glass. When the music finished, everyone applauded and walked to their own tables with their partners. I looked out the window. The rotating hall was now facing the western suburbs. The last lights flickered out one by one, leaving only a vast expanse of darkness.

The sudden silence made me feel nervous. I drank my juice and said, "I should go back to school."

The band started playing a tango as we walked across the hall. Only a few couples stood up to dance. The elevator door opened before we pressed the button, and two men stepped out.

Something about them made me grab Bruno, who was about to enter the elevator. I watched them walk to the table where the girl in the red shirt was sitting. One of them tapped her shoulder. She looked up, and I saw her body stiffen in anticipation of a fight. But she just stood up, said something to her bearded partner, and followed the two strangers into the elevator. As the door closed behind them, my heart filled with fear. On the surface, nothing had happened. They seemed to know one another quite well. Neither Bruno nor the bearded guy were upset. But I knew something was wrong. The two men were not her friends.

Bruno asked me to have dinner with him the next day. I thought about it and told him I couldn't, but I would certainly see him again before he flew back to Rome. As I pushed my bike through the gate where the security men were sitting outside their office to enjoy the cool night, I laughed at myself for being oversensitive. What did I have to worry about? I didn't do anything wrong. I pedaled my bike. It didn't move. I looked back and almost fell off. Two men were gripping the back seat.

"What do you want?" I asked calmly. Somehow I was no longer afraid.

"We want to have a word with you in the office. Come with us quietly." The man spoke in a low voice. I recognized him by his extraordinarily small head and the pinched features on his face. He was the same one who had taken away the girl in silver tights.

"What's your relationship with Bruno Berio?" he asked as soon as he sat down behind his desk. I stood in front of four security men. Two of them had rushed over when I was brought into the room. The girl in silver tights was sitting on the bench against the wall.

"Friends," I said.

"What kind of friends? Midnight friend? Bed friend?" They laughed. "How much money did he give you?" he asked again when the laughter subsided.

"I don't understand your question."

"Ha, she's a good actress. How innocent she looks!" He turned to a young man standing behind him. "Little Sun, hand me her pretty little purse. Let me see how generous that Italian guy was."

"Yes, Old Liu." Little Sun stepped forward and put his hand on my shoulder. I turned away and took my bag off my shoulder.

"Take your time," I said sarcastically.

Little Sun handed it to Old Liu. He turned it upside down. Dante's Inferno fell out, together with my ID. He picked up the book, thumbed through it, shook the bag upside down again, then turned it over to look inside in disbelief. It was a simple one-pocket straw bag without a zipper, just big enough to hold the book. He turned to me in disgust and anger, looking me up and down, as if to find out where I had hidden the money.

"Sorry, I have no pockets." I opened my arms to show them my T-shirt and skirt.

"Impossible," he murmured. "She must have dropped it somewhere on the street."

"How could I? I didn't even know who you were when you got me from behind," I taunted.

He picked up the book again and turned the pages. "Old Liu, I just looked through it. There're no dirty pictures in it," Little Sun said.

"What's in the book? Yellow poems?" He rummaged through it with a deep frown.

"Why don't you read it for yourself?"

"College student," he roared, "you can be smart with me now, but soon you'll end up like her." He pointed at the girl. She had slipped onto the floor, her head buried between her knees. The power and pride had vanished from her.

"She was tougher than you. But when we called the Cannon Bureau for a prison van to take her away, she started crying like a little girl. Now if you're wise, tell me how much foreign exchange money you got from him. You know our party's policy: leniency to those who confess their crimes and severity to those who refuse to."

"But I didn't commit any crime. You've searched my bag.

Why—you want me to make up a story?"

He looked at me in disgust. "So you let him screw you for nothing, you cheap whore?"

"I didn't sleep with him," I shouted, my patience all exhausted. "We're just friends—friends, do you hear? Why can't you believe that friendship is possible between a man and a woman, even between a foreign man and a Chinese woman?"

"Shut up," he roared, leaning over his desk and grabbing my T-shirt. "Don't you forget where you are, college brat. If you don't know how to behave, I'll teach you. I'm sure your departmental party secretary knows how to fix you." He waved my student ID.

I became silent. You Shan and Jiang would be delighted to hear the news from Old Liu, who couldn't be older than forty. He must have earned the respectful title *Old* by being in the security service longer than anyone else.

Sirens. A red van drove in and stopped right outside the office. The girl in silver tights cried out and curled herself into a ball.

"Don't, don't," she wailed.

Nobody paid attention to her. The four men ran out to greet the driver. Then they all came back and surrounded the girl.

"Stand up," Old Liu shouted, and kicked her. She looked pathetic as she propped herself up against the wall, her legs trembling, her cheeks stained with mascara and tear. "Well, are you ready to talk?"

"If I talk, you won't send me away?" she asked meekly.

"Depends on your attitude," he said triumphantly, giving me a meaningful glance.

"I, I was bad."

"How bad?" he asked. "Speak loud, so that every one in this room can hear you."

"I wore makeup and seductive clothing and danced with foreigners."

"And?" Old Liu raised his eyebrows. Even he realized that the content of her confession made the scene ridiculous.

"I received money from foreigners," she added quickly.

"Why did they give you money?"

She bent her head. Old Liu grunted and asked, "How many did you sleep with?"

"About three or four."

"How many exactly?"

"Four."

"Do you realize that your behavior has stained the image of our country?"

"Yes."

"Do you truly feel remorseful for what you did?"

"Yes."

"Do you think it fair to receive the penalty of four hundred yuan in foreign exchange money?"

Four hundred. I was shocked. Did she really make so much? The girl in silver tights looked up with her pleading eyes.

"But that's all I have."

"You think it's too much?" Old Liu said angrily. "No, even four thousand isn't enough to repair the damage you've done." He signaled Little Sun to return her purse.

She took out the money, counting each bill twice before she gave them to Old Liu. When he reached out his hand, she said, "Can I get a receipt?"

He flared up. "This is it! You had your last chance. Now keep your filthy money and go to jail. This will teach you a lesson for not trusting the party and the government. What do you need a receipt for? To prove to your pimp mother that you didn't eat up the money?" he shouted at the top of his voice, his mouth frothing.

She screamed as she was dragged into the van. "Shut up, you pig! You're a pimp, and your whole place is a filthy whorehouse. I'm cleaner than all of you!"

There was a dead silence in and outside the room. Through the window, I saw Old Liu giving instructions to the three young security men, who nodded and returned to the main building. When he came in alone, he glared at me with hatred.

"You've seen the end of stubborn resistance. I hope you've

learned a lesson from her. Now tell me when you entered his room."

"It's on your register book."

"I want to hear you say it," he roared.

What the hell? I thought. *Just tell him everything.* I really had nothing to hide.

"About ten, I don't remember exactly. I stayed in his room for about ten to fifteen minutes. Then we went to the ballroom for some drinks and stayed for forty-five minutes. Then I left the hotel."

"What did you do in his room?"

"He read Dante in Italian. That's all."

"That's all?" he laughed. "We'll find out. Who the hell is Dante? What kind of poems did she write? They must be dirty ones. Otherwise, why would he spend time on them? A businessman, as far I know, is interested in two things: money and women. So don't tell me that your businessman friend did nothing but read a poem while you were alone in a nice room." He leaned on his chair and laughed.

"Dante is a man," I said, trying not to laugh. "And the book he read from is called *Inferno.* In Chinese, it's called *Diyu,* prison underground, or hell."

"Mm," he nodded thoughtfully, "that sounds interesting." He suddenly sat up. "Were you both naked when he read *Diyu* to you?"

"What?" I couldn't believe my ears.

"Ha, I got you, didn't I? You were naked, weren't you? After the reading, you had sex. How did he enter you, from the front or back?"

He must be insane, I said to myself as I stared at his excited face.

"How long did it last?" He didn't wait for my answer and continued his monologue, his eyes narrowing. "Did you do anal and oral also?"

"I don't know what you're talking about," I said in despair.

"Oral means you lick his cock with your tongue. And anal, he fucked your behind, your ass." He wet his lips and his eyes became glassy. Suddenly he raised his voice. "Don't you dare play games with me. Haven't you done it with your Italian devil?"

"No. The only time we touched is when we shook hands."

"I don't have much patience, college whore!" He hit the table with his fist. "If you say no to me again, I'll let the police or your department deal with you. They won't be just talking to you, understand? Now, answer me nice and straight. How long did your intercourse last?"

I fixed my eyes to the floor, aghast at his question, but lost courage to say no again.

"I'm asking you a question, Miss College Student!"

"I don't know. I don't have a watch." As soon as I said it, I bit my lips angrily, realizing I had just acknowledged his charge.

"Let me help you then," he smiled triumphantly. "You said you stayed in his room only fifteen minutes. I won't question how you figured that out without a watch. I think you stayed there more than fifteen minutes, at least half an hour. Greeting, taking off your clothing, and reading the poem took about five minutes, and putting on clothing and departure also about five minutes. That would leave twenty minutes for the hanky-panky, am I right?"

I had never heard the term *hanky-panky*, but I knew what it meant from his gesture and expression. The only thing I could do was to keep my silence.

"What's so embarrassing, eh?" He laughed with satisfaction. "You've done it, you've enjoyed it, now you have to pay for it. Did he use a condom?"

I almost jumped. For a moment I thought I was talking with that sleazy guy from the Peace Hotel again.

"Or do you take pills? Probably it's the condom. Those foreign devils are afraid of diseases. OK, the man used a condom for birth control." He read to himself as he scribbled the words in his book. "What size did he use? Large, probably. The devils do have big penises. Purpose of the sexual intercourse," he looked up at me, bit his pen, and continued writing without bothering to wait for my answer, "for the porno book and money. The amount received—still under investigation."

He sat up in his chair, threw his pen on the table, and looked into my eyes. "Sign what you've acknowledged. If you cooperate with us, we'll think about ending your case here and now, and I promise it won't go any further than this room. Think about it. You're going to graduate soon, right? You don't want to be assigned to some remote province and be buried there all your life because of an awful scandal, the worst kind for a girl? All you have to do to avoid the disaster is to sign the paper and pay your penalty. I can talk to my supervisor about giving you a discount, since this is your first time and you're still a student."

He stopped to catch his breath. Slowly he pushed the record book toward me. He had written two full pages of our conversation—actually, his own monologue. His handwriting was small and cramped just like his face. He pointed with his forefinger to the place where I was supposed to sign. I noticed that his nails were bitten down to the flesh and the finger joints were big and crooked. Other than the fantastic story about sex, everything he had said was true—I couldn't afford this kind of scandal. Yet signing this nonsense was out of the question. What could I do to get out of this terrible situation? This Old Liu was a maniac. It was impossible to talk reason with him at all.

"Do you need some time to think it over?" he whispered in my ear. He had quietly moved behind me and placed his hands on my shoulders. I leaped up in disgust and wiped the place he had touched.

"Keep your hands off!" I hissed.

He grabbed my hair from behind and turned my face toward him. "You should feel lucky I touched you, college whore. Are you going to sign it or not?"

"No!" I screamed at the top of my voice.

He slapped my face and threw me down into the chair. "You've got to make a decision before dawn. I mean what I say." He jerked his head backward and walked out, slamming the door behind him.

I was left alone again. Nobody seemed to worry that I would try to escape. They had my ID. A call to Beijing University and the campus security men would get me immediately. I looked at the clock. It was 4:10 A.M. What was Bruno doing? My heart suddenly raged against him. Was he a devil or a friend? Since the moment I had met him on the train, troubles had been haunting me. Now he must be sound asleep in his comfortable bed, oblivious of the deep shit I was in.

The doorknob turned. Little Sun came in, sat down behind Old Liu's desk, and looked at me thoughtfully.

"Well, have you decided yet?"

A touch of gentleness in his voice made me look up. He was only in his early twenties, his eyes still clear and expressive, quite unlike the harsh and indifferent eyes of the old security guards. Hope rose in my heart.

"I really didn't sleep with him," I pleaded. "How could I? I knew it was late, so I stayed only a few minutes."

"Why did you come to see him if you knew it was late?"

I sensed his sincerity and told him how I met Bruno, including what had happened at the Peace Hotel. When I finished, he was quiet for a while before he spoke.

"You should learn to be more careful. It's not that we want to take every woman who goes out with foreigners for a prostitute. The fact is that there's too much prostitution going on in every hotel. We've been working overtime on these cases. Old Liu is a very experienced and well-respected security officer."

"But he can also make mistakes sometimes," I interrupted.

He raised his hand to stop me. "We all respect him," he repeated, "and admire him. True, he might be wrong. But I don't think you should feel angry about being here. Think about it. Is it appropriate for a young woman to visit a single foreign man in a hotel at midnight?" He stared at me with his scolding eyes.

It was ten in the evening, not midnight, I said to myself. *Besides, what's wrong with visiting a man at midnight?* But I bent my head, pretending that I was ashamed. He was my only hope.

"Only you know what you did in his room. We don't have any evidence. We must depend on you to tell us the truth, and you must depend on us to believe you." He tapped his pen on the desk.

"I told the truth," I said, seized by despair again. He was right. It was up to them or to Old Liu to believe me or not. My fate was totally in their hands.

"I don't want to say I trust you," Little Sun said slowly. "But I do want to give you a chance, since it's your first mistake." I looked up at him quickly, then moved my eyes away, afraid that he would change his mind. "I'll talk to Old Liu about your case. You might not have to sign the paper. But you must admit your mistake and pay the penalty."

"Fine," I said. *But how much would they charge me?* I asked myself.

"Don't be too optimistic. I have to talk to Old Liu first. If he says no, I can't do anything about it. He's in charge. But I'll get his supervisor involved. Old Liu listens only to him. You stay here and take it easy." Before he closed the door, he added, "Don't worry too much."

I was grateful to Little Sun. If he could get me out of here, I would never forget him.

Oh god, how much would they fine me? Four hundred yuan? I had only fifty in foreign exchange money that Zhou had given me and about five yuan from my monthly allowance. Where could I collect the money?

I dozed off and was awakened by Little Sun. He gestured for me to follow him. It was getting light outside. He led me into a big office in the main hotel building. A gray-haired man looked up sternly from his desk.

"So you're Ni Bing," he said with authority in his voice. I nodded. "Do you realize what you have done?"

I bit my lips. My eyes met Little Sun's. "Yes," I said.

"Do you feel sorry?"

"Yes."

Satisfied by my submissiveness, he turned to Little Sun. "Since she has admitted her mistake and since it was her first time, we should give her a chance. Fine her four hundred yuan in foreign exchange money and let her go."

He straightened his back, ready to receive gratitude from me. I didn't move.

"I don't have that kind of money. I'm just a student!" I cried out with all my courage.

My boldness astonished him. He took off his glasses and studied me as if I were a beast.

Little Sun rushed to him and whispered something in his ear.

He nodded, thought a while, and said, "The penalty is necessary. But according to your situation, we'll reduce the amount to two hundred yuan. Little Sun, give her a receipt when she pays."

"I still can't pay right now. I have nothing on me except my ID. You have to give me some time to collect the money."

He frowned and said nothing. I added quickly, "You have my ID. I'll be back within two hours. If not, you can call my department."

He seemed unhappy to have to make this compromise. "I'll let you do this only once," he said. "I hope I won't see you here again. Why don't you devote your energy and time to your studies and work? Even if you can't control your desires, why do you have to meddle with foreigners? There are plenty of Chinese men."

"I didn't meddle with any foreigner the way you think. And I don't want to meddle with any Chinese man. I'm innocent." I turned to Little Sun as if he would support me. But he pulled me out of the room.

"Don't be stupid," he said sharply. "Just go and get the money."

I pushed my bike out of the Xiyuan Hotel. Rage throbbed in my temples and clouded my eyes.

Calm down, I told myself. *Think hard. You need two hundred yuan in foreign exchange money in two hours. How are you going to get it?* I looked at my old Seagull watch. It was worth fifteen yuan at most. I had purchased my bike a year ago for thirty yuan from a graduate student. Now even if I gave it away for free, no one would take it. I could sell some of my books and dictionaries, but what I needed was two hundred yuan in foreign exchange money in two hours.

The thought of Old Liu calling You Shan and Jiang in the department made me sick. The sidewalk seemed to sway beneath my feet. I breathed deeply and leaned back against a pay phone. The solution to the problem suddenly seemed obvious to me: I was going to sleep with Bruno and get money from him. This was my only way out. This was that the policemen on the train, the guy from the Peace Hotel, and Old Liu from Xiyuan Hotel called whoring. But wasn't that what they wanted? Ever since I had met Bruno, all the forces, visible and invisible, had been pushing me in that direction. *All right, I'm going to whore and make that two hundred yuan in foreign exchange money for you,* I said aloud to the empty street, laughing and coughing at the same time like a lunatic in the dawn light. Finally I picked up the phone and dialed the Xiyuan Hotel.

So Bruno became my first Western lover. We stayed in bed for two hours. I screamed, cursed, laughed, and bit him like a wildcat. He was delighted, thinking I was having orgasms, and my shouting was a sign of ecstasy. He wanted to see me again when he came to China on his next trip, but I just smiled and ran out with the money. In the hallway, I sobbed bitterly, but no tears came out. Where were the security guards? Why didn't they catch me when I was whoring?

When I went to the office to pay the fine, I couldn't stop myself from laughing into the faces of Little Sun and Old Liu. What a farce! I was a whore handing my pimps their cuts.

Chapter Eighteen

MY HEART POUNDED like crazy when I saw the thick letter from New York lying on the concierge's desk. Zhou hadn't forgotten about me! I tore open the envelope. A pile of application forms for Baruch College fell out, together with Zhou's letter.

"Sorry it took me so long to write you. Busy with my stores and kids. I hope you'll start the processing and come to New York next year. If you need anything, don't hesitate to write me."

The big, childish characters danced before my eyes. I quickly stuffed everything into my bag and went directly to the library to see Old Guan.

"What should I do with the forms?" I asked, standing over the desk where Guan was filling out library cards. He had lost all his hair during his hard years, the pink smooth scalp dotted with brown spots, which always made me smile. It had been only about ten days ago that I strolled into this newly opened foreign reference room. The moment we saw each other, his dim eyes sparked, the wrinkles on his face opened and smoothed, and I felt I had known him for a long time. He showed me around the shelves that stored the novels, poetry, anthologies, and theory books that the foreign professors had ordered from the West. The departments didn't want these books to circulate among the stu-

dents, nor did the library want to put them on the regular
shelves. So they cleared this room, shoveled the books in, and
appointed Guan to take care of them. Only faculty members,
graduate students, and seniors from the foreign languages
departments were allowed to enter. This was a perfect position
both for him and the English Department. He had already been
an associate professor in the late fifties when he was sent to work
on numerous farms as a Rightist, an antirevolutionist, and an
American spy. He was rehabilitated just a few months ago. We
talked until the library closed. The next day, I went back with a
bag of Shanghai candies. When he opened the bag and saw what
was inside, he laughed, tears running down his battered face.
"You're proud," he said, "but you've got a damn good heart."

I would have died for him at that moment. Practically no one
on the campus talked to me. The hotel security sent a report to
the English Department. I was lucky that the department merely gave me a demerit in my records instead of expelling me. But
I became known as a girl who had slept with an Italian businessman for money. My classmates avoided me. My roommates in
the dorm acted as if I were invisible. Huli spat at my feet whenever she passed by. Even Mr. Steinberg looked at me with sad,
pitying eyes and told me that he'd always remember me as the
girl who had written a beautiful story about Ma Ao Village. He
sounded as if he were mourning for my death. I almost grabbed
him and shouted that I was still alive.

And now this stranger was telling me that I had a good heart.
"You're the first person to give me anything in the past thirty
years, and you hardly know me," Guan said.

We both laughed, knowing that his second statement was not
totally true. We must have met each other somewhere in our
previous lives.

GUAN LOOKED at the paper through his glasses, which had
slipped down onto the middle of his nose. "Well, fill them out.
You need any help?"

"But it's not that simple." I stamped my feet like a little girl. How great it was to be able to act willfully sometimes! "How about the Translation Company? I just got the job and it's the best one I can find right now."

The company had been founded about five years ago by the Foreign Language Bureau to translate all the UN documents from the major European languages into Chinese. All the work was paid for in US dollars. After the bureau took most of its profits, the company still had enough left to give its employees good bonuses and benefits. Everyone in my class, except for those who were going to graduate schools, wanted this job. They couldn't believe that I, who had such a terrible reputation and record in my file, was picked by the company. It did give a big boost to my shattered ego. Everything seemed to have fallen apart: my relationship with Yan, the demerit in my political file, and my failure in the graduate entrance exams, although I knew the first two were not completely my fault, and the failure in the exams was a deliberate act. When Xiao Jia, the assistant manager from the Translation Company, told me at the end of our interview that she would highly recommend me to the manager, I swore to myself that I'd work really hard to prove that she had trusted the right person. How could I tell her that I was planning to go to America even before I started the job?

"Is that all you want, a good job?" Guan asked in a funny voice. "Is that your purpose for giving up grad school?"

I gave him a quick look and bent my head. Every time I got tangled in my own thoughts, he would poke through the mess and let some light in. Of course I chose to fail the exams so that I would not have to go to Hangzhou. No matter how powerful Yan was, he could never find me a job and have me transferred there. Hangzhou was one of the most difficult cities to move to in China. My department offered to enroll me in a special one-year program to be trained as an English lecturer at Beijing University. They hinted that if I did well, I could be sent to England or the US to get further training. It was true that I couldn't bear the idea of living the rest of my life with my pigtail in the hands of You Shan and Jiang. I also knew that they would not be in the department forever. But I still declined the offer without a second thought. I wanted out badly.

But where?

"You need to get out," he said after a long silence. "I'm not saying this country, this land, isn't good for you. On the contrary, it's one of the best you will ever find. You'll know what I mean when you've lived in another country for several years. But right now it's cursed, especially for you. You're too strange, too alien, for the old customs here. And you don't know how to bend, or maybe you don't want to. Sooner or later, you'll be shattered.

"Go to New York, Ni Bing," he raised his voice. "It's a tough place. I know because I lived there for four years. But I'm sure you'll survive and learn to like it. Grow strong and then come back. Don't hesitate. Talk to Xiao Jia. You need her permission and support to start the whole process. Go, my child. The faster, the better."

My heart stopped for a second, then thumped hard. *My child,* he had just called me, *my child.* But there was more than that. We must have met somewhere, far away and long ago. I took his hand. It was old and wrinkled, yet so warm and youthful, just like his face. Pressing it to my lips, I wanted to call him everything at once: grandpa, pa, brother, friend. But all I could say was "Thank you."

He smiled. "Ni Bing, I have a few hundred yuan the English Department gave me when I was rehabilitated. Any time you need it, just tell me. I'm sure it will come in handy for you."

XIAO JIA WAS truly happy to see me. "Hi, what brought you here? I thought you were already on your way to the south. You know you have two months vacation, don't you? Ah, you're worried about your things? They're fine, wrapped and hidden behind the couch in your office. You want to take a look?"

Her beaming smile and singing voice relaxed me. Perhaps it wouldn't be as hard as I thought. "Can I have a talk with you privately?" I said, looking around at her office, which she shared with four other people.

"Sure. Come to the conference room with me."

We passed the office where my luggage was piled in the corner behind the beige sofa. On September first, this room, shared by five other translators, would be my office during the day and my bedroom in the evening. The Translation Company was still building apartments for its employees. When Xiao Jia sent a white Toyota minivan to the campus to pick up my belongings, she promised me a one-bedroom apartment as soon as the building was completed.

"So, what can I do for you?" Xiao Jia asked warmly as she put a cup of jasmine tea in front of me.

"I'm thinking of applying for graduate school in New York. I know I shouldn't bring this up before I start working, but my cousin wants me to get into the program for the fall semester next year. So I must begin the procedure now, and I need your permission letter." I pushed Zhou's letter and the applications toward Jia.

Her beaming moon face turned pale, and the smile froze at the corners of her mouth. "Well," she finally said, "you've certainly planned everything."

Her words whipped my cheeks. She was implying that I had tricked her into this whole thing. "No, you misunderstand me," I said. "I really didn't plan to go to New York when I applied for this job, at least not so soon. My cousin had mentioned it, but I had never believed he was serious. I'm really sorry it turned out like this. But if I start my job now, I can still work here for more than a year."

"Do you know that your salary doesn't begin till September first?" Her voice was less cold. *Perhaps there is some hope,* I told myself.

"I know. I don't mind that at all. You can use me as an intern. You'll see how hard I can work, and how well."

She smiled and sighed. "Xiao Ni, do you know the new policy from the Central Committee? Any college graduate must work for two years before he or she can apply for schools abroad."

It was my turn to become aghast. Another two years! How many two years had I waited and how many more would I have to? I clenched my teeth. "Then I'd like to ask permission to start the application in two years."

She shook her head slowly, her eyes fixed on me with pity and sadness. "So you're really determined. Well, I can't make the decision by myself. I need to talk to the manager and other assistant managers. Wait here for me."

It took her a long time to come back. Before she said anything, she poured me another cup of tea. I sensed something was wrong.

"Xiao Ni, we want you to understand our difficult situation," she said, her voice the tone of business. "It took us two and a half years to negotiate and bargain with our authorities to let us hire a new translator and expand our business. You don't know how many signatures and seals we had to get through from the Foreign Language Press and the Ministry of Culture. We wouldn't have done it if not for our urgent need for a new hand. And we had hoped that this new person would work here at least two years."

"But I am willing to work for two years," I was practically shouting. She raised her hand to stop me.

"I'm sorry, Ni Bing, we have no other choice. If we hire someone who has already planned to leave before she begins to work, we'll not only have a harder time getting a new translator from the authorities, but we'll also set a bad example for the other employees here. Everyone wants to go abroad nowadays. Believe me, we all have some connections overseas. If we let people come and go as they please, this place will fall apart in no time."

A terrible thought came to my mind. I dared not ask, but I had to do it. "Are you saying that I shouldn't come to work at all? Does it mean I'm fired?"

She avoided my eyes. "Not exactly. You're not on our official staff till September, and it's only the end of July. I'm really sorry, Xiao Ni. I hope you'll understand our difficulty. If you have no further questions, I'd like to go back to work. We're busy here." She stood up.

I wanted to stand up with her but couldn't move. My mind turned blank. How did this happen?

"Xiao Ni," Jia said in a soft voice, "perhaps you can get another job through the English Department?"

I shook my head. I couldn't imagine facing You Shan and Jiang again.

"But it's their responsibility. I'll talk to them if you want." She was at a loss for what to say and looked relieved when her secretary peeked in the room and told her she was wanted by the manager. "Well, I'll try my best to help you. Don't worry about your things here. I'll keep an eye on them. Take care, Xiao Ni. I'm sure things will work out for you."

I stood at the gate, gazing back at the square building of the Translation Company. This place had been my only official connection with reality. The company had my residence registration card, my files, and all my belongings. Once I had started working, I'd have been given an ID card, a salary, a room to sleep in, and all the other things I needed to survive. But I'd just been stripped of everything. I was now a homeless person.

OLD GUAN and I sat facing each other on the bare bunk beds. On the desk was a Dezhou roast chicken and the smoked bean curd he had brought for this dinner. But neither of us had any appetite. It was July 31, the last day for all the graduates to clear out of the dormitory. I looked around the room where I had spent four years with nine other students. We used to complain about how small and crowded it was. Now it seemed alarmingly empty, with nothing to hold onto. Someone had left a flask behind. The bamboo shell looked fine from outside. When I picked it up, I realized it was shattered inside. Still, it was the only object that reaffirmed my four years on the campus. For a moment, I wished that I had bought the yearbook and gotten everyone's signature. I didn't do it for fear that no one would sign mine. Also, I came out like a blur in the group graduation photo, my facial features barely recognizable. I tore the picture into pieces.

"Try the chicken. It's the best roast chicken in the north." Guan tore off a leg and wing and put them in my bowl. Watching me nibble at the meat, he asked, "Are you sure you can stay with your friend until you find a new job?"

I nodded, my mouth full of the chicken I couldn't swallow. I had lied to him so that he wouldn't worry, but actually I had no place to go. Guan would have sheltered me if he hadn't lived in a one-room apartment with his bad-tempered wife.

"Did you see Professor Wang? Can he help you find a job?" Guan asked.

Again I nodded, pretending I was too busy chewing to answer his question in words. I had nothing to tell him but bad news. He had suggested that I go to see Wang, the only person in the department who had the means and heart to help me now. I had been to the department and asked the secretary if the Translation Company had sent back my file. She answered yes, but the department no longer had the responsibility to locate a new job for me. Once I was out of the department, I was out forever. Didn't I know that spilled water couldn't be collected?

Guan assured me that Wang would help. I agreed because he had given me an A-plus for the paper I had done for his modern English poetry course. He had also been in charge of the 1979 year students while I was the academic student representative. We used to meet weekly to discuss the needs and problems of the students. He seemed to be understanding and warmhearted.

I went to his apartment. His five-year-old son answered the door. When he recognized me, he looked as if he'd seen a ghost and banged the door shut. I heard him shouting inside: "Dad, it's the girl, it's the girl." So they'd been talking about me, the girl who had sunk so low. The door opened again; Professor Wang held it firmly to keep me from entering. He stared at me through the crack, a big frown on his face.

"What do you want?" he finally asked, his voice filled with irritation. My lips trembled. I tried to open my mouth, to tell him that I needed his help, but my voice failed. I couldn't remember how I left his apartment. Somehow Professor Wang's rejection shattered me. So I really was bad, cursed, outcast. A brick lay in the middle of the street. I saw it but still crashed into it at full speed on my bike. I flew into the air and landed on the dirt road, face down. I lay motionless under the bike, indulging myself in the physical pain, which was easier to bear than the torment in my soul. A man rode by. He stopped to lift the bike off me and to help me sit up. He cried out when he saw my bloody elbows and knees and offered to take me to a clinic. I shook my head, walking away slowly while pushing my bike. A job was what I needed, not a doctor. Then I remembered that I hadn't thanked him. I turned and saw him moving the brick out of the road.

Now I was wearing a long-sleeved shirt to hide the infected wounds on my elbows. Every time I moved my arms, the scabs would break and bloody pus would ooze out. Guan sighed. "I heard that there's a new policy now," he said. "A college graduate can look for a job on his or her own instead of being assigned to a company through the department. Why don't you try that? English teachers are badly needed. With your grades and background, I'm sure many places will grab you instantly."

But I have two major problems, I wanted to say. *First, people would immediately wonder why I gave up the position in the Translation Company. Second, who would want to hire somebody who could work only for a year or two?* Well, I didn't have to tell them about my plan to study abroad until I got the job, but I was tired of telling any more lies. There should be no more compromise. "That's what I plan to do tomorrow. I'll visit colleges and high schools," I told Guan.

Guan put the other leg in my bowl. "Eat it. You'll need lots of energy."

Someone knocked on the door three times. I jumped to my feet. Only Yan would be knocking like this. But it couldn't be him. He should be in Yunnan collecting materials for his research. Before the semester had ended, he asked me to travel there with him in the summer. I still had no guts to say no to him; instead, I wrote him a letter saying that I had to go to Shanghai to take care of Waipo. She was sick. I had hoped that my lie would at least prevent him from coming to Beijing.

More knocks, gentle but persisting. Perhaps it was just the security guards checking on the students. I gestured for Guan to go behind the mosquito net before I opened the door. I didn't want to get him into any trouble.

Yan staggered in, a traveling bag on his shoulder. He looked about the room with his drunken eyes, then turned to me.

"I can tell I'm not welcome here," he said, glancing at the dishes on the desk. "At least I deserve a cup of water."

I poured him a cup of tea from my flask.

He blew away the leaves floating on the surface and tried to sip the tea. His hand shook and the hot water spilled on his pants. He smashed the cup on the floor.

"What kind of play are you putting on?" he shouted.

I stood before him. *It will end today, finally,* I told myself. Oh, how ugly he looked!

Guan walked out and stood by the window. Yan nodded to him.

"It's what I guessed," he said.

I almost burst out laughing. Yan was hinting that Guan was my lover! He had to be mad. Guan looked more than sixty years old. He had lost all his hair and half his teeth. The only thing youthful were his eyes, which shined through the wrinkles.

"Can I have a talk with you, a man-to-man, honest talk?" he said.

I bent over laughing. The word *honest* just didn't sound right coming out of Yan's mouth. When I looked up, they had already gone. I sat down on the bed and stared through the corner of the curtain. Somewhere in the darkness, two men were making a decision about my life. What could he possibly tell Guan about me? It was absurd that Yan had to believe I had another lover in order to break up with me. But what did I care what he thought about me as long as he left me alone?

The door opened. Yan came in first and stood in front of me. I looked up, propping myself up with both hands behind my back. Guan remained at the door.

"You're certainly a remarkable actress." He hissed out each word.

"And you're a fine director," I replied, smiling in order to keep my boiling anger under control.

He headed for the door, then he turned to me, his hand on the knob, his head up dramatically, and shouted, "Without me, you're nothing!"

His footsteps faded in the hallway. I opened my hands to Guan. "So it's all over. Just like that. And how terrified I had been, awaiting this moment!"

He stood still at the door, looking very pale.

"What did he tell you?" I suddenly felt the old panic creeping back to me. What if Yan had also turned Guan against me?

He smiled. "He warned me that you're not to be trusted. What happened to him may happen to me. Someday I'll enter your room and find you eating chicken with another man."

"Isn't it funny that he took us for lovers?" I laughed. "But it's great, it's really great."

He gazed at me for a long time and turned his head with a sigh. Then he took an envelope out of his breast pocket. "Take this. You'll need it for food and transportation. Ni Bing, no matter what happens, remember your grandpa Guan is always behind you. And never forget your strength. Good night, my child."

And he disappeared into the night.

Chapter Nineteen

I STARED UP at the building of the Translation Company from outside its iron gate. In contrast to the brightly lit, noisy streets, the building crouched in the pitch dark and dead silence like a hunting animal. It was the evening of October first. Only a mad person would still be working in the office while everyone else was out on the streets celebrating the thirty-fifth National Day of New China. But I kept waiting. In the past two months, I had learned patience and humility. I needed warm clothing for the autumn, and the twenty yuan cash I had hidden at the bottom of my trunk for an emergency was still in the office. I could have come on a weekday, but it would have been awkward to face Xiao Jia and the other employees there. I was hoping to find someone who had to sleep in the office—as I would have been doing if I hadn't been fired—get my stuff, and leave quietly.

I was hungry. I had been trying to make my money last as long as possible by eating only bread and by walking or biking. Still, the two hundred yuan Guan gave me had dwindled at an alarming speed. Yesterday I'd spent my last fifteen fen on a stale steamed bread from a food stand. Sleeping in subways and train stations didn't cost money, but everything else did. In the past two months, I had visited almost every college and middle school in Beijing, even some elementary schools. They all got excited initially, then showed suspicion, and finally shook their heads when they heard my plan to go abroad in a year or two.

Only two months ago, I had been received like a princess inside the Translation Company, surrounded by the manager and assistant managers, who couldn't stop telling me how they looked forward to my work there. Now I was standing outside the gate, homeless and penniless, cold and starved, not knowing what to do next or where to go.

I'd seen Guan only once. Without my saying a word, he knew things were not going well. He suggested that I consider transferring my residence registration back to my parents' place as an unemployed youth and get the permission letter to start the graduate school application process from the neighborhood committee. I shouted to him that it was the dumbest idea. After I calmed down, however, I wrote a letter to my mother asking her about the possibility. But I didn't get any response.

Someone switched on the light on the second floor, turned it off, then on again. Whoever was there seemed to be playing some game. No matter. I'd go in and get my things, then buy myself some hot pork buns. I shook the gate, hoping the lock was just a fake or not working. To my surprise, a small door in the gate opened. Someone had forgotten to put the chain through the bars. I walked in and up to the second floor. Again, to my surprise, I found that the room where the light had beamed through the window was the one where I had checked my baggage. As I knocked softly, I heard music inside. It was the Hong Kong singer Deng Lijun singing "Don't pick wild flowers on the road."

No one answered.

I knocked again. The music stopped, and the door opened a few inches, showing a flat red nose, a thick mouth with a mustache, and a frowning forehead. I recognized him as one of the assistant managers.

"Who are you?" he asked sternly. "What do you want?"

"My name is Ni Bing. I was assigned to your company as a translator, remember? We shook hands." I leaned against the door, for I could tell that he was ready to shut it in my face, and I was not going to let him do it. I needed my money. The frown on his forehead deepened.

"You don't belong here anymore. What do you want at this late hour? Why don't you come back tomorrow? We'll sit down and talk, eh?" He was pushing the door toward me, but I had already placed my foot in it.

"Don't worry," I said, trying to keep my voice as soft as possible. What was he afraid of? "I want nothing from you. I'm here to get some winter clothing from my luggage in this room. Would you please let me in?"

"What luggage? I don't know anything about it. Why should we take care of your things since you're no longer our employee?" His voice became hysterical. "Besides, how do I know who the hell you are? Do you have an ID? How can you prove you're Ni Bing?"

"You know exactly who I am. Why can't you let me in? What are you hiding there?"

In his panic, he tried to slam the door, but I had already pushed my shoulders in and flung it wide open. A naked woman screamed and jumped up from the couch, covering her sex with her hands.

He grabbed the phone and shouted, "Hoodlum, hoodlum, get out, get out, police, where's the police!"

I backed out of the room and ran as fast as I could. A cop was already waiting at the end of the hallway. He pulled my arms behind my back, handcuffed me, and pushed me into a van. The siren wailed all the way to the police station. I was pulled out and shoved into a dark room. I stumbled down the steps. The iron door banged behind me. When everything became silent, I looked up. It was a semibasement, just big enough for a narrow bed supported by two benches. A toilet pit stood three inches above the floor at the end of the bed.

I was now in deep trouble. The cops were super-sensitive on the thirty-fifth National Day. They had been clearing all the homeless, hoodlums, and non-Beijing residents out of the capital. I had no papers or ID to justify my stay in Beijing.

I got up from the damp floor and stretched out on the bed. The wheat straw rustled under my weight. It was not as soft as the rice straw I used to sleep on in Ma Ao Village, but it was much better than the cold chairs and stone steps in the subway and train station. If not for the dread of the inevitable interrogation and being thrown out of Beijing, the prospect of staying there for a few days might not have been so frightening.

A deafening explosion of fireworks. Thousands of chrysanthemum flowers opened while rising into the sky, hung there for about three seconds, then fell reluctantly back to earth. The government was using the most extravagant fireworks for this anniversary. Tiananmen Square must be packed with people. When I was a little girl, my grandparents used to take me to the People's Square in Shanghai to watch the fireworks. We could never make it all the way because of the crowd. I would jump up and down in some narrow alley, its exit and entrance blocked by the swarming people. Waipo told me that when I grew up, I would watch fireworks on the rostrum of Tiananmen. Instead, I was watching them from a jail cell window.

The voice of the anchor from the Central Broadcasting Station came through the loudspeaker in the courtyard: "The rostrum of Tiananmen, where Chairman Mao and other national leaders had announced the foundation of the New China on October 1, 1949, is now open to the public for the first time since the liberation. The national leaders and representatives of all the various nationalities are mounting the rostrum one by one: Deng Xiaoping, Ye Jianying, Yang Shangkun, Wang Zhen, Chen Yun . . ."

More fireworks cut through the dark, smoky sky, more flowers bloomed in the darkness, mixed with shooting stars and parachutes. The air stank with gunpowder. Did heaven also smell that bad? If so, I'd rather go somewhere else.

The door opened. A policeman came in with a bowl and locked the door behind him. His hooked nose and close-set round eyes made him look like a bird of prey. All the cops had that look. He put the bowl on the floor. It was soy sauce soup with two pieces of Chinese cabbage floating on the surface and a piece of corn bread impaled on the bamboo chopsticks.

"Eat," he said, pointing to the food with his foot.

I sat still on the bed. I was starved a moment ago. But now he'd have to kill me to make me bend over and pick up the bowl between his shoes.

"Is the bread too rough for your tender throat?"

I remained silent. He reminded me of Old Liu. They both talked in a cynical, sarcastic tone, full of hatred. His chilling gaze made me shiver.

"Are you going to eat?" He stepped forward. I smelled the cheap alcohol on his breath.

"I'm not hungry."

"This is not a rest home. Whether you're hungry or not, you must eat. I'm not going to let you waste the food." He took the bread and shoved it into my mouth. "How's that? Not too bad, eh?" He laughed like a hyena.

I swallowed the bread and laughed with him, louder and crazier.

He opened his eyes wide. When he finally realized I was laughing at him, he grabbed the rest of the bread and pushed it into my throat.

I closed my teeth before he had time to withdraw his fingers. He screamed. I bit harder. I wished I had sharper teeth to cut those filthy fingers into pieces.

He punched my nose. I fell onto the floor and passed out. When I came to, he had already wrapped his hand with a handkerchief. He circled around me, his eyes shiny with excitement. Finally he bent over to pull me up by my braid, his thin lips squeezed into a crooked smile.

"Laozi is teaching you a lesson today."

He twirled my braid around his hand to have a better grip, and slapped my face. Left, right, right, left. His movements were slow, calculated, as if he wanted to measure the effect of his torture. Soon I began to feel as if I was being torn apart from the inside of my brain. But I kept smiling. I would not satisfy this man who called himself *father* with tears or begging.

"Stubborn, stubborn," he shouted, driven wild by my silence and my smile. "I can't believe you can be more stubborn than my fists." He clenched his hand. His punches landed on me like thunder claps. "Beg, beg for mercy. Laozi can't believe he can't open your mouth." He was screaming and punching himself into a frenzy.

Suddenly he stopped and held my chin to turn my face to the light. "Nice skin," he murmured, chuckling and stroking my cheek with the back of his hand.

Goose bumps started crawling all over my body. I tried to push his hand off my face, but he grabbed my hands and pressed his stinky mouth on mine. I jerked my head away, spitting on his owl face as hard as I could. He raised his fist intuitively but stopped in midair as he saw me standing defiantly before him instead of dodging his blow. He let go of my arms and moved to my back. Before I could figure out what he was trying to do, he caught me by the collar and ripped my shirt apart, the buttons flying off in all directions. I froze in my utter vulnerableness, my hands crossing over my bare chest like a mummy. He kicked at the crooks of my knees. I fell like a tree but felt no pain. He bent down to turn my stiff body over.

As he tried to unbutton my jeans, I screamed. "Hit me, don't touch me. Hit me, don't touch me." But my voice came out like a croaking frog.

He knelt over me, his legs clutching my hips from each side. "Say it louder," he shouted, and laughed when he understood what I was saying. "Ha, you're begging. Laozi finally got you begging." He handcuffed my hands, pulled them off my chest, nailed them above my head on the floor. "Once again, once again, let laozi hear it again," he repeated in a singing tone as he stood above me triumphantly, his feet dancing on each side of my waist.

I raised my right knee and kicked into his crotch with all my remaining strength. He curled up, his hands covering his balls. When he got his breath back, he jumped on top of me. The last thing I saw was his frothing mouth and his hands coming down on my hair. Hundreds of firecrackers exploded in my ears as he smashed my head on the cement floor. Then everything went black.

Mama, my head is on fire.

I powdered my hair with a whole box of benzene hexachloride, then soaked it in kerosene. Lice, thousands of lice were sucking my blood, and more eggs were hatching. For weeks, my scalp had been itching as if an army of ants were marching around under my hair. That night I scratched my head with a comb. Three tiny creatures fell on the book I was reading and crawled around in panic. I pinned them against the page with my fingers and twisted. Three red streaks on the white sheet. I went on reading. Suddenly I jumped up. Lice! I had never seen them, but I knew. I took out the mirror in the drawer. Each of my hairs was lined with white eggs. O shit shit shit, I moaned. Su Feng came in while I was tearing my hair frantically. She suggested using BHC and kerosene to kill the lice, a folk recipe among the peasants.

I rolled from side to side in bed, bumping my head against the wall in my agony. Su Feng had blown out the lamp. She didn't want my kerosene-drenched hair to catch on fire. But I could endure any kind of pain as long as the lice were being killed.

Wherever I ran, children chased me away. "Foreign devil, foreign devil," they screamed as they threw stones frantically at me.

"But I'm not." I tried to reason with some of them who had adult faces. In fact they were my mother, father, Nainai, and Waipo. "Look at my black hair, my slanted eyes, my yellow skin. I'm one hundred percent Chinese."

"Doesn't matter, doesn't matter," the child with Nainai's face said. "It's what's going on inside that makes you a foreign devil. You're too wild and stubborn. That's not good."

More stones. I was being buried alive in the stone pile. I reached out my hands. "Mama, where is my mama?"

I ran to the building where I grew up with Waipo. It was about to collapse. There was a big hole on each floor. Pieces of plaster fell on top of my head. But I kept running in to fetch my things. Trivial things—combs, toothbrush, safety pins, old underwear, buttons. How helpless I was!

I OPENED MY EYES. In the purple-and-orange dawn sky, there was a small window barred with rusty irons. "Jail," I murmured, and instantly felt the cold cement floor against my skin. I tried to sit up but couldn't move. Blood had glued my hair to the ground. I touched my forehead. Blood on my fingers, fresh and sticky. I stared at my hand till it turned black and congealed. Little by little, I tore my hair off the floor and sat up halfway, supporting myself on my elbows. A warm stream gushed out from my scalp and trickled down my cheek. Thick, dark clouds wrapped me.

Nainai appeared in her black silk grave clothes. "I'm sorry, Nainai," I cried. "I couldn't visit you in Weihai as I had promised at the Shanghai Port. I was too tangled up in the mess."

She nodded. "You're not happy, my daughter. Why don't you come with me and live again, a real life, like a bird?"

She turned to leave. The soles of her bound feet were worn out. The separated uppers opened and closed like two hungry mouths. It couldn't be Nainai. She had always worn shoes made of black velvet with red silk flowers embroidered on each side. No matter how busy she was, her shoes were always spotlessly clean and tidy. She would never put her feet in such wretched things, even if there were no thread or needles in the other world. And why did she call me her daughter?

I followed her along the country road. The fields around us cracked like the patterns on a turtle's back. Nothing remained in the burning soil. Thunder growled in the depths of the earth. We walked in the direction of the drums. Someone was getting married. The bridegroom looked like my father. The bride had raven black hair that reached to her waist. They were escorted to the altar and told to kneel in front of the god's picture. A noose slipped down from a slant-necked tree and caught the neck of the bride. She dangled instantly in the air, her red lotus shoes kicking back and forth. A crowd gathered, most the kids from the navy compound, throwing stones and spitting at the corpse. No one was shocked. Too many people had hung themselves or jumped into lakes or off buildings during the Cultural Revolution. Revolution is not a banquet, Chairman Mao had said, but a thunderstorm. *Someone cut the rope. The corpse fell with a heavy thud. A man kicked and spat. "What a beauty snake!" She lay on the ground, motionless, her arm raised and bent over her head, as if to protect herself. I stared at her and saw my own face.*

I wanted to scream and run, but my feet were stuck in a puddle of blood that trickled from the bride's mouth. I couldn't tear my eyes away from her. Her tongue protruded slightly from her blue lips. Her nostrils seemed to be quivering like the wings of a fly. I held my breath. Perhaps she would stand up again. Then what? What would they do with two Ni Bings, or two brides? The crowd covered the body with a white sheet and put her into a coffin. She's not dead, I shouted. Not yet! I'm still breathing. I tried my best to shout, but I had lost my voice.

Cold and stiff Mama the jacket you gave me doesn't keep me warm it's passed on to you from Waipo the cotton as hard as rocks I need a new jacket Mama the place I'm going to is dark and cold when I leave please don't cry I'll be a speck of dust drifting on the ocean on the waves in the rainbows of the dusk clouds drifting in the earliest morning fog of spring please don't cry for me Mama drifting in the magnificent rolls of October clouds don't cry for me last night I dreamed again the numerous iron doors along the tunnel I walk and walk I open one door after another endless my wrists ache but the last door won't open I keep bumping against its metal surface it stays silent I dig into the cracks my fingers bleed but still this awful silence

I woke up again when someone lifted me from the floor. I forced myself to open my eyes. A woman was looking at me through a pair of square glasses with silver metal frames, her dark almond eyes shiny with tender tears. She bent her smooth, long white neck over my face, her soft short hair covering her round cheeks, like a mother swan dipping her beak into the sacred water. *Mother,* I whispered. *Ni Bing,* she called out with a great relief. I felt dizzy with a sharp disappointment. The woman was Xiao Jia, the assistant manager from the Translation Company.

"Ni Bing, I apologize to you, the whole company apologizes to you," she said. I gazed at her face. How fast her lips moved! "This was a complete misunderstanding. Hold onto my shoulders. Keep your eyes open. I'm taking you out of here. We're going to the hospital. Look at me. I'm Xiao Jia. It's all over now. Ni Bing, don't close your eyes. You'll be fine. You'll find a job. You'll go to New York. Just hang on there. Do you hear me? Do you hear the ambulance?"

Chapter Twenty

THE MOMENT I DISCOVERED that the magic herb my father gave me three and a half years ago had decayed, I knew that something bad had happened to him.

I had kept it inside my pillowcase. I liked to sleep on it and wake up with the bitter smell of linzhi, although the hard mushroom often left a red mark on my cheek or forehead. That morning, no scent drifted into my nostril through the fabric. I shook the pillowcase. Pieces of linzhi and some brown powder fell out. Yesterday I had felt it, and it was as hard as a stone. How could it decay overnight?

Mother's letter arrived at noon. "Since your nainai passed away, your father has gone insane. He refuses to talk to me, as if I were her murderer. Then he disappears without saying a word to his family. I went to Zhoushan Television Station, where he had been working since his retirement. They told me he'd quit and showed me his resignation letter and his request to be assigned back to Shandong, his native land. And even they didn't know where he was now. I almost fainted on the spot. It was awful what he had done to me, to us. The only explanation for his behavior is that he has lost his mind because of his mother's death. He finally wrote to me and told me that he had settled down in Zhao Zhuang, a coal mining area. What the hell is he doing there? Ni Bing, I know I shouldn't bother you when you're busy trying to get your passport and visa for America. But I'm at my wits' end. Our family can't go on without your father. Do something. If you have time, please come home and plan what to do to bring him back. At least write to him. Perhaps he'll listen to you. You're our only hope."

I went to Party Secretary Tian's office and informed him of my immediate departure. I had just given the final exams to my two classes and would grade the papers when I returned from my trip. It wouldn't be long. A week at most. It was a family emergency.

He looked at me with a smile and nodded. "Take two weeks if need be," he said, "but return in time for the departure banquet the school is planning to give in your honor. If you need financial support, please do not hesitate to ask."

I thanked him wholeheartedly and ran to my room to pack. I had been teaching under his auspices at the Institute of the Administrative Staff of the Cultural Ministry for ten months. When I came out of the hospital on October 5 last year, Xiao Jia took me directly to Tian. He had been her old boss and was now a good friend. We walked into his office and settled everything within ten minutes. The school was expanding. It needed English teachers to train the people from the Cultural Ministry before they were sent abroad. I told Tian about my intention to study in New York within a year or two. He smiled and handed me the textbooks for the morning's classes. Perhaps he didn't believe I could get all the materials ready for America in such a short time. In any event, he gave me two notes for the personnel director—one to get me a room, one to Beijing University requesting the release of my transcripts. I was dumbfounded, as if struck by a miracle. The whole summer I had been running around like a headless fly. Suddenly everything I wanted was granted: a job, a home, and the approval to apply to American schools.

I turned to Xiao Jia and Tian. If only I could embrace them! *Wait and see how I'll work for you, Old Tian. And Xiao Jia, you won't regret having recommended me,* I said to myself.

I took over the most difficult and time-consuming classes and devoted all my energy to the students. Tian was pleased. He was an amiable old man who loved life and his vices, cigarettes and liquor. When I visited him each month, I brought him a carton of Marlboros or a bottle of whiskey. Each item cost me about seventy yuan, my monthly salary. I taught two English classes at a night school to make up my expenses. Guan had slipped fifty yuan in my pocket several times. Tian accepted my gifts with graciousness. He truly appreciated them. When I told him about my progress in my application to graduate school, he always laughed and said, "Good, good, young people should have ambitions. As soon as you get the admission letter, I'll discuss the matter at the party meeting." His quick promise made me suspicious. It was hard to believe that things could run so smoothly.

In May I was expecting the admission letter from Baruch College. By the end of the month, it still hadn't arrived. Twice a day, I went to the storehouse for my mail. Old Shang, the woman who was in charge of supplies and mail for our school, shrugged her shoulders as soon as she saw me run in. I started going to the general office in the main building for the incoming and outgoing mail for the Foreign Languages Bureau, to which our school belonged. One day, Little Wang, a young girl in the office I had befriended, asked me if I'd received the letter I was expecting. She had seen a thick brown envelope from New York. She knew the words because her aunt lived there. Too bad there were no stamps on it. Must be official mail. She'd put it on top of the pile for our school. Didn't Old Shang give it to me?

I thanked her and ran to the storehouse.

Old Shang stared at me with blank eyes. Nope, nothing for me. Yes, there was a thick envelope, but not for me. Little Wang must be mistaken. She didn't know English, and she wasn't very smart. I left without saying a word, took out all my savings, and went to the Telephone Building to call the admissions office at Baruch College in New York. The letter had been sent out three weeks before. I requested another notice and an I-94 form and had them mailed to Beijing University Library, care of Professor Guan Yu.

When it arrived, I visited Tian in his home without any bombs and grenades, the local slang for cartons of cigarettes and whiskey bottles for gifts. I entered his apartment and presented him the admission letter. He took a look at it and went back to the TV screen without saying anything. I sat down on the chair near the door, waiting patiently. By eleven o'clock, he started dozing off on his sofa. His wife woke him up and told him to go to bed. He stood up, looked at me and sighed, "OK, I'll summon a meeting tomorrow to discuss your case. Go home now."

I returned the next evening. He didn't mention the meeting he had promised. I sat at his door like a ghost, a shadow. Tian remained quiet but certainly felt the pressure of my presence. He squirmed in his sofa, nodding off and waking up with a jerk in front of the TV. By eleven-thirty, I said good-bye politely. The next day, I went back again. This lasted a week. By the eighth evening, he looked at my face and sighed. "So, you're determined to leave, aren't you, you mule?"

I pressed myself against the wall, nodding. I didn't have to tell him that I would come here every evening until he let me go. He could see it in my face. He shook his head and took an envelope out of his breast pocket. "What a pity! You're such a good teacher. But I guess our place is too small for you. Take the approval letter. Take it and leave before I change my mind."

I grabbed his hand and planted a kiss on its back. His eyes opened wide in shock. I ran out before he could say anything.

With Tian's approval letter, I was able to apply for a passport from the police station, then enter the American Embassy to apply for a visa. I had to get up at three A.M., only to stand in line all day *four times* before I could get in. Too many people wanted to go to America. But I had no complaint. Because yesterday, finally, the tall, blond consul stamped a visa on my passport.

I WEIGHED THE PASSPORT in my hand before I zipped it into the inside pocket of my bag. I was going to show it to my father. Would he realize what I had gone through to obtain this little book with a stamp from the American Embassy? But why would he care about it as much as I did? We had different agendas. Mine had always been to leave—leave home, leave the countryside, leave the island, leave Hangzhou, leave the country. And his secret longing had been to return to Weihai, his laojia. I had known it since I was a child. That was why I wasn't so surprised that he was moving to the north. What worried me was the decayed linzhi. I hoped it was only a sign of Nainai's death. She'd passed away on October 1 last year. By the time my mother wrote me, Nainai had been buried outside her village for two months. Perhaps this was the time to visit laojia, my native homeland, and Nainai's grave, once I had seen my father. I took out a map and found Zhao Zhuang. It was a tiny place, far from Weihai, although both were in Shandong Province. Why did he go there instead of Weihai?

I took the express to Xuzhou, where I could take a local train to Zhao Zhuang. I was going to visit my father, to say good-bye to him before I left for New York, to persuade him to return to his family on the island, and finally, to settle the question that had been haunting me all my life, the question no one in my mother's family would answer: *Who was my mother? Who was the woman who gave birth to me?*

The question had poisoned my childhood. In my adult years, I had managed to suppress it. But recently it again leaped out at me when I filled out the forms for the embassy. The Americans wanted to know when my parents got married or divorced.

I called Waipo. I couldn't reach my mother through the phone on the island. Even in Shanghai, one could be reached only through the public phone service, which was located at the gate of her apartment building block. When I called, the service lady told me to hold on, and she ran off to my grandma's building to inform her of the call. It took twenty minutes for Waipo to come to the phone. I said hello and immediately asked the date of my parents' marriage.

My grandma had a photographic memory for dates and numbers. But this time, she was silent. *What's the matter, Waipo,* I almost shouted, *I need the information for my visa.* Reluctantly, she gave me the date. My parents were married on February 13, 1958. I thanked her and hung up. The call had cost me a fortune.

Suddenly something exploded inside me. I was born on July 15, 1958, of the lunar calendar, about six or seven months after their wedding. Did that mean I was born three or four months prematurely? But Waipo had never talked about it. Instead, there was so much mystery and silence about my birth. And the word *sin* had once slipped out of her mouth. Who was my mother? Who was I?

A few hours after I got onto the local train to Zhao Zhuang, the raw smell of coal began to sting my lungs. The passengers who boarded the train at each stop looked as if they hadn't washed their faces or clothes for years. The black dust seemed to have settled permanently into their wrinkled faces. *I'm getting near Zhao Zhuang,* I told myself, my heart beating wildly. It dawned on me that I had always had questions about my mother but never about my father, even during the years when I wasn't talking to him. *Perhaps I didn't want anyone else to be my father,* I thought.

Zhao Zhuang was unmistakably a coal mining town. The air was pungent and heavy with black dust. The bare mountains looked as if they had been turned inside out. And the sun seemed to have been sealed behind the gray clouds forever. But I didn't feel gloomy. The area was charged with a kind of raw energy. I found the hotel where my father was staying. The manager told me that he was working in Mine No. 5 and gave me directions.

"He's your diedie?" she asked as I was leaving.

I turned to her, surprised and pleased at the same time. We didn't look alike. It used to hurt me when our neighborhood women pampered my two sisters, exclaiming how they looked exactly like my father. But they never mentioned me. I stood there, as if unseen.

How did this woman recognize our relationship?

"Well, it's not your looks," she explained, seeing the question in my eyes. "It's something about your expression, the way you move your eyes and mouth, the way you walk and talk. Not only that. There's a fundamental similarity, a connection, a qi, I don't know what to call it, between the two of you. This kind of common qi is often seen in couples who have been living harmoniously together for many, many years. But since you're so young, you have to be his daughter. You two must get along really well."

I nodded and turned to leave when she stopped me again, a pensive look on her face. "Little Ni, maybe you should tell your dad to take it easy. It's really tough down there, even for young men in their twenties. He seems to be quite sick. I hear him moan at night, as if he is in terrible pain. I'm worried about him. He's a nice man, you know. He gave me some of his magic herb. He doesn't have to work down there at all, with his credentials and rank. He could easily sit in the office. I told him several times, but he's a stubborn mule."

I thanked her and ran all the way to Mine No. 5. The lift had just arrived at the entrance. The round steel can opened and vomited out a group of miners who immediately scattered in different directions. It was the end of the day shift. I stopped one miner and said my father's name. He thought for a second and pointed into the pit. I squatted at the entrance. The lift grumbled as it went up and down inside the stomach of the earth, spitting out the exhausted miners every fifteen or twenty minutes. The sun behind the peak had set the thick layers of clouds on fire with its last rays of light. Now the entire mountain had become a stove stuffed with wet coal, slowly burning the sky into a deep orange. Bats darted noiselessly from mountain to mountain. They were the spirits of dusk.

The lift stopped at the entrance and opened its steel mouth. Nothing came out. I stood up and approached the lift. It was empty inside. There was a shrill drilling noise deep in the pit, accompanied by a deep, slow puffing and blowing sound. *The mountain is breathing,* I thought. The lift shook impatiently, inviting me to enter. I stepped in. My father was down there.

I looked up as the lift slid down. The sky was giving off its last tinge of orange light. How deep did I have to go in order to find my father? Time seemed to have stood still. Perhaps it was pressed into something concrete in the heart of the earth, like the soil that was crystallized into black coal under thousands of years of pressure. The lift jolted as it touched the ground. I walked out. Under the dim light, I saw nothing except for the scattered tools on the ground and three entrances to tunnels that extended horizontally. I peeked into each of them. It was pitch dark inside. In which tunnel was my father? A drilling noise came from the central tunnel. The wooden frames shook with each vibration. I hesitated for a moment, then bent my head and went in.

All my life I had been terrified of tunnels, in reality and in dreams. My nightmares had always involved underground scenes: crawling in tunnels, being pulled into them and buried alive, getting lost inside them, or running away from them. Now that I was really inside one, I was no longer afraid. I was in a familiar atmosphere, although I'd never been in a mine before. The drilling had stopped. What led me on now was the sound of digging, or the vibration of digging, its rhythm going at the same beat as my heart. I kept my head down in this tunnel; sometimes I had to crawl. The darkness here was dense, with a weight of its own, like the damp air of a coming storm. It pressed me from all directions, but I was not afraid. Soon I smelled my father. His sweat, which had always combined the odors of the sea and soil, was more concentrated here.

The tunnel made a sharp turn. I saw a light and a figure kneeling in a pile of coal lumps, lifting a pickax above his head. "Hey," he shouted, flinging the tool into the wall. A huge piece of coal fell off and broke at his knees.

"Father," I called.

He turned to me. The light on his hat shot into my eyes and

forced me to squint. "Ah, you're back," he said, picking up a towel from the basket next to him to wipe his sweat. He turned the basket upside down and gestured for me to sit. He sat on the other basket. He was naked above his waist. His stomach protruded prominently. But it was not fat. It swished, as if full of water. And the ribs lined up neatly on his thin chest. He had lost too much weight. If not for the smell, I would barely have recognized him.

"I'm going to New York next month." *But this is the least important of all the things I have to tell and ask him,* I thought, as I handed him my passport.

He wiped his hands on his trousers before he took it. "Good," he said, flipping through the page, then stopped to stare at my photo. I had loosened my braid in that picture. My hair hung over my shoulders like a dark curtain. The photographer had painted my eyebrows with a pencil to accentuate my features. The darkened brows extended like a pair of wings. They made my nose bridge look higher.

"So you'll live among the foreign devils, marry one of them, and soon become one yourself," he muttered. I couldn't figure out if he were joking or serious.

"But Father, I've always been a sort of foreign devil. In fact, that was my nickname when I was a kid." I tried to adopt the same tone he used.

He seemed shaken by what I said. His gaze moved from the passport to my face.

"Yes, you have been a strange girl," he said, "and still are."

We stared at each other. Something about him made me think of the decayed linzhi. It was the whites of his eyes. They were tinted a dirty yellow. They used to be sparkling white. Sitting on the upturned basket, he looked ancient and drained. My father was very sick. I trembled with fear.

"Who am I, Father?" I burst out in despair. If he refused to tell me the truth, I'd never have another chance.

"You're Ni Bing, my daughter," he said, his back straightened like a soldier ready for an attack.

"I know that." I waved my hand impatiently. "Actually, I want to know who my mother is. She never liked me. I don't have to go into details with you. You saw how differently she treated me from my sisters. I felt rejected all the time. I couldn't feel part of the family, not completely. And I feel foreign wherever I go. It's terrible, father. You must tell me why I was born about six months after you and Mother got married. What was going on? I have the right to know. I'm your daughter. I'm going to a foreign country. And I don't know when I'll see you again. I must know who I am, who my mother is! You owe this to me." I was already out of breath from shouting.

And he just sat there, as silent as the dark around us.

"Father," I called again.

He looked up. "I'm not your father," he said.

I don't understand, I really don't understand, I wanted to say, but my mouth opened and closed several times in vain. Inside me, two voices argued back and forth. One said, *Of course, Ni Bing, that explains everything: Nainai's hostility toward you when you were a kid, your lack of similarity in looks to your father, and your mother's capricious moods.* The other retorted, *Nonsense. How do you explain the connection between the two of you if he's not your father? Of the entire family, isn't he the person who cares for you the most, the one you feel closest to?*

"I'm not your father," he repeated, his gaze now turned to the wall. The light from his hat made a bright spot on the coal. "Your mother was truly beautiful and lively when she was a girl. She still is. The first time I met her was at a dance party the City Youth League arranged for the navy officers in Shanghai. When I followed General Zhao into the hall, I was his most trusted bodyguard at that time. She jumped into my sight like the spring sunlight. She was dancing with a young officer. The red bow at the end of her long braid flew up in the air. She was about sixteen, her tall, slim body not completely developed, yet full of life and joy. My boss squeezed my arm and made a gesture with his chin in her direction. I could see at one glance that he wanted her and that he expected me to get her for him. I had helped him to get together with several young women after we came to the city. I was young and handsome. Women seemed to enjoy talking to me. Once we started talking and dancing, I introduced them to my boss and left him to handle the rest. He was married, his wife a veteran revolutionary. Her rank was actually higher than his. He loved young women but dared not divorce his wife, so all his affairs were carried out secretly. I had never given this task a second thought. I was just carrying out orders. But this time, I did mind it. She was too beautiful for this old toad, yet I had to obey—I was a soldier, his bodyguard. His wishes were my duty.

"When the music stopped, I walked to her table and bowed to her. She stood up with a smile. It was pure sunlight. Oh, how she looked at me with trust and delight! She thought I was inviting her to dance. But I was merely taking her to that old lech. I wished I were the ugliest man on earth so that she would reject me. I walked her to General Zhao's table, feeling like a murderer. I watched her face darken for a second when he took her hand, then it brightened up immediately. We were heroes to these innocent young girls. We beat Jiang and liberated the whole country. General Zhao carried authority in his look and manner. Although he was in his late forties, he could have had any woman he wanted.

"At first, she looked constantly in my direction, hoping I'd ask her to dance again. I stared at the far corner of the hall to avoid her eyes. Gradually, she gave up and let him take her spinning, one dance after another. I stole a glance at her. She looked pale. I hoped Zhao would feel pity for her and let her go. When I looked up again, they were gone. *Damn, she's finished,* I cursed to myself. *He must have taken her to the lounge.* It wasn't a bathroom but a special place for the high-ranked leaders to rest and to take naps with their women friends. Lots of things took place there. I cursed myself till they finally reappeared. He was holding her arm. She looked like a bud stamped into mud before it had a chance to bloom. I felt like weeping when I saw her trembling lips and tearful eyes. My boss looked content. Rubbing his hands, he ordered me to take Comrade Chen Chun home in his jeep. She was feeling dizzy. Not used to the waltz. 'Needs more practice,' he laughed, rubbing his fat greasy hands. I wished I could punch him in the face or put a bullet through his round belly. But all I could do was to take her home in silence."

He suddenly stopped. His last words echoed in the tunnel. I stared at the only lit spot on the wall, waiting. I had come here to prove that my mother was not real. Instead, I had been given this incredible story. Did I want to hear all of it? Did I have the nerve? This was too bizarre, almost like a cheap drama or some mystery story. How could I relate this to myself, to my father and mother? But who was my father? I jumped when he started talking again.

"I've sworn to myself to bury this past forever. But you're right, I do owe the truth to you, and you only. That night when I took your mother home, I made a resolution that I'd never do this again for my boss. The next weekend, however, he told me to get ready quickly. He had to pick up a friend for dinner. General Zhao never picked up anybody. He always sent for the person he wanted to see, or they begged to see him. And he had never bought flowers for anyone. But he was holding a bouquet of roses in his arms when he got into the seat. He gave me the address. I got pale. It was where your mother lived. 'What's the matter, Xiao Ni?' I heard his icy voice. 'Have you forgotten the way already?' I turned the key. *Coward, coward, coward,* I cursed myself all the way. I had my old mother in the north. She had suffered so much all her life. If I died, what was she going to do in her old age?

"She was waiting at the gate when we got there, holding onto her mother's arm. She didn't want to get into the jeep, I could tell. But her mother, your waipo, nudged her in our direction. She called General Zhao shouzhang. It was what all the civilians called high-ranking officers at that time. Nothing special, but she had such a smile on her face. His authority and rank made a deep impression on her. I disliked her immediately. Perhaps that's why we could never get along.

"Your mother got in. We drove to a restaurant on Huaihai Road. I waited in the jeep. Then I drove them to his office at headquarters. There were a luxurious bed and bathroom there. General Zhao often spent nights in his office. The next morning, I drove her home again in silence. This happened once a week, then two and three times a week. General Zhao seemed to be obsessed with her. His need to see her became more frequent, until one day his wife called me into her office."

He paused again, as if he knew I'd been holding my breath. When I breathed normally, he went on.

"She stared at me with fury and sadness. *Damn, she must have heard of everything,* I said to myself. I had known General Zhao's wife Liu Xiang longer than I knew her husband. Actually I started my revolutionary career working as her bodyguard and secretary. She used to call me xiao gui—little ghost, an endearment term for young soldiers. I was sixteen then. She taught me how to use different weapons, how to read and write, and all the other stuff. I called her da jie—big sister, and she was like my sister, and my hero, because she was a great warrior.

"Then she sent me to the battle fields. She wanted me to be independent and distinguish myself in action. And I did. I became a company commander within half a year. I was about to be promoted to a battalion commander when Big Sister Liu called and asked me to work for her husband, who had been appointed as head of the navy headquarters in Shanghai. I couldn't refuse. I owed everything to her. Soon I realized why she wanted me around her husband. He liked women, young women especially. She wanted me to keep an eye on him. That put me in a funny position. He was my direct boss. I had to do what he told me. The only help I could give her was to report his activities. But what was the point? She couldn't stop him. To know everything would only give her more grief. Besides, General Zhao had a bad temper. If he knew I spied for his wife, he'd finish my career in a second. Even Big Sister Liu couldn't help me, unless she wanted to break up with him. But she would never do that, not for me.

"'You betrayed me, both of you,' she finally said, her voice choking with tears. 'I've given you everything, everything I could give.' *Is she talking to me or to her husband?* I thought. *She should let him go. What is the point of clinging to someone who doesn't want you?* I pleaded silently to her, my head bent over my chest.

"'I'm sorry, Da Jie,' I said.

"'Now what are we going to do?' she suddenly screamed. 'She's two months pregnant. And she won't have an abortion. Worse, my dead old man won't let her go. He wants to marry her. Such a mess! If you had reported the truth to me earlier, things wouldn't have gone so bad.' She stamped her feet in despair.

"I froze in my chair. 'Sinful, sinful,' I muttered. This was what my mother said when she heard something awful. Who was sinful, though? Me, General Zhao, or the girl? My brain got all tangled up. I stared at her like an idiot.

"After circling the room for a long time, she suddenly stopped in front of me and grabbed my shoulders. 'Am I still your da jie?' she asked me fiercely. I nodded my head, trying not to cry out in pain. Her sharp nails were digging into my shoulders as if she wanted to claw out my heart to prove my loyalty. 'Good. Da Jie has a favor to ask you.' She whispered into my ear, 'Marry that girl.'

"'No!' I jumped from my chair, throwing her to the floor. 'Absolutely not,' I shouted. 'How am I going to live like a man for the rest of my life?'

"She stood up from the floor and sat down on the chair with a sneer at the corners of her mouth. 'Without me, you'd never have grown into a man. Remember, when you joined the army twelve years ago, you were nothing but a sick, illiterate country boy. I gave you a new life. Now it's your turn to do something for me. That girl is dragging him into an abyss. Only he's too bewitched to see it. But I'm not. I won't allow that. Our lives are tied together. He goes down, I go down. Do you understand? If we're ruined, so will you and the girl be. Now it's up to you to save all of us. Xiao Ni, I'm not asking you for a favor now. I'm ordering you—Marry her and take her away. You're going to be transferred to Zhoushan. We're setting up the East China Sea Fleet on the island. Ten brand-new warships from Russia. You'll be one of the captains. Of course you'll spend two years study-ing in the Navy Institute. You love ships, don't you? Here's your chance. You'll have a ship and a family there. I want you to have a career.'

"'But I've been engaged, Da Jie. She's been living with my mother for the past twelve years,' I pleaded.

"'You ran away from her. That's what you told me when you begged me to take you in the army. It was a feudalist custom to have a child-would-be-wife, anyway.'

"'But I've grown to like her. I'm planning to . . .'

"She cut in. 'If you really liked her, you'd have gone back home and married her. How old are you, twenty-nine? And she's three years older, right? You don't make a girl wait till that age if you love her. Now you have to tell your mother and the girl that it's for the revolutionary cause that you're marrying another girl. They'll understand. I'm not going to waste any more energy. You are getting married tomorrow and you are leaving with her the day after. I've arranged everything.'

"I squatted down, holding my head with my arms, and howled into my crotch. If I could crawl into the crack on the floor! I was just a worm. That was where I deserved to be. She was stroking my hair. 'Trust me. Da Jie has never treated you shabbily, has she?' she murmured. But I was disgusted with her, General Zhao, and most of all, I was disgusted with myself. Because, to tell you the truth, I was tempted. The ship, the beautiful girl, I actually wanted them both. What a despicable person I was!"

He sobbed. Black tears washed his coal dust-covered cheeks. His skin was the same dirty yellow as his eyes. My father was very sick. He had been suffering too much. Pain without end. No one was spared. Was that what we came into this world for? How I longed to sob, like my father, but my eyes were dry! I didn't know how to cry. Suddenly I thought of something.

"What happened to her?" I asked.

He knew I was asking about the girl, his child-would-be-wife. "She hung herself," he said, his voice filled with guilt and self-reproach. I slipped onto the ground from the basket as if a huge hammer had hit me on the head.

"What did she look like?" I asked sternly.

He pulled out his wallet from his pants pocket and put it in my palm. A girl smiled at me through the scratched plastic. She was in her early twenties. Her thin slanted eyes and delicate mouth made her look sweet and obedient. But her nose, straight and high, gave away her inner character as a strong person. I'd seen her, I told myself, searching my memory like mad.

I heard him say, "She was stubborn. Liu Xiang, my boss's wife, sent her three hundred yuan and said it might be useful when she got married. She replied that she had been married since she was nineteen and that was it. If her man was not happy with her, she'd just take care of her mother-in-law, then become a nun. She returned the money to Liu Xiang without a day's delay. It was a lot of money at that time. She probably had never seen a ten-yuan bill in her life."

I stared at the face. She had painted her lips and cheeks with red ink on the black-and-white picture. She had wanted to please her "husband." I had seen her somewhere. Not just once, but many many times. In my dreams, nightmares, day fantasies. Since my memory began. But who was she? Why did she kill herself if she had vowed to take care of Nainai for the rest of her life?

"Liu Xiang was probably mad at this rejection. No one dared to disobey her, not even her husband. That's why he conducted his affairs secretly. When your mother had only a month left till her labor, the navy hospital on the island suddenly informed me that they could not admit my wife for labor. I called Liu Xiang and cursed her on the phone. It had to be her trick. She didn't deny it. She said that she just wanted my wife to have the child as far away as possible to prevent her husband from seeing the mother and baby. I asked sarcastically where my wife was supposed to deliver the baby, on the moon or on Mars? She answered shamelessly that she had arranged for the best hospital in Qingdao, the city near my hometown. I could send for my mother, if I wanted to, to take care of my wife, since she was an experienced midwife. We could leave within a week.

"If I had been single, I would have brought a grenade to bomb her and her damn husband into meat jam, then I would have killed myself. But what about my wife and my mother? I was their sole protector now. And she loved me so. She was willing to go to the farthest corner on earth as long as we were together. She said the first time she set her eyes on me, she had fallen in love with me. She almost fainted with joy and excitement when she thought I was going to ask her for a dance. But . . . *All's well that ends well, right?* she kept asking me. Maybe all the torture was necessary for our union. All I could do was smile at her, my heart filled with pity, disgust, and guilt at the same time. She looked so fragile and beautiful. And liveliness had again returned to her after we settled down on the island, away from the evil and misery. How could I not love her?

"But every day she was growing bigger with a child by another man, by my boss. And every night I heard the poor girl I had abandoned weeping far away. When that happened, I became powerless. I couldn't be intimate with your mother. She was very hurt but endured it stoically. I swore to myself that I would protect this sweet girl for the rest of my life.

"So we went to Qingdao by the boat. Your waipo went along. After we settled down in the navy guest house, I sent for my mother. She had never met her new daughter-in-law, and I figured that my wife's pregnancy might make their meeting less difficult—no one could really shout at a woman who was about to give birth. In my letter, I had only told my mom that I had married another woman in Shanghai and that I was sorry I had disappointed Yuan Mei. That was my fiancée's name. I didn't say anything about why and how we married. My mom would have killed me, probably both of us, if she had known the truth. She was that powerful at that time.

"As soon as they met, my mother spat on the ground and stalked out. I ran after her. 'Yaojing, yaojing, you're bewitched by a yaojing,' she screamed at me when I finally caught up with her.

"I tried my best to calm her down.

"'You could have done so much better, my son. Now you're totally ruined by that creature,' she said.

"'But I'll be a captain, Mom. Even if I won't be promoted in the future, it's fine because I love her.'

"She pointed her finger at me, murmuring, 'What about her? She waited twelve years for you, working like a mule to take care of me and your younger brother. And you let her go for a yaojing. You know well what you've done to her, my son. Another life ruined!'

"'You can't call her monstrous, Mom,' I said. 'She's just an innocent girl.'

"'Innocent, ha!' she shouted. 'You'll have plenty bitterness to swallow in the future.'"

I stared at my father. He sat still on the upset basket, his face animated by the speech. I had never heard him speak continuously for longer than two minutes. At home he was silent most of the time. Mother and my sisters did all the talking. Now words rushed out of his mouth as if he were possessed by another spirit. I heard Nainai's tone of voice when he played her role.

"It was a mistake to get everyone together at that time. Your waipo and your nainai fought nonstop whenever they were in the same room. And your mother couldn't get along with my mother. I wished you could be born as soon as possible and we could all go our separate ways.

"And you were. You came suddenly, giving no sign or warning. It was storming outside. No one was around. The navy jeep driver who was supposed to drive us in an emergency couldn't be

found anywhere. I ran in and out, but there was no public transportation. No bus, no rickshaw. You were pushing hard from inside. Your foot was already an inch out. Your mother was screaming. The bed underneath was soaked in bloody water. I ran to my
mother's room and pounded on her door. She had been terribly
sulky and hysterical for the past three days, shutting herself in
the room and chanting words that no one could understand.

"'Mom, you've got to help us. Something is wrong. The foot,
the baby's foot is coming out.'

"She flung the door open and rushed to your mother's bed. She
took a look at the mess and immediately ordered me to bring her
hot water and soap, muttering 'sinful' to herself as she washed her
hands. When she was ready, she told me to leave the room. 'The
blood from a childbirth brings bad luck to men,' she said.

"I waited in the hallway. I didn't know how long. Endlessly. You
know how time plays tricks on us. When I finally heard noises, it
wasn't your crying, but your waipo's shouting for help and my
mother's screaming: 'Evil creature, give back my child.'

"I broke in. I didn't care about the bad luck stuff. I'd already
hit the bottom. How much worse could things go? I opened the
door. Your waipo had just snapped you away from my mother's
hands. She looked insane, I mean my mother. Her bun had gotten loose from her head, her bloody hands were wringing the air
as if she were strangling the neck of an invisible enemy.

"I grabbed her arms. 'Mom, Mom, what's the matter?' I yelled
in her face. She looked at me with the whites of her eyes. 'She's
gone, my poor baby is gone,' she said in a hoarse voice, and burst
into sobs. I didn't know what she was talking about at that time.
It was days later that I realized she was mourning the death of
Yuan Mei. She had hung herself that night. But I didn't know. I
thought my mother had seen that the baby didn't look like me at
all and started to go crazy.

"I took her to the next room, made her lie down, and rushed
back to see your mother. She lay on the bloody sheet, her eyes
closed, exhausted from the labor and the drama my mother had

created. My head was muddy from the confusion and commotion. Your waipo touched my elbow. 'You want to see the baby?' she asked timidly.

"I took the bundle from her hands. You looked tiny and ugly. Your face was covered with blood and white foam, and your eyes, nose, and mouth were all squeezed together, as if you were about to sneeze. I held you in my hands. I didn't know what I was supposed to feel. Hatred, disgust, love, sympathy? Suddenly you opened your eyes and looked straight at me. I almost dropped you to the floor. You looked at me like a fairy, an angel. It was weird. I instantly felt a connection with you that I had felt for no one else. I felt we had been friends for many, many lives in the past.

"All of a sudden, nothing mattered anymore. All the hatred, disgust, and confusion were wiped away by the look you gave me. I held you against my chest. And the warmth from your little body melted the ice in my heart. I looked at your mother. For the first time, I felt intimacy and connection with her. I knelt next to her and kissed her pale lips. I said to myself: *Here's my wife. Here's my daughter. No one can take them away from me.*"

I tried to see my father, but my eyes wouldn't open. My eyelids were heavy, weighed down by tears that couldn't be shed. I laid my head on his lap. I heard the familiar echo of bubbling water again. It came faintly, then fled, luring me into the deep darkness. I followed it without hesitation. This was the sound I heard when I first learned how to swim. Alone in the middle of the pool, I floated on the surface of the water with my arms and legs stretched out and my head half-submerged. This echo, mysterious and celestial, whispered to me from an abyss below, promising me the most precious gift. I chased it. I had to have it. When I was pulled out from the bottom of the pool, my serene, almost happy expression puzzled the lifeguards. They suspected I was a half-wit.

"Bing Ah, Bing," someone called me gently, rubbing my ears with his coarse hands. The echoes rolled over me, then receded as if pulled back by an invisible force. I heard him say, "Look at me, Bing."

And I looked up. "Diedie," I said. My Shandong accent came to me naturally. It was the way my father, Nainai, and all my other ancestors spoke. "Diedie," I called again, more confident this time, and tears flooded my face. I sobbed for the first time in front of another human being. How comforting crying could be! Through my tears, I saw my father nodding his head, as if encouraging and acknowledging my acceptance. We were father and daughter, connected by something deeper than blood. And nothing could take that away from us. I wiped my face with my sleeves. "Diedie, come home with me."

He shook his head. "I am home."

"But Mother and my two sisters need you."

He smiled. "Hao and Shuang have grown up and will be as strong as you. I don't have much time left. I need to do some digging here."

He saw the anxious inquiry in my eyes. "Bing Ah, you must not grieve. I have cancer in my liver and have only a few months to live. We all come and go. This is as natural as the sun rising and seting and the river flowing from east to west."

For a moment I thought I was hearing Yan. Yan had once told me that he had liver cancer, but it was just a game. If only my father could also play the same trick! I stared at his yellow skin and eyes, his stomach filled with water, the beads of sweat trickling down from his face to his bony chest, and the handle of the pickax pressed into his liver to reduce the pain. I had grown up seeing him push himself against a table corner, a doorknob, things that had a hard edge. We had all thought he suffered from xinkou teng—heartache, or stomachache, a common problem for many people. I remembered the magic mushroom that had decayed overnight in my pillowcase. They say everything in existence has a reason. What was the reason for my father's cancer? He was only fifty-seven. What was the reason for us to meet here, in the womb of the earth? And what was the reason for all the pain and suffering that had no end?

He wiped my face with a white handkerchief. Amid the sharp

odors of the coal dust, I smelled on his handkerchief the faint Fan brand soap I had liked as a kid, and his sweat, which made me think of the ocean and earth at once. I inhaled, imprinting the smell of my father on my olfactory memory.

"Diedie," I sobbed, "why did you have to go through this? Why do we all have to go through this? What have we done wrong? It's so unfair, so unfair. I can't take it anymore."

He sighed, his hand lying still on top of my head. Finally he picked up a lump of coal from the pile he had just dug. It shone like gold. He weighed it in his palm. "Ni Bing, do you know that this lump holds millions of lives and many millions of years? Those trees and plants, birds and animals, they once lived on the surface of the earth, bathed in the sun, the wind, and the rain. Then they fell, died, rotted, turned into fossils, and were buried deep in the earth, waiting, waiting silently for a moment when they could be lit and burst into flame. This day may never come. Even if it does, the fire lasts only for a few minutes, maybe an hour, then it's all over. Nothing but white ashes remains. Is it worth it? Absolutely!" He pressed my scalp. A hot current of energy flowed from his fingertips. I stopped trembling. My father was transferring his life into me. He wrapped the coal in his handkerchief and put it in my pocket.

"Bing Ah," he said, patting the pocket as if to seal it. "You'll live in a strange country. But I know you'll do fine. Those foreign devils will suit your wild spirit. You used to get upset when your sisters called you foreign devil. Well, we're all devils to some degree. But I would say you're a devil with a great soul. And don't you ever forget that!"

He lifted his pickax and resumed his digging. I stood behind him, watching the shoulder joints rise and fall in his back as he flung his tool. My father was sick and old, his half-naked body smeared with coal dust. But he was the most dignified, most free person I had ever seen. "Good-bye, Diedie," I said silently, and turned to leave.

Night had completely fallen over the mountains as I crawled

out of the pit. But I could see every movement in the air clearly. Bats were making circles before their return to the cave, their intensely dark shadows crisscrossing in the night sky. "It is possible to add more darkness to the dark, after all," I said aloud.

Chapter Twenty-one

THE OLD RUSSIAN PLANE had been sitting on the runway for over
fifty minutes. It had backed away from the gate, but after it slid
a few hundred meters, the engine suddenly died. The stewardess
announced that we'd take off again as soon as the runway was
cleared. The plane had only about forty seats, all taken. The air
stank of stale sweat, sneakers, and smoke. I was taking this plane
to Guangzhou. From there I'd enter Hong Kong by train and
spend a night with Zhou's friend before I took the Northwest
Airlines plane for New York. This was the cheapest way to get to
America, although roundabout and exhausting. I wanted to
reduce Zhou's cost as much as possible.

The temperature in the plane became intolerably high. Sweat
streamed down my back and soaked my T-shirt around my waist.
I unbuckled myself and pulled out my bag from under the seat,
looking for my handkerchief. My jeans were too tight to pocket
anything. The bag was heavy with books and the coal lump my
father had given me. When I settled down in New York, I would
stuff it in my pillowcase. I had taken with me only a few things:
an English-Chinese dictionary and a Chinese-English dictionary,
two pairs of jeans, some T-shirts and sweaters, and the farewell
gifts I had received from my colleagues. In the school basement

I had stored the two carton boxes of my belongings: books, notebooks, clothing, blankets, and the other things I'd accumulated in the past twelve years. Old Tian had patted his chest, saying that he'd personally keep an eye on them until I returned. For some reason, everyone in the institute assumed that I'd come back with a Ph.D. degree within two years, whereas my mother, sisters, and Waipo believed that I'd marry a foreign devil and have a bunch of half-foreign-devil kids. The only people who had never asked me when I'd come back were my father and Guan.

Guan had taken me out to a Yangzhou restaurant for a farewell dinner. During the meal, he told me endless stories about New York and New Yorkers, some funny, some scary and sad. I listened and looked at his face, wrinkled like the folds of an ancient mountain. *You old, old angel,* I said to him silently, *you're teaching me how to survive in a foreign country. But you know I'll survive, and survive well, don't you?*

We parted outside the restaurant. He didn't offer to see me off at the airport as everyone else I knew in Beijing did. He'd be with me for the rest of my life, his endearing eyes shining on my soul wherever I went.

I said good-bye to everyone. All my relatives were delighted that I was going to New York. Waipo threw a party for my birthday and departure. Mother was also there. She had just returned from her trip to Zhao Zhuang to see her husband. She looked exhausted and exhilarated at the same time. She didn't mention her husband. Instead, she talked on and on about a chigong master she had met on the train and how his qi had transformed her. She was going to learn the art and become a healer. The master had told her she had the potential. My aunts and uncles looked at one anther with sarcastic smiles. They had always thought my mother was a bit crazy. I felt mad at them, because I heard my mother's passion and devotion for life in her voice, something I had ignored before. She had struggled hard, as I had, as we all had. I was glad that she had finally found a way. I felt the potential for her to become a great healer, too. She had the energy and passion.

I looked at her face, scarred by frostbite. Warmth flowed through my body and I longed to reach out to touch her thickened waist. *She is my mother,* I said to myself. There was no mistake about it. And I loved her. The affirmation was comforting and reassuring. She might not be the best mother for me, but she could be a great mother for many others. And I was happy about that.

Yan had completely disappeared from my life. Occasionally, I thought about him, about our stormy relationship, wondering how so much passion and hatred could vanish like smoke. My classmate from Hangzhou Teachers' School told me that he was back in Hangzhou University as a Ph.D. student and that his wife was with him. Perhaps something good had come out of our break. We had both loved in our own ways. That was the most important, after all, to have loved.

I met Huang Ming at the free market, by accident. He was selling jeans behind a stand. He called my name. I looked but couldn't recognize him, couldn't connect this skinny peddler with the great student leader of Beijing University. We grasped each other's hands, trying to feel the electric tingling we had once felt, but nothing happened. I gazed at his gray hair, his sallow, dry skin, while he stammered about writing me letters that he had never mailed and that he had been looking for me since he returned from Tibet.

All I could say was, "What are you doing here?"

He smiled with such sadness. "My lungs collapsed in Tibet, and I was allowed to return to Beijing. After I recovered, I couldn't find a job. My friends helped me get the license for this stand. I have to live, you know."

We were both at a loss for how to continue the conversation. A customer wanted to see a pair of Levi jeans. The stand was full of fake brand jeans, all hung on the ceiling. Huang Ming took the jeans down with a bamboo pole and spread them on the counter. The customer inspected them carefully, shook her head, and pretended to leave. When she didn't hear Huang call her back for a bargain, she looked back in amazement, then shrugged her shoulders and walked to the next stand.

"I'm going to New York tomorrow," I said.

"Congratulations!" His voice sounded cool and flat as he turned to hang the jeans back up near the ceiling. The bamboo pole shook in his hands. Finally the jeans slipped off the hook and fell with a heavy thud.

"I'm making money, lots of money," he exploded, stamping his feet on the jeans. "And I'm opening another stand. Soon I'll be a millionaire. You know what? I'll go to New York, too, and I'll go there with the dough, so I don't have to wash dishes in some sorry restaurant. That's what really counts there, the money, isn't it? And how many dollars are you taking with you?"

"Twenty-five," I said, trying to hold back my tears.

He laughed, stamping his feet and snapping his fingers like one of those peddlers who became obscenely rich by selling clothes on the streets.

"Ming, your lunch." A woman came with a tin box and crawled into the stand under the counter. She looked at me, then at Huang Ming, and opened the lunch box. Steam rose from the four white buns. She was in her early thirties, her stocky body radiating warmth and strength.

"My wife, Li Lian," Huang said in a rushed voice. "Without her, I'd probably have been buried for months already."

She smiled and pulled out a stool. "My husband is thoughtless. Sit down, please. Would you like a pork bun? It's still warm."

I thanked her and fled. I couldn't bear the guilt and confusion on Huang Ming's face. How I had worshipped and loved him!

Seated now in the plane on the runway, I touched the smooth cover of my passport. The certificate with the stamp of an American visa was the link between my past and future, between the old land where I had lived for twenty-seven years and a strange city on the other side of the earth. Was this what all my struggles and sufferings boiled down to? Was this all life was about—forever on the point of no returning, forever in the process of losing? I had wanted to leave so much, but now my eyes were heavy with tears.

I looked out the plane's window. The blue sky of early September spread endlessly, speckless, like a piece of virgin silk. Soon it would be shredded open by our old, ugly plane. Far away, smoky blue mountains extended until they merged seamlessly with the sky.

I had seen the two blues merge like this before. I had been seven years old, alone at home with Nainai. My mother and sisters were in Shanghai. Father suddenly came home from the sea, exhilarated by his miraculous escape from an August typhoon. He took me to the Peach Blossom Island to see the ocean. There were only mud beaches along the coast of the East China Sea. But the Peach Blossom Island had a small golden sand beach. We took off our shoes and sank our feet into the hot sand. After the storm, the ocean was quiet and shy. "Just like my pretty little Bing," my father said. He folded a red boat, then a white bird to fly over it, supported by a thin wire. We set the boat to sail. The current carried it away fast, and soon it went out of my sight. I sat on my father's shoulders, watching the boat and the bird sailing between the sea and the sky. There was something unusual about the ocean that day. I looked up and down, down and up. And I became more confused: I couldn't tell which was the sky and which was the sea. This had never happened to me. Suddenly I shouted, "Dad, the sea is blue today."

My father laughed. "Silly girl, of course it's blue."

"No," I insisted. "it's yellow, sometimes gray. Only today it's blue like the sky. How come?"

He thought for a while, and said, "Xiao Bing, someday I'll take you to Weihai, your laojia. There the ocean is always as blue as the sky, the apples as red as virgins' cheeks."

"But why, Dad? Why do they have the same color?"

He was silent for a long time, gazing between the two blues as he murmured, "Why are you my daughter and I your dad? Why do seagulls always follow boats? Why do the sky and ocean stare at each other? And why are all the mountains and rivers, the pain and joy, without end? I don't know. Perhaps there's a reason for everything. Perhaps nothing needs a reason. But what's the difference? Or as your nainai would say, it's bu er—the same difference."

I didn't understand what he was saying at the time and felt embarrassed because of my ignorance. So I picked out a white hair from among his thick black curls. I pulled, patting his head with my other hand so that he wouldn't feel the pain. He jumped and said, "Naughty girl." I showed him the white hair. He laughed, and I laughed with him.

THE PASSENGER ON MY LEFT was clearing his throat. I turned and saw him eyeing me with curiosity as I wiped my tears and sweat with a white handkerchief. I must have looked funny laughing and weeping at the same time. Twenty years. I thought I had completely forgotten that scene with my father, but nothing really gets lost in memory.

My fellow passenger had garlic breath, and his new gray Western suit, which hung loosely on his skinny body, smelled sour from sweat. I looked at his face. He reminded me of someone I couldn't name. I glanced at the neighbor on my right. He was also in his forties, also in a Western suit, which my foreign professor from Beijing University had called a "monkey's suit"—he also looked familiar. I turned around. Men and women, old and young, everyone seemed to share a common hallmark. I looked hard at these tense, tired faces. Like me, they were flying abroad, and for this trip they had all put on their best clothes. But no clothes could hide the pain and struggle they had gone through. Every experience was carved into their faces which had stiffened into masks. Yet occasionally, when they didn't pay attention, when they thought no one was looking, sparkles jumped in their eyes, and smiles swept across their lips. Yes, they had been suffering, and they had been silent, but they had never stopped fighting for hope and joy, however transitory, and they never would. That was the hallmark they all shared, the hallmark we all shared. *Give it a spark, just a spark, and the coal lump will burst into a flame,* my father's last words roared in my head.

Something happened to me at that moment. My body was on fire. My whole being was on fire with a feeling I had never experienced before—gratitude for being alive and connected to others. The sensation was new, unfamiliar; it put me all in a fluster. I laid my hand on my belly, breathing deeply. Warmth flowed from my fingertips into my womb. With a slow, steady motion, I moved my hand upward, silently naming each part of me—this is my stomach, liver, heart, breasts, lungs, neck, chin, lips, nose, eyes, hair. I was carressing myself and it was no longer disgusting, no longer shameful, the way I had always felt whenever my hands came across my body by accident. For the first time, I stopped feeling like a ghost. For the first time I could feel the weight of myself, feel my flesh and blood, its warmth and smell. My finger stopped at the scar on my scalp. I shuddered as the face of the cop who had knocked me out in jail surfaced. I was feeling a sharp pain, but for the first time, I didn't try to push it away. I pressed each of my scars. My body, yes my body was here, in this stifling airplane, solid, grounded, though terribly scarred. From here on I would learn how to feel, be it anger, pain or hatred. Then I would learn love, how to love my family, my friends, my fellow passengers in "monkey's suits," perhaps even those who had made me suffer. It wouldn't be easy. But once I began to love, I would love with gratitude and dignity, because it would come from an abyss of hatred, from someone who had tasted despair and emptiness. From there, I would learn joy.

The sensation of caressing was burning me into ashes and dissolving me into the tiniest elements. But I was not afraid. I was willing to sacrifice anything for this moment—the moment of embracing my own being, the moment of ecstasy that had come the hard way. It wouldn't last long, yet it would live with me, with my memory, which would be the source of my life, which I could retrieve whenever I needed. This I knew.

I felt the weight of the coal lump inside my bag. I used to hate coal, hate hauling a fully loaded cart of coal dust from the store and making coal balls with my bare hands. Now I carried a lump of it as I had carried the magic herb linzhi. No matter how high and far I went, this lump of coal would anchor me to the ground, to the land where my ancestors had been born, grown, and died. That was my lao jia, my old home, born in my blood.

I was waiting, waiting in the steamy airplane to soar into the sky while my father was digging into the black womb of the earth. But what difference did it make? All directions were the same direction. Past, present, and future, sky and earth, time and space—all were one. Someday and somewhere, we would meet, my father and I, and would immediately recognize each other from our hallmark—the pain and joy that were imbedded in our faces.

"It is worth it, Diedie," I said aloud.

The engine was humming again. Fresh air rushed into the cabin, into my lungs. The plane hesitated before picking up speed on the runway. Finally, with a sudden quiver, we took off into the blue.

COLOPHON

The text of this book was set in Perpetua, with Koch-Antiqua display. It was printed on acid-free paper, and smyth sewn for durability and reading comfort.